# HOBO: Volume 1

## By Pete Garcia

First and foremost, this book is dedicated to my Lord and Savior Jesus Christ. Secondly, to my family who endured the long days and nights I spent working on this, instead of giving you the time you most richly deserve. Last but not least, my amazing wife, who has patiently put up with my crazy writing obsession.

Artwork by Ramsey Robin Rye

Editing by Michael Valentino

As long as what you are afraid of is something evil, you may still hope that the good may come to your rescue. But suppose you struggle through to the good and find that it also is dreadful? How if food itself turns out to be the very thing you can't eat, and home the very place you can't live, and your very comforter the person who makes you uncomfortable? Then, indeed, there is no rescue possible: the last card has been played.

**-C. S. LEWIS,** *Perelandra*

# INTRODUCTION

The genesis of this book began in the fall of 2013 when I was on my second deployment to Afghanistan. Somewhere between the cramped bus rides to the airfield, and my long walks across the base (Kandahar), I wondered where we would go if the US collapsed and no help was on the horizon. Afghanistan was a landlocked country, with hostile nations on at least three sides, not to mention some of the most inhospitable terrain and weather known to man.

Intrigued by this idea, I went back to my CHU (Container Housing Unit) and began writing out my ideas in a Word Document. I had intended on it initially being a nonfiction, but as I was working out the possible scenarios for how this could happen, Tristan came to life and I began writing it from his perspective. Little did I know that eight years later, a very similar scenario would emerge in America's longest war.

Admittedly, there are some liberties taken here. I have purposely misrepresented some of the military aspects, as not to give any information (either intentionally or unintentionally) to those who would use it for ill gain. While some of the locations are real, other places are not. My intent is not to create a so-real scenario that it would be used for any other way than as background for this fictional story. While the story has not changed since 2013, I did include a recent, real-world event to add to the story.

While this is a work of fiction, there are theological and supernatural truths interwoven into this storyline. These are biblically based beliefs that were prophesied between two-three thousand years ago. The Rapture, the War of Gog and Magog, the Two Witnesses, the Third Temple, the Beast, and the Mark of the Beast are just a few biblical concepts that span millennia and considered Christian orthodoxy, and are still future events that are destined to occur.

Another liberty I took was in the insertion of the "gap" in time between the Rapture and the start of the 70th Week of Daniel (i.e., the Tribulation). The fact is that the Rapture does not begin the Tribulation. The covenant confirmed between the Antichrist, Israel, and the many (Dan. 9:27) is confirmed. I do not know how long that gap is, but my estimations put it around two to three and a half years.

Respectfully,

Pete Garcia

12 OCT 21

# PROLOGUE

Barachiel scanned the dark skies below him cautiously; he knew this would be his most dangerous assignment yet. He had been flying above the earth for hours now, seeking a point of entry, but the enemy had the planet's atmosphere locked down behind a seemingly impenetrable defensive network. *They know something is afoot*, he thought, referring to the frenzied activity of fallen angels below him. His mission was to protect a human; an unredeemed man by the name of Tristan, but for what purpose, he did not yet know. Then he saw what he was looking for, as a small opening appeared over the Indian Ocean.

He lowered his wings and leaned forward to sharpen his angle of attack. He then reached out as if to grab the air in front of him and immediately shot forward like a bolt of lightning. He plunged into the Indian Ocean at a speed virtually undetectable to the naked eye. Although he knew another angel could not kill him, he could be unnecessarily delayed or potentially thwarted should the adversary get wind of his assignment. Thus, he decided to trade speed for discretion as he plunged into the ocean's surface.

The air was the primary domain of Satan and his fellow fallen angels. Angels could not kill each other, but they could fight, and delay, and repel each other when time was of the essence. He knew he could survive in any physical environment; however, moving underwater would afford him better concealment from the enemy as he advanced towards his objective. Although Barachiel could move underwater at incredible speeds, he decided slower was better. This was not due to friction or obstacles; the world's oceans and seas had their own, unique perils.

The angelic hierarchy is incredibly complex for both the holy and fallen angels. Most fallen angels chose to live in the second heavens, i.e., the earth's atmosphere. They do this because they know what dreadful future awaits them in the end the eternal blackness of hellfire. Given the choice, most chose to avoid anything that reminded them of their dark, dreadful fate for as long as possible. However, some did not. This told him that on one hand, while nefarious and malevolent, at least the airborne fallen angels had enough common sense to enjoy their freedom while they still had it. This also told him that those who chose the darkness of the ocean deep were completely insane.

Out of the complex hierarchy of fallen angels, the water dwellers, or *Leviathan* as they called themselves, were only slightly better off than those already confined to the abyss. They lived in the unexplored places of the ocean deep. They especially delighted in causing disasters at sea and stirring up massive storms that wreaked havoc upon the islands and coastal cities around the world. Although he had never fought one, those who had told him their centuries in the dark, watery, underworld had warped them beyond recognition. Still, there were far fewer *Leviathan*, so his odds of traveling undetected and unmolested were better than moving through the atmosphere.

Just then, he saw movement out of the corner of his eye. He drew his sword and spun around to see his brother in arms, Turiel, drawing up beside him.

"Greetings in the name of the Father," Turiel said.

"Greetings, brother," Barachiel replied, "in the name of the Son."

"And in the name of Holy Spirit," they both replied in unison.

"What brings you here?" Barachiel asked.

"I am sent to accompany you to your target," he replied. "You have dangerous roads to travel."

"I am glad for your company, and will gladly take it as long as you can give it. The deep waters are not a nice place to be."

"Neither is where you are headed," Turiel said.

"Yes, the Hindu-Kush Mountains; I am to wait there until my mission arrives."

"Ah, deep in enemy territory. Let us pray the *Prince of Persia* does not find out about your arrival or your mission ahead of time. I think my follow-on mission is connected to yours somehow."

"Oh really?"

"Yes. I am to head to Kansas after I'm done escorting you."

"And yes, the longer I can keep my presence from the fallen prince, the better."

"I will see you there then," Turiel said. "May God grant us safe travels."

"Amen," they said in unison.

At this, they sped off together through the murky waters.

# Chapter 1

*If the world had a landfill the size of a nation, Afghanistan would be it*, Tristan thought. However, the view from 35,000 feet was not so bad. At least at this altitude, the air was cool, but he knew what awaited him upon landing; the end of a long, hot Afghani summer. Afghanistan was not a landfill because of the pollution, although, probably preferable. Afghan culture encompassed some of the worst aspects of humanity: widespread ignorance and illiteracy, tribalism, perpetual warfare, landmines, and unchecked brutality. There was no question to why this rugged, landlocked country was given the nickname, the 'Graveyard of Empires.' *If you'd ask me, they have earned it*, answering a question in his mind no one asked. All the heavyweights have tried their hand and failed here. Alexander the Great. Genghis Khan. The British. The Russians. The United States? Whoever had the bright idea to come here should have taken a lesson in history. Afghanistan, historically speaking, is in love with being a failed state.

Afghanistan is a land with two fixed social constructs guiding everyday life: rigid tribalism and a medieval devotion to militant Islam. This has made living here unnecessarily cruel and difficult, and why the average lifespan does not often exceed 50 years of age. Although they briefly flirted with Western modernity in the 1950s and 60s, it was short-lived. The Soviet Union's military incursion in the 1970s to spread the *Gospel of Karl Marx* caused the locals to rebel and resort back to their more primitive ways. Hard to make genuine progress in a country where everyone wants to go back to the good old days, especially if those days were steeped in the Dark Ages.

After twenty years of military operations with little to show for it, the US was finally getting the hint it would fare no better than the Russians had a generation earlier. *If you want genuine change here, you are going to have to play the long game and change their religion* he thought. Unfortunately, Uncle Sam was not interested in actually fixing this place. They just needed somewhere they could use to justify a bottomless budget. He knew how the game was played but he was too close to retirement to start making waves by saying it aloud. *Just do my time and get out while I am still sorta young and vertical.*

This was his fourth deployment and hopefully, his last. He thought briefly of his wife and kids back in Kansas. He did not want to dwell on them too long, because it was too early into the deployment to go and make himself heartsick. He hated being forced to leave them again but was hoping this final trip would at least set them up financially so he could retire right at twenty-years.

All these thoughts kept racing through his mind as he looked out over the sea of his camouflaged comrades in the Air Force C17. These were the principal forms of movement for troops coming in and out of the Afghani-Theater. While pressurized, they were Spartan in their accommodations for passengers. Soon enough, the short two-hour flight from Manas Airbase in Kyrgyzstan, to Bagram Airbase, Afghanistan would come to its abrupt end. All of his mental exercises in theorizing about the stupidity of this deployment would be over and he would soon be living it.

There is one truism every soldier understands; the worst part about deploying to war was not being there, it was getting there. It was living in transit until you could get somewhere you could call your own. That does not happen until you unpack your rucksack and make your bed… regardless of what that bed actually looked like. Once you were there, the only two things you had to worry about was your family back home and making it through the day. Wash, rinse, repeat.

He could tell they were starting to descend because he could feel the temperature getting warmer. Just then, the Air Force pilot came over the intercom to announce they would be landing soon. He knew all too well their quick descent and rough landing was not based on bravado, but fear of being shot down. A fast descent and rough touchdown was just what his stomach did not need. *Oh well*, he thought. He laid his head back and toasted the air in front of him with his lukewarm water bottle as if to say, *here is to another turn in Afghanistan.*

**Chapter 2**

National Capitol Region (NCR)
**Late August**

The massive, scarcely lit corridors inside the Pentagon were mostly deserted at night. Every so often, a uniformed person would pop out of an office, and walk down the hall briskly with a Starbucks cup in hand heading quickly toward another office. After 2020, the hallway traffic was lighter than ever, even during the day, with many adopting the new normal of working virtually. A group of Colonels and Generals were the exception to the rule this particular evening. They quietly headed down the main hallway and stopped in front of a nondescript door.

Conference Room 10A, on level 2, could have easily been mistaken for a broom closet, if not for the steady stream of people filtering into it. This section of the building had taken the brunt of the hit during the 9/11 attacks, so during reconstruction, the Pentagon asked for a special room where top-level, classified business could be conducted. Colloquially dubbed *the tank*, the National Military Command Center (NMCC) was the joint operations center for the Pentagon outfitted with the latest multimedia technology and every seat provided maximum viewing capacity for over a dozen high definition, flat screens.

The screens themselves could display either separate pictures, or a single one depending on how you wanted to view an event. Today, the screens formed one giant map of the greater Middle East and Europe, overlaid with moving graphics. A smaller image appeared in the corner and doubled as a video teleconference, with an unnamed agent narrating the graphics courtesy the EUCOM (European Command) headquarters in Stuttgart, Germany.

The room filled with four-star combatant commanders as well as service chiefs for each of the respective branches and chaired by the Pentagon's Director of Operations, the J3. He called the room to order, and promptly handed the controls over to the person on-screen. "Gentlemen," a voice addressed the gathering, "today we are faced with perhaps one of, if not, the most significant threats we have ever faced as a nation." The map focused in on Southern Europe, with Greece and Spain glowing dimly.

"You'll notice both Greece and Spain in red. These two countries represent the current 'guinea pigs' for the EU Central Bank's latest efforts to beta-test their new central bank digital currency. This new currency is called the *Kredit*."

Before he could continue, a voice within the tank spoke out.

"With all due respect, agent, crypto and digital currencies aren't necessarily new, news. So how exactly is a digital currency a threat to the most powerful nation in the world?" a NORTHCOM (Northern Command) Air Force general asked impatiently.

The screen then showed a series of lines beginning to shoot out from Greece and Spain across their respective borders in all directions.

"Sir, it's true that digital currencies in and of themselves, are not a threat. Cryptocurrencies have been around for nearly 20 years. However, what we are concerned with in this particular situation is the way this digital currency spreads. Encrypted with an aggressive new form of AI, or Artificial Intelligence, it has proven to be quite troublesome here, and we fear, has the potential to disrupt the global markets in an unintended way. The lines represent a simulation of the spread, but the software they are using is unlike anything we have ever seen before. The algorithms in their software, allow that particular format to spread wirelessly and aggressively through both Wi-Fi and cellular networks similar to how an airborne virus spreads."

"Are you suggesting we are facing some form of a digital-pandemic?" a General asked half-jokingly. The mere suggestion of the word 'pandemic' after 2020, made many in the room suddenly uncomfortable.

"Exactly correct, sir," replied the agent with a straight face.

"Again, and forgive my ignorance on the subject, but I'm not following the logic. The EU is beta testing a new form of currency. It spreads wirelessly, and is perhaps troublesome, but why is this urgent? Isn't this more of a

Treasury issue, rather than Defense?" the NORTHCOM General inquired, more serious this time.

"Well, if I may be frank, if our money gets corrupted or the market seriously disrupted, you will no longer have the funds to run the Department of Defense, or any other departments for that matter. Imagine an AI program that aggressively takes over any smart device. It also does this by overriding any safeguards you had, such as password or biometric protections. That is what this technology does. It makes any wireless device convert to this new currency. It changes any currency linked to a device, into the EU *Kredit,*" the agent explained. "In other words, it converts all valued currency linked to a device, into an un-valued *Kredit*, as if the other currencies never existed."

"How did your team even come to discover this new financial revelation? I thought you were working the Lebanon operation for us," a General from SOCOM (Special Operations Command) asked.

"We were. However, we followed one of our leads back to the island of Santorini, and then onto Athens. It was in Santorini that we first noticed our cell phones and tablets started acting funny. It almost felt like someone was on our network shadowing us. Our team IT specialist noticed this new, subtle programming change and asked us if any of us had uploaded or downloaded any new software, and none of us had.

"At this point, we thought we might be compromised. At least, it felt like it. We felt like we had wet, slimy eyeballs watching our every move. By the time we got to Athens, we knew we were compromised. We decided to bundle our entire tech into a safe room, while we kept spotters on the original target without any tech. They are writing everything down by hand, and sending runners to us while our *quarry* went to ground.

"Meanwhile, we focused on the bugs in our tech. Our initial assessment was that the Turks or Russians were hacking us. However, the more we pulled on this thread the more worried we became. The software seemed passive, yet morphing on our system and bypassing all of our safety and encryption protocols. Even using a Virtual Private Network (VPN) did not seem to stop it. Apparently, the *Kredit* requires minimal Wi-Fi or cellular signal before it invades an electronic device.

"It was only by sheer, dumb luck we caught a snippet about it on BBC News while we were waiting at the hotel. We put two and two together and concluded it was not a *hack* in the traditional sense of the word, but some new government initiative.

"At this point, we put a tactical pause on hunting ISIS, and we started investigating this to give you a SITREP regarding this new development. At the rate it's spreading, and if we are correct in the fact that it spreads wirelessly like a network virus, across any network, it's only a matter of days before it jumps over into Bulgaria, France, and the rest of Europe."

The men, mostly senior officers, began talking amongst themselves. The NORTHCOM General looked over to the Cyber-Command Admiral and asked, "What can you tell us about this digital currency?"

"I am familiar with the Europeans flirting with the concept, but did not know they were this far into development…or deployment I should say. Our knowledge of it has been peripheral at best. We have not been read-in on the execution of this particular program by the EU or anyone else, until just now. Come to think about it, we knew (he said making the hand gesture of the group at large) as much as any of you did. We knew they had a digital currency program, as many nations currently do, but our Intel community has only been able to watch from a distance. All we definitively knew, was it was very high-level, *Above Très Secret UE*, or *EU Top Secret* classified. This could be that. As far as financial matters go, I am interested in the topic as a hobby, but it is not my area of expertise. However, I am familiar with similar technology we attempted to use years ago in Project *Glitter Dust*."

"Project *Glitter Dust*?" asked the puzzled NORTHCOM General.

"That was the unofficial name. But glitter, because it gets everywhere and is dang near impossible to get rid of," the Cyber Commander replied. "Anyway, we knew the Europeans were looking to roll out a major software update last year that would impact all their systems. Even then, we only knew about that because they sent out a vague courtesy letter to all NATO partners telling us their HTTP Protocols were about to change. However, with the COVID-19 pandemic and subsequent global fiasco, they postponed it and life moved on.

"Nevertheless, *Project Glitter* was supposed to be used as an offensive/defensive weapons program, ran by an intuitive AI software system designed to disrupt an enemy's information pipeline. That is why it spread wirelessly. We tested it in a closed system, and it worked almost too well, but ultimately, it was canned it because it was deemed, too disruptive. There wasn't any real way to control it. Now, I am not one to ascribe motives to people, but if this is what our European allies are using, they probably did not intend for it to evolve into what it apparently is now. How could they? They knew it would be like setting a bomb off in the global markets."

"Are you saying they somehow hacked our technology, or otherwise found a way to use it once we ended our project?" the NORTHCOM General asked.

"It is possible they developed it concurrently with ours, but it is also possible that they somehow got ahold of our technology and created their own Frankenstein," the Cyber Admiral acknowledged with a shudder.

"You also said it spread wirelessly and that it was both offensive and defensive?" a high-ranking civilian official asked inquisitively. "Could you expand on that?"

"It was a computer virus designed to spread like an airborne virus," the Cyber Admiral said. "That was the offensive nature to it. Alternatively, the defensive nature was giving our systems and our troops the *inoculation* (he said signaling air quotes) beforehand by way of an electronic tattoo, or a chip. In theory, this would have let us tap into an enemy's information system without negatively affecting our own," the Cyber Admiral said.

"Chipping? Like an RFID tag or a microchip?" another asked.

"Yes, well, nanotechnology is a more appropriate a term," he said and then paused. "Remember, gentlemen, the end-goal for all of our programs and initiatives was to ultimately move the technology out of the smart device and into the user via bio-technological means."

Then, as if a light bulb went off in his head, his eyes widened in recognition and he leaned forward. "This is going to sound a bit wild and fringy, but as they say, *hindsight is 20/20*. It reminds me of the *Great Reset* initiative they promoted at the World Economic Forum back in 2018 at Davos, Switzerland. The idea being, they could get rid of the *Euro*, which has struggled since its inception, and replace it with an all-encompassing bio-currency. It was supposed to eliminate the need for passports, local identification documents, and local currencies."

"I remember that too," another General said. "That is why that name sounded so familiar." There was a collective remembering amongst the group, most of whom had been inundated with all the changes since COVID-19, but were still not familiar with the World Economic Forum.

The operative on the screen finally got the chance to speak again.

"Gentlemen, the Cyber Admiral is spot on. From what we have come to find out here through our own investigations, and frankly, what we are seeing now on the ground is only the beta-test of the *Kredit*. It is a two-stage process. The first stage is rolling out the software to smart devices, to which, my team here, are currently struggling with. The second stage, as the Admiral correctly noted, is the application of the technology into the user. We are starting to see advertising for this as the next best thing. What we can say definitively, is that the *Kredit* is part of a EU Central Bank initiative, internally managed by this new AI program called the BEAST. That stands for Bitcoin Enabled Artificially intelligent, Structured Technology. It is all predicated on Machine Learning/Deep Learning technology they have been working on now for a dozen years."

"So how was that different from Project Glitter?" the Deputy Commander for EUCOM asked the Cyber Admiral.

"Glitter focused on the transmutability and transmissibility of the AI program. Glitter didn't have the block-chain technology attached to it," he replied. "They may have taken these and merged them to make something even more frightening."

"So they've been letting us do all the heavy financial and manpower lifting for NATO all these years while they spent their energies perfecting artificial intelligence?" another Admiral asked the Deputy Commander for EUCOM.

"Yes. Why wouldn't they? Why should they spend all that money on their own defense when the Americans would do it for free? Besides, they believe AI is the wave of the future and were willing to bet big on it. They did the same thing with CERN (The European Organization for Nuclear Research) years ago, and it has paid off in big dividends."

"Sir," the agent on screen asked the Cyber Commander, "are we being tracked?"

"I think it's safe to assume you are, at least passively. However, by who specifically, and to what extent, we cannot say for sure. However, since none of you have the accompanying RFID tags in your persons or equipment, you may be showing up as anomalies in their systems."

"So they can see us, but we don't register in their systems, so we appear as blips on a screen?" the agent asked.

"My best guess is yes," the Admiral replied. "However, once they roll it out *carte blanche* to all Greeks and Spaniards, those 'blips' are going to stand out even more profoundly."

"I have a feeling this is going to roll out faster and further than anyone expects," the agent said guardedly. "It is on our equipment and we don't know how to get it off. Who's to say that if we catch a flight to the UK tomorrow, and take this with us, whether or not it spreads from there?"

"This *Kredit* does in fact create a new problem set for us," the EUCOM General said rubbing his chin. "The loss of anonymity, presumably across Europe in the months and years ahead, means a certain denial of freedom of operational movement we have enjoyed for decades."

"I'd say loss of anonymity is a pretty serious issue," another Admiral added.

"Just to play devil's advocate, how do we know for certain that this is the new EU *Kredit* AI program, versus, some good old-fashioned tech-spoofing operation by the Russians or Chinese?" the Army Futures Command (AFC) General asked.

"Although we can't rule their involvement out entirely, the fact that the BBC did the program on it, and the fact that it didn't happen until we got to Greece, leads us to believe it is a legitimate, state-sanctioned initiative, albeit, with some unintended side-effects. Honestly, we were all surprised at the turn of events and how this seemingly insignificant thing has derailed our entire operation," the agent told the group.

"All we know now is that it is some kind of wireless, or perhaps even, an artificially intelligent, wireless virus that is feeding all kinds of information back to somebody. Based off the Admiral's comments, we can now know with a reasonable degree of certainty that this is an EU initiative, however, we don't know where else our information is being fed back into," the unnamed agent concluded.

"We will need some more specifics on this before we send up a red flag to the *Joint Chiefs of Staff* (JCoS)," the Vice-Chairman added.

"Roger that, sir. Honestly, we did not want to alarm anyone about this, but we felt it warranted a report back to this body (pointing to them). As far as we can discern, this new *Kredit* seems to be everywhere here in Greece, and seems to be causing some issues here. If our theory on this being some form of digital virus that spreads wirelessly is correct, it is inevitable it will spread beyond the borders here and work its way back to the US. We couldn't let all the secrets of the swamp get out now could we?" the agent said jokingly attempting to lighten the mood.

"Careful now, some of us have to live and work in the swamp," a grim-faced General replied with a grin. Some nervous laughing broke out across the room.

"Well, sir, this is why we brought it back to you to seek further guidance," the agent said. "We have no confidence that we can continue to conduct our mission clandestinely anymore without fear of being compromised by unknown entities."

"So, just for clarification, the tech you're using now is compromised?" the Vice-Chairman asked.

"We believe it is. We even believe our SIPRNet (Secret Internet Protocol Router Network) computers are as well."

There was a collective gasp in the room as if all the oxygen had just been sucked out…then silence.

"Sir, this was just two days ago, and I believe it has spread to any wireless device in the area. This has the potential to become a digital pandemic, very quickly."

With 2020 still fresh in everyone's memories, the use of the word *pandemic* brought back painful memories of just how sour this thing could go.

"Honestly, sir, it may already be too late. Infected phones and laptops seem to act as carriers the minute power is applied to them. Assuming there are flights still coming over many times a day from Greece and Spain, we should assume that this tech is already in the US."

"But, we still don't know if it actually damages anything, right?" a senior Air Force General asked.

"Well, sir, that's just it. We do not know. It has not changed the functionality of anything as of yet, except with the currency conversions, but we just do not know whom it is feeding information back to. If this tech gets in the wrong hands, and we can't get it off our gear, and we have really smart IT guys with us…it has the potential to be used in some kind of massive cyber-attack."

"Thank you for this very informative report, agent, you were right to bring this to our attention," the head General said looking around the room. "We need to draft a summary of this report ASAP, and get it to the Vice-Chiefs for informational awareness. Keep the spotters on our Hezbollah target, save what you can by hand, and destroy the tech. Again, thank you for the update, be safe out there, and for the love of Pete, don't bring any tech back with you."

"Roger, sir, Bravo Team out."

## Chapter 3

Early September
Afghanistan

Bagram Air Base sat in a topographical bowl in northeastern Afghanistan. Snow-capped peaks and the rocky brown slopes of the Hindu Kush Mountains surrounded the base. The mountains ran from northwest in Nepal, to southwest in Afghanistan forming a natural barrier separating the country in half, save for a few narrow valleys, which cut through east west. Since its construction by the Americans during the 1950s, Bagram had changed hands frequently.

First taken by the Soviets in the 1970s, and then fought over by the Taliban and the Northern Alliance in the 1990s, it was eventually secured by the Brits early in the post-9/11 invasion. By 2003, it was back under U.S. control again and served as the main headquarters for the Regional Command-East (RC-East)--or now, the Train Advise Assist Command-East (TAC-E) mission. Tristan supposed the new name had more of an administrative vibe to it, but the old one sounded cooler.

Two weeks into this deployment and everything was already becoming like the movie *Groundhog Day*. He was getting used to the smells again, a telltale sign he was acclimatizing to his surroundings. The only thing that separated his days now, were the meetings he attended. He was walking along Disney Drive to the dining facility for breakfast when he noticed several old concrete buildings built by the Soviets, standing next to the newer wooden and metal American counterparts. *Remnants of a bygone era* he thought, *I wonder if ours will still be standing forty-years from now.*

Disney Drive was Bagram's main road and ran parallel to the airfield runways. Disney had all of the major support amenities, which made life on Bagram even remotely bearable. There was a food court, which consisted of portable buildings topped with familiar banners like--Pizza Hut, Burger King, Green Bean Coffee, and so on. With *General Order #1* in effect prohibiting the consumption of all forms of alcohol, the closest thing to *going out* on a Friday night was getting a latte at the Green Bean.

The dining facilities, or DFACs, were all ran by the same company, Kellogg, Brown, & Root (KBR), the major military contracting support and logistics company. They hired *third-country nationals*, commonly referred to as TCNs, from around the world to work the DFACs. It was apparent to Tristan, judging by the quality of the food that the TCNs neither knew nor cared how the food actually tasted.
To most of them, even the worst food was probably a gourmet meal. He grabbed his tray and moved out.

Although his back was facing the entrance, Tristan spotted his friend Jack Gregory immediately, primarily because he always sat in the same spot every day. He appeared to be in a trance of sorts, staring at the wall mounted television screen. He had a fork of reconstituted scrambled eggs frozen halfway to his partially open mouth. *Two weeks into the deployment and Jack is already struggling to put the food in his mouth* Tristan thought with a chuckle.

Tristan did not blame him. He too often found himself struggling to force a fork of powdered, yet slightly soggy eggs towards his own mouth. He tried to apply some empathy here, but he seriously doubted eggs, bacon, omelets, and French toast were ever on the TCN's menu back home. Therefore, he did not necessarily fault them for not getting it right. Still...

Tristan walked over to the table and noticed Jack's fixed gaze. He then glanced at the television screen himself, half-expecting images of tornado wreckage or maybe another school shooting back in the States to splash across the screen. Instead, all he saw was some stuffy reporter interviewing another stuffy person in a crumpled suit—apparently discussing some economic situation in Europe. According to a scrolling line of closed captioning at the bottom, the economist was talking about multinational conglomerates in Europe attempting to introduce a new form of currency. Tristan set his tray down and parked himself across from Jack, careful not to block his view.

"I'm disappointed in you, chaplain. Watching the news when you could be reading your *book of magic*. And at breakfast too? You are setting a bad tone for the rest of your day; I can see your brain atrophying right before my very eyes."

"And a very fine morning to you as well, Major pain in-my-neck," Jack said without breaking his gaze from the television. "If I understand this correctly, it looks like the Europeans are trying to introduce a new currency in the EU. Something they are doing in coordination with the UfM. Ever heard of it?"

"No, I have not heard anything about anyone doing anything. I try not to discuss global economics before my first cup of coffee of the day, regardless of how terrible it might be," he said as he exaggerated a grimace of his first sip.

Jack nodded in agreement. "I get a distinct feeling though that this will not turn out well. It could translate to work-related troubles for us in the not too distant future."

Tristan started scraping butter onto his toast. "See, this is why you usually eat alone. Nobody wants to hear that sort of negativity first thing in the morning."

Jack looked at Tristan and smiled. Tristan was tall and thin, with dark hair, a domed forehead, with deep-set, heavy-lidded brown eyes that could go from pensive to sharp in an instant…as they did now.

"Have I told you I'm glad you're here?" Jack asked. "In Bagram, I mean. I'm sorry for your sake--I know you'd rather be home with the family--but I'm looking forward to the nine months of your thinly veiled insults and pithy remarks."

Both he and Tristan would be spending their forty-sixth birthdays here in what had been universally dubbed by the military as, 'the Stan.'

"My insults are thinly veiled? I must be slipping." Tristan took a bite of toast, then added, "It's good to see you too, reverend. Your presence here is a bright spot in what promises to be a long and dull deployment."

Tristan was a borderline atheist, so he found it ironic that the one person he hit it off with instantly was an Army Chaplain. This was irony of the highest and most paradoxical order. Tristan jerked his head toward a young lieutenant who had just made it through the chow line and was now covertly eyeing tables while loading up on coffee creamers.

"Look at that kid over there, Sokowski. He thinks he is back in high school looking for the *cool* table in the cafeteria. He wants to sit with us but he's afraid we're too cool for him."

Jack's eyebrows lifted. "Oh, are we cool?"

"I'm very cool. You are just cool by association.

"Man, is he a pink-faced baby or what? Do you think we were ever that young?"

"Pretty sure I was. You were grown in a lab somewhere I think."

Tristan raised his voice. "SOKO!"

Sokowski glanced over. Tristan made a come-here gesture, and Sokowski complied, looking relieved.

Before Sokowski could speak, Tristan grabbed Jack's empty coffee mug and held it up. "More coffee please," he asked with his best poker face.

Sokowski froze, looking confused. Tristan laughed.

"Just kidding, LT. Have a seat."

"That was male banter," Jack said helpfully as the lieutenant set his tray down beside Tristan's. "He's taking a mildly adversarial stance as a demonstration of camaraderie and goodwill. Perhaps you should respond in kind, with a jocular insult with gratuitous overtones of preening to Major

Zavota's age. However, be careful not to overstep the bounds of hierarchy and respect. That would be bad form."

"I take back what I said earlier," Tristan told Jack. "*This* is why you always eat alone."

"What? I'm helping the lieutenant navigate the tricky social ritual of male bonding in a highly-rigid, hierarchical military construct." Jack turned back to Sokowski. "It's all right, Lieutenant. You do not actually have to insult Major Zavota about being prehistoric."

"What's new, gentlemen?" Sokowski asked.

"I was just about to tell him about the news-bomb that dropped today--no, not a literal bomb. I'm speaking metaphorically," Jack replied.

"Hold on." Tristan took a swig of coffee and let out a sigh. "Substandard food- *check*, watered-down coffee *check*," he said feigning disgust. "All right, professor, proceed. Tell us about this metaphorical bomb."

"They just announced that the EU was testing out a new currency."

"So are they replacing the *Euro*?" Sokowski asked.

"Nope. If I understood the broadcast correctly, they are augmenting it with something called the *Kredit*."

"What do you mean? What kind of credit?"

"No, *the Kredit*, with a K. That is the name of it. It is some new, digitally based block-chain cryptocurrency controlled by artificial intelligence. Apparently, the European Central Bank has been fine-tuning it for the past few years. It was just introduced this year in Greece and Spain."

"Why there?" Tristan asked skeptically.
"Well, given they are the weakest economies in the European Union, I supposed they figured why not," Jack replied.

Tristan tore open a salsa packet and poured it over his eggs. "Exhilarating," he said sarcastically. "I remember hearing something about it last year I think. I guess it was shelved when the whole COVID-19 thing happened. This reminds me of the time when Secretary Rumsfeld announced the US Department of Defense lost track of a trillion dollars on September 10th, 2001. Of course, 9/11 happened the next day so the story ended up being buried for a few years."

"Don't talk about that too loudly, someone might think you know where it is," Jack nodded with a wink.

"Sir, you said this currency is digital? What is it, on a card or something?" Sokowski asked.

"No," Jack said. "From what I understand, it is an AI powered software program. Apparently, they wanted to put it in the form of an RFID tag and inject it into the user; however, it had a couple of hiccups. First, the technology keeps progressing so rapidly, they keep finding new ways to do it. I mean, RFID technology has been around for years; it has been used to chip everything from pets and livestock, to products and vehicles. Secondly, while 'chipping' tested popular in the Nordic countries, the southern Mediterranean nations were not thrilled with the idea of it."

"The *Kredit* chip was actually supposed to be implanted into the user's hand?" Tristan asked. "I don't blame the Greeks; that is creepy. But aside from that, what makes this special?"

"Well, RFID technology is not new. However, what this new *Kredit* was proposed to do was tie the user's unique biometrics into a database."

"So they turn the person into the hard drive, then?" Sokowski asked.

"Yeah. Only this thing is not external, it is internal. The chip is just a conduit. The actual information is stored in your DNA."

Tristan choked on his eggs. "Wait, what?"

"That's right. Digital data is now being stored at the cellular level. In theory, it is incredibly practical--impossible to hack, and very efficient. When you think about it that is what DNA already does, it stores data. It is an amazingly compact system, with far greater data density than actual hard drives. You just assign binary values to the TGAC bases, and there you are."

"Sure, there you are," said a confused Tristan. "Easy-peasy."

"Well, that was the original plan. As I said earlier, it did not test well in southern Europe. Therefore, for the time being, the chip is voluntary. For everyone else, it is being patched into their smart devices."

"So this *Kredit* being a wireless AI program is better than the actual RFID chip?" Sokowski asked inquisitively. "I guess that makes sense, I mean, we can already pay with our phones and watches."

"Have you ever heard of a *gateway drug*?" Jack asked Sokowski.

"Yeah, sure," he replied.

"Essentially, they are one in the same program from what I understand. This wireless AI system is simply the first step toward the RFID biometric chip. Since most people are already addicted to their smartphones, the next logical step is to get the smartphone onto or into the human body. Ergo, if these global bankers cannot get everyone chipped now, they will use smartphones as the gateway. Then, once everyone becomes dependent upon having it on their smartphones, they will figure out a way to crash the smart devices or make them unusable for this currency. At that point, people will demand you give them the chip."

"Ah, the old *Hegelian Dialectic*," Tristan said suspiciously. "Thesis, Antithesis, and Synthesis."

"Who is the professor now?" Jack eyed Tristan.

"One of the few things I remembered from my philosophy class many moons ago."

"But why would they need to chip people if they can just use smartphones?" Sokowski asked.

"The body is the last frontier, as it were, with regards to technology," Jack replied. "It will solve the problems of identity theft and national borders. It will be hailed as the next medical breakthrough. While the data is noodling around in your cells, why not have it do early detection for cancer or other degenerative diseases? Hospitals and first responders in Greece and Spain already have reader devices that can tell blood type, allergies, and preexisting conditions, as well as have complete access to the user's current medical state before they ever do anything to a patient," Jack said.

He continued. "With healthcare in such a sorry state of affairs these days, preemptive medicine has become all the new rage. Insurance agencies have gotten seriously interested, which at least over in Europe, helped underwrite some of the costs to get the *Kredit* program off the ground. Other nations want in as well—hence the big announcement today. This technology is going to spread. I can see this going global. The days of fiat currency are numbered."

"Man," Tristan said. "The whole thing sounds like something out of a bad science fiction movie."

"It sounds like an extremely plausible scenario for the *end-times*," Jack replied.

Tristan suppressed a sigh, *here we go.* He had walked right into that one.

"And there it is," Tristan said. "Everything always gets back to the Bible with you, doesn't it, Jack?"

"Well, yes, and for good reason. Ultimately, everything does get back to the Bible, whether people realize it or not. Moreover, the *Book of Revelation* makes it clear that economics will play a central role in end-time events. The *Mark of the Beast*, submission to the Antichrist--it is all about buying and selling. Think about it. If the *Kredit* system went worldwide, and you refused to get on board, you would not be able to buy or sell anything...eventually. Paper dollars, credit cards, the gold bars people have saved and slaved for, none of it would be any good. You would be dead in the water, unable to buy gas for your car or food for your family. Economic forces are powerful. They make the world *go round*. And those who pull the strings have everyone else over a barrel."

The conversation had gotten uncomfortable. Lieutenant Sokowski suddenly became engrossed with his biscuits and gravy.

Hoping for a distraction, Tristan looked at Jack's books. This morning's tomes included the Bible (standard wear for an Army Chaplain) and a book that lay open to an image of what looked like a penny, but with a pipe-smoking skeleton in place of Abe Lincoln. The skeleton had one of those bundles tied to a stick slung over his shoulder.

"What's this?" Tristan asked, pointing.

Jack took the bait.

"It's a book about post-Civil War America. Fascinating stuff. Did you know the whole period between the Civil War and World War II was a social and economic maelstrom? Interestingly enough, this is where the "hobo" phenomenon came into play. You had westward expansion, the transcontinental railroad, and industrialization all happening at the same time and feeding off each other. In addition, one recession after another, and financial panics, and not one but two depressions. Labor became more seasonal, and displaced workers took advantage of the railroads' free transportation to find jobs. Being a *hobo* became this huge subculture, with as many as one and a half million traveling the country at any given time. That was like three percent of the total population back then."

Tristan silently congratulated himself on getting Jack to change conversational directions. Back in high school, he had been highly skilled at manipulating certain brainy but absent-minded teachers into going down rabbit trails and all but abandoning the lesson causing the class-time to run out. Jack was the same way, easy to play when you knew which buttons to push. Jack was an *ideas* man, a big picture guy;

always fascinated by the relationships between seemingly unrelated events. Conversations with him tended to get big, fast. He could start with the most mundane topic and bring in history, sociology, quantum mechanics, semiotics, linguistics, and biology, and wrap it up with something about how it all ultimately sprung from God's creation, and boy wasn't it glorious.

"What made you study hobos?" Tristan asked jokingly.

"Part of my Master's degree curriculum on post-Civil War America."

"But you're a chaplain, aren't you supposed to be getting like a Bible degree or something?" Tristan asked.

"Already have one," Jack replied. "This one is on me. I love history. In addition, when digital currencies like bitcoin and lite coin were introduced a couple of years ago, I started doing a lot of reading about currencies. The *Federal Reserve Act of 1913* was the origin of the whole notion that governments ought to micromanage their economies. Increased government intervention in the domestic economy led to protectionist policies, which, in turn, caused problems between nations, which led to the Great Depression.

"When you think about it, most wars are caused by economic competition over land and resources. Nowadays, we are all about international collaboration as a means of preventing war. Globalism is presented as a sign of progress, with all humanity working together toward a common goal, but biblically speaking that sort of thing never ends well. It's nothing more than organized rebellion against God--man manufacturing his own salvation."

He was skating close to the end-times topic again. Time for another diversion.

"Strange word, *hobo*," Tristan said pointing towards a chapter heading. "Where does it come from?"

*A masterstroke of genius, bringing in linguistics* Tristan thought.

Jack's eyes fairly gleamed.

"Unknown. There are several theories, but ultimately it is an etymological mystery. It might derive from *hoe-boy*, as in a farmhand. On the other hand, it may have derived from a greeting, like *Ho, boy* or even *Ho, beau,* which is something railroad workers used to say. The most compelling theory, I think, is that it's an abbreviation for *homeward bound.*"

Tristan nudged Lieutenant Sokowski. "I hope you're taking notes, Lieutenant. There'll be a test at the end."

The lieutenant looked dazed. "You guys lost me back at the chip being a gateway drug."

Tristan looked at the book again and saw an image of a coin in the picture. The whole idea of homelessness made him a little uneasy. He had a distant uncle, a Vietnam veteran, who had become homeless after the war. The family used to hear from him every few years, but eventually, the calls and postcards just quit.

"So a whole subculture of combat veterans turned into a transient labor class?" Tristan asked. "Not exactly something you'd think the government would want to commemorate with a special-issue coin."

"Oh, the coin wasn't minted that way. It was just a regular penny carved that way. Coin engraving was a popular art form in the early twentieth century--especially among hobos since all it took was a coin and a knife. You start with the design that is already on the coin and just shave away parts of it to make it look like something else. The Buffalo Nickel was the most popular coin to work with because the big Native American head gave the artist a lot to work with.

This penny design, carved out of a tiny Lincoln-head, is really fine work."

Tristan leaned closer to the page. "For real. Some itinerant day-laborer with a knife did all that?"

"Amazing, isn't it? I see it as a form of symbolic irony. By defacing the currency, at least in their minds, they symbolically control the economic forces that had run roughshod over their lives. Corporate capitalism had made them homeless, but they could still take a knife in hand and change the face of a coin." His brow furrowed. "But here is the irony. A hobo-coin is a piece of currency that man has modified. The *Kredit* is a piece of currency that modifies the man."

Tristan looked at his watch and stood. "On that cheerful note, gentlemen, I must take my leave. I am off to a series of exciting meetings today. Chaplain Jack, if the U.S. economy collapses and a worldwide apocalypse starts before I see you at lunch, do not do anything I wouldn't do. Remember, actually eat something, okay, Chaplain? Trust me, you need the calories."

# Chapter 4

Bagram Airbase, Afghanistan
Late September

Since September 11, 2001, the American military, primarily
Army and Marines, have endured an endless rotation of
deployments to both Iraq and Afghanistan. The first few
years of a conflict usually meant 'Wild West' rules…or few
rules, because of the fluidity of the fight. However, as the
war matured and things began to settle down, the dreaded
process of 'Garrison-ization' begins to kick in. This meant
increasingly draconian and ridiculous rules as time passes.
Bagram 2021 was no different.

Garrison-ization begins largely due to the monotony
of the routine in deployments. You did the same things, ate
the same food, and worked with the same people every day.
There were no weekends and no holidays. Monday was often
just as busy as Sunday and the only difference from day to
day was the meetings. However being a field grade officer
also required Tristan to attend at least at three different
meetings every day, all dealing with variations of the same
thing…the Drawdown.

How do we get 10,000 troops, aircraft, equipment, and everything else, out of a landlocked country like Afghanistan with minimal casualties and loss of sensitive equipment? How do we do that while trying to prevent the Taliban from just taking back over the minute after we leave? Should we even care? Granted, Tristan wasn't the only one there dealing with this, he was simply one of many who would be expected to work 16 hour days, trying to figure it out.

After breakfast with Chaplain Gregory, Tristan had to make it to the 0900 update brief with his brigade commander, Colonel Price. This was where the key staff briefed him on their progress regarding the particular projects they had been assigned. Tristan walked into the meeting early to make a coffee and review his notes. Although he had not been involved in the Iraq drawdown in 2011, he had heard horror stories about it. Those stories mostly centered on the chaos and lawlessness that kicks in as the base authority structure starts to collapse when the Army pulls out.

He rather expected the same thing here...except worse. The Afghans were a much tougher breed than the Iraqis. The Afghans were an accumulation of many fiercely independent tribes, the largest being Pashtun, who had a millennia's worth of fighting experience under their man dresses. Even if you were pulling out of a location, they would not just wave to you or flip you off as you're leaving. They would spend every bullet they had shooting at you and trying to blow up your convoy on the way out.

With Afghanistan being landlocked between Pakistan to the south and east, Iran to the west, China to the northeast and the former Soviet satellite nations to the north, almost everything would need to be flown out. While the US still had access to the Pakistani port at Karachi, they only sent the stuff there you could afford to be pilfered…because it most likely would.

The brigade commander walked in and everyone jumped to their feet as the brigade executive officer (XO) called the room to attention. The commander sat down and said, "As you were." The XO began discussing the drawdown agenda, but Tristan glanced over to the boss and noticed he seemed distracted. Tristan had known Colonel Price for a long time, going back to their days in the 101$^{st}$

Airborne Division. Either it was by luck or good fortune, Tristan wound up here under his command with the First Infantry Division. Tristan liked him then, and even more so now. It definitely does not hurt to have spent time chewing the same dirt as your boss either.

Tristan's thoughts drifted back to his breakfast conversation with the chaplain, and he wondered if his boss's current distractions had anything to do with that. For some reason, the idea of 'pagers' came to mind. He remembered back in college when pagers were all the rage. Of course, this was the early 1990s, and cell phone technology had not evolved yet, so that was the only way to stay in touch with your friends. However, when cell phones did come out, pagers instantly went the way of the dinosaur. Except now, the US Dollar was the Pager, and the *Kredit* was the IPhone 12.

He had heard somewhere that advancements in technology were doubling every 24-28 months. This meant even the IPhone 12 would be obsolete in a few years. What was unique about the *Kredit* though according to Jack, was that it tapped into something that has not changed in six thousand years (plus) of human history…our DNA. He wondered what that would do to our economy, and even more so, to his family back in Kansas. However, reality came crashing back when he heard his name called.

"Major Zavota," a voice spoke out, "what are your initial assessments for closing FOB Patriot?"

Tristan looked up to the overhead flat screen that served as their briefing template and then back at Colonel

Price. "Sir, to be perfectly honest, of all the FOBs that have to close down, I see Patriot as being our most challenging." "Why is that?" he asked.

"Patriot represents the largest of the small, forward operating bases we have remaining in theater. Like most everywhere else, Patriot has accumulated a lot of additional equipment and vehicles over the years, and will require a greater effort to get everything out we cannot destroy in place. With the smaller FOBs, you could convoy-out most everything you brought with you in one trip. However, Patriot would need some major readjustments there to get more than one Chinook into it at a time. It is going to be challenging to try and maintain security while flying and driving back through the valley to get here," Tristan said.

"Wow, that was profound," the XO replied sarcastically.

Tristan shot back his best 'I could karate-chop your throat' look at the XO and said, "It is as profound an assessment can be without having ever been there."

They were both Majors and it was not uncommon for staffers to come to verbal fisticuffs given their respective positions. Deflecting the sarcasm and not allowing the XO to get the better of him, Tristan continued.

"Furthermore, and I'm sure Captain Johnson can attest to this, the fight is starting to escalate there, which makes moving things out by ground equally challenging."

Captain Trevor Johnson was the Brigade Intelligence officer, and a friend. The boss looked over at him and Trevor nodded with approval.

"Major Zavota is correct, sir," Trevor confirmed. "Although historical records have shown the north to be relatively calm, connectivity seems to be escalating rapidly."

"How so?" Colonel Price asked.

"Our field intel reports show an increase in Russian made ZPU's and DShK's entering into recent actions, which as you know, are particularly nasty weapon systems designed to hit aircraft and vehicles with effective stopping power," he noted. "These are preliminary reports, of course, but the ground guys are saying it's like these two particular weapon systems are flooding in from the Stans," he added, referring to the former Soviet-bloc nations to the north of Afghanistan. "We have also seen the reintroduction of MANPADs, particularly higher-order Iranian Misagh variants."

"Very interesting indeed," Colonel Price said as he looked at the handout Captain Johnson handed him. "XO, confirm with higher and see what we can find out about Kunduz and in particular, FOB Patriot, and see why the sudden spike in that particular area. It would seem, if my gut is correct, the Russians are doing to us, what we did to them back in the 1980s."

The Colonel was alluding to the CIA-backed support of the mujahedeen forces in the 1980s that were fighting the Russian occupation of Afghanistan. The mujahedeen were disorganized and getting beat solidly until the US began feeding them Stinger missiles and AK-47s, along with tactical training on how to hurt the Russians even as they began withdrawing. Now, thirty-plus years later, it would seem, at least based off the influx of Russian weapons coming from the north, the Russians were returning the favor. They were funneling weapons through their former Soviet satellite states to put the *coup de grâce* on the US as American forces began withdrawing. Revenge by proxy. *This had Cold War 3.0 written all over it* Tristan thought.

"Folks, I'm going to have to cut this meeting short. I have a briefing with the Division Commander here in about thirty-minutes. Tristan, I want you to go to Patriot as soon as possible and personally assist Major Thompson up there with the drawdown plans. XO, you have the meeting."

"Yes, sir, I'll make arrangements right away," Tristan replied.

"Roger, sir," the XO replied.

Colonel Price stood up and saluted the group as the rest of the room did likewise. "As you were."

Tristan also started making his way out the door behind the brigade commander as the XO began going through the remainder of the briefing with the rest of the staff.

## Chapter 5

Bagram Airbase, Afghanistan
Late September

Tristan caught up to Colonel Price outside the meeting and asked, "Sir, do you have a minute?"

"I've got approximately five before I head to Division HQ for a briefing with the boss," he said. Colonel Price had been referring to the Commanding General (CG), Major General Rickards, who was the Regional Commander for both RC-E and North. In the past, each RC had its own Regional Commander, but with the drawdown, the Army's reduction in forces made it unnecessary to have a whole lot of brass in one spot. Besides, things were heating back up in Iraq again with the new ISIS on the move and Syria becoming an even larger quagmire than it already was.

"What's on your mind, Tristan?" he said as they moved into his office.

"Sir, I was sitting with Jack this morning at the DFAC when we caught a report on BBC about the EU moving to test a new currency. At first, I did not think much about it, but Jack made it seem like this was likely to have serious complications for us in the not-too-distant future. Like the US Dollar could crash and collapse the economy. Just wanted to get your thoughts on it."

"It would seem that Chaplain Gregory is correct. In fact, that is what my meeting I'm leaving for is about…at least, in part." His gaze drifted off again towards a plaque hanging on his wall as if it was the most interesting thing in the world. "It would seem," he started again, "that our drawdown will happen a lot quicker than we anticipated."

"Sir, how do you mean?"

"Look, Tristan, this is pretty serious stuff. I mean, I wanted to brief the whole group this morning, but the CG has made it all *close-hold* information. I cannot tell you much more at the present, but I will say, if I were you, I would tell your wife to get back home to her family as soon as possible. If this goes the way I think it might go, she's not going to be safe at Riley for too much longer…even if she's living on the base."

Tristan was beyond shocked. He thought he would be breaking the news to his boss, not the other way around.

"Roger, sir, how though? I cannot just have her pack everything on her own, with the kids, and haul everything back to Texas on her own. She's still running the FRG."

"Tristan, look, I've already told my wife to get back home to Virginia. It is your family, you do what you want, but we go back quite a few years, and I am just giving you an unofficial heads-up. Take it for what it is."

"Roger, sir," and with that, he began making his way out of the Brigade headquarters with the Colonel in tow, also heading out to meet his driver and head to Division HQ. It would be pointless to call her now, being twelve hours ahead of her time zone; he would have to wait until later this afternoon or early evening before he could get on Skype with her to talk things over. An email for something of this magnitude simply would not suffice.

"Sir," Tristan said as Colonel Price was walking to the driver's side of his vehicle, "if things are going to get as bad as you think they are, when are we putting this information out to the troops?"

"Soon," Colonel Price responded. "Very soon. I expect to within the next day or so."

# Chapter 6

Bagram Airbase, Afghanistan
Late September

Tristan's discussion with Colonel Price left him feeling a deep sense of unease. Although Tristan was not even sure why he asked his colonel that, he thought perhaps he wanted some level of validation to dismiss Jack's concerns over this *Kredit* issue. He wondered what would actually happen if the US currency collapsed. Images of *Mad Max* flashed across his mind. One thing was for sure, if the US Dollar did collapse, it would trash all of the legal and financial agreements we currently had with partner nations. Everything would need to be renegotiated either by the *Kredit*, or by the barrel of a gun. This meant it could affect all points of entry and exit as well as carriers for personnel and equipment.

More to the point of his present assignment, it would mean the planes they needed to fly people and equipment back, could not pay for the gas. Military personnel could potentially be stuck, until some political or otherwise arrangements were made. Even worse, American soldiers, contractors, and other defense personnel would not be paid, which obviously did not bode well for the families back home. Hence, the warning from Colonel Price. Finally, the whole world relied on the US Dollar as the stabilizing currency for their own currencies. This had the potential to drag the world's economies down almost overnight.

Any nation who relied on the US Dollar as a reserve currency, or held a lot of our debt in bonds, would encounter serious issues of their own. Seeing this was just now breaking on the news, and seeing how the news broke only after the people in the know already knew what was coming, it was probably too far-gone by now. No putting the genie back in this bottle. However, seeing as this would have broken in the US late last night, most of the people there would not be tracking this as a major story until they woke up tomorrow morning. Anxiety got the better of him and Tristan decided it was worth waking his wife up. However, he would have to take care of some travel arrangements here first, before he could break away.

Later that afternoon, Tristan made it back to his room and sat down at his computer to get his internet connection up and get Skype running. The internet on base was notoriously slow, so he was impatiently waiting for the connection to dial her up when a knock came at the door. He answered the door, half-expecting to see Jack or maybe

Captain Doring wanting to see if he was going to hit the gym.

Instead, it was the brigade commander's driver, Sergeant Austin.

"Sir, I was instructed to come collect you and some of the other key staff for an impromptu meeting with Colonel Price back at the HQ," he said hurriedly.

As a staffer, Tristan was usually not important enough to be issued a phone here, hence the personal invitation.

"How soon?"

"Right away, sir," he said.

"Roger, give me about five minutes, I need to send the wife a message ASAP."

"Alright, sir, I'll be out front in the vehicle. Please do hurry though; Colonel Price was intent on this happening very quickly."

"Ok."

Tristan sat back down and would have to settle for sending a quick, cryptic note to the wife instead of trying to raise her by phone. He began typing...

\*\*\*

The ride back to the brigade seemed surreal. He had a sinking feeling of growing desperation in the back of his mind that the world was about to take a turn for the worse; this meeting was proof positive. This sinking feeling was not just at the geopolitical-level; he felt it on a personal level. It was as if he had some kind of ghostly albatross hung about his neck and he could not shake off the curse. Increasingly, he felt like he was never alone, like something or someone was constantly watching him, and it began to become a little unnerving.

In the dying light of the day, the airfield seemed to take on a more ominous feeling with the sun fading in the west. The mountains no longer looked majestic…but daunting. The perimeter no longer secure…but flimsy. He imagined if he were rattled by the thoughts of the implications of a potential collapse to the current world order. He began to freak himself out a little too much, so he turned his mind to other things.

Brigade Commanders were privy to a lot of information that even their field grade staff officers were not. They attend the 'big boy' meetings, where operations are hashed out, not so much with PowerPoint briefs, but with cigars and fifty-year-old Scotch. If the closed-door meeting his boss attended today were in fact discussing the end of the

United States, the Scotch would have been flowing for sure, because at this point, what does it matter.

"*Gah,*" he muttered in disgust. "*I'm beginning to sound like Jack and all this 'end of the world' stuff.*"

"Sir?"

"Oh nothing, sorry. I was just talking to myself," he said halfheartedly, as he glanced out the dusty window. "Who else were you instructed to pick up or notify?" Tristan asked the driver.

"Just you and a few others, sir. After you, I need to grab the Command Sergeant Major (CSM), the Chaplain, and the Battalion Commanders."

"Why me though?" he asked.

"Sir, couldn't tell you. He just mentioned you at the end, after listing off the rest of the leadership. I grabbed you first since you were the furthest away from the HQ."

Although flattering, he imagined that it was because Colonel Price already knew that he knew. He would bring the Chaplain because in this realm of "multi-domain operations," he (the Brigade Commander) would have been stupid not to include the spiritual domain as a factor. The Battalion
Commanders and the CSM, because this would now become a significant leadership challenge known as a SEE (a

significant emotional event). He shuddered at what those challenges might entail.

They got to the building, and instead of heading into the conference room as he anticipated, the driver pointed to the roof. The roof of the TOC was like most buildings in this country, flat with a raised curb around the edge one could sit on, and often used more for recreational purposes, especially in the evenings. Cigar smoking, coffee drinking, and card playing were the more traditional events held for rooftop gatherings. However, Tristan figured today had more to do with privacy than just the scenery.

He made it to the top via the outside stairwell, and the wooden benches were already in use by the battalion commanders. He only knew them in passing but had heard good things. They seemed a bit surprised at his being there.

"What brings you here, Major Zavota?" Lieutenant Colonel Huggins asked.

"Sir, I was asked to be here by the boss," Tristan replied.

"You know what this is about?" Lieutenant Colonel Freeman asked.

"Sir, I have an inkling. And we are probably not going to like it," Tristan responded.

He sat down and noticed a smorgasbord of cigars someone had brought.

"Anyone mind if I grab one?" Tristan asked. "Knock yourself out," Lieutenant Colonel Consiglio replied.

Just after lighting up, the Brigade Commander and the Chaplain came into view as they made their way up the stairs. Aside from the privacy, the boss probably chose this spot because it offered a macro view of the airfield and of the surrounding area. He and the three Battalion Commanders stood up as he walked toward them and immediately picked out a cigar.

"Thank you for all coming on such short notice, but I felt this information needs to be actioned as soon as humanly possible. It couldn't wait until Wednesday's meeting.

"As you know, I've been with the CG this morning, well, for most of the day, along with the other Brigade Commanders discussing these issues with them, on what we are about to discuss now."

The battalion commanders' ears perked up and began to lean forward a little as if to denote their increased curiosity. Being a commander was all about information management. In order to be a leader in your organization, you needed information. Therefore, this conversation seemed right up their alley. However, Tristan reckoned this kind of information, was not going to be the kind they were going to be able to disseminate right away. They would have to think carefully about how to construct the message to their respective formations so as not to start a panic or stampede. They were first going to have to absorb it themselves. It was highly likely they were not tracking the news either.

Colonel Price cut the tip of the cigar off and began lighting it. He took a long drag off it, blew the smoke out, and stared off into the distance; as if his attention span were as wispy as the smoke he had just exhaled.

"Sir, what's going on? What's got you distracted?" one commander asked.

Colonel Price exhaled again and looked over each of their faces and said, "Are any of you familiar with *Xenophon and the March of the Ten Thousand*?"

Blank stares and silence filled the air.

"How about something more recent then. Does the fall of Saigon at the end of the Vietnam War ring a bell?" To this, there was shared acknowledgment.

"Well, let me begin by paraphrasing Mark Twain here, *history doesn't repeat itself, but it sure does rhyme.*"

# Chapter 7

Fort Riley, Kansas
Late September

Katy's biological alarm clock went off at 0645 with its usual, cruel regularity as baby Emma cried out for a diaper change and a bottle. She seemed destined to be an early riser just like her father. Katy got up and made a bottle for her, and came back to change her diaper to see if she could somehow coax her back to sleep for another blessed hour. Thankfully, it worked, and just as she cozied back into bed, she noticed a message on her phone from Tristan. She picked up her phone and with one eye cranked open allowed her sight to adjust to the brightness of the phone as she opened her Facebook message.

*"Katy, I need you to see about going to your parents for a while. If you leave, it will need to be tomorrow or the next, but no later. Can't talk about much now, but you need to make sure you grab the important stuff in the house. Sorry, can't divulge any more than that at the moment, but I'll call later. I love you. Tristan*

"What the heck?" she muttered. *This is odd. Tristan would never ask me to up and head to my parents like this unless it was something serious.* Her parents lived eight hours away and moving three kids and three dogs wasn't a task she really looked forward to doing on her own; especially on such short notice. She began typing back-

*This better be good. Call me when you get back in. Love, Me*

She lay the phone down and closed her eyes again as thoughts began to pour into her exhausted mind. *Why would he ask me to do that?* Knowing Tristan, who was an unbeliever, and a devout realist, he wouldn't ask her to do something like this unless something was seriously amiss. Maybe it was a terrorist threat or some kind of virus outbreak he got information about. Living on base, with all of its conveniences, at the very least, offered a semblance of security. However, try as she might, she was not able to turn her mind off and go back to sleep. It is virtually impossible to do while you are worried. *Oh, he is going to pay for this,* she thought as she finally succumbed to the plush pillow as sleep drifted over her eyes again.

The early morning darkness and stillness floated over her home providing the perfect environment for deep, peaceful sleep. However, Katy's mind shifted from Tristan's message to the uncontrollable stream of consciousness flow of random images, to that of dreamlessness. It was here in the dark stillness of the early morning, a vision flashed across her mind; Washington, D.C. was crumbling, and thick with overgrown weed and fauna. Her vision panned out and all across America, massive explosions in every direction were brilliantly juxtaposed against a darkened horizon. The last image she saw was of Tristan walking down the road away from her toward the explosions. Although she could not see his face, she knew it was him, except, he was different; changed somehow. With this, she sat up in the midst of a mild panic attack. *Oh, Tristan, what is happening*!

## Chapter 8

Bagram Airbase, Afghanistan
Late September

"Sir, are you suggesting the United States is going to collapse, and Bagram here is going to be overrun?" LTC Consiglio asked.

"No, well yes, but not exactly how you're thinking" COL Price replied. "These are two separate issues, which are intricately connected. To the first, what I am saying is if our currency collapses, things are going to start spinning out of control rather quickly. If it happens, getting out of Afghanistan is going to be challenging, to say the least. And those aren't my words; those were the CG's words."

"Sir, respectfully, this is crazy. I mean, the United freaking States is the most powerful nation in the world, with the greatest economy the world has ever seen," LTC Freeman said emotionally. "That simply can't happen. We are far too diversified financially."

"Our economic interests are very diversified. However, what do they all have in common? The US Dollar. Apparently, Cyber Command has been tracking this as a potential issue for at least the last two years. They have always had contingency plans in place for such an event, but like us, no one ever really took it seriously. Just like everything else we do here, we need to come up with some serious options for what to do next. We need the best, worst, and most likely *courses of action*. Secondly, we need to consider the reaction from the troops once they find out they may not be paid anymore. It is not like in the past where we had budget delays and temporary government shutdowns. This is, never being paid again, at least in US Dollars.

"I mean, soldiers are going to do what they need to do here, to get home. However, the minute we hit US soil, they are going to be scattering to the four winds like a giant zonkhorn going off. I cannot imagine many if any soldiers would stay in formation if they were no longer receiving paychecks. How could they take care of their families or pay their bills? At a more strategic level, how we are going to pay for the fuel and planes to fly ourselves home, if our currency, credit accounts, and all the like become null and void?" LTC Huggins added.

"That's true, sir, but don't we own the fuel and the planes?" Tristan asked Colonel Price, "We should be able to fly ourselves out of here and back to the US if everything falls apart."

"Yes and no," he replied. "Yes, we own the Air Force planes, but our fuel, fuel stops, and ports have all been contracted through various agencies and countries, and those contracts were predicated on our ability to pay handsomely for them. Imagine if you are Spain, Kyrgyzstan, or Romania, the US military is leasing real estate from you to move people and equipment through, and the US can no longer pay you. They charge us, or rather, overcharge us exorbitant rates to use their real estate. How interested are they going to be in helping us if we can no longer pay the bill? How long do you think they'll still honor those agreements without any promise of future payment?

"Not only are we dealing with the logistical nightmare of getting our folks home, but getting back and around the US while it's in full-tilt meltdown, is not going to be a piece of cake either," Huggins added. "It's like walking into a family reunion on the verge of a civil war."

"True. Then add all the disgruntled and worried soldiers, who have family scattered all over the US, and in varying states of financial readiness, medical needs, living conditions, and the like, and we are going to quickly be in over our heads. We need to warn the troops, but we also need to keep everyone's head in the game here so we can all make it home in one piece," Colonel Price said. "I know you guys have been busy fighting the war and executing the drawdown mission along with doing the RIP/TOA, but I've got the CG's word our mission here, shortly, is going to change significantly. Tristan and Jack here were the first two to notice it by watching the news at the DFAC this morning. BBC I believe?"

"Yes, sir," both Jack and Tristan confirmed.

"Well, if you two saw it, you can bet your bottom dollar other soldiers have seen it. The rumor mill is going to go into full effect tomorrow, with the bad news picking up steam faster than a juicy political sex scandal."

"Sir, what do you want our priorities to be?" Freeman asked.

"First things first. The CG's priorities are mine. I want a full laydown by tonight of where all of your soldiers and contractors are. I need a complete laydown of vehicles, equipment, and aircraft as well. That includes how many you have here on Bagram and any of the forward team sites. Moreover, because this in-depth accounting will invite all kinds of questions from your company commanders and First Sergeants, you need to, collectively, standardize a brief (hands out pieces of paper to all around) to brief them. Let us keep it simple and not start a panic, which is what this *Memorandum for Record* (MFR) does. We need to reassure the soldiers, NCOs, and officers we know what is happening, and we have a plan.

"Lastly, I need you to know my wife will conduct town hall meetings with all of your families back home virtually. Chances are, they watch the news, and as the bad news starts to spread, they need to be the ones the spouses can rely on for solid information. Remember, nothing specific, but you need to inform them there is the potential for things to be expedited regarding our return."

"Sir, not to sound like a skeptic, but aren't we getting ahead of ourselves on this? I mean, the news just dropped.

That in and of itself does not mean the US is going to collapse overnight does it?" Lieutenant Colonel Huggins asked.

"Lieutenant Colonel Huggins, sir, I do not want to sound like a conspiracy theorist about this," Jack added, "but I would be willing to bet, that if BBC, CNN, and other major news outlets are reporting it, they are only releasing half the picture. All I am saying is that there is probably a lot more to this story than what we are being told publically."

"Thanks, Chaplain. I believe you are correct. Look, the bottom line is I do not have all the information, and neither does the CG. All we know for now is that this mission is being cut short, and this financial experiment by the Europeans is causing DOD to freak out. I will get Captain Johnson to start digging through the SIPRNET to see what information is being passed on the high side. If the Secretary of Defense issues an all-points bulletin on this, it would behoove us to take it equally as seriously. Get your initial assessments to the XO tonight no later than 2200 for personnel and aircraft accountability so we can pass it back up to Division, and do not begin having those discussions with your spouses and command teams back home until the troops here have been notified. Remember, I need calm and resolute leadership from you all now, and throughout this entire process. As for the day-to-day operations, the only authorized air missions tomorrow will be those directly related to the drawdown, MEDEVAC, and the Quick Reaction Force (QRF). Everything else is on hold until we get word back from division headquarters. That is all."

**Chapter 9**

Bagram Airbase, Afghanistan
Late September

After the huddle, Tristan headed back to his room again. He figured by now Katy would have gotten his message, and probably had a million questions. To be fair, he was not exactly sure what to say…since this news would only be breaking in the States in the next day or so, and with all the media spin and bias, who knew how people would react. It could be the sky is falling and either everyone goes into survival mode, or the story is buried under the other ten thousand news stories of the day. It is not going to get the reaction from the general population, until either hyperinflation or massive deflation, starts to hit. However, he was not an economist, so his knowledge of this was superficial at best.

As he walked in, he noticed the little 'message' icon on his computer and immediately began the process of Skyping with her. It was still morning in the States, but by now, she had been up for at least an hour or so and would have had some time for coffee and breakfast. Dialing. Connection.

"Hey, morning, hun," he said.

"So what is going on?" she asked. He could hear the kids in the background running, with a mixture of laughing and fighting. "Is the world finally coming to an end?"

"Umm…I….don't think so, but I can't definitively say it's not either at this point."

Just then, Sofia came up and injected herself in between Katy and the phone to show her daddy a picture she drew.

"Oh that's great, *hunny-bunny*, what is it?"

"It is horses," Sofia replied.

"It's supposed to be the *Four Horsemen of the Apocalypse*," Katy added.

"Aren't they a little young to be learning that?" Tristan asked cautiously.

"It's a very basic overview her class is doing in BSF, she is proud."

"That is really great artwork, Sophia. Thank you for showing me."

"I'll add it to your pile on your desk for when you get back."

"Ok, thanks hunny-bunny." With that, Sofia ran off and joined her sisters in the other room.

"So what is really going on?" Katy asked.

"Well, without getting too technical about it, the leadership over here feels the US currency might collapse soon." *Whew…bombs away.*

"Wait, what? How? When?" she asked.

"Well, that's just it. They are not sure. Word around the head shed (the Pentagon) was based on some geopolitical-economic posturing, our currency may not be viable for much longer."

"Now, say all of that again, in English this time."

"So, other countries use our currency, to stabilize their currencies…if that makes sense. Recently, the European Union has decided to use a new, digital currency. This currency has caused major disruptions and is causing major disruptions, across the board. Some organizations, oil organizations being the largest, have decided instead of just selling their oil in US Dollars, which made our currency stable, now they will sell it in this new digital currency."

"So when is this supposed to happen? I mean, when does our dollar 'collapse'?"

"That's just it. The news only broke over here today, and primarily out of the British news, so I'm not sure what is going to happen there in the States on your time. I mean, it could be the leading story, or it could go over like a wet blanket. All I know is the people *in the know*, i.e....economists, military leaders, business leaders, government politicians...those kinds of people, are freaking out now. Anyway, Colonel Price suggested to the leaders here, they might have their families go home to live somewhere safe for a while."

"Aren't I safe here on the base?"

"Yes, but think about it this way. If our currency collapses, then we, along with everyone else in the military, are not going to be paid. How long do you reckon soldiers will willingly stay in an all-volunteer Army when they're no longer receiving a paycheck?"

"Ahhh.....oh yeah, that sucks. That means we aren't going to get paid." The light bulb went on. "Maybe you should have led with that first, instead of all the other *fluff*."

"Point taken." Anything not directly to the point about a matter, to Katy, was fluff. "Anyway, let's assume that our money becomes worthless and everything, I would feel better about you and the kids being at your parents' ranch, than on the base."

"Me too. Look, let me start getting the kids sorted out. I will call Mom and let her know we are coming, and then I gotta get packed, loaded, gassed up, and on the road. I'll call or message you when I'm on my way there."

"Look," he said, "see if someone from church can help. That is a lot to do in a short period. Make sure you grab all of our important papers, guns, clothes, etc. Whatever food we can take without it spoiling and valuables."

"I got it. What about the TVs and electronics?"

"Leave it. Your parents got televisions. Well, at least bring the iPads for the kids. But, hun, you need to be on the road before noon, if you want to make it there at a decent hour. Also, try to minimize your fuel stops. You should only need to stop once. I know it sucks and the kids are going to go crazy, but things may get scary."

"That's why I always carry my .380. We will stop at that place south of Wichita. All right, I am going to get ready.
Love you, babe, be safe!"

"I love you too, hun. Keep me posted. I'll stay up here as long as necessary."

"Ok, bye."

Tristan laid in bed and stared at the ceiling. He could not turn his mind off. Just imagine the massive amount of work Katy was going to have to do just to get herself, the kids, and the dogs, along with all of their important stuff, out of the house and on the road in three hours. He knew she was capable, but he did not envy her now. He didn't know if anyone from church could make it in time, but he toyed with the idea of asking on her behalf.

He was never a big 'church' guy. He went because she insisted on going, but he didn't know what he believed in exactly. After their son miscarried, he gave up on God. How could a good God, allow my unborn son to die? He decided to channel all that anger and frustration into focusing on his military career. She could keep all of the 'religious' stuff if it made her happy. He figured he was a good enough person. He tried to do right by his wife and kids. If there was a 'God,' surely, that would matter and he would make it through the old *Pearly Gates*. God would have to give him some more definitive proof than just some *dusty old Book*.

Just then, he felt his heart give him a sharp pang.

*What was that?* he thought as he rubbed his hands on his chest. He had never had problems with his ticker before. Although he was 45, he had been in decent shape most of his career. This, however, scared him. He didn't know when he was going to take the time to get this checked out before he left, but perhaps he could get the Physician's Assistant at Patriot to give him a quick check-up after he arrives.

He began to think about the worst-case scenarios…like what if he had a heart attack while he was up there at Patriot with limited medical resources. What if had one here, and couldn't leave the base by air due to his medical condition? He had heard stories in the past where patients in Bagram's combat hospital couldn't be flown to Landstuhl, Germany because of altitude limitations.

What if he was in surgery and their enemies decided to storm the base? Surely, they are also hearing the news that the US, aka…the 'Great Satan,' was collapsing. That might explain the rash of Russian weapons flooding in from the north now. Heart attack aside, where would he run if they did try to storm the base? Would they make a last stand here like the Alamo? His mind was racing through a hundred scenarios, and before he knew it, his eyes closed like heavy coffers, and he was out. Sleeping like the dead.

# Chapter 10

Katy had ended the Skype session and immediately got on the phone while walking outside to call her mom.

"Hey."

"Hi sweetie, how are you doing?"

"Good. Was wondering if it would be ok if the girls and I came and stayed with ya'll for a bit?"

"Of course. Is…everything ok between you and Tristan? Or you just getting lonely?"

"Oh, yeah, everything is good between us. He actually recommended I come see ya'll. There is some news about to break here today or is breaking now I suppose, he's a little worried about."

"What news?"

"Something to do with banking, the US Dollar, and currency and all that."

"Well, I hadn't heard anything, but you and the grandbabies are always more than welcome to come stay with us anytime. You don't need a global crisis for that."

Katy smiled. "Thanks, Mom, we'll be down there later tonight."

"Alright, sweetie, see you guys then."

Katy hung up and began walking back inside. The house they lived in on base was built in the 1930s, so the solid brick and stone, while beautiful, made for terrible cell reception. The kids were playing upstairs and she hollered up to them, "Girls, now I want you to go pick out your favorite toys, and some movies. We are going to Nana's house tonight." At that news, the girls hollered in delight and took off in the direction of their rooms.

Katy wandered to the office and immediately went to their row of binders, which had all the important medical folders, birth records, and other important information on each of the kids. She found a plastic tub and began loading them all in. She grabbed Tristan's "I Love Me" binder, which had all of his achievements, orders, evaluations, and so on, as well. She worked her way methodically through the rest of the office to grab anything she might think was important.

At about that time, her next-door neighbor Michelle knocked on the front door.

Katy answered, "Michelle, how are you? Come on in."

Michelle entered, but she looked worse for wear.

"What's going on?"

"Have you talked to Tristan?" she asked.

"Actually yeah, just now. He told me about what is going on and wants me to go stay with my parents in Texas."

"Yeah, Preston just did the same for me, except, I really don't feel like driving to Utah," she said lingeringly. "I mean, do you really think we should leave? The base seems like a safe place to be if everything goes to hell in a handbasket...excuse my language." Michelle, Preston, and their seven children were Mormons, and he deployed overseas with Tristan as well.

"Yeah, that is a bit of a further drive than we have to make," Katy said. "Do you have any family that could maybe meet you halfway and help drive the rest of the way back?"

"Not a bad idea actually. Even better would be to fly my parents out here and get them to help me drive it. I think being a solo parent with seven kids on a long road trip, is, if I am not mistaken, one of Dante's *circles of hell*. But I could be wrong!" she said while laughing nervously.

"Hey, I thought all you Mormons had this "large family" thing down pat?" Katy replied jokingly.

"Well, in theory, yes. Still a lot of work. And I'm already exhausted," Michelle said.

"Look, I know you're Baptist and I'm Mormon, but would you pray for me? This seems a bit overwhelming, and the way Preston made it sound, a little like *the end of the world*."

"Absolutely. Tristan did not sound alarmed, but then again, he wouldn't know the difference between *the end of the year* from *the end of the world*. He is not very religious if you hadn't picked up on that already."

"Oh, I had no idea. But truth be told, I've been stuck in my own personal *circle of hell* as of late," she said letting her laughter die in her throat. "I better get going, I'm going to call the parents and see what they can do."

"And, Michelle, I will keep you in my prayers. Primarily for sanity, but also salvation," Katy said with a mischievous smile.

"You Baptists are all the same, always trying to convert everyone," Michelle quipped while walking.

"You know it, girl!"

Katy immediately whispered a prayer before she got busy and forgot: *Dear Jesus, please watch over this family and their journey going forward and for their salvation. Also, please watch over us as we head out as well. Please watch over the families who stay behind here and make this place a refuge for those who come to seek shelter in the days and weeks to come. Please watch over Tristan, help him come to know You as Lord and Savior, and bring him home to me in one piece. Amen.*

## Chapter 11

Paradise, Texas
Late September

Paradise, Texas was Katy's hometown. She was born and raised there all the way up through college. By the time Katy reached her teenage years, the lack of anonymity small-town life provided was a compelling reason for her to want to leave. Everyone was always in your business and she longed for the day to break out of Nowhere, USA, and make her mark upon the world. Well, life did not exactly work out like that but having married Tristan and signed up to the Army life now going on fifteen-years, she always got a little nostalgic going home.

Being an Army family was a bit like being a gypsy, or a carny she supposed because as soon as you settled into a place, made friends, got a job, you had to move again. You were typically only at a location for two or three years before getting orders to a new location. That was so different from how she grew up. She had four generations of family still living within a 100-mile radius of Paradise, and there was never any shortage of family to see or things to do.

As she finished packing the girl's suitcases, the idea of the US economy collapsing raced across her mind like a lightning bolt. She could understand why Tristan wanted her to go home. Her parents lived on a ranch. They had cattle for meat, a water well, and a robust garden for vegetables. Nowadays, they could be labeled *preppers*, although, back in the *good old days*, it was just called being *self-reliant*.

*Why do we have to label everything these days anyway?* she thought. It is not as if they had the garden in case a zombie apocalypse broke out. Besides, the garden was more hobby than prepping. They grew carrots, peppers, tomatoes, zucchinis, and squash. If everything did go to hell in a handbasket, they would at least have to get more serious about their selection. However, probably the biggest advantage was the ranch was conveniently located in the middle of nowhere, squared. It had originally belonged to Katy's grandfather, but as he grew older, he began bringing on more of his children to help run it. Nevertheless, she could see Tristan's logic in the sense that at least she would have a good support structure there for her and the girls.

With three girls packed, she started packing herself and made sure to grab her .380 and the shotgun they kept.

This all seemed so crazy to her. Who would have thought the US would ever be in the situation it now finds itself. She was not the history buff Tristan was, but she had listened to enough of his ramblings to know every empire, no matter how great, eventually came to its inescapable end. Some of those endings came suddenly, others gradually, but either way, it was presumably not fun living through the final moments of an empire in decline.

Two hours later, she had the kids situated in the Suburban, the suitcases and dogs loaded, and she was doing a last walk-thru of the house. There was a decent chance they never came back here, which seemed disconcerting. She had grabbed some snacks and bottles. She grabbed her own personal folder Tristan had made her, which contained all her important documents. It had a *Power of Attorney*, insurance policies, and other paperwork she would need if it ever came to it one day. Although, if the economy and the government collapsed, she figured it probably wouldn't mean much anyway.

Driving off base, and getting on the highway, she had also called a couple of her girlfriends, some from the Army and a few from the church, who apparently were not tracking any of this. She had begun to think she and Tristan were perhaps being overly paranoid about the whole thing. She hadn't been ten minutes on the road before she realized her kids were asleep, mouths open and dead to the world. Normally, she would take advantage of the peace and quiet, but she turned on the news radio to see if anyone was talking about this. To her surprise, she caught Rush Limbaugh talking about it; so, apparently, it was not just Tristan's paranoia.

*Folks, let me tell you…do not let the drive-by media skew your perception on what's really happening here. This is a coordinated attack to take down the United States. They knew they couldn't beat us in open conflict, nor could they compete with our economic engine. Therefore, they decided to hit us where we are weakest, our national debt. Let me summarize here: we have the EU, essentially, diving*

*headfirst with this digital currency. We've got OPEC and the member states of the Union for the Mediterranean, minus Israel, as well as many other transnational organizations, collectively ditching the US Dollar for this new digital currency. Not only this Kredit, but also throwing in with a 'basket of currencies,' primarily because of the debt we've got tacked on to our economy. We have this massive debt, because Congress has kept the printing presses on overdrive.*

*It was never just a matter of if, but when. I am holding in my formerly nicotine-stained fingers, the most recent copy of our national debt numbers....*

She turned the volume down to process what she'd just heard. She supposed Rush got charged a lot with fear mongering over the years, and she was a fan, but he was not wrong on this. She had been following the national debt for a few years now, mainly because she wanted to know what kind of future her kids would have to live in. However, being a mother to three young girls, most of her time was spent either listening to *Strawberry Shortcake* or *My Little Pony* for the ten-millionth time. However, it was nice to hear another adult talking about adult things. So if Rush was talking about what it meant, about 20-million other Americans were also hearing it. If this was true, and things really take a turn for
the worse, she wondered how long it would take before things started to truly spiral out of control?

She stared down the highway looking at all the cars coming and going. How many of these people were doing the same thing she wondered? How many were in Texas, or heading to Kansas from Texas, to get away from whatever calamity they thought was coming? Her calm thought processes were interrupted when she saw the sky change from bright blue, to smoke-filled and overcast. The landscape around her also changed instantly. Instead of the rolling green Flint Hills of central Kansas, to a nightmare landscape that was charred black and on fire. She saw bloated bodies lining the road as far as the eye could see. The road was increasingly becoming littered with abandoned vehicles, many of which were also on fire. She swerved to miss one only to snap back to reality at the last second nearly jerking the car off the road. The skies returned to their brilliant blue, the landscape green and rolling. No cars or bodies littering the road. As soon as the vision started, it was over, and she was beginning to question her sanity. She pulled over to the side of the road.

*Oh God, I don't know what that just was, but I pray You are not you showing me the future.*

## Chapter 12

Bagram Airbase, Afghanistan
Late September

Tristan woke up early the next morning, still wearing the uniform he had worn the night before. His mouth dry, thanks to the air conditioner in his room blowing directly at his face.

He stretched and stood up, tasting his mouth, then cupping his hands to smell his breath. *Ugh, morning breath* he thought. First things first, brush your teeth and take a shower.

Heading to chow later that morning felt like déjà vu all over again from yesterday's eye-opening discovery. Well, to be fair, every day deployed felt like déjà vu all over again. He half expected to see Jack sitting at the same table, staring at the same television. He was not. In fact, the place looked deserted. He looked at his watch and realized he was a good hour earlier than he normally went. With all the information and business of yesterday, his mind was overwhelmed and he must have hit the bed earlier than usual. He normally only needed about six hours a night, and going to bed early always meant getting up early. He grabbed his tray of food, found an empty corner of the DFAC with the television on the news, and began remedying his food with liberal doses of salt, pepper, and hot sauce. There was scant mentioning of *the Kredit* on the news Perhaps they were all overreacting.

However later that morning, the TOC was abuzz with numerous sidebar conversations discussing current events. Many of his field-grade peers were sneaking over to their financial websites, trying to see how the stock market was doing in light of recent news. Although he never got involved with stocks and bonds, he had toyed with the idea.

It was not that he did not have the money; it was just that he did not understand it and he never felt comfortable handing over his hard-earned money to things he could not wrap his mind around. He walked over to Sam and said, "How is your portfolio holding up these days?"

"It's crazy right now. They're all over the board. I tried to do the prudent thing and diversify my holdings, but the things that should be up are down…and things down that should be up."

Sam was an old friend of his and a Major. He worked in FUOPs, or Future Operations. It was everything they planned outside of a 96-hour window. So, most of his projects would not happen until the next week.

"I never got in the market myself. I don't really understand all of it, so I just invested in some land down near my wife's parents' place."

"That's probably the safest thing to do these days. That and gold maybe. They are not making any more land you know…except, if you live near an active volcano or something. I bet real estate is really cheap next to one of those things," he said with deadpan humor.

They both cracked up a little at that.

"Sam, your wife going to hang out there back at Riley?"

"Oh no, she went back just before we left to come over here. She's with her parents right now in Virginia."

"That's good" Tristan replied. "If things get crazy, at least she's with family."

"Yeah," he said allowing his gaze to drift off into the furthest part of the office...as if he had been too preoccupied with his portfolio to even consider Sarah might actually be in harm's way.

"Well hey, aside from the small talk, the reason I came over, was to see if the boss had any follow-on information about the impending drawdown and if it's going to be expedited?"

"He hadn't told me or Steve anything yet. However, Steve has been in his office feverishly working on something. I went in earlier to ask him something and he never took his eyes off the computer. He just muttered something so I figured if he needed something bad enough, he'd come out and yell."

Major Steve Lyons was the Brigade Operations Officer. This meant, he worked directly under Colonel Price and dealt with all the day-to-day, and week-to-week operations the Brigade would be doing. In civilian language, a Brigade Commander would be akin to a president of a company or the head of the board of directors. The Brigade

Executive Officer would be a program manager over things like equipment, staff, and logistics.

The Brigade Operations Officer would be like a program manager who was in charge of various actionable, agile, projects who all reported to him for daily status updates. A very, very demanding job he would not wish on his worst enemy. However, if you did a good job at it, you could write your own ticket, which apparently, Steve was doing. He was an extremely smart and likable fellow. What was a little weird, was he was the same rank as Tristan and Sam, but outranked them by position, which meant they worked for him.

"Alright, well, let me know if you hear anything. I'm trying to start the drawdown plan for FOB Patriot up in the Kunduz region, and I need some guidance on how exactly they want to execute it…which will most likely fall in your lane, being FUOPs and all."

"Roger, WILCO," he replied robotically. Again, they laughed at that.

"Hey, false motivation is better than no motivation," he added.

"True dat!" Tristan said as he threw up some fictitious gang signs. "Peace out."

Again, they laughed at the ridiculousness of it all. Although Tristan supposed, being in the Army really was like being in a gang…a really big, well-armed gang, with all the best toys. He walked away and decided to drop in on Steve to see what was going on.

"Hey man, you got a second?"

"I don't. Boss has got me working on some stuff, and I'm running out of time," Steve replied mechanically.

"This about the economic situation?"

Steve stopped and looked at him. "How do you know?"

"We talked about it yesterday morning after the CUB. And then later, with all the BN Commanders on the roof last night."

Steve looked a little confused. He was the Operations Officer and was supposed to be the right hand man, along with the XO to the Brigade Commander. Tristan was a staffer, how did he…Tristan could see all this playing out on his face and in his eyes as if there was a flashing neon sign spelling it out across his forehead.

"Look, man, don't hate me because I already know. I just happened to be the first one to bring it up, and only then, because Jack had caught it on the news at the DFAC over breakfast yesterday.

"Still, now I'm having to do cheetah-flips to get three different contingency plans drawn up before the meeting this afternoon…and I'm only hearing about a rooftop huddle last night, this morning."

"Why didn't you farm it out to us lowly staffers?" Tristan asked.

"He (the Boss) told me to keep this close-hold. He wanted some solid planning done before we start broadcasting an expedited departure."

"Fair enough. Sooo….where are you at now on the planning, and where do you want me to start?"

"I think we do the least likely, most likely, and most dangerous courses of action, should the economy crash."

"Well, before we do, I believe we should bring in Jack."

"The Chaplain?"

"Yeah. He is the real subject matter expert on all this. He's the first one that I know of that brought me up to speed on what's going on here."

"Ok, grab him, and let's reconvene in the conference room in 20 minutes."

# Chapter 13

Paradise, Texas
Late September

Katy arrived at her parents' house early in the evening, completely spent, and ready to get out of the car. Long distance traveling with kids and dogs was tough with both of them driving and borderline hellish, doing it by herself. Still, it was a good feeling pulling up her to her family's property and seeing everyone again. It was a win-win-win situation for all. Her parents got to see their grandbabies, her daughters got to see their *Nana* and *Papaw*, and she got some rest.

After they were unpacked and the kids were out running around, she snuck off to the bathroom to see if Tristan had called her, or left a message on Skype. Nothing. What gives? She told him to call her that night, so it would have been early the next morning for him, so something must be up. Even though Tristan wasn't a religious man, he was religious when it came to calling her…so for him to miss a night meant he must have been very busy indeed.

Her mom Janice came in… "Is everything alright?"
"Yeah, just seeing if I could get ahold of Tristan."
"This economy thing?" her mom asked.

"Yeah. I thought maybe Tristan was going crazy over there, but I heard it on the radio. People are talking about this as if it were a sure thing."

"Well, your dad and brother are gonna do some runs to the store in a bit to stock up on some essentials, you know, *just in case*," she said with a wink.

"I got a list of things I need for the girls, diapers, medicine, and whatnot. Don't let em leave before I can get it to them."

"Ok, but hurry, they'll not be here for much longer."

"I will, Mom, thanks."

She walked into the kitchen and found a sheet of scratch paper, and began jotting down things she needed. Her mind drifted back to 2020 and all the craziness during COVID-19. She added toilet paper to the list.

The local Wal-Mart was busier than normal. Not quite as bad as your typical *Black Friday* level of busy, but definitely more than your average work night. Katy's dad Carl, along with her brother David parked the truck and began making their way in.

"Reminds me of the great toilet paper crisis of 2020," David said sardonically. *Seems news of the impending economic apocalypse had already hit their small town news wire and people were beginning to panic shop* he thought.

"Just wait until it becomes a mad dash," Carl said. "So, let's split up. I will take the groceries, and you get all the non-food stuff. Meet me back here in about 45 minutes."

"I hate shopping. We should have let the ladies do this."

"I know, but with Katy having just driven nine hours, and the kids and all, they may not have made it in time. Just stick to the list. You get what you need, but Katy was very specific about what she needed."

David rolled his eyes. Shopping was like going to the dentist, boring and painful. Mostly because he hated dealing with all the people in the store. He put in his earbuds and turned on some music. *At least I have some tunes.*

"Alright, see you back here at 45."


**Chapter 14**


National Capital Region (NCR)
Early October


The President listened intently to the intelligence update briefing from his Chairman of the Joint Chiefs of Staff and his agency chiefs. Most of these intelligence briefs usually consisted of bad people doing bad things in some faraway place. On the other hand, sometimes his agencies were just catching onto nefarious globalist plots they needed to thwart. Either way, he could handle that type of briefing.

He could even handle a hurricane or a terrorist attack. However, an economic attack that threatened the stability of the US Dollar, which had the potential to dismantle their entire economy…was new. His administration would need some type of response before things began to happen, which could not be undone. One thing he knew was true above all others- you mess with people's livelihood, and their ability to put food on the table and a roof over their head, and you risk civil war.

However, this time, there was something different in his chief's and staffs actual briefing. He could usually pinpoint what kind of emergency it was, before they even started talking, just by their demeanor. They would then proceed to tell him, who the main perpetrator was, and what kind of response the government should sanction. However, something was now amiss. Something was not being said during their Intel briefing, that perhaps, they did not even fully understand. Then it hit him. There was fear and panic behind their eyes.

*They were far too professional to wear their emotions on their sleeves* he thought, which is why he didn't initially catch it. He had seen the same look before when the doctors came in and told them his daughter had breast cancer. Even before the doctor said anything, he already knew what they were going to say. It was hopelessness mingled with the unknown. Either way, in a situation like this, there was no real military response that could fix this dilemma. This was something that would require a high mix of economic genius and a generous dose of miracles to sort out, which did not suit these people very well. Nevertheless, they still managed to mask it somewhat during the brief. A new president would not have understood the gravity as quickly as he did.

"So why don't we cut to the chase here, and get down to what's really bothering you," the President said.

"Sir, we have reason to believe, there will also be some type of imminent cyber-attack on our networks due to this massive economic vulnerability. In fact, I would venture to say, it's already begun."

"Who is it, the Iranians? North Koreans? Chinese? Russians?"

"No, sir, the EU."

"What? How is that?"

"We don't know yet if it is intentional, or just a byproduct of the software they're using for their replacement of the *Euro*. It seems to be some sort of Artificial Intelligence

(AI) attached to their software programming. It basically attaches itself to every kind of electronic device imaginable."

"You mean this is in regards to their *Digital Kredit* they launched in Greece and Spain?"

"Yes, sir. I think they made it, and this is just an assumption, but we think they made it this aggressive to make it easier for those economies to adapt to the total digital systems they are pushing by using this proactive form of software. Somehow, the software code they are using has gotten a mind of its own and is able to make its way past almost any firewall and security systems by rewriting itself."

"Is this the *Great Reset* they were talking about at Davos, Switzerland last year?" the President asked.

"It could be," the Chairman stated.

"So, aside from being annoying as hell, what is the real damage with this?"

"Sir, we don't really know yet. We've reached out to the EU Central Bank, and economic chiefs there and they claim they don't know either.

"This is either a science experiment gone wrong or the work of a brilliant rogue hacker, sliding those AI programs and functions into it without anyone knowing. I mean, if this was something sanctioned by the EU without fully understanding all of the ramifications, then we should hold them wholly responsible.

"As of right now, they claim this was only supposed to be a test-run with Greece and Spain. They don't know how or why it's spreading like it is."

"But what does it do?" asked the President. "Is it like STUXNET?"

"No, sir. STUXNET was rudimentary compared to this software. Imagine what would happen if *Siri* or *Alexa*, something in most everyone's phones and laptops, went rogue, and autonomous. Some just of the preliminary studies on this have shown it is able to get into most everything with no physical connections. Whether someone on the other end is exploiting this information and I mean, all information; confidential, secret, top-secret, and above top secret…we don't know."

"Jeez Louise. Didn't those *geniuses* over there in Brussels realize if they tank our dollar, it would drag the rest of the world economy down with it? What do we have to counter it?"

"Right now, we have our team at DARPA studying it in an enclosed, off-circuit environment to see. However, the AI is pretty advanced. Not even we have this stuff."

"Make sure we got this to the DSA, NSA, and Cyber Command to also get in on this. Those guys can usually make this science fiction stuff up before noon without breaking a sweat."

"They are, sir. We also have some of our teams at MIT and Harvard working it, in particular, what it is going to do the New York Stock Exchange."

"And you said it was a form of Artificial Intelligence?"

"Yes, sir. There are three recognized types: weak, strong, and super AI. The weak is a program, which can do one thing well, like play chess…but that is all it can do. Strong AI is like Siri or Alexa on an iPhone or Amazon device. You can ask it questions and it can get it right most of the time. However, it does not reprogram itself or think autonomously. Super AI, is anywhere from at least as smart as or smarter than the smartest human on the planet, to thousands of times smarter."

"So which of these do you believe it is?"

"Sir, we think, and it's still a little too early to pinpoint, but it's either between strong and super, or it's a form of super."

"Does this have the potential to cause a mass panic?" the President asked.

"Yes, sir, it does."

"I want you guys to also bring in some folks from the industry. Microsoft, IBM, whoever. At this point, we cannot afford to be subtle anymore. See what they know about it and what impacts it will have on their devices. Have someone reach out to Jim Bonnichsen; he is a friend from Apple. Let's see if we have the ability to counteract this thing before this administration gives its first official response."

## Chapter 15

Bagram, Afghanistan
Early October

Tristan lay in his bed thinking about all the *courses of action* they had been laboring over all week. As tired as he was, his brain was still racing 100 miles per hour and he couldn't shut it off even if he tried. For all the years he had been in the military, this was by far, the craziest situation they ever found themselves. They had been tasked to wargame, the collapse of their nation. He was not great at many things, but he could *what if* it with the best of them.

It reminded him of a paper he had read once while attending Command and General Staff College (CGSC), which was the Army's graduate-level equivalent for advanced learning. He pulled his laptop up to his chest and typed in a quick search. *Ah, there it is* he thought. *A World Lit Only By Fire*, by William Manchester. A part of it had always intrigued him. He did a quick word search and then found it.

*Europe had been troubled since the Roman Empire perished in the fifth century. There were many reasons for Rome's fall, among them apathy and bureaucratic absolutism, but the chain of events leading to its actual end had begun the century before. The defenders of the empire were responsible for a ten-thousand-mile frontier. Ever since the time of the soldier-historian Tacitus, in the first century A.D., the vital sector in the north— where the realm's border rested on the Danube and the Rhine—had been vulnerable. Above these great rivers the forests swarmed with barbaric Germanic tribes, some of them tamer than others but all envious of the empire's prosperity. For centuries, they had been intimidated by the imperial legions confronting them on the far banks.*

*Who were the barbarians at their gates* he wondered? Well, here in Afghanistan, it was the Taliban, Al Qaeda, the Haqqani Network, and about a dozen other ne'er-do-well local groups. Who were the barbarians at America's gate?

The Chinese? The Russians? Even the European Union? Every nation that longed to be the number one shot-caller in the world was our modern day equivalent to the Visigoths or the Huns. Nevertheless, how does one knock off the world's premiere superpower? Obviously, a military attack would be foolish. Look what happened to the Japanese in 1941.

A political attack was possible, but the US power structure was all checks and balances. Political sabotage had been tried many times, and each had failed. Economically, the US was energy independent. While she had given away much of her manufacturing base, getting it turned back on would not take much. No, if you wanted to take out America, you had to take out the one thing that everything revolved around- money. However, if you went after the US Dollar, regardless of our staggering national debt, you threatened to drag down the entire global economy. Global economic suicide was certainly the perceived end state, unless, you were the one doing it, and had anticipated the crisis and prepared.

Thus, the *worst-case scenario*: the US economy collapses and drags the rest of the world down with it. The collapse of the United States would definitely send the world back to the Dark Ages. How do you plan for that? Tristan had to treat this entire situation like a crime scene. He, along with Steve and the others, backward planned the entire event. How does the US get its forces from out of the middle of Afghanistan and back to the US without the use of money; land lease agreements, fuel, commercial airliners, etc. all required payment. This required retrograding their forces abroad in a tactical retreat.

The *Worst-Case Scenario* envisioned a fight all the way home. It even envisioned a fight once their troops made it back stateside. The *allied* nations, from which they leased land, ports, and fuel, would most likely not continue to honor any agreements, primarily, because there would be no promise of future payments. These nations would also be facing their own onslaught of problems if the world economy nose-dived. The key element of this scenario would be surprise and force. US Military would have to move back by force, and take the fuel, food, and resources from those places that were unwilling to give it up per their prior agreement. Of course, it did not seem like the American thing to do, but desperate times call for desperate measures. While they may not have had any money, they did have a lot of firepower if push came to shove.

The *Best Case Scenario*: was in Tristan's mind, also the least likely. This was where the economy tanks, but the world is slow to notice what is actually happening. The scenario relied on speed and confusion. They would also be dependent upon these nations being embroiled in their own problems, to care too much about the US Military moving back through their airspace. What the team had envisioned here, was even though the global economy was beginning to crash, there would be enough time to get their people home before those nations really started to grasp just how serious things would become.

The *Most Likely Scenario* was a mix of both. Somehow, with this pending financial apocalypse at hand, they would not be able to make any assumptions about the way things had been done in the past. They would have to strategically think through every step of this plan and account for significant equipment losses. They would plan to land at their strategic fuel stops, prepared to take over airports if necessary to get their aircraft refueled and back in the air. They would require a great deal of speed and seriousness as to their purpose, so to give any would be problematic bureaucrats or other banana-republic officials, any reason to get in their way. In and out before anyone was the wiser. Their overarching guidance had been to hope for the best while planning for the worst.

Although he also recognized *hope* was not a military strategy, he thought maybe they would need to make an exception this time. It was not every day that the world's lone superpower collapses. Therefore, after many hours, they balanced out the worst and best case scenarios, which left them the *Most Likely Course of Action* (MLCOA).

This was also the most difficult, because they were in effect, preparing for a financial meltdown, but attempting to deal with it through a military response. The expectation was that there would be significant turmoil around the world, but the worst of it would be confined largely to the major urban areas. Since none of their ports were located in major cities along the way back to the US, he thought maybe they had that going for them. Major cities were always potential hotspots for violent flare-ups, primarily in regards to looting and rioting. The response from local law enforcement would be quick he hoped, with areas enacting various forms of Martial Law.

Granted, this only held true if the various national law enforcement agencies and militaries held together without the promise of payment or help from their own leadership. Where their planning cell came up short, was what the reaction would be elsewhere around the world. One assumption was if the US and NATO military bases along the route back, were to remain friendly, then they could still utilize their help to retrograde back to the States. They still did not have a solid solution on security while in the air. All of a sudden, he felt very vulnerable.

Nevertheless, if they were limited on food, beds, or space in general, or if the host nation themselves were in full meltdown, things might get dicey. A less than optimal choice, being they were going armed to the teeth, was if they had to occupy an allied location by force, preferably with minimal loss of life. The brigade logistics officer and the support operations officer (SPO) would handle how to get there and ensure they were ready to go with fuel, food, transportation, water, and lodging requests in reverse order of travel. Between their plans to move troops out, and the supply people working the necessities, in theory, their plan would get everyone back stateside safe and sound.

There were also the much-feared international *black swan* events. These unplanned, unforeseen events they just did not see coming. This could be anything from India and Pakistan kicking off a nuclear exchange, to Russia and China taking advantage of the chaos and making massive land grabs. If things turned for the worse, he half expected Martial Law to be declared in most, if not all fifty states. They had all hoped the government had a plan in place to restore order promptly because if they did not, things would get ugly very quickly.

Although this economic apocalypse had only just recently broken on the news, the fear of it was already spreading faster than a wildfire on a dry Kansas plain. The military leadership there in Afghanistan had done their best to filter it out to the soldiers and contractors currently deployed there, but it was contagious. He did not know how much of this had sunk into the American public psyche as of yet. They often could be oblivious to things outside the confines of their continental borders. However, he imagined the movers and shakers in Washington, D.C., Wall Street, and other major financial centers were hurriedly making plans to either cash in on or hoard whatever assets they had in this coming crisis.

Here he was, caught somewhere in the middle of all this, separated from his family by thousands of miles. *Of all the times this could have happened, it had to happen while I was deployed* he thought. *What kind of God would allow this? How did God not see this coming? Isn't America supposed to be God's chosen people or something?* He was mad all of a sudden. If there was a God, he did not like this God.

# Chapter 16

The next morning, the TOC was pulsating with talk about a potential meltdown. It was weird because not even a few weeks ago, most folks would have considered this kind of talk *tin-foil hat* conspiracy stuff. It was like living in a bizarro-world, where everything was upside-down and inside out. Before all the craziness kicked off, the only person who normally did talk about this stuff was Jack; now everyone was. Like he was a carrier for some kind of airborne *doomsday* virus, and now everyone has the bug.

The normal order of things, such as the war effort, also seemed to come to a halt as everyone pretty much disengaged from their routine jobs to call, email, text, and Skype with loved ones back home. Instead of being glued to SIPR feeds and communication systems, folks were glued to the network television. The boss had hoped to keep a manageable lid on this and stay ahead of it, but the 21st century was the *Information Age*, and news like this would not stay quiet for long.

Tristan grabbed a cup of coffee and sat down next to

First Lieutenant Jorge Rosario, the Brigade Assistant Intel Officer. He had been in the Army for less than three years and was on his first combat tour. "Bummer of a first deployment," Tristan said to him. "You may not even get a combat patch for all your efforts."

"For real, sir," he replied. "Everyone is focused on what they're going to do once they get back to the States. I am just trying to figure out how we get out of here first."

"Well, there is a plan," Tristan said flatly. "I mean, depending on how this all turns out, is going to depend on whether we walk to the plane or run to it."

"How bad do you think it will get?" Jorge asked.

"I don't know."

"I'm not sure if this is relevant, but during our RIP out-brief with the 101st, their S2 had told us in the Two-Cell, there had been a slight uptick in Small Arms Fire (SAFIRE) a month prior to us getting there. We'd been watching it, and getting the intel-dumps from the units and battalions, and it seems the upticks have continued to rise," Jorge said.

"The boss is tracking."

"Yes, sir, but we all figured being the end of the summer; the Taliban were just trying to get their licks in before winter hits."

"But?" Tristan sensed the hesitation in his statement.

"But what if they knew?" he said. "What if they were just softening us up, or probing, for what they knew was coming."

"Who, the Taliban? The Haqqani-Network? ISIS? Al Qaeda? I mean, if they knew what was actually going on, they would already be surrounding this place," LT Rosario said.

"It's possible. I doubt your local Taliban fighter watches CNN or the BBC, but they could be getting fed info from the Pakistani Intel agency ISI." Tristan added, "Keep an eye on it. This could be an early indicator of things to come."

"Roger that, sir," Jorge replied with an almost renewed sense of purpose.

With all the talk of the economic situation, they were forgetting that they were still in a war zone. It made him think of the old quote, *whatever happens, the enemy still gets a vote.*

## Chapter 17

Bagram Air Base:
Mid-October

It had been at least two weeks since Colonel Price first confirmed the news both he and Jack had watched that fateful morning at the Dining Facility. Taking a mental inventory while he was walking back to his office, he surmised thus far, he had moved his wife and kids back to her parents' place in Texas. The boss had huddled with his battalion commanders and a few select others on the rooftop to confirm what he and

Jack had seen on television was what the Commanding General was briefing the senior leaders in the Afghan theatre. Their planning cell had done their best hasty analysis of what might happen, and the news of it seemed to be going viral around the base. The enlisted Warrant Officers and Commissioned Officers of the Air Force, Army, Navy, Marines, and Contractors…did not matter; everyone seemed to be feeding off the anxiety of the uncertainty.

Air Force flights out of country started to pick up, and people were not being as congenial about making the passenger list as they had in the past. Contractors were starting to leave in droves…, which was weird. Defense contractors were usually military members who either got out or retired and then been hired by some defense company to come back over making double what they had been making in the military, oftentimes doing the same exact job. If they were leaving in higher than usual numbers, foregoing hefty paychecks, something indeed was *rotten in Denmark*. Tristan thought about some of the fights that had broken out at the passenger terminal and if things were getting bad here amongst America's finest, he feared the worst for those back in the urban areas of the US.

The TCN's or Third Country Nationals (usually from places like Bangladesh, Pakistan, India, and Nepal) were seemingly unaware of the theater-wide anxiety. Most of them spoke little to no English, so aside from the thinning out of personnel, it was unclear how much they understood. Truth be told, if they left, the base would really be screwed. They worked in the Dining Facilities, did the laundry, drove buses, cleaned the restrooms, and all the jobs no one else wanted to do. However, these were the jobs that made living there, livable. Maybe they knew, but decided going back to *Whereverstan*, was still less preferable. Tristan did not know, but he wondered how they were going to be worked into their varying courses of action, in case things got dicey.

The Brigade Deputy Commander, Lieutenant Colonel Harmon, walked in. He was in charge when Colonel Price had to leave for official business.

"Zavota, weren't you already supposed to have headed north to Patriot?"

"Yes, sir. Between the air threats and the maintenance, all flights outside of our immediate AO were put on hold. However, we got the green light this morning. We are ready to go."

"We?"

"The chaplain asked if he could go with me. I told him I would ask."

"No problem. Get with Second Battalion and see if you and the chaplain can get on a flight up to FOB Patriot. We need to do an emergency resupply for food and water, but also, I need you to help them break things down and start moving it back here to Bagram."

"Roger. How long do we have?"

"96 hours or less."

"Roger, sir, I'll head over there right now and see what's heading that way."

"If they don't, since we've limited our flights across the brigade, generate a flight on my authority. I will approve it. But you need to get there today, and expect to stay until they're mission complete with drawdown."

"Will do, sir. I'll let you know right before we pull pitch."

FOB Patriot was up in *no man's land*, and it was a postage stamp of a base. While Mike Thompson was a good leader, he tended to stress a lot about little things. I suppose they need me there to keep him focused and levelheaded with this last-minute mission. He jotted a message down on his Facebook messenger app to his wife and would have to wait until he got somewhere with Wi-Fi to send it.

With that, he was out the door and heading toward the flight line.

## Chapter 18

Bagram, Afghanistan
Early October

Second Battalion was down the street on Stallion Ramp. Tristan walked toward their flight operations center and walked up to their front desk.

"Hey, what's flying north today?" he asked the flight operations clerk who had been staring intensely at her computer.

"Nothing yet, unless a MEDEVAC or attack happens," she said without looking up.

"I need a flight north to Patriot, who's up on QRF?"

She looked up finally and immediately shot up. "Sorry, sir, I thought you were somebody else."

"No problem, just don't let it happen again," he said as he gave her a sly wink.

"You need to go to FOB Patriot, sir?"

"Yes."

"We have a *purple team* on standby, but you'd have to ask the Colonel," she said.

"He in his office?"

"I believe so, sir."

"Thanks, I'll head over there to see him, but this is top-down orders, so notify the crews to be ready to go in two hours."

"Roger, sir."

Tristan walked out of flight operations and over to Second BN's headquarters. He knew Lieutenant Colonel Jake Huggins would authorize the flight, but it was courtesy to run it by him before launching his crews. He walked in, headed to his office, and knocked on the frame of the open door.

"Hey, sir, got a minute?"

Lieutenant Colonel Huggins looked up… "Sure, I understand you need a lift?"

"Roger, sir. The DCO asked me to help out with FOB Patriot's closure."

"You'll have three days. I'm to bring you back on

Friday."

"Good. I was just instructed 96 hours or less, so we will have to work quickly. Hoping things go smoothly," Tristan said.

"You know hope isn't a strategy right?" Lieutenant Colonel Huggins said with a smile.

"Yes, sir, I know. Nevertheless, these are unprecedented times we are in now. I'll be applying liberal doses of hope and luck on everything we do."

"Safe flight then."

"Thanks, sir, I'll check in on the backside. Sir, you mind if I borrow your Tata truck for about thirty minutes. I need to run back to the room and get some clothes and stuff before heading out?" Tristan asked.

"Sure, go ahead. I don't need it until tonight," Huggins replied.

Tristan headed out with the keys and got in the Tata. Tata's were Toyota Tacoma knock-offs which were apparently very popular in these neighborhoods. He started driving back to the barracks and spotted the Chaplain doing his power walk between the brigade and the coffee shack. He pulled over.

"You need a lift, sexy?" Tristan did his best 1970s ladies' man impression.

"Far out, man. Where'd you get the sweet ride, I'm digging it?"

"Ok, no more seventies for you. Where you heading, brigade?"

"Seriously, where'd you get the truck? Are you saying a lowly assistant staffer gets a ride to drive before essential, ministerial special-staff do?" he asked sarcastically.

"No, not mine. Lieutenant Colonel Huggins. I am actually heading back to the room to grab some essentials before we head up to FOB Patriot. Going to be up there a few days helping them with closing the base. Supposed to be back Friday," Tristan offered.

"We?"

"Yeah, you and I."

"Which means I need to grab my stuff as well."

"Yes. Get in."

"Sweet, I haven't been to Patriot yet."

"I already got you approved by the Brigade Commander and the DCO, so hop in.

"Just like olden times eh?" Tristan said.

"Gotta love last-minute missions, this is when the most interesting things happen," Jack added. "Hey, let's swing by my place first since I have my 'go-bag' already packed."

"Roger."

## Chapter 19

RC-North Afghanistan
Early October

Two hours later, they were airborne and flying over steep ridgelines marked with tiny villages and dirt roads. Forward Operating Base Patriot was small and strategically speaking, not very valuable. It was supposed to be a midway point aircrews and ground convoys could detour to on their way up to Mazari-Sharif -- the regional center and largest town in the area. Both plugged into the cockpit conversations via their 'Davy Clark' headsets. They were instructed to look out the left side of the Blackhawk aircraft to the road to their 10 o'clock position.

"You seeing what I'm seeing?" the left seat pilot asked the other.

"Mark the location on the GPS and we'll send it back as a *spot report* to higher," the other replied.

"Who are they?" Tristan asked.

"Beats me, sir, could be Taliban, Haqqani, or just one tribe going to go have dinner over at another tribe's village. Whoever they are, there is a lot of them."

Below them, for what looked like a mile or so, there was a column of people walking along a dirt road heading south. What they could not tell from the altitude they were at, was if it was all men, men and women, or families. Afghanistan was elusive when it came to hiding the large populations that lived there. Because the country was so broken up by terrain, one would assume not many people lived outside of the major cities of Kabul or Kandahar. However, if one had attended a Shura (key tribal leader meeting), all of sudden, hundreds of men would appear as if they were coming down from the highlands to reveal they actually existed. Whatever was below, it appeared to be hundreds of people, all moving away from something…or towards it. Tristan, who was only carrying a 9-Millimeter Berretta pistol, felt naked all of a sudden.

They arrived at Patriot within the hour, and not having been there before, they were expecting to be completely underwhelmed by the size of it. Although it was small, it was a tightly secured base, surrounded by high Hesco barriers and ninety-degreed corners marked with guard towers and a decently sized helipad. The buildings were wooden and had a distinct, 'frontier' feel to them. Except for this time, they had traded Comanche and Apache Indians for the Taliban and Al Qaeda.

Getting out of the helicopters, they made their way with their gear to the small flight operations building. Behind them, the aircraft picked up and turned back towards the way they came. Someone walked out of the building to greet them.

"Hey, didn't know you were coming up here!" Major Thompson bellowed out to them as they greeted each other. "To what do I owe the pleasure?"

"How read-in are you on the situation?" Tristan asked.

"You mean the drawdown? Only that it is being expedited. I guess we are the first on the chopping block."

"That is one way to put it," Tristan replied. "We need to be out of here completely by Friday."

The expression on Thompson's face was a mixture of horror and bewilderment.

"Friday?"

"Yeah. The DCO asked if we would come and help here where we could. Where are you at now with the drawdown?"

"Well, I'd be lying to say we are where I'd hope we'd be, but then again, we only got notification of the move last week. With today being Tuesday, I'd say three days would be a very tight timeline indeed," Thompson responded while chewing on his unlit cigar. "Any news about why this was expedited so quickly?

"There is a lot going on that I am going to have bring you up to speed on. What are you tracking thus far?" Tristan asked as they began making their way towards the porch of the flight operations.

"We don't get a lot of news out this way. The Wi-Fi is spotty at best. News on SIPR has been cryptic as well, but I see an uptick in our efforts to get out of here. What are you tracking?"

"Well, the US is in a pretty dicey situation economically. The EU dropped some new form of digital currency into the market and it is wreaking havoc everywhere. The experts are saying this will have some serious ramifications on our dollar. Leadership at Bagram and Kandahar want to make sure we *tighten our shot-group*

126

here on the ground in case we need to make a quick exit," Jack offered. "That is about the gist of it.

"Let's meet up in 30 minutes and go over the exit plans you have so far. In the meantime, where can we throw our gear and grab a bite to eat?" Tristan asked.

"I got you the guest rooms in the building behind the flight ops there, and I'll have the runner go grab some MREs (Meals Ready to Eat) from the chow hall. After you eat, come upstairs above flight ops and we'll sit down in the conference room where we can get started."

## Chapter 20

Paradise, Texas
Early October

Katy had just finished making breakfast for the girls when her dad walked in with a furrowed brow. The kids were busy making designer animals out of their pancakes and Katy leaned against the kitchen island taking small sips out of her coffee.

"What's going on, Dad?" she asked.

"Was driving back from work this morning when I heard on the radio the government was considering implementing some kind of *Martial Law* in certain places."

"Why would they announce that, I mean, wouldn't that create an unnecessary panic?" she asked worriedly.

"Don't know for sure, but I think they are preempting a state of emergency, like when they know a hurricane is going to hit the coast or something. I guess so they can begin posturing the National Guard, police, and other federal and state agencies ahead of time if they had to."

"Who is going to pay the state's emergency funding if our dollar goes bust? For that matter, who is going to pay the National Guard and law enforcement to go implement Martial Law? I doubt seriously they are going to work for free."

"I don't know. Maybe they might pay them in gold, silver, food, land grants, wampum, who knows. However, they must have some resources stockpiled they can use as bargaining chips with the necessary professions like police, doctors, electricians, and so on. Perhaps they were floating the idea to see what the public and media reaction would be first. The woman on the radio did not necessarily call it

*Martial Law*; they called it an amber on the advisory scale Homeland Defense uses. I think they said it was similar to going to DEFCON 2."

"Wait, amber, like an Amber-Alert?" Katy asked.

"No, like the color amber- or orange."

"Wait, you are confusing me. So they didn't actually say the words *Martial Law*, but it's essentially the same thing?" she asked. "*Martial Law* seems like a very loaded term, which would cause strong reactions in people," she further added. "I don't think they would throw that around loosely. However, I could see them doing Threat Level Orange. I think the threat is high with all the uncertainty going on."

"Pretty much. We better keep stocking up. They haven't issued anything for Texas as of yet, it was just for the major cities on the east and west coast, but I would not put it past people to start panicking and making runs on the stores again. People are dangerous when they run in herds."

\*\*\*

Tristan and Mark were sitting around the map table, which
had the layout of FOB Patriot drawn out to scale, while Mark
was busy explaining his exit plan. Jack had stepped out
earlier and was doing his chaplain thing by going around and
checking on everyone. Considering the US Army had in the
past, closed a number of smaller FOBs strewn throughout the
theater, they had a general idea of the order of how things
needed to go.

Secure the people.

Secure the sensitive items and weapons.

Destroy anything they were not going take with them.

Beyond that, they just needed to ensure any loose
ends were tied up. An FOB this size did not seem too
daunting a task. The FOB had a manning roster of around 93
people. That included soldiers, contractors, and TCNs.
Patriot did not have many things to begin with; it was, for all
intents and purposes, a minimally staffed way station. Tristan
hoped he did not have to repeat this exercise with the other
half dozen small FOBs still operating in theater. However, it
made sense now why the brigade commander had him

brought into his roof top *soiree*. He needed him and Jack up to speed so they could pass along the most accurate information possible to the outlying stations.

"And that's it. Doesn't seem too bad," Mark said, finishing his plan with a large swig of coffee.

"Well, we have till Friday, so where do you need me?" Tristan asked.

"I'll send a runner out to gather all the Platoon Sergeants and contract leads to have our folks start packing. I figure they can have most of their personal and pro-gear buttoned up by this evening. We'll start a burn-party tonight for the stuff we don't intend to take with us," Mark said matter-of-factly.

"Wouldn't it make a huge smoke plume?" Tristan asked instantly thinking back to all his military training on light discipline. Fire at night on an exercise was bad. "I mean, if the enemy didn't know something was up before, they will surely know something then."

"Yeah. I mean, well, the best I can do is burn at night. At least there is hardly any illumination tonight; the smoke will not be visible from very far away. And this place isn't important enough to warrant an incinerator."

Large, well-defined smoke plumes tended to make excellent markers to shoot at for the Taliban's homemade mortars and rockets. However, given the options, tonight offered the best opportunity with no moon to burn all nonessential paperwork and equipment that could not leave with the Americans. It would have to work. He hoped it would not draw too much attention.

Just then, Jack walked in briskly and said, "Gents, we might have a situation."

"What is it?" Mark asked.

"We've got a significant amount of local nationals gathering around the FOB," Jack said. "Is it normal for here?"

"Not really. I mean, we have done some MEDCAPs in the past where we provided some immunization shots and free dental and optometry services. Even then, it was not more than twenty or thirty at a time. How many people are out there?" Mark asked.

"Venturing a guess, I'd say more than a hundred, less than two," Jack said hesitantly. "I mean, they don't appear hostile or threatening, but I'd bet a pretty penny every last one of them is at least armed with an AK-47 and a full clip."

Major Thompson immediately bolted out the door and headed toward flight operations, which also doubled as his operations-cell. He immediately began barking out orders.

"Sergeant Richardson, get on the horn with Brigade and give them a situation report (SITREP). We need to put their QRF on request. Specialist Cofield, talk to Second Squad and get a drone up. Let's see how big this crowd is and what they're hiding. Everyone else, on my command, put your vests and Kevlar's on and lock and load."

## Chapter 21

*Two major problems in the world's financial system have to be addressed: 1) the demise of the U.S. dollar as the world's reserve currency, and 2) the almost uncontrollable growth in debts and in central banks' balance sheets. For all of these issues, central banks have only been buying time since the start of the credit crisis in 2007. But given how sensitive this issue is, nothing can be said in public. Any official comments about a new 'Plan B' will crash financial markets (Plan A) immediately. Central planners know the only way to plan a reset is to do it in total secrecy.*

**Willem Middelkoop, <u>The Big Reset</u>**

Washington, D.C. Early
October

Back in Washington, D.C., the time was in the middle of the
night, or, *zero dark thirty* as the military often refer to it. A
dozen or so Congressmen huddled in a conference room in
an unnamed and unmarked building not far from Capitol
Hill. They spoke quietly as if to consciously highlight the
need for confidentiality.

"What should our response be?" one asked the others.
Although Wall Street and the markets had not yet tanked, the
storm clouds were looming ominously overhead.

"The President just ordered Homeland Security to
elevate the threat level to amber. I think once we see one or
two cities start to have issues, he'll raise it to red and declare
martial law," another offered in reply. "He'll have good
cause, too, which means Congress and the courts can't
challenge it. We all know what's at stake."

"This is the perfect opportunity to get rid of him,
finally," another said in disgust.

"Well, if the dollar does crash, how is that going to
anyone to help us unseat him from the White House? How
do we pay those law enforcement officers and security

personnel? They aren't going to work for free while having their own families left to fend for themselves," another quipped sarcastically. "And who here is talking to the Europeans? Don't they realize they just opened Pandora's Box and let out every worst-case scenario possible? We have very little wiggle room on this."

"The team and I are in touch with our counterparts over there. They still maintain this tech-virus-pandemic was not intentional, however, they see this crisis as an opportunity as well," the central figure said. "They wanted to slow-roll this *Great Reset* out to help unveil their new *Kredit* implementation in Spain and Greece. But now, it's already in London, Paris, Istanbul, Baltimore, Chicago, New York, and Atlanta."

"This is bad," another added. "Maybe even apocalyptic."

"What are our options?" the man in the center asked.

"I think we really only have two," the representative at the end of the table said. "Either we embrace this *Kredit* publically and act as if we were in full support all along, or we fight it. If we support it, then it may help stabilize the markets and prevent people from making runs on the banks."

"And if we fight it?" another asked. "You know once we replace the dollar with something somebody else controls, our sovereignty is gone."

"Well, then we run the risk of basic societal breakdown in every minor and major urban area across the nation. It will so spook the markets, people are going to be pulling out as fast as they can; anything that even smells like US dollar will be replaced with gold, silver, land, physical resources, etc.," she added grudgingly. "It's not just going to be our currency that crashes, but everybody. The way I see it, we are about to see trillions wiped out in every major holding across the globe. This is not just people holding stocks, bonds, certificates because they own because they can afford to, it's 401Ks, retirements, life savings, etc. Everything not already linked to the *Kredit* is going to get their knees cut off from under them."

"We also have troops stationed around the world, which we will need to marshal back here to the States," another member added.

"They will have to wait," she noted coldly. "Trillions of dollars are at stake here, which takes precedence over a few thousand military members in Combat Zones. Besides, they are heavily armed. They can fight their way out if they have to."

"Wow, that was cold, even for you," another remarked jokingly.

"Maybe," she said. "But if we don't get ahead of this now, they won't have a country to come back to. We'll be just like Pompeii; a smoldering pile of ashes."

"Well, if you ask me, the Dollar was dead a long time ago," another member added. "We've managed to keep this charade on life support with smoke and mirrors, but with it already carrying twenty-seven trillion in debt, not to mention the one-hundred trillion in unfunded liabilities; it became unsalvageable a long time ago. I say we join the cause and turn this crisis into an opportunity. I say we take a vote."

"All in favor of converting to the *Kredit* say *aye*," the speaker at the center said.

Every hand shot up minus one.

"All against dumping the dollar for the *Kredit* say *nay*," he continued.

The lone dissenter raised his hand. "This will mark the end of America," he noted somberly.

"The ayes have it. Get with your party members and organizations tomorrow, and let them know which way we are leaning and start messaging it. Bring in your core teams and get them on board first. After that, we will start working on the outer rings through our partners at the media. We need a majority vote on this no later than Wednesday during our Emergency Session," the speaker at the center concluded. Adjourned.

The group got up and began making their way out of the smoke-filled room.

## Chapter 22

FOB Patriot
Early October

FOB Patriot sat on the remains of a faded old Soviet base, which had been built back in the early 1980s. Although largely built up with wooden structures, it still had three remaining Soviet concrete structures (gym, bathhouse, and jail). Two roads just north of the base crisscrossed leading northwest to southeast, as well as northeast to southwest depending on which direction you were heading. Portions of the Hindu Kush Mountains surrounded the base, and a small river ran northeast-southwest, naturally following the base of the mountains. Of course, the roads and the rivers contorted themselves to the mountainous terrain all around them, so nothing here was ever in a straight line.

The area immediately surrounding the FOB was poppy farmland and relatively flat. It reminded Jack of the terraced rice paddies in China and Vietnam, but definitely not as organized. Of course, the poppy was the key ingredient of heroin, which is what they made and used the proceeds to continue to fund their endless jihad. It did have some natural terrain features that offered both cover and concealment, should the enemy need it. Today it seemed as though they needed it. The groups of local natives, which had been gathering the days prior, had begun to back themselves up and start setting up what appeared to be defensive positions all around the FOB.

Jack had been making his way around to the different guard positions checking on the soldiers. He asked them how they were holding up and if they'd had a chance to call home yet. Most had, but Jack could sense the seriousness in their gazes and speech patterns. Since Jack was an Army Chaplain, he was considered a non-combatant by the Geneva

Convention and thus prohibited from carrying a weapon. However, he sure wished he had one right now. Things were starting to get tense outside the FOB and he definitely felt underdressed. This was the first time in his eight-year career as a chaplain where he intended to violate the Geneva Convention charter and arm himself. Besides, he did not think the Afghan Taliban were party to those *gentlemen's rules* anyway.

While he had been on the northwest corner, Jack noticed the direction of the wind had shifted and was now blowing strong from the northwest to the southeast. He also noticed an odd scent in the wind. It wasn't marijuana, but something like it. After a few whiffs a very pleasant lightheadedness began to come over him and it dawned on him they were burning something to get everyone there high. He was not the only one who noticed it. One of the soldiers said they frequently burned stuff to annoy the Americans there, but only did it when the winds would be sustained in the base's direction. The soldier had been flying a small drone around outside the wall about 200 feet in the air. He was feeding visual information back to the TOC inside.

Jack also noticed the movement along the outside. The locals were moving back but not leaving, as if they knew something bad was about to happen. That was when Jack began moving toward Mark and Tristan to let them know what was happening.

Major Thompson went into a closet and after a few minutes, came out with two gas masks still in their wrapping. He gave one to Jack and the other to Tristan. Apparently, this was not the first time they'd tried to use smoke.

"Man, I never thought I'd have to wear one of these things over here," Tristan said untangling the webbing in the back as he went to put it on.

"Me either," Thompson said. "But these guys love to burn stuff when the wind is blowing our direction."

"What are they burning?" Tristan asked. "It kind of smells like weed."

"Hashish probably, or whatever it is they use to get high," Thompson replied. "Initially, we thought they were doing it to just annoy us. You know, make it as unpleasant to be here as possible. Back then, they would also burn trash when the wind was blowing this way. Then we noticed they were also doing it to mask their movements from drones. Now it seems, they're using it for both, and adding in drugs to make us high and not want to fight back when they attack."

"So you think they're getting ready to att…" Jack said being interrupted by a large explosion outside.

"Yes I do," Thompson said running toward the front entrance.

Tristan donned his mask and grabbed his M-4. Jack donned his mask and then found a large, thick broom handle he could use as a staff if he needed it. The radio in the ops was going off very loudly and the ops team was speaking frantically to the folks back at Bagram.

"Roger, we are under attack! You need to send air support now!" the operator yelled into the radio.

"Roger that," the voice replied. "QRF enroute, ETA 30 minutes. We've also requested A-10 support that may get there sooner."

"What is the SITREP?" the voice on the other side of the radio continued to ask.

"We have around 150-200 fighters who have taken up position around the FOB," the operator said. "They've just started firing at our entrance with their rocket-propelled grenades (RPGs). We are also receiving indiscriminate mortar hits as well as small arms fire."

***

Tristan had been following Mark, moving low and fast. The sounds were overlapping and very loud "pop pop pop" sounds followed by frequent explosions. Smoke was now coming over the Hescos very thick, as well as from a small fire that had ignited in one of the buildings.

"Mark, I'm heading to that building to see what was damaged and to help put that fire out!" Tristan yelled as he peeled off in the direction toward the building. He didn't know if Mark heard him or not. Mark peeked back and gave him the thumbs up as he continued toward the main entrance.

Each of the four guard towers was lighting up the late afternoon with their M-60 machine guns. They were ripping through the perimeter terrain like a rain of hellfire. Jack could see the RPGs zipping past them, fortunately, most of which had not had any effective hits, at least not yet. RPGs were notoriously inaccurate, with no guidance systems built into them. They were point and shoot, and hope you hit what you were aiming at.

As soon as an RPG zipped by, the guard tower would swing their M-60s toward that direction and evaporate everything in that general direction. Furthermore, there were soldiers along the wall who were firing their SAW machine guns as well as M-4s, laying down heavy suppressive fire. As soon as someone stood up to fire an RPG, they were immediately cut down and their RPG being launched as a result of their trigger reflex while falling meant those rockets were being fired all over the place. It was a picture-perfect definition of chaos.

Tristan raced inside the building where a mortar had struck. Fortunately, there didn't appear to be anyone inside since everyone was outside along the wall. It appeared to be sleeping quarters. Part of it was an open bay, the back half had some closed-off rooms, presumably for the higher ranking NCOs and officers. The mortar had knocked the power out of the building so the dark helped identify where the fire was burning. Tristan pulled out his flashlight and scanned around for a fire extinguisher. Within a minute or two, he'd found one and took the pin out. The fire was not out of control, but if left unattended, could easily catch and threaten the rest of the structures within their FOB. He directed the hose toward the base of the fire and squeezed off a large spray of white, cloudy retardant.

He worked his way through the rest of the room doing touch-up sprays on places that were still burning. Thankfully, he'd kept his gas mask on so the smoke wasn't overwhelming, but he was now sweating profusely and feeling somewhat claustrophobic. Finishing inside, he found his way back outside just in time to see another building on the other side take a direct hit from a mortar. He saw Jack huddled with some contractors in the bunker and he raced toward them. He chuckled a little bit about the irony of putting out fires. It had become such an overused pun; he never actually thought he would literally be putting out real fires.

Jack saw Tristan and began moving toward him.

"Hey, come help me put this fire out!" Tristan yelled through his mask. "I hope you can use that staff like Moses!"

"Ah, we got jokes at a time like this, let's go, *Fireman-Sam*," Jack said as they both began moving in the direction of the new fire.

## Chapter 23

FOB Patriot
Early October

With his QRF sorties of AH-64s and UH-60s launched, Colonel Price stayed in the Brigade's TOC listening to the radio reports coming out of Patriot. He requested they leave their comms on an open mic, so they could hear everything going on and free up the ops Specialists to work on other things like providing the QRF team's coordinates and updates.

"Hey, Specialist Q" (Q was Quintana's nickname), "where are Major's Thompson and Zavota?" Colonel Price asked.

"Sir, the last I heard, Zavota was putting out fires, and Thompson was at the front entrance helping secure it," Q said.

"Roger," Colonel Price stated impatiently. "Let me know the minute they get back to the TOC."

"Roger, Sir, WILCO," Q replied.

Colonel Price stood there brooding for a moment. His own TOC was abuzz with activity as other outlying FOBs were reporting similar reports of unusual activity outside their bases. He didn't have enough aircraft and crews to cover every one of them, so he gave the request up to the Air Force for as much support as they could muster.

He sent a similar request to the Navy teams that were currently flying out of Bagram but figured they would be tied up supporting the few remaining Marine units still operating out of Kandahar and in the Helmand. He decided instead to spend the next few free moments to send a SITREP up to the Division commander. Just then, the *big voice* (the airbase speaker system) began its robotic notification that mortar attacks were starting to hit Bagram airbase.

Bagram was a sprawling base with two, ten-thousand foot runways. Along the runways, you had the tarmacs and dozens of hangars and tenant units. Furthermore, most of the varied units were arrayed along Disney. The base had two outer layers of security. A ten-mile wide outer layer with a complicated series of triple-concertina wires, as well as antivehicle defilades, and an inner barrier of Hescos.

You then had the base itself, which was comprised of a series of fences and Hescos. It was a secure, miniature, self-contained city. Therefore, unless the mortar hit was in your direct vicinity, you probably were not going to hear the explosion. Nevertheless, it seemed the enemy was directing its biggest weapons systems to get the Americans' attention concentrated over here instead of the outer FOBs. Just then, a new report came in of a pair of vehicle-borne improvised explosive devices (VB-IED) attempting to ram their way through the gates and have the suicide bomber/drivers detonate. The Taliban were trying to force their way into Bagram.

"Captain Grimes, didn't the aircrews that took Major's Zavota and Shaw up to Patriot; report a significant amount of human traffic heading south?" Colonel Price asked.

"They did, Sir. Do you think it's who's hitting us now?" Captain Grimes asked.

"Very likely. Do some digging and see what the chatter has been around theatre, and get back to me within the hour."

"Roger, Sir" Captain Grimes replied.

"Once they give us the reverse grid coordinates for the mortar rounds, let's get some birds in the air and send some rounds back to them courtesy the Spartan Brigade," Colonel Price said in a huff.

Within minutes, the coordinates were broadcasted on the mIRC chat windows, for which all the operations rooms across theatre would use. The Brigade Battle Captain, Major Anderson asked and received the final verbal approval from Colonel Price to launch the QRF. Within a minute, a pair of AH-64 Apache helicopters were in the air heading to the presumed launch coordinates from the last spate of mortar rounds. Computer simulation modeling based on the impact zone could be reversed within minutes to determine how far out the shots had been made from. It was not an exact science, but it was dang close.

The only drawback was it took a few minutes. The Taliban had become very proficient at setting up mortar tubes, launching some shots, and then abandoning their position before any response would come. They could not launch them very far, and these homemade tubes were wildly inaccurate, but every once in a while, they hit a building or something and got lucky.

The AH-64s found the abandoned mortar site and did a couple of slow and low passes to survey it with their camera. The site was surprisingly out in the open, and apparently a quick set up and not really worth the cost of one Hellfire missile, but they also couldn't leave it set up, so they pulled back and fixed their target. "Here goes a $100K down the drain," pilot one said as he launched a single Hellfire anti-tank missile.

Just then, four men jumped out of the grass half a football field away from the aircraft. They had hidden under some false terrain and they quickly set up and fired four RPGs. Four smoke trails were seen heading toward the hovering aircraft. They were coming from each cardinal direction, in an attempt to cut off the aircraft from heading out in any particular direction. The RPGs slammed into the aft portion of the first Apache causing it to career into a fierce tailspin.

The second Apache pulled pitch and immediately began to climb letting the remaining RPGs pass underneath. It then quickly nosed forward, down, and began to increase speed and circling on a right-hand departure. In the process, the pilots began to both make emergency calls back to their brigade as well as shooting strafing rounds from its 12.7 mm machine gun, mounted to the side of the aircraft. The first aircraft continued its spin until it crashed hard into the ground with a metallic thud and whirring. The second aircraft had already picked up speed and was flying at 75 feet at 60 knots in z patterns lighting up anything that moved underneath.

"Spartan 1, this is Cav05, we have one aircraft down. I cannot see anyone moving, but I cannot land either. Still have hostiles in the area. Need to send ground forces out to secure the site and requesting more QRF to hunt down these bastards," the Pilot in Command from the airborne Apache said angrily.

"Cav05, keep your speed up and you are free to go weapons hot," the radio replied. He'd already been weapons hot (firing freely) but now it was officially legal. He keyed the mic back twice to indicate he understood. Both he and his co-pilot were scanning feverishly but could not see anyone or anything moving down in the tall, waving grass.

"Sir, it seems like the mortar fire was a ruse to get us to launch our QRF to this specific location," Captain Grimes reported to Colonel Price. "They knew our response and anticipated it."

"So is this a one-off event, or is it just the beginning?" he asked the Captain.

"Sir, it is too early to tell, but given what is going on at Patriot, I'd say they were connected," Captain Grimes responded.

"I'm thinking the same thing. Somehow, they know what is going on back in the US and are going to try to exploit this opportunity to hit us as hard as they can. Their intel most likely is coming to them through the Pakistani ISI," Colonel Price said. "I want to pull our forces back to Bagram ASAP. Get me on the phone with MG Rickards."

# Chapter 24

The Green family sat around the television that afternoon
watching the President deliver a state of the union-style
address to the nation. Normally, these would be at night at
the most optimal prime-time slot, but not during
emergencies. Katy's mother, father, brother, and daughters
all watched the president deliver his comments about what
was currently unfolding.

*My fellow Americans. Recent events have come to
light about a rather dynamic and significant economic
development that will have significant impacts on our way of
life. The European Union has decided, rather unilaterally I
might add, to create a form of currency, which was intended
to replace their current Euro, which is failing in many
regards. This replacement was a new form of digital
currency, backed by block chain technology, a global
internet system, and an advanced form of Artificial
Intelligence, or AI.*

*Their intent was simply to test this new currency, and its accompanying technology with Greece and Spain, considering their outstanding national debts and significant economic problems, however, this technology has slipped beyond their borders. This advanced and aggressive form of Artificial Intelligence was supposed to implement a form of instant conversions for all of their local currencies into a single one called, the Kredit. This, however, has begun reacting to everything, far beyond the boundaries of Greece and Spain.*

*My European friends have assured me, this was in no way intentional, nevertheless, it has begun spreading through every European country, Turkey, North Africa, and is even now in the US. My administration is working tirelessly to understand the ramifications of this situation. Even now, it is being called a digital pandemic, and at present, it is still uncertain as to how it will affect our markets and our economy. I ask you do not panic, nor rush out to pull all of your money from the banks. We will ensure our markets remain strong and viable. I am charging each of the governors to prevent or stop any price gouging for fuel and other necessities. May God bless you, the United States military, and the United States of America.*

With that, the media spokesperson came back on to begin their partisan analysis of what the President just said. Katy turned the volume down and asked, "I guess Tristan was right? Should we panic?"

"I don't know. Anytime the government comes out and says…hey, everything is going to be ok, it's usually right before everything falls apart," David replied.

"Reagan once said *'the scariest words you will ever hear is that we are from the government, and we are here to help,'*" her dad added with a nervous laugh.

"I mean, I still don't get all the hubbub," Katy said. "How does this change everything?"

"If I go to the bank, and pull out a hundred dollars, will it now simply give me a hundred dollars' worth of *Kredits*?

"Well, it's digital, so you wouldn't be able to pull out any cash I would think," Carl said.

"I'm confused. You remember when we went to Germany a few years ago, and we had to go to a machine where you could convert your US Dollars into Euros? I put in a hundred dollars; we would get back, like eighty euros, depending on the exchange rate at the time. Is that the same thing we're talking about now?" Katy asked.

"You just said it yourself. It depended on the exchange rate. The *Kredit* doesn't have a rate yet, to my knowledge," David replied. "It's an untested currency that exists purely on the Internet."

"I guess it would throw a lot of turmoil into the markets," Carl added. "All I remember though, is right after 9/11, President Bush said the same thing. That we should not panic but we should keep spending our money. He didn't want 9/11 to crash the economy."

"Bush didn't want Wall Street and the stock markets to fall apart. However, in terms of economic destructive power, the 2008 mortgage collapse was far worse than 9/11," Katy's dad said. "We don't think about it like that because we aren't in the markets, but trillions were lost across numerous industries. Hundreds of thousands of stock portfolios, retirements, 401Ks, and so on were wiped out I read."

"Yeah, but remember September the 10th, 2001?" David asked. "When Rumsfeld came out and announced they had lost track of over two trillion dollars. No idea where it went. Then the next day, everyone forgot because of 9/11."

"So what are we going to do here if it happens?" Janice asked.

"We need to get the gardens going. We need to start canning what we have. Need to check the water-well and see what we have. Stock up on things we cannot make, like oil and batteries. Probably buy another generator. Get some solar panels wired into the house for backup," David added.

"And stock up on guns and ammo," Katy added.

"Need to set up a meeting with the family and let them know where to come to should things start to fall apart," Katy said to her dad. "Uncle Tony and Nathan, and Mom's side as well, need to come out of the city and at a minimum, park their travel trailers out here."

"Probably wouldn't hurt to go talk to the neighbors all around as well. At least get some kind of neighborhood watch going," he added.

"This is all so crazy," her brother noted blankly while staring at the television. "Who would have thought it was going to end like this?"

"End?" Carl said.

"Yeah, as in the end of the American dream. I always thought it would be an asteroid or super-volcano that did us in," he added.

"Or the Rapture," Katy said matter-of-factly.

He looked at her, rolling his eyes. "You and that Rapture thingy. I thought you quit believing that stuff when we got out of Sunday school?"

"No, still believe it. Tristan does not. He has kind of lost faith in everything since we lost Paul." She was referring to their baby boy whom they lost in miscarriage.

"Speaking of, have you heard from Tristan?" he asked.

"No, he's on a mission he couldn't really talk about but said he'd be back on Friday. He'd try to email from where he was going, but he said their internet was spotty."

"Well, in the meantime, pray for the Rapture, but prepare for the collapse, and we'll see which happens first," her dad added calmly. "That's all we can do at this point."

The newscaster began broadcasting images from several major cities around the US that were seeing some looting and protesting starting to happen.

"So it begins," her mom said.

## Chapter 25

FOB Patriot
Early October

The main entrance was guarded by a series of ten-foot-high concrete T-Wall barriers, which were normally whitish-gray. They now had a charred look to them as numerous RPGs had exploded into them. Most service members serving in Afghanistan and Iraq from 2003-2021 had undergone some form of indirect fire (usually RPGs and mortars). Not to say one became immune to them, but this attack was extremely ambitious. The only other time Tristan could recall an attack this brazen was at FOB Wanat back in 2008. He wondered if this was going to be the new Wanat.

He and Jack were still running from building to building making sure no fires were left burning, and using whatever they could to extinguish them. It was only an hour or so into this attack and he was already exhausted, although his adrenaline was helping him push through it all. They'd come to the last building to hit, the coffee shack, and saw the northwest corner had been blown out. Tristan carried his fire extinguisher around toward the base of the smoke and let loose.

Jack had been bringing whatever gray water they could find to use on the more stubbornly burning places to drench it. He knew he couldn't use their drinking water (which was about a week's worth left), and only used it on the spots the extinguisher couldn't quite get out. Specialist Quintana came running out of the TOC and saw them, and made a bee-line to them.

"Sir," he said, speaking to Jack who was nearest. "Bagram did have QRF heading our way, but said they had to be recalled due to their own ongoing attack."

"What?" Jack asked. "So are they saying no one is coming up to assist here?"

"Roger, Sir, at least for now. It seems we are on our own," Quintana said.

"We got to find Major Thompson," Jack said dumping the last of his water container on the remains of a smoldering wall. "Tristan, let's go find Thompson. We got bad news," Jack yelled loudly into the shack where Tristan was spot touching small fires.

"Why, what's up?" Tristan yelled back.

"Bagram is under attack as well," Jack yelled back with a sinking feeling in his stomach.

Up until this point, Tristan had faith in the system. If you attack a small FOB like Patriot or Wanat, help is going to come, and it is going to be overwhelming. A-10s, F-16s, Special Forces, Infantry Battalions, drones, the whole nine yards were going to be at your disposal. Now, they really felt alone knowing help would not come. Not that it was not coming, but that it probably could not come. If Bagram were under attack, it would be the number one priority. If Patriot fell to the Taliban or Haqqani Network or any of the other dozen or so terrorist/rebel groups, the mission would continue. If Bagram fell, well, they would have lost all of northern Afghanistan. They found Thompson on the northern wall guard shack directing fire toward various areas in their perimeter.

"Mark!" Tristan yelled up to him. "We gotta talk, bro!"

"Can it wait, I'm a little busy at the moment?" he replied.

"No, it can't. Get down here!" Tristan yelled back to him.

Tristan did not outrank him, but as a fellow Major, he felt he had enough just cause to pull him from that situation and bring him up to speed.

"What the heck, man, what is so import…." Mark said trailing off as he noticed the grim expressions on Tristan and Jack's faces.

"No help is coming. Bagram is under attack," Tristan said soberly.

Mark repositioned his cigar and stared off into the distance.

"We got two options then: either we bug out and head toward Bagram, or figure out how to hold up here for the long run," Mark said still staring.

"I think we need to make a run for Bagram. No telling how long they will stay engaged. It will be dangerous, but with forces gathered here and there, the movement in between may not be as bad. Plus, the closer we are to them, the greater the chances they will be able to help us out and bring us in safely," Tristan said.

"Jack and I can run and gather all the food, water, and ammo we can gather, but we need to conserve as much as we can. We don't know how long we'll be without support."

"Wanat," Mark said.

"Yep, except, they got support eventually. We may not," Jack replied.

They had all been in theatre together with the 101$^{st}$ back in 2008 when it happened. Even though that happened over ten years ago, it was still very fresh in their minds.

"I need to call back to Brigade and ask for further guidance. Do we stay here and fight, or abandon and or rendezvous at a more defensible location."

"I'll do it," Tristan said. "You and Jack stay here and continue directing the fight. Just keep the guys from going *full-Rambo*. You don't have limitless ammo and we're going to need some for the trip."

They split up and Tristan made his way back to flight operations. He could hear the spatter of small arms fire break the periods of intense silence. The explosions had died down somewhat, but it was getting dark. He knew the Taliban could not fight at night, not as the Americans could, so they would soon resort to the indiscriminate mortar attacks. *If they land a direct hit on flight ops, we will be screwed,* Tristan thought. He made his way through the doors and was instantly overwhelmed with non-stop radio chatter.

"Sir, it seems like every FOB is getting hit," Quintana said.

The other NCOs and Specialists were running around, looking at computer screens and answering radio calls back to Bagram.

"Q, give me the best breakdown of who is getting attacked and where," Tristan said. "But first, get me on the phone with Brigade."

"Yes, Sir," Quintana replied. He quickly moved to the satellite phone and punched in the number. Tristan was highly impressed with this soldier.

Quintana handed him the phone and began moving toward his computer to begin working on Major Zavota's request. "Sir, it's ringing," he said.

"Spartan BDE, this line is unsecure, how can I help you, Sergeant Jenkins speaking," the voice on the other end stated in rapid-fire sequence.

"Sergeant Jenkins, this is Major Zavota, please get me the XO or the Commander," Tristan said.

"Sir, hold on, let me find them. Things are a bit crazy at the moment," Jenkins replied even less formally.

"Yeah, here too," Tristan told him. "Things are crazy all over."

Tristan could hear the phone being placed on the desk as Jenkins walked away. Their TOC sounded even busier than here. He could hear multiple radios going off, and even the rattle of gunfire coming through one of them. Finally, after what seemed like forever, a familiar voice got on the line.

"Tristan, Colonel Price here."

"Sir, please tell me things are going better there than here?" Tristan asked.

"Not much better, unfortunately. How is Patriot holding up?" he asked.

"Sir, Jack and I are helping Mark and his team out here best we can. Been putting out fires from the mortars. Jack is working with a couple of their NCOs here to consolidate and account for all classes of supply."

"Send that back to us once you have it," Colonel Price replied. "I don't know when we can send relief and support up to you. The attack here has been heavy and sustained. It seems like they know the US is otherwise preoccupied and are attempting to take advantage of the chaotic situation."

"Roger, Sir. I know you can't say on an open-line, but could you send me any rendezvous locations on the high side should it come to it?"

Tristan was asking for the *scatter plan* to be sent on the secure SIPRNET.

"Will do, Tristan. You guys stay safe up there. We will get you support as soon as we are able to, if not, check your SIPR. Price out."

## Chapter 26

Washington D.C
Early October

It was 4:00 a.m. and the National Military Command Center was abuzz with activity. All four services (Army, Air Force, Navy, and Marines) had their top geographical combatant command officers, civilians, and enlisted personnel working 24/7. People were running from room to room hurriedly and the general tenor was bordering on panic. One particular conference room was packed as well, as the Chairman of the

Joint Chiefs of Staff (CJCS) at the head of the conference table sharply asked, "Status report?"

The Navy's Combatant Commander (COCOM) began addressing the group. "Gentlemen, the situation is more dire than we could have anticipated," the Admiral stated soberly. "We are being challenged on every front. However, we still maintain freedom of maneuver at sea. Unfortunately, the major constraint we are now facing is the ports we normally utilize and that were under long-term Military Interdepartmental Purchase Request (MIPR) contracts. Host nations like Singapore, Japan, Australia, Bahrain, Qatar, and Spain have now threatened to close them without the promise of future payment." After this, the Admiral sat down and nervously shuffled his notes.

Next to speak was the Air Force's COCOM General who stood up and said, "We too, maintain dominance in the air and space. However, our bases in Turkey, Spain, and Italy have been given notification we will lose them within the next two months if we cannot gain a rectification of future payments. Refueling operations have pretty much come to a halt awaiting further renegotiations throughout CENTCOM, INDOPACOM, and EUCOM's areas of responsibilities (AoRs). OCONUS-based service and resourcing contracts, both long and short term, are being called into account by virtually every vendor."

The Marine's COCOM general rose and spoke. "Sir, we have been requested by Homeland Security to assist in whatever assets we can muster to shore up defenses at all of our CONUS-based installations, especially those housing missile units. We still maintain our sea-based Marine Expeditionary Units (MEUs) with the Navy and have one Regimental Combat Team (RCT) in Afghanistan supporting operations in RC-South."

Last was the Army General. He was the Army's Chief of Staff, directly under the civilian Secretary of Army. "Sir, we are spread thin throughout every major Area of Responsibility (AOR). Most pressing is our troops in Afghanistan and Syria. We need serious options and support for pulling them out. We are getting reports every FOB is under varying stages of attacks, from Kandahar to Bagram. We have begun redirecting all soldiers coming out of Initial Entry Training to four bases: Bragg, Campbell, Hood, and Lewis. We have consolidated all of our Korean Forces (KFOR) to Camp Humphreys, just south of Seoul. Our

European troops are being consolidated in Ramstein, Spangdahlem, and Wiesbaden should we need to move them expeditiously."

The Chairman of the Joint Chiefs, also an Army General, looked at the Admiral. "We need your 7th Fleet directed towards Korea and the Diego Garcia. We may need to look at flying our troops out of Afghanistan to the ships there for repatriation back to the US. Work with our Indian counterparts to see where we could secure a port for their extradition. Our waypoints in Kyrgyzstan and Spain are drying up. You have 48 hours to come up with three viable courses of action."

"Yes, Sir," the admiral replied. He turned to an aide and whispered something and then the aide was off.

"We are going to need some long hauls from both Kandahar and Bagram flying as much of the sensitive items and people we can get from those two locations. If it means tapping into our strategic reserves for the aerial refuelers, so be it. The Commander in Chief will authorize it. Afghan and Syrian AORs are our top priorities. You have 48 hours as well."

"Yes, Sir," the Air Force general said as he too turned to an aide.

"I want a full accounting of your Marines and where we have them stationed here CONUS. You can prioritize your assistance to NORTHCOM as Colorado Springs, White Sands, and Minot, North Dakota, in that order."

"Yes, Sir," the Marine general replied.

"Get your troops to either Bagram or Kandahar. Close the small FOBs, retrieve your people and as much of the equipment as possible. We do not want either of them falling into the wrong hands. You will notify me personally every six hours on the progress."

"Yes, Sir," the Army general replied. He turned to his aide who took his instructions and moved out quickly. "Gentlemen, we are all about to face a serious issue of desertion. Without the promise of payment, I do not know how long our forces will stay put. We need to come up with some viable incentives for them to stay. Any suggestions?" the Chairman asked.

"I think we offer them free food and housing," the Army general said.

"Free healthcare," added the Air Force general. "Technically, they already get free healthcare, but this needs to be an incentive we actively beef up. It will come in handy down the road."

"We'd have to keep the providers in service for that to work," the Admiral added. "At least our military providers, not sure what we will do about all of our civilian providers."

"Free food at the Dining Facilities for as long as we have it to give. Then it will have to go to our Meals-Ready to-Eat (MREs) once we exhaust those. Unless the food contracts can be renegotiated," the Army general added.

"Still, we should anticipate a good 30-40 percent of our forces deserting once they realize payment is no longer tenable. We either need to go to more draconian measures in place, and reinstitute martial law on base, or we work with what we have," the Chairman added. "Particularly tough will be those folks who live out on the economy and have families off post. Rumor has it, Congress is looking to implement the *Kredit* here since it seems to be the currency of the future. I have it from a good source that is the way they are leaning. The bottom line is this, people: Bring the families inside the wire, and give them food, housing and medical care as with the troops. Play the patriot card, you stay with us you have a part in the solution. You desert; you are on your own.

Remind them that during the Revolutionary War, Washington's troops went long stretches without being paid."

"Sir, if we go to this new, digital currency that would mean the end of American sovereignty," the Marine general said soberly.

"Yes, it would, but we've all known the dollar was in trouble for a long time. Once we crossed the $20-trillion debt threshold, we were at the point of no return. We have a decent idea of what is coming. We should be anticipating a full-course meltdown from all four corners of the economic sectors: retail, real estate, banking, and manufacturing. DHS and Army North are working with state and federal law enforcement to shore up law and order here in the States. However, we should anticipate criminals and gangs, particularly the Mexican Cartels and Far Right groups trying to make land grabs in less governed areas. Reinforce the message to your service members, those who stay on board with us will be taken care of, and once things stabilize, will automatically promote them up to two rank-grades."

"Do we have any idea of how long it will be?" the Army general asked.

"Once they make the announcement public, I figure anywhere from three to six months," the Chairman responded. "People, you know your missions, make it happen. That is all."

**Chapter 27**

FOB Patriot
Early October

A local Taliban rammed his Tata truck into the outer Hesco barrier causing it to catch fire. Major Thompson did not see any way of moving the truck without getting his team shot up, nor did he want to waste the water on trying to extinguish it; he decided to let it burn itself out. Hescos were, after all, just burlap, wire, and rock (or sediment) all packed together. *At least they quit burning the hashish,* he thought. He had three Buffalo Up-Armored troop trucks, along with six Up Armored MRAPs, and about the same in HMMWV (pronounced Humvees). Getting everyone out would be tight if they had to make a run for it, and even still, would need to drive at least thirty minutes to get around the mountains for the straightaway for another hour to make it within eyesight of Bagram. Thankfully, they had enough firepower to fight their way to Bagram if need be. However, they did not anticipate making this convoy without air support or MEDEVAC. He called his officers to himself.

"Guys, listen up; I want the vehicles loaded and ready to go. Just take what we can carry- food, ammo, and water. Everything else, we burn or blow in place."

"Sir, what about our personal gear? Laptops, books, linen?" a lieutenant asked.

"No room. It all stays. Even our pro-gear and equipment. My main priority is to get you out and carry all the weapons I can haul out of here. Everything else stays. If things continue as they are, we will need to make a serious run for it and we can't let anything slow us down. I need you prepared for that eventuality. Bagram is getting hit, along with everywhere else."

"Run to where, Sir?" a captain asked.

"Bagram," he replied.
"I thought you said it was under attack?" the captain asked.

"It is, but it is the best chance we have," Major Thompson replied. "If there is going to be any sort of national rescue mission, it will be to Bagram and Kandahar. Any of the outlying FOBs are being brought in, as they are able. Plus, we will be able to get air support around Bagram."

Several hours later, Tristan and Jack were finishing consolidating all the food, water, and ammo they could scrounge. They began loading them into the vehicles. Although they had not gotten a green light to go just yet, the longer they stayed, the worse it was going to turn out. More and more enemy fighters were joining their comrades around FOB Patriot it seemed. Like a twisted tailgate party that began getting out of control. "We better make one last sweep through the buildings to check," Jack said. "If you see any small, personal items of value like pictures or sentimental items, grab em. We'll make sure the soldiers get it when we get back to Bagram."

They went back through each building beginning with the one closest to flight ops. The Ops team were rigging the place with explosive charges. There was no way they would be able to grab all the equipment if they had to make a run for it. Jack did quick sweeps through every other room. They covered the open bay rooms with a sense of urgency, and it was in their last building it happened. An explosion rocked the building. The sound was deafening. Both Jack and Tristan felt the shock wave hit their bodies as they were thrown to the floor. The last thing Tristan remembered was seeing Jack's legs going past his own with smoke, dust, and bits of wood flying through the air.

Major Thompson instinctively ducked as the explosion happened behind him. He looked around at the collapsed barracks building, and knew in his heart it was time to leave. If anyone was in there, he was not going to have time to get them out. Not only had the enemy gotten better at targeting their buildings, but their numbers were continuing to swell outside the gate. Their numbers were growing, but they had not formed a cohesive barrier around the base yet. His people had done a good job of keeping the exit open with heavy amounts of M60 fire and grenade assaults.

The plan was to have his mortar teams set up a heavy barrage along their route out to clear a path. Their buildings had all been rigged with C4 and claymore mines. Once they cleared the base, they would set the explosives off leaving virtually nothing but rubble for the bad guys. He had not seen Jack or Tristan in a while, last he knew they were loading the vehicles up. He looked up at the wall and watched his men returning fire and maintaining their trigger discipline. They had a lot of ammo, but it was not limitless. He knew they would have to leave and they would need whatever ammo they could carry for the trip back.

Another building toward the south end of the base was hit by an explosion. The Taliban now had an easier time aiming because of the huge clouds of smoke that guided them. They did not need to try to rush the FOB; they could just mortar the place into oblivion. They must have felt confident there would be no air support today. If the Americans were going to leave, it was now or never.

*** 

Tristan opened his eyes and could tell he was lying under what appeared to be a large chunk of wood. He wasn't sure how much time had passed since the explosion, but everything was eerily quiet. Too quiet in fact. Either that or he was now deaf.

The building they were in must have taken a direct hit during the last mortar barrage. He reasoned that the enemy must know they didn't have air support coming and could take all the time they needed to set up their attack. He felt the crushing weight of wood and debris on him but he was still able to breathe and move his head around. He turned his head to the right and could see Jack laying near him, also under wood and rubble and he gently pushed on Jack with his hand. Jack began to stir.

Jack turned his head and looked at Tristan. He pointed to his ears. Tristan nodded. He could feel something wet and warm and at first thought it had been sweat. They had been going hard at it for the past few hours putting out fires and collecting supplies. He went to wipe it away and looked at his red-stained fingers; it had been blood. He began to feel around the sides and back of his head looking for a cut or scratch, but did not feel anything. Jack started talking but all Tristan could see was his mouth moving. Then he noticed the ringing in his ears.

"What?" Tristan mouthed.

More muffled talking. "What?" Tristan mouthed again.

Jack shook his head. He pointed directly to his own ears and then pointed to Tristan.

Then Tristan understood. The blood had been coming from inside his ears. The explosion must have blown his eardrums, or something close to it. *That is just great,* Tristan thought. *Not only am I stuck in a Third World crap hole, not only is the US on the verge of collapse, not only might we soon be on the run against angry terrorist mobs, but now I'm deaf too.* Jack found a scrap of paper, took the pen from his sleeve, and jotted a note.

*Dude, this is not permanent. Your hearing will come back. This happened to me when I was younger during a firework accident. All I can hear is ringing. But we have to be quiet; we do not know who's around.*

Jack put his fingers to his lips to make the *shush* sign. He then pointed toward the outside and Tristan noticed some lights flashing around. Jack took back his note and penned something else.

*That must be what is left of the Taliban mob. I think Patriot was just overrun.*

Tristan took the pen from Jack and penned back.

*When? How long have we been knocked out?*

He handed it back to Jack. He looked up at Tristan, shrugged his shoulders and wrote.

178

*We must have been out for at least an hour or two.*

*Thompson and his team must have thought we were dead.*
They laid there for what seemed to be an eternity.
Jack could still hear a little; after a while, he took the note
and began writing again.

*My hearing is coming back. It sounds like they're
starting to move out. Thompson must have blown this place
up pretty good on the way out...if they made it out.*

Carefully and quietly, Jack and Tristan began to
move the immediate debris off themselves and could turn
over to look for the best way out of this mess. They made
their way out of what was left of the building on their hands
and knees, immediately shrinking into the shadows. The
place still had some local stragglers looking through the
debris for anything of value. Occasionally, one of them
would start shouting "Allah Akbar" and start shooting their
AK-47s into the air.
Jack looked at Tristan with terrified eyes.

Jack, still holding the pen and paper, scribbled
something quickly, *how much longer do you think we will
have to wait?* Tristan shrugged and looked up into the sky.
They had finished loading the vehicles around five that
evening. It had started getting dark on the last sweep through

the buildings. Then there was the rocket blast. Once they got completely out of what was left of the building, they looked behind them. The blast had leveled the building. Somehow, they had lived through a direct hit, and Mark and his team must have thought they were killed and left. Then the reality of it set in; they had been left behind.

## Chapter 28

Escape from Patriot Early
October

Walking out of a destroyed FOB Patriot proved to be no small feat. Tristan and Jack would have to wait for the cover of full darkness to do anything. Still, they would have to move through the roving hordes of Taliban who would be wound up all night following their supposed victory over the Americans. Thankfully, the crowds of pillagers had already begun to dissipate as the darkness settled in and the temperatures dropped. While the debris from their collapsed building had become almost unbearable and uncomfortable, it was a minefield of sharp, jagged, and charred wood and nails and advantageous for cover and concealment. At least the ringing in his ears was starting to subside and his hearing was coming back.

After another hour, it was fully dark. A few Taliban remained behind, mostly huddling around a makeshift campfire drinking tea near what used to be the main gate of FOB Patriot. After what seemed like centuries, they were finally able to crouch their way carefully out of the debris and moved toward the Hesco wall to the rear of what used to be the building. They had to move slow not just due to the noise, but getting a cut here could easily become infected and slow them down considerably.

They moved quietly along the base of the Hesco wall away from the front gate. The plan was to find some rope or sheets and use the guard tower at the southeast corner to climb out from if possible. However, as they began making their way to the southeast corner, they noticed one of the collapsed buildings made a sizeable dent into the Hesco barriers. This made for a convenient exit strategy and preferable to climbing down a wall exposed. However, once they cleared the wall, they were not entirely sure where to go. If they headed due south, they knew they would eventually get to Bagram. However, they would have to make their way through heavily infested Taliban-territory.

Therefore, even if they got close to the base, there was no guarantee they could actually make it to the base. A full-length burqa would come in handy right about now.

"Jack," Tristan whispered as he climbed over the opening in the Hesco wall, "we need to head west." "Why?" Jack replied in a whisper.

"We aren't going to make it Bagram, not if it's surrounded like this place was," Tristan whispered back.

"What's west of here?" Jack asked.

"More Hazaras, Tajiks, and Uzbeks," Tristan whispered back.

"Is that good or bad?" Jack asked.

"It's better than Pashtun, which is what most of the Taliban and Haqqani are. The Hazaras, Tajiks, and Uzbeks do not particularly like or trust the Pashtuns, who make up the majority. So we are more likely to find safe passage through their territory than we are here or south of here."

"How far till we are safe?" Jack whispered back to him as he continued down the outside Hesco wall.

"Maybe a couple of days' walk, that is, if we strictly travel at night," Tristan whispered. "I should have eaten that last meal; I just couldn't stomach another MRE. Had I known it was going be my last one…?" he said trailing off softly.

"You didn't see any MREs on the way out did you?"

"No. We picked this place clean before the Taliban attacked. What we didn't get, you know they did," Jack said thumbing back toward the remaining guards. "Besides, God will provide. Remember, you're rolling with a man of the cloth."

Tristan chuckled quietly at this. "Even at a time like this, you still manage to find a way to evangelize me." "What else can I do? Gotta keep our spirits up or else we're doomed."

They began moving out hunched and low to the ground. Their eyes had already adjusted to the moonless night. Afghanistan lacked the ambient lights from any kind of city or modernity, so it was seemingly darker than anywhere else was in the world. They would have to go slow until they found some kind of path or road. Tristan looked at the base and knew it was situated north to south, so he began heading out toward the left.

# Chapter 29

Paradise, Texas
Early October

Paradise was like most small towns in Texas. There were a couple of gas stations, a Wal-Mart, a local grocery store, some fast food, and local restaurants. Although there was not much more to the town than that, it primarily remained viable because it straddled the only major highway coming out of Fort Worth up to Oklahoma and to West Texas. It was just far enough away from the big city to keep most of the riffraff from coming to bother it, and close enough for the folks in Paradise to make the trip into the big city if necessary.

Sheriff Adam Flannery and his deputies did their best to keep Paradise and the rest of Smith County free from the crime and problems endemic to big cities like Fort Worth and Dallas, but it was getting worse. More people meant more problems. Small cities all over the state were swelling up as people began to flee not just city-life, but also other states after all of the last year's draconian COVID-19 lockdowns. This reverse migration was causing all sorts of exponential growing pains in small towns whose infrastructures were not prepared to handle them. Especially now that the economy was going crazy. More and more people seemed to be fleeing the city and trying to find refuge in Paradise and the other small towns of Smith County.

As Sheriff, he rarely went on patrols anymore due to all the other engagements he had to keep (city council and mayor meetings, key leader engagements, and the day to day running of the county jail), but he decided to cover the shift of one of his deputies who had come down sick with the stomach bug.

"Sheriff, this is Deputy Car 19 on highway 36, over," the voice on the radio said mechanically.

"Go ahead, 19," Sheriff Flannery responded methodically.

"Sir, we've got a lot of people starting to RV-squat out here near Jackson's Creek Road. They're not hooked up to sewage or electricity, and its public land, but I don't think they're supposed to set up residence here," the deputy replied.

"Alright, I'm heading your way," the Sheriff, responded. "Hold fast until I get there."

As he began driving in that direction, Sheriff Flannery started mulling over all the reasons why people were suddenly interested in coming to Paradise. The only reason he could figure folks would come this way, was to get away from the craziness brewing in the cities. Perhaps all this hubbub about the economy being in a free-fall of sorts was true. *People are starting to get nervous and want to get away from the big cities, which will put a huge strain on the tiny towns.*

There is no civility anymore. At the slightest inkling of political unrest or public outrage, looting and rioting seemed to become the normal response. *Maybe folks are seeing the storm on the horizon and are trying to get out of the path of it. If that's the case, these few dozens are just the tip of the iceberg. We need a more permanent solution than Jackson's Creek,* he thought. Yep, the city council and the mayor are not going to like this problem.

***

Afghanistan, West of Patriot
Early October

Moving out in the dark in a place like Afghanistan was very arduous and dangerous. There were so many natural hazards such as rocks, crevices, ravines or wadis, snakes, and insects, which almost made you forget about the human hazards like the Taliban and other bad actors out there who would just as soon cut your head off than let you pass. The going was going to be slow.

About an hour after leaving Patriot, they had located what appeared to be a path heading in a generally westerly southwest direction through what they thought to be the Baghlan Valley. Jack was interested in this valley because it would eventually dump them out in a valley just west of the famed city of Bamyan, which once was home to the giant Buddha statues. That was until the Taliban blew them up several years back. The valley they were traveling through had a dirt road about 100 yards to the left of the center. Tristan had recommended they not use the actual road due to any unexploded IEDs, which may still be buried there for NATO and US troops. It would seem as though fate had smiled briefly upon them. They had stumbled upon a path the locals used.

Both this *local's road*, and the main one, were running parallel through the natural valley separating the northern and southern strands of the Hindu Kush Mountains. The valley between them started wide, but would soon narrow the further west they travelled. At a certain point, the mountains would box them in naturally. Traversing through a steep valley separating the northern and southern fingers of the Hindu Kush mountain range while directing them west, would make navigating at night easier, but it would also severely limit their choices during the daylight hours. They would need to find good places to hide during the day.

Tristan was not tracking any villages in the valley itself but there were likely some crossroads they would have to pass. These roads would run through any natural breaks in the mountains that would lead to other villages. He expected the Taliban and the other tribes to use the narrower portions of the valley as natural choke points. From there, they probably set some of their tribesmen to act as gatekeepers of sorts.

They had been walking on the local's road now for at least two hours, and thankfully, had not run into anyone. The nights during October and early November in Afghanistan, was where chilly started turning cold. They only had the clothes on their back, and had not had time to bring any cold weather gear with them. Nevertheless, between the adrenaline pumping through them and the mountains naturally blocking the wind blowing out of the north, they had not had time to complain about the cold. It was right around this time they could make out a light in the far distance. Although it only appeared to be a simple campfire outside of a mud-hut, the light from it might as well have been a nightclub as dark as the valley was. They contemplated their next moves.

"How are we going to get past them?" Jack asked.

"We might have to find a place nearby and hole up, then watch and see when the best time to slip past them would be. Maybe in a couple of hours they'll go to sleep or do a shift change or something," Tristan replied softly. His hearing had been recovering as the ringing in his ears had completely subsided. "I can't tell if it is a shadow, or a small cave," he said pointing to a dark spot at the foot of the mountain about a hundred yards ahead. There was just enough starlight out to catch glimpses of potential hideouts. "We should make for that and keep an eye on them for a bit to see if they establish any kind of patterns."

"I can't see this cave you're pointing to, but going there and staying put could take forever. We don't have any food or water, so whatever we do, we need to conserve our energy, but also get to a place where we can find some of both," Jack replied.

"Seriously?" Tristan asked softly. "You can't see where I'm pointing at?"

"No. I know you're a pilot and all, and supposed to have 20/20 vision, but dang, son, you must have some owl blood in you or something," Jack said sarcastically. "Are you part Owl?"

"I don't know if it's a cave, it may just be a shadow from a larger rock with the campfire light hitting it the right way. But it looks like a cave from here."

"I hope nothing is in those caves," Jack said looking around the expanse of the valley they were in. "Like mountain trolls or something."

"Careful Chaplin, your fear of the supernatural is showing through, although, I thought you didn't believe in anything other than *angels,*" Tristan whispered suspiciously.

"I don't. I believe in God, and I believe there are angels and demons, but I do not expect to run into them anytime soon. However, I believe we might be breaking into the cave-home of snakes and other creepy crawlers that go bump in the night," Jack replied tensely.

Just then, they heard a weapon being charged behind them.

They turned slowly to see two men who had been sitting on a large boulder to their right. Apparently, they had been so fixated on the light from the guard hut ahead, they did not notice two men who remained motionless and silent the whole time. This reminded Tristan of the Anglerfish that lives at the bottom of the sea, which uses light at the end of its angler to distract and draw in its prey. *We are the prey now,* he thought sadly. Both he and Jack raised their hands. Jack tried in his best Pashtun to give the Muslim greeting *Salam Alaikum,* but the two tribesmen kept their weapons pointed at them.

The two guards worked their way down off the rock, taking turns to keep their weapons trained on Jack and Tristan. They began yelling for their compatriots down at the shack, who by now had their attention focused in their direction. Although he doubted they knew what was going on globally, they knew enough to know two Americans traveling alone in their valley, was either extremely fortunate, or the Taliban's campaign plan of attacking all the bases was working. Either way, this was not looking promising Tristan thought. They needed a distraction so he could draw his weapon and put some distance between these guys (and their friends) and themselves. With raised hands in the air, Tristan looked past them and tipped two fingers to the right as if he was subtly telling people behind the guards to attack.

They bought the ruse.

One of the guards saw his subtle movements and took his attention off them to glance back. The other guard, who had been focused on Jack, now turned to his friend to ask what he was looking for. Tristan drew his .9-millimeter Berretta and fired hitting the second guard square in the chest. He was already squaring his sights on the first guard who seemed to freeze at the sight of his friend falling backward and what was happening didn't seem to register in his brain. Tristan squeezed off two rounds hitting him in the stomach and chest. He went down as well like a sack of potatoes being thrown on the floor. By now, the other guards from the shack had heard the noise and started making their way toward Jack and Tristan. They were still a good 600 yards off when Jack and Tristan collected up the AK-47s from the dead guards. Jack turned and squeezed off two, three-round bursts in the general direction of the approaching guards in the hopes of either slowing or dissuading their new would be attackers.

# Chapter 30

The "Cabal" as they were called by conspiracy theorists, were a real clandestine group of congressional representatives and senators from both parties, who met in secret to make the impossible happen. At present, they had been discussing the unfolding economic crisis stemming from Europe. The world's markets were moving quickly and reacting wildly to the spread of this digital virus. The *Euro* was in a freefall now. The *Ruble* was tanking even faster than it had before the outset. The *Yen*, *Won*, and *Rupee* likewise, were all crumbling. They were all failing in varying degrees due to the aggressiveness of the *Kredit*. It was here the Cabal came to discuss the fate of the US Dollar.

"Ladies and gentlemen," the voice at the head of the table said. "We are at crunch time. By this time next week, the US is going to be completely saturated with the *Kredit*. Every smartphone, every bank, every stock market portfolio is going to be attempting to convert every known fiat currency to this new *Kredit*, and there isn't much we can do to stop it. The last time we met, we agreed to embrace this change, even if it meant the death of the Dollar. You went back to your respective committees and parties, and we are still at an impasse, haggling over this, that, and the other. I need you to report on where we are since last we met."

A representative seated closest to the head of the table spoke next. "The majority of my Democratic colleagues support the conversion. We need to stay at the forefront of this, or we'll be left behind begging for scraps."

The man opposite spoke next. "I only have around a quarter of my Republican colleagues who will go along with the measure. The Conservative Caucus will not get behind it. The usual (referring to the RINOs, or- Republican in Name Only) Republican factions will, however, support this."

The table head spoke again. "And of the rest of the 75%?"

The man spoke again. "They will not support it. They see this as the death of the Constitution and have vowed to fight it *tooth and nail*."

The rest of the group shook and nodded their heads and began whispering amongst themselves as to the quandary their *Cabal* seemed to find themselves in.

"Well," the head of the table began saying, "nothing creates change faster than a crisis. If we let this play out

194

accordingly, we will whittle away the majority of your party (pointing to the Republicans) down to get this passed, legally.

The people would never accept this through fiat or mandate. Crisis moments also make people desperate. We do not want to risk a civil war over this either. However, we are relying on the fact most people do not want to give up their air-conditioned jobs, streaming television services, or grocery stores. In fact, if we let this crisis worsen, the people will *demand* we embrace it or risk losing our way of life."

Again, the group was whispering and nodding their heads in agreement. A man at the end of the table spoke next. "I understand why you say we need to embrace this new currency, but what happens if we don't. Remember Y2K? Everyone thought at the stroke of midnight, computers around the world would crash causing the world to end overnight. However, none of that happened. Aren't we glad we didn't panic then? Is it safe to say, we are being a little too preemptive in our desire to play God?"

There was an awkward silence.

"The Independent colleague at the end of the table brings up a legitimate concern," the head of the table spoke again. "However, we are 300% more connected to the

Internet today, than we were 20 years ago. We have managed to get smart devices into practically every home in the nation. Upwards of 70% of our *Fortune 500*, companies are transnational and primarily in emerging markets. We simply cannot, *not* do anything. This is going to affect us. It can crash our economy if we do not embrace this crisis and turn it into an opportunity. There are already problems out in flyover country. People are getting all *apocalyptic* and stocking up for the end of the world. If we don't make some type of public announcement soon, things could get violent," the head of the table concluded.

"We will take it to the president in the morning. If he agrees, fine. If he doesn't, then we will be forced to take more drastic action," the speaker at the center said. "Are we in agreement?"

The "Ayes" were unanimous.


There is the moral of all human tales;

'Tis but the same rehearsal of the past,

First Freedom, and then Glory- when that fails,
Wealth, vice, corruption- barbarism at last.

**-Lord Byron, Childe Harold's Pilgrimage (1812-1818)**

***

Afghanistan, West of Patriot
Early-Mid October

Tristan and Jack began moving toward those guards from the shack with their weapons at the ready. Each AK-47 only had ten bullets apiece left; not nearly enough to engage in any kind of sustained firefight. They would have to take their shots carefully.

"This feels so weird," Jack said. "You know chaplains are not allowed to carry weapons in the military."

"Wow, I didn't know that," Tristan said sarcastically. "Hey, these aren't necessarily precision weapons. They're more 'pray and spray' type weapons. Just point them in the general direction when it comes time."

"No issue with the praying part, not sure I'm cut out for the spraying part," Jack whispered back.

"Look, if we wound them, we might as well kill them. The Afghanistan medical resources here are both slim and none. They'd probably rather be dead than crippled," Tristan continued.

"I don't know if I can take another person's life. I mean, I am a chaplain for Pete's sake. I didn't sign up to shoot people."

"You didn't sign up for the *end of the world* either did you, bud?" Tristan retorted.

"No, not that either."

As the two groups drew closer, both Jack and Tristan, and the approaching guards began taking up opposing defensive positions. It was extremely difficult to judge the distance at night in the dark, but Tristan figured they were at what appeared to be the lengths of a football field. As far as he could tell, there were only two guards at the hut. If they radioed for help, there would soon be many more. However, with the terrain narrowing in upon them, they were walking into a bit of a *Mexican-Standoff*.

"Look, if things go south, or one of us is wounded, killed, or captured, the other has to make it home," Jack whispered. "One of us has to make it back to the families to let them know what happened here."

Looking at him, Tristan had not even considered they both would not make it out alive. Especially after getting out of Patriot. Nevertheless, he was right. The likelihood of both of them making it all the way home was not good. It was not as if they could just hop on a plane once they got out of Afghanistan. Getting home was going to be an almost insurmountable challenge, especially if either of them were wounded. Something as simple as a fractured leg would make the journey virtually impossible.

They hunkered down behind a large outcropping of rocks. Since the Taliban guards had that fire at the hut behind them, it put them at somewhat of a disadvantage. Any time they moved, their shadows formed silhouettes signaling their direction of movement. Jack and Tristan on the other hand were completely shielded by darkness. The guards were not sure where they went, but they kept moving in zigzag patterns.

"We're going to have to have to make the first move. We can't stay here all night trying to wait these guys out," Tristan said. "Time is definitely on their side. I'd expect their replacements to show up around daybreak, so we run the risk of doubling the number of people we have to fight to get past."

They got low and started to move left, putting as much lateral distance as possible between themselves and the guards. The narrow valley did not give them a lot of room to move. It would be impossible to low-crawl over the jagged rocks and brush; they crouched and moved in three to five second bursts. Their advantage, the light was behind the enemies. Their disadvantage, the narrowness of the valley.

"Hey, we just need to get close enough to take these two clowns out," Tristan said, noticing the increasingly worried look on Jack's face.

"That's not all I'm worried about," Jack said.

"What else?"

"They probably know where all their landmines are," Jack whispered back.

Tristan hadn't even thought of that. Chances are if they were going to take the trouble to make this a choke point for travelers, they probably have some surprises out there as well. Those two guys back at the rock were probably only there to extort the locals by serving as guides through here.

At this point, fear began to paralyze the two Americans. Neither wanted to move.

"Look, if God got us this far, He can get us past this checkpoint," Jack said in a low voice.

"I don't think God pays too much attention to this corner of the world anymore," Tristan said in an equally hushed voice.

"We'll see," Jack said. "Let's move."

Jack stepped forward and felt it before he heard it. It was the feel and sound of a metal button clicking down under the dirt. Jack looked at Tristan who also heard it. Their eyes went from normal to the size of small dinner plates and knew instinctively this was not going to end well.

## Chapter 31

Paradise, Texas
Early-Mid October

Sheriff Flannery pulled up to the impromptu RV park where he saw some of the squatters stepping out of their RVs to address the arrival of law enforcement…armed.

"Folks, I'm going to have to ask you to leave here," he said stepping out of his vehicle. "You aren't allowed to set up camp on county land like this; it's simply not designed to support long-term situations."

"Sheriff, we had to get out of the city. Things were starting to get ugly there. So if we can't stay here, where can we go?" one said.

"Yeah, you said it yourself, this is *county* land, which is public land," another squatter replied. "Besides, you ain't got any other places set up."

"True, it is public land. However, our county ordinances do not allow just whoever to come set up wherever they want. What we can do is re-open the old Carswell RV campgrounds for the time being," Sheriff Flannery said anticipating these responses. "And there, you'll have electrical and plumbing hookups for your vehicles. You ain't got that out here. I don't need a bunch of grass fires starting from all of your campfires. I ain't got the manpower to fight it at present."

He turned and pointed down the road. "Folks, just take highway 21 into town, turn left at County Road 38, and you'll see the signs for Carswell RV Park. My deputies are there, as well as the city water and power company, who are in the process of turning everything back on. I'm just asking you to work with us and be patient. No need to go flashing firearms."

This new information seemed to diffuse the situation for the moment. Sheriff Flannery had to call in some quick favors on the way over to make this happen. The Carswell RV Park had shut down a couple of years ago after a major human trafficking hub was discovered there, and it had been shut down ever since. However, if this were a sign of things to come, human trafficking would be the least of their problems. He got back in his car and got on the radio to his deputy there.

"Deputy Walsh, how's it going at the RV park?" Sheriff Flannery asked.

"Sir, we got everything back on. However, this park only has 32 parking spots. How many folks are out there?"

"I count a dozen RVs. Not sure about the total count of people. Maybe 30 or so," Sheriff Flannery responded.

"What are we going to do when all these spots are taken?" Deputy Walsh asked.

"I don't know. I need to call the mayor and the city council and have a discussion. Stay put for now. Folks should be heading your way shortly. Help them get in and settled.
Flannery, out."

Sheriff Flannery put his mic down and picked up his cell phone. He dialed up the mayor. It rang for what seemed like an eternity.

"Mayor Trumbull. Sheriff Flannery."

"Sheriff, what can I do you for?" Mayor Trumbull responded.

"We need to call a meeting tomorrow. You, the County Regents, the City Council, and the City Manager."

"Why? What's the crisis?"

"I'll explain in depth tomorrow, but we're starting to see an uptick in the folks moving out of the DFW-metroplex, and coming this way."

"That doesn't sound like a 'tomorrow crisis.' Why don't we set them up with some realtors and I can get my secretary to get us set up later next week? My Friday is already booked solid."

"Dammit, Bob, I know where you spend your Fridays. This thing is more important than your golf-outing with your buddies."

~silence~

"Alright, Adam. My conference room at 10. I'll get the council and the manager, you get the regents," Mayor Trumbull replied.

"Thanks, Bob. Look, I didn't mean to snap. But I got a bad feeling about all this."

"Don't worry about it. We'll get it sorted out."

He hung up. He had known Bob Trumbull since they were in middle school together. Good guy. Decent mayor. Terrible golfer. However, tends to live in a bubble. If it does not happen inside of Paradise, he does not much care. Like most folks here, they have moved out here to get away from the craziness of the city, and the world. Nevertheless, just because they chose not to move into the world, did not mean the world wasn't going to move into Paradise.

His phone rang this time. He looked down and saw it was his wife. *Probably wondering where I am and if I'm going to make it to dinner,* he thought.

"Hey, Hun."

"Nope. Yep. No, I'll be there. Dinner at six sounds perfect."

He hung up. He looked out his windshield again. The first of the RVs were pulling out and heading into town. *I will remember this day. The day when everything started to change.*

*** 

Hindu Kush Mountains, Afghanistan

The metallic click of the landmine indicated it was activated. The second Jack moves his foot will cause it to detonate and the force of the explosive will be pushed up and out. Tristan stood still next to him, with his weapon aimed in the direction of the two advancing guards with beads of sweat starting to form on his forehead.

"Tristan, you should go."

"No way, man, I'm not leaving you here like this."

"You have to make it home and to your wife and kids. You have to be a witness to all that has transpired. People have to know what happened here.

Tristan was panicking so hard now his heart felt like it was going to beat itself free of his chest. "For the guy stepping on certain death, why are you calm and I'm a wreck. I thought you said God was going to save us?"

"I am beginning to think God has a different plan in mind for me," Jack said. He stood there looking off into the distance for a moment with his eyes pitched upwards intensely staring at something in the distance somewhere over Tristan's head.

"Jack. Talk to me, buddy. Snap out of it, what is going on in your head?"

"Tristan, this is where my journey with you ends, but I know where I am going. Death is not the end for me," he said with a smile.

"That is lunacy, Jack. How can you know for sure you're going anywhere just because some old book says so?" Tristan said shaking his head. "We need to figure out how to get you out of this."

"God has a grand plan for you as well; He is not through with you. He is going to use you."

"Use me for what? I don't even see how I am going to make it out of this god-forsaken country."

"Don't worry, God will provide a way. Here, take my ammo," he said carefully handing Tristan his single ammo clip. "Even though this is where our journey together ends, this is not the end. I will see you again. Now, start backing up opposite of me. Let me be the distraction. I will make a scene here. Those guards will start coming my way to investigate it, and then I will release my foot. That's when you run."

"Maybe we can find a rock or something, and swap

your foot for the rock, like in an *Indian Jones* movie," Tristan said attempting poorly to add some humor to the situation.

Jack could hear the emotions overwhelming his friend's voice even at a whisper. Jack began to pray aloud.

*"Dear God, please use my life and my death to show my friend Tristan here that You are real, and you love him. Watch over my family. Watch over my friend here, and protect him on his journey home."*

Tristan took the clip and began moving backward carefully. He never took his eyes off Jack. There was something unnerving about his eyes; a steely-edged resolve he'd never noticed before. Not defiance to the situation, but a calm, steady determination to see it through. Jack knew without a doubt, where he was going the second he lifted his foot. Tristan has seen a few men die over the course of his life. Most were terrified or babbling nonsense. However, Jack was calm and resolute. Tristan, still moving back, was startled back to reality when Jack began singing a hymn as loud as he could.

1. *"When peace, like a river, attendeth my way,*

   *When sorrows like sea billows roll;*
   *Whatever my lot, Thou hast taught me to say,*

   *It is well, it is well with my soul.* o   *It is well with my soul,*

   > *It is well, it is well with my soul.*

2. *Though Satan should buffet, though trials should come,*

   *Let this blest assurance control,*

   *That Christ hath regarded my helpless estate, And hath shed His own blood for my soul.*

3. *My sin—oh, the bliss of this glorious thought!— My sin, not in part but the whole, Is nailed to the cross, and I bear it no more, Praise the Lord, praise the Lord, O my soul!*

4. *For me, be it Christ, be it Christ hence to live:*
   *If Jordan above me shall roll,*

   *No pang shall be mine, for in death as in life Thou wilt whisper Thy peace to my soul.*

5. *But, Lord, 'tis for Thee, for Thy coming we wait,*
   *The sky, not the grave, is our goal; Oh, trump of the angel! Oh, voice of the Lord!*

*Blessed hope, blessed rest of my soul!*

6. *And Lord, haste the day when the faith shall be sight,*
   *The clouds be rolled back as a scroll;*
   *The trump shall resound, and the Lord shall descend,*
   *Even so, it is well with my soul.*


Sensing movement nearby, Tristan dropped to his knees and knelt there. He could make out movement coming toward Jack in spurts now. Their shadows from the fire behind them were the telltale sign. He looked back at Jack. For the briefest of moments, Tristan thought he saw someone standing next to him, but he could not quite be sure. Tristan rubbed his eyes. Jack stole one last look his way as if to say with his eyes, *goodbye.* However, just as soon as Tristan thought those words in his mind, Jack's voice, clear as day, echoed in his ears. *God is not through you yet my friend.* Jack's voice was as clear as if he were standing right next to him.

The two Taliban guards were now upon him. At this point, they began encircling him with weapons trained on him. They were shouting at him in Pashtun.

Then Jack knelt.

A blinding flash of light matched the ear-shattering explosion. Even though Tristan was more than fifty feet away now, the force of the blast threw him backward. Worse yet, he was momentarily blinded. He should have covered his eyes, but he could not, not stare at his friend. The two guards had made it within ten feet of Jack when the blast all but evaporated them. After the blast, all he could hear was unearthly quiet. His ears were ringing again. Tristan picked himself up and began moving slowly back toward the same path the two guards had walked toward them on.

Once he found their path, he picked up his pace. The blast area was now about ninety-feet behind him. He stayed as low as possible and moved quickly behind the hut so the campfire would not reveal his whereabouts. The blast had been extremely loud, and if there were other bad actors out there, they would surely be coming in this direction to investigate.

Once he passed the hut, he found a path along the northern side of the valley that appeared to be well traveled. He picked up his pace to a jog, relying on his eyes night adaption and the ambient starlight available to move quickly along the path.

After thirty minutes or so, his hearing returned to normal, and he came to a stop. He found a clear spot to sit down and dropped with minimal resistance. He was exhausted both physically and emotionally. They had now been on the run since 8:00 last night. His watch said it was approaching 5:00 a.m. and he still had not had time to process Jack's sudden demise. He needed to find a place to hole up before daylight or he risked falling asleep out in the open. He picked himself and started walking again, scanning both sides of the valley for a place to hide.

At that point, the valley was starting to open wider, which meant he was getting closer to the opening of the Bamyan Valley. Still, he did not think he would make it there before sunup and he did not want to be caught out in the open during the day. He needed a cave like what they saw earlier before their Taliban encounter. Just as he began to form the word in his mind, a dark spot appeared along the wall, which caught his peripheral attention. Tristan stopped, and then made a straight line to it.

## Chapter 32

Come to Me, all *you* who labor and are heavy laden,
and I will give you rest. **Matthew 11:28**

Afghanistan, West of Patriot
Early-Mid October

While the valley was very dark even with the available
ambient light, the inside of the cave was pitch black. Tristan
had to enter slowly like a man seeing with his hands, and felt
a great sense of trepidation settle over him as he inched his
way in. Although he could not see where he was going, his
feet told him he appeared to be on a declined path of sorts.
The entrance to the cave amplified sound; this allowed him
to hear what he thought to be men talking further down the
valley. Their muffled voices gave no indication of distance,
but he did not want to risk staying close to the entrance.
Advancing deeper into the darkness, he began to think
perhaps this was not such a good idea after all.

Although he could not see it, he sensed the cave
opening up the further he moved into it. It was far more
spacious than the tiny entrance led one to believe. Walking
in, he could feel the ceiling just above his head. Now it

seemed to have opened up into a small cavern. Exhausted, emptied of adrenaline, and emotionally drained, he dropped to his knees. The ground was littered with small rocks, which immediately sent a sharp jab of pain emanating from where he had just planted his knee. He cleared the floor out underneath him, continued down, and spread himself prostrate out over the ground. He dropped his head and began to cry.

It was not a loud wailing cry or uncontrolled sobbing, but the soft whimpering of a broken man. He was a man, seemingly, without a country. He was stranded in a Third World hellhole. His only friend here had been blown up right before his eyes. Although they had known each other for years through mutual acquaintances, they had only gotten close this past year when they began planning this deployment. Ironically, after hardly knowing each other for years, they became fast friends. Life in the military was like that.

Serving in the military was like being a gypsy. You constantly uprooted your life and moved every two to three years. Nothing was ever permanent. People constantly flowed in and out of your life. One of the unsung powers service members often developed was a sixth sense about selecting friends due to the compressed timelines everyone found themselves under. Seasoned military folk became experts at filtering through the good and bad, and finding those few others they deemed worthy of kinship. Even though it had only been a year, Jack could have been Tristan's brother.

As if perfectly timed, he immediately felt that familiar pain rip across his heart. The first time it had happened back at Bagram, it had scared him a little, like a warning shot. Now, he knew without a doubt that it was a heart attack. This time, he knew it was due to the immense amount of physical, emotional, and psychological strain he was undergoing. He seized his chest as if to lessen the pain, but the pain would
not subside. If he died here, it was very likely that no one would ever know. The Army probably already assumed he and Jack died back at Patriot if Major Thompson even made it back to Bagram alive. If he were lucky, some local Afghan would find the remains of his body several months from now and try and sell his *body* back to the next American they saw.

The pain began throbbing through his entire chest as his life flashed before his eyes. He had heard that that happened to people right before they died, but he didn't really believe it. Now, he was seeing images of his wife and children through the varying stages of his life like snapshots in time, which only served to compound the heartache he was already enduring. He thought about Jack's eyes and expression right before he died. He had always considered himself fearless, but his newfound mortality had exposed this as a complete charade. He was about to step off into an unknown eternity and it terrified him fiercely. He wanted what Jack had; a resolute certainty about what comes after.

After a minute of intense pain and unable to move under his own power, the pain in his chest began to ease. Laying there exhausted in the complete darkness, he was not entirely sure if he was still alive, dead, or somewhere in between. He felt extremely vulnerable at this moment, sure, that if an eighty-year-old man came in here with a cane looking to fight, he would get his butt kicked.

His thoughts, which previously were littered with jumbled images of his life, now seemed to focus in on the person standing next to Jack right before the explosion. *Was that real, or was I just seeing things?* He was trying to grapple with what his eyes and ears had heard, and of everything he thought he knew about the world.

*Perhaps*, he thought, *I am losing my mind after all.* He pulled out his 9 mm and began seriously contemplating putting himself out of his own misery before he suffered a stroke, or worse, was caught by the Taliban. Behind him in the dark, shadowy figures continued to whisper how hopeless the situation was, and how he would be better off ending his own life rather than dying slowly.

Just then, he remembered Jack's last words…*God is not through with you yet.* Then in utter grief and anguish, he surprised himself when he heard a voice speak out softly and broken; surprisingly, it was his own.

*Jesus, I am here in some nameless cave in a forgotten part of the world. I am quite literally at the bottom and I have nowhere else to turn. I have no rank, no name, no possessions, no country, and no family…I have only what I am wearing. I don't even know if you're real, but I want to. I am sorry I have put you off all my life. I am sorry I didn't take my wife seriously all those years. I resisted her every attempt to bring me around, all because my pride wouldn't allow it. God, why did you have to take Jack? He didn't deserve it, I did. Please forgive me. Save me. Help me to see my family again.*

No sooner had he whispered those words he felt a tremendous burden lifted off him. The feeling of being watched immediately dissipated. His heart, which had been throbbing only moments before, now seemed calm. He opened his eyes and noticed that although he was still physically exhausted; his mind was beginning to clear. He was beginning to understand things differently. It felt like his heart was finally liberated after forty-six years of bondage. He felt free. The veil of skepticism, which had blinded him for so many years, lifted not from his eyes, but from his mind. He no longer had the threat of an uncertain future hanging over his head like a dead weight. He could not explain it, but he knew it through and through.

The cave, while still pitch black, became a little less menacing. He could move his fingers again. After a few minutes, he tried his arms. He somehow found the strength to sit up. It was then he saw it. From the back of the cave, which he still could not tell how far back it went, seemed to be faint glowing light. It appeared to be growing brighter and brighter with each passing moment. It looked like the warm glow a candle gives off as if a person were approaching him from a long, darkened hallway.

Just then, the hair on his neck and arms stood up. Goosebumps rippled out across his body. Out of the corner of his eye, he perceived someone staring at him. Slowly, he turned his head just as a face appeared out of the darkness. A giant glowing face.

*What the*.....Tristan fell backward and his eyes grew wide with terror. An uncontrollable fear gripped his entire body and again, he entered into that surreal state where he was not entirely sure if he was awake or dreaming. He could not be sure he could trust what he was actually seeing. Nevertheless, the giant face materialized out of the darkness into the form of a giant man. A giant man with wings furled who seemed to be radiating softly.

"Son of man," the voice said reassuringly, "the Lord has heard your cry and has redeemed you. He has sent me to you as a guide."

The voice, although not loud, penetrated through his bones. Every fiber of his body could feel the words echoing throughout his being.

Instinctively, Tristan turned and made himself prostrate before him. The giant man immediately touched his shoulder, causing him to stand up instantly and effortlessly.

"Do not bow before me," he said in a voice that was still reverberating through Tristan's body.

"Only God is worthy of worship."

"Who…what…are you….are you a ghost? An angel?" Tristan heard himself ask.

"Yes, I am a fellow servant like you; a messenger and guide. And yes, I am what you would call, an angel."

This angel being could have easily been ten feet tall. However, he was not tall and skinny like a professional basketball player. He was built solidly to be ten feet tall. Proportionate in every way; Tristan could tell this angel must have been very powerful.

"How are you here with me?" Tristan asked tentatively.

"The *Alpha and Omega* has heard your prayer, and has sent me to guide you home," the Angel responded.

"Home? Why me though?"

"The Lord has a special mission for you." "A mission?" Tristan asked.

"I cannot tell you right now, but you will see," the angel responded.

"What is your name?" Tristan asked.

"It is Barachiel," he replied.

"How am I going to get out of here? How am I going to get out of Afghanistan? There might be some US forces left in Kandahar, but the bases up north here were all overrun," Tristan said.

"Are you familiar with *Elijah the Prophet*?" Barachiel asked.

"Who?" Tristan replied looking puzzled.

"The *Prince of Persia* still runs these lands, so we must make haste, but first you must rest and replenish your strength. Take and drink, you will need the strength." Barachiel smiled as he produced a carafe of water out of thin air and handed it to Tristan.

*And Ahab told Jezebel all that Elijah had done, also how he had executed all the prophets with the sword. Then Jezebel sent a messenger to Elijah, saying, "So let the gods do to me, and more also, if I do not make your life as the life of one of them by tomorrow about this time." And when he saw that, he arose and ran for his life, and went to Beersheba, which belongs to Judah, and left his servant there. But he himself went a day's journey into the wilderness, and came and sat down under a broom tree. And he prayed that he might die, and said, "It is enough! Now, Lord, take my life, for I am no better than my fathers!"*

*Then as he lay and slept under a broom tree, suddenly an angel touched him, and said to him, "Arise and eat." Then he looked, and there by his head was a cake baked on coals, and a jar of water. So he ate and drank, and lay down again. And the angel of the Lord came back the second time, and touched him, and said, "Arise and eat, because the journey is too great for you." So he arose, and ate and drank; and he went in the strength of that food forty days and forty nights as far as Horeb, the mountain of God.* **1st Kings 19:1-9**

## Chapter 33

Paradise, Texas Mid-October

Back home, Katy was waking up after the craziest and most vivid dreams she'd ever had. It was like something straight out of the book of Revelation. She hardly ever remembered her dreams, but this one was like a high-definition movie playing in her mind. She dreamt of Tristan running. She dreamt of angels busily moving *to and fro* from heaven to earth. She saw the world's oceans, but instead of it being full of water, they were full of people. They were all jostling and fighting each other to climb out onto the land. She saw a monster rising up out of the ocean of people and devouring them all.

Just then, she felt a chill streak across her body and noticed she was soaking wet with sweat. She got up and went to the hallway bathroom. She found a towel and quickly began to dry herself off. She'd always loved her mom's towels because they smelled like Lilac and reminded her of growing up here during simpler times.

She looked into the mirror and a verse immediately came to mind, *for now we see through a glass, darkly; but then face to face: now I know in part; but then shall I know even as also I am known.* She knew it was from the Apostle Paul and one of his letters to the church in Corinth, but she could not remember the exact verse. She was just surprised to have remembered that much of the verse, especially having just woken up.

She lay back down and let her mind drift around, searching for the dream again. She wondered what it meant if anything. *I hope Tristan is ok.* She had not heard from him in almost two days. The only thing she knew was he was traveling to a different base to help them close up shop, but that was the last thing she heard. She tried to stifle her growing anxiety over the matter. *Look, Katy,* she told herself, *every time Tristan went to a different base in theater, it always took him time to get some kind of internet to send a message back. Chances are if he went to a smaller place, they either had very little bandwidth or none at all. He is fine. This is not your first rodeo.* She finished a short prayer and immediately fell into a deep and peaceful sleep. Above her house, perched like a hawk on the hunt, Turiel kept watch.

***

Central Afghanistan-Hindu Kush Region
Mid-October

Barachiel reached out his enormous hands and some food-like substance appeared in them.

"What is that?" Tristan asked cautiously.

"This is manna. Take and eat. You will be sustained for the long journey ahead."

Tristan reached out and took it. He had been too exhausted to realize just how hungry he actually was. He ate. The food was bread-like, but not bread. It tasted like meat was cooked into the bread itself, then served nice and warm. Having finished his first one already, Barachiel handed him a new carafe of clear, cold water. Tristan drank again. Immediately, he began to feel rejuvenated. He was still tired, but not exhausted. He was not full, but he was also not hungry. Barachiel then stood up to his full height again, for which, the cave seemed to mysteriously accommodate.

"It will be daylight soon, so you must wait here and rest until dark. Then you will go back out and head west. Your legs will have strength in them to run. Your eyes will see the dangers long before you cross them. You do not stop running until you come across your own. You will know." "What do you mean *my own*?" Tristan asked. However, Barachiel was already gone. One minute he was standing there, all ten feet of him, and the next, he was simply not there. Had Tristan not been holding the remains of the manna and the small carafe of water, he would have thought he had hallucinated all of this. Nevertheless, their presence in his hands remained behind as evidence of a supernatural event he had just been party to, and he was relieved.

*Jack and Katy were right. God exists. Angels. All of it. I have been so foolish and stubborn all these years not to believe it. He thought of Katy. She has no idea where I am. How am I going to get to her from here? Nevertheless, the angel said to wait until dark, and then run until I see my own. What does that mean? My own what? People? Family?*

He lay down and glanced out toward the entrance of the cave. It was growing brighter with daybreak. He lay back and closed his eyes. The ground suddenly fell away from him as if he were floating on the softest bed in the world. The last thoughts he had were of the Angel standing watch over the entrance to the cave.

**Chapter 34**

Central Afghanistan-Hindu Kush Region
Mid-October

Tristan opened his eyes to complete darkness. At first, it took him a second to remember where he was. How long did he sleep he wondered? Had he dreamed all of this? His thoughts drifted to Jack and the explosion. He still could not wrap his mind around all that had just happened. He sat up, still expecting to see the angel there, but he was not. He glanced toward the entrance to the cave and saw it was dusk, about to turn to night.

Barachiel had told him he had to run until he ran into his own. He still was not sure what that meant exactly, but he got up and dusted himself off. He glanced over at a bag and saw some of the manna-stuff sitting there with another carafe full of water. He went over, dropped to his knees and thanked God for his meal. He ate and again, felt power surging through him, as if he were eating a delicious cake made out of pure caffeine. He finished the manna and drank long and hard from the carafe. Finishing it, he put it down and then headed toward the entrance and poked his head outside.

Looking left and right, and allowing his eyes and ears to adjust to the fading light, he listened for the sound of movement. Hearing none, he stepped out and went right. Although he was not sure how he knew, he figured he had about forty miles to go before he would clear the valley he was in presently. He began walking at a brisk pace and then found himself jogging. Amazingly, he could see in the fading light as if it were in the middle of the day. Before long, he found himself running easily clearing hurdles and wadis that would have otherwise slowed him down in the past. He ran and did not feel winded or tired. Nor did he feel the aches

227

and pains he had acquired over the past two days in their escape from Patriot.

After a while, he glanced down at his watch to see how long he'd run and was shocked to see four-hours had passed. Before long, he had noticed he was running out of mountains on either side of him and was now coming into the opening on the western side of the Hindu Kush heading towards the Afghani city of Herat. He did not know how he knew exactly but assumed this is what Barachiel meant *by knowing*.

He kept his pace up and then noticed some movement peripheral to himself along what appeared to be a road on his right some 500-yards away. The movement was a vehicle and looked to be moving along at a good speed. He did not know how fast he was running, but amazingly, he seemed to be keeping pace with the vehicle as the two paths began to converge. His movement must have caught their eye as well because they slowed down and began pointing towards him. Tristan watched as the vehicle continued to slow down and converge over toward his path.

Tristan slowed to a jog, then finally, to a walk. The vehicle stopped about fifty feet ahead of him. All four doors of the SUV opened simultaneously and four, monster-sized men got out of the vehicle each wearing night-vision goggles on their helmets. It was as if someone went back to the eighth century and dragged some Nordic Vikings into the future. Tristan was 6'1, and these guys made him feel small. Clearly, seeing an American soldier running out in the middle of the night in nowhere Afghanistan made Tristan an easy target to spot. They looked like they were either some kind of special operations team or mercenaries, perhaps Delta Force or Navy SEALs. Whoever they were, they looked like serious men.

"Hello, gentlemen," Tristan cautiously said with a shallow wave of his hand, "I am an American."

"We figured that much judging by the uniform," one of the large soldiers responded. The rest of the men did not respond, but instead, moved slowly to encircle him.

"You know how fast you were running back there?" the same soldier asked.

"I don't know. How fast?" Tristan replied.

"Like 45 kilometers per hour. Or almost 30 miles per hour," another one replied.

"That's pretty good right, I mean, for my age?" Tristan asked satirically.

"Usain Bolt's world breaking record was 27 miles per hour," the first one said.

"How are you running that fast? And for how long?" the driver asked.

"I am not sure. Maybe four hours or so. I lost track of time," Tristan said. "My name is Major Tristan Zavota, and I've just escaped from a bad situation with barely my life."

The commando squad looked at each other hesitantly and then lowered their weapons. Like a light switch, the mood instantly lightened. "Dude, that was awesome. You should've been in the Olympics," one of them said. "Or Delta."

"Is that who you guys are with?" Tristan asked.

"Yeah, we cannot confirm or deny anything. Suffice to say, we were part of a distinct Joint Special Operations Command team out on a mission when everything started going south. We tried getting back into Bagram, but that place is a *dumpster fire*."

Tristan wondered if Thompson and the soldiers from Patriot made it in. "What about the embassy at Kabul?"

"We didn't even bother trying to get into the embassy. Those jokers are trying to get out of there to get to Bagram before Kabul tears itself apart. However, Bagram is completely surrounded. No one is getting in or out of there. At least not by ground," the largest of the Delta team members responded. "What about you?"

"I was at Patriot when it got overrun. My friend Jack and I were sent up there from Bagram to help them close the place down when it happened. We were buried under a building after it took some indirect fire, and the troops that were there left, most likely assumed we were dead and beat feet out of there. Either way, we made it out after cover of darkness," Tristan said staring off into the shadowy valley he had just emerged from thinking back to Jack's last moments.

"Where's your friend Jack?" one asked.

"He didn't make it, landmine. Back that way," Tristan said pointing towards the valley from which he had emerged. It seemed like forever ago, even though it had only been a matter of hours.

"Sorry, brother, tough break. I'm Tiny by the way," he said. Tiny was presumably one of those satirical operator nicknames he was called, given his enormous size. He then turned to introduce the rest of the team. "This here is Red, who was blonde-headed and blue-eyed and looked nothing like a Native American; "Izzy," who was the smallest of the bunch; and "Phil" was the only one who, even though still large, looked like he could pass for an average guy if he tried hard enough. They all had beards and wore civilian, tactical clothing.

"Look, we are heading to Herat to see if there are any US assets left to fly us out of theatre. You're more than welcome to come with us."

"Thanks. I will definitely take you up on that generous offer," Tristan said. "Besides, I don't know how much more my boots could have taken." He lifted up his boots to show the sole of his boot worn down nearly to his socks.

"Alright then, let's roll," Tiny said.

With that, they all piled back into the SUV under the cover of darkness with Tristan offered the front seat. Herat was another fifty miles or so, and judging by the stretch of roads up ahead, would take at least an hour and a half. Tristan climbed in and settled into the front passenger seat, and he found his eyes immediately growing heavy. Tristan thought of the quote by George Orwell in that *people sleep peaceably in their beds at night only because rough men stand ready to do violence on their behalf.* Within a minute, he was sound asleep.

## Chapter 35

Western Afghanistan
Mid-October

Herat was the furthest western major Afghan city and bordered eastern Iran. As it turned out, the trip to Herat turned out to be a bust. The US Compound in Herat was abandoned and looked like its former tenants had abandoned it with great haste. The gates were thrown open and the local *burn and loot* crowd had worked the place over hard. Tristan slept through all of it. He woke up three hours later to discover they were not even in Afghanistan anymore.

"Where are we?" Tristan asked as he stirred and looked around while simultaneously rubbing his eyes.

"Morning, sunshine," Red said without smiling.

"There wasn't anything useful left in Herat. So we are pushing west," Izzy, said who was sitting behind Tristan.

"Look, I'm not Mr. Geography or anything, but isn't Iran west of Herat?" Tristan asked hesitantly.

"Pretty much," Red said.

"Isn't that a bad idea?" Tristan asked. "I mean, we are their sworn enemies aren't we?"

"Yes and no," Tiny responded. "There are plenty of indigenous and Nomadic tribes living in Iran who hate the Ayatollah and the leadership in Tehran even more than we do. If we stay to the south and clear of any major urban areas, we should be able to move freely until we make it to the Kurdistan border. From there, we will head into Erbil. We should have reasonably safe passage through Kurdistan if we stay well north of Mosul. From there, we'll link up with some Yazīdī Kurds we worked with in the past who can hopefully get us safe passage through to the Syrian border."

"Assuming we have any US-assets left to meet up with," Phil said from the far back.

"Also assuming we don't run into any pro-Ayatollah militia groups like the Basij or Revolutionary Guard folks along the way," Tiny added.

"Yeah. We assume we would rather not run into them. Not that we couldn't deal with the situation," he said tapping his Heckler and Koch M4 submachine gun, "but it sure makes moving easier when they don't even know we are there."

The team continued to move west. Ahead of them, unbeknownst to them, another squad began clearing a path for them. Tristan looked outside and thought for a moment he could see Barachiel flying alongside their truck. He wiped his eyes still unsure if he was awake or still dreaming. He looked out a second time and it was Barachiel, but not just he.

Tristan leaned forward and looked up through the windshield to see that there were two more above and to the front of their vehicle. There seemed to be several other angels all flying in concert with their vehicle, as if providing some kind of divine, angelic overwatch.

"What are you looking at?" Red asked.

Tristan thought about this for a second and was not sure exactly how to answer, without sounding crazy.

"I don't think you'd believe me if I told you," Tristan replied.

"Dude, I've been Delta now for almost ten years. I've seen my share of crazy," Red said chuckling.

"Alright then. It seems we have an angelic escort of sorts," Tristan then said flatly.

"You mean, like wings and harps angels?" Red asked.

"Wings, yes, harps, no. These fellas are big. They make you guys look like children, no offense," Tristan said cautiously.

Red repositioned his hands on the steering wheel and rubbed his chin. He then peeked up through the windshield but saw nothing but the glow of the sun beginning to rise over the desert horizon.

"I know it sounds crazy," Tristan added. "Trust me; I was not a believer in them either until just recently."

Tiny leaned forward from the back, having eavesdropped on the conversation, and asked, "Did you talk to one back in the valley?"

"Yeah. He actually guided me to a cave and I hid out there for a few hours. Even gave me some food and water. Then, when it was time to leave, I got, I don't know how to say it, superpowers or something. That is how I was able to run as I did. I guess I ran at 30 miles per hour for nearly four hours until I met you guys."

The SUV had grown uncomfortably quiet. Tristan thought perhaps they might stop and kick him out for sounding like a nut-job. Then Izzy asked a question.

"What was the angel like?"

Tristan turned his body in the seat so he could face backward.

"His name was Barachiel and he was sent by God to escort me home. He was probably like 9-10 feet tall. Solidly built and he had ethereal glow about him." More silence.

"I know it sounds crazy, but it's true," Tristan added shaking his head.

"It's not that," Phil said, "I think it's the shock of it is what we, I, am struggling with. We all saw you effortlessly running faster than any normal human can physically run."

"Yeah," Izzy added. "I used to go to church a long time ago, but being in this job now, I've seen too much ugly in the world. It callouses you…you know?"

"When I got to the cave, having just watched my best friend get blown up, I was a wreck," Tristan said staring out his window again. "I just got to the cave and prayed and asked God to save me. The second I asked, I felt this weight lift off me. Shortly thereafter, Barachiel appeared. Scared me half to death. I didn't know what to make of it either."

The Delta squad each sat in their seats reflecting on what Tristan just said for a few minutes. It was, arguably, a lot to take in.

"I guess, extraordinary times call for extraordinary measures," Phil said finally breaking the silence. "It's still shocking. It's in the same category like definitively proving Bigfoot exists, or knowing without a doubt who killed JFK."

"What proof?" Tristan asked curiously.

"Dude, we watched you run at superhuman speeds for at least half a mile," Tiny said. "Clearly, you're not Usain Bolt, so running at that pace for that long, means either you're jacked up on some kind of steroid/meth mix, or you're getting some supernatural help."

"Thanks for the vote of confidence," Tristan said jokingly.

"No offense, but you're no spring chicken," Izzy added.

The team was well inside of Iran now, and so far, the only border crossing they had passed was virtually nonexistent. A shack and a metal bar lay across the road, which the team conveniently drove around to avoid.

"That's odd when thinking back upon it," Red noted. "The border crossing behind us usually always had a few Revolutionary Guard rejects there, if for nothing else, pretenses. I even brought extra money to bribe the guards. But it was completely abandoned."

"Not odd, but Iran is probably tracking what is going on with the US and is recalculating their options now," Phil added.

Tristan then realized he had not called home in a while. His wife was probably freaking out by now. He asked, "Say, you guys wouldn't happen to have a satellite phone I could use would you?" Tristan asked. "I'd like to let my wife know I'm still alive."

"Sure do," Phil said as he handed up one. "Just press the 01-first for the country code and then your number. The call will be encrypted, so she's not going to recognize the number."

Tristan dialed up his wife, and as advertised, she did not answer. She probably saw this number, did not recognize it and ignored it. Instead, he left a voicemail.

"Hey, Hun, I'm alive. Crazy story though. I am with some friends heading west. I will call again in a few hours. Kiss the girls for me, love you."

Using their GPS, the team aimed their truck toward the center of Iran and continued moving westward avoiding the major highways. Above them, a squad of divine angels formed a protective shield above and beside their vehicle, as they moved straight through the heart of enemy territory. This ancient land belonged to a dark force whom the Bible only refers to once, the *Prince of Persia*. Unbeknownst to the team, their vehicle was being obscured from the prying enemy eyes of man. However, to the spiritual realm, four angels escorting a lone vehicle through the heart of Persia drew all the wrong kinds of attention.

## Chapter 36

Paradise, Texas Mid-October

The influx of new people into the town by way of the RV camp was beginning to make news amongst the locals. This meant the rumor mill was kicking into high gear. Stories began circulating the whole of Fort Worth and Dallas would begin moving outside of their prescribed boundaries of

Highway 820 and I35. Of course, most folks were now tracking the major news stories of the day concerning the financial apocalypse the US was currently walking into. The arrival of the new people was just proof-positive things were about to get scary.

The last time Texas had a major influx like this was before, during, and after Hurricane Katrina, when displaced Louisianans by the thousands, were resettled throughout Texas. Although, that was different. It used to be, living along the coast was your problem. Now, with the potential collapse of the dollar, it was everyone's problem. Since Katrina, the government at both the state and federal level started to crack down hard on price gouging. Now, even they were not able to stop the inevitable price gouging, which would inevitably follow. The year 2020 showed us what a little panic would do to our toilet paper and Lysol inventories.

As usual, the "experts" on television were all saying they had been predicting this for years, although, the media pundits routinely failed to follow up on verifying those claims. Although some had predicted a financial downturn, no one really saw the *Kredit* coming. That technology had been the European Union's top-secret project, and did not see the light of day until it was ready for prime time.

Towns like Paradise rarely get involved in the outside world, however, the day the newcomers arrived at the abandoned RV camp, the world just got involved in Paradise. Rumor had it the newcomers were just the first wave of people that would be fleeing the big city and swamping the surrounding towns that were ill equipped to handle the doubling of their populations.

Locals began to stock up at the grocery stores and store shelves started to go bare. The threat of the *Kredit* and the collapsing dollar, introduced much fear and anxiety across all markets. Both manufacturers and distributors were hesitant to restock their service lines, due to this uncertainty. Gas lines began to form at all the gas stations. The restaurants and nightlife also suffered as more and more people stayed home. From what you were seeing, you would think a cat-5 hurricane was on its way to hit Paradise.

Even worse were the non-physical changes that were beginning to take place. Paradise had always been a very friendly place. However, with the arrival of the 'first-wave,' the locals started to become less and less friendly. There was a growing air of suspicion around town as a survivalist-based paranoia spread like an airborne virus. Of course, these symptoms of collective paranoia were not unique to Paradise.

Small towns across the nation were beginning to feel the burden of the increasing population of outsider 'city dwellers.' These people had begun evacuating their former urban domains with the onset of the breakdown of civil society.

Katy had been driving through town with her kids and her brother and had commented on the subtle changes she was seeing.

"Is it me or does the town seem very different these days?" Katy asked her brother. The kids were busy watching cartoons on the minivan's onboard entertainment system.

"No, you're right. Things are different," he said. "Ever since the new folks arrived at the RV park, the economic issue went from being a faraway problem, to at our doorstep."

"You know, things are hardly as bad as the media often lets on. I guess what I mean is, the media will build up a problem so much, the reality of it hardly ever lives up to its hype," David said. "However, when the media doesn't hype up something, and it just happens, that's when you know it's going to be bad."

"So are you saying this economic mess over the dollar collapsing is more hype than hurt?" Katy asked.

"Yeah, I mean, I think so," he said. "When is the last time the media ever got any crisis right?"

"True," she responded. "However, Tristan always said the financial markets were ruled by herd mentality. Therefore, if the markets are spooked, then there was great potential to make things go from bad to worse when people start to panic. Remember when we were trying to buy a house back in 2008, and all the stuff with the *Mortgage Crisis* and banks *too big to fail* was going on?"

"Yeah, I remember," David nodded.

"We couldn't get a loan to save our lives," Katy replied.

"Well, I think that was more of the sub-prime market collapsing rather than just the herd panicking," David replied.

"I didn't mean the people panicked, I meant the bankers and investors panicked," Katy said. "I think this is a lot like that, instead of an overinflated mortgage market, we are talking the US Dollar and our overinflated national debt."

"Do you think this is it?" he asked. "Are we in the last days?"

"I don't know, we could be in the opening stages of it," Katy said. "I always believed the first thing that would happen would be the *Rapture of the Church*. Then a gap in time where everything went to hell in a handbasket. But since the Bible is silent about the greatest *Christian* nation in the history of mankind, it's kind of hard to say where we are exactly."

"Post-Christian," he said correcting her.

"For sure. We haven't been a *Christian* nation in decades," she replied.

"Wow, our conversation turned morbid pretty quickly," he said.

"Kind of hard not to get morbid when you consider the collapse of your own nation," Katy said soberly. "I mean, if that's what this turns out to be. It reminds me of the Roman Empire in the 4th-century. I always wondered what it would have been like to live in Rome when you had the barbarians at the gates."

"Let's change the subject. Tristan is still deployed and you have not heard from him in a while. I do not want you getting all worked up and worried, especially since they announced the pullback of all troops overseas. You worried about Tristan not being a believer and the Rapture happening?" David asked.

"Yes. I would be lying to say I was not. He's coming around slowly," she responded looking off into the distance. "Maybe."

"He will come around. We have been keeping him in our men's prayer group now for months. God will reach him somehow."

"I pray he does," she said. "He's not going to want to be here for what comes after the Rapture."

"Hey, I got a voicemail," Katy said looking down at her phone curiously. "I didn't even hear it ring."

## Chapter 37

Eastern Iran

Mid-October

Then said he unto me, Fear not, Daniel: for from the first day that thou didst set thine heart to understand, and to chasten thyself before thy God, thy words were heard, and I am come for thy words. But the prince of the kingdom of Persia withstood me one and twenty days: but, lo, Michael, one of the chief princes, came to help me; and I remained there with the kings of Persia. Now I am come to make thee understand what shall befall thy people in the latter days: for yet the vision is for many days. **Daniel 10:12-14**

"The Prince of Persia was a title given to one of

Lucifer's top lieutenants. An ancient, territorial demon, filled with immense power, and wickedness. He serves Lucifer by keeping spiritual darkness over these lands, from Afghanistan through Syria," Barachiel said to Tristan as they were traveling westward in the vehicle.

Tristan swapped places with Izzy and was now in the far back and pretending to sleep with his head resting against the window when Barachiel gave him that bit of uncomfortable information. Barachiel was outside but keeping pace with their SUV as easily as if he were simply strolling in the park on a Sunday afternoon.

"How does that work?" Tristan asked at a whisper so faint, it was only detectable to Barachiel. "Does each country have its own angel or territorial demon? Like does the US have its own?"

"Yes. Satan cannot be everywhere at once. Thus, he has command of vast legions who take up posts around the world who form the principalities, powers, and rulers of darkness. He is the *prince of the power of the air*, and those below him form a highly complex hierarchy of territorial commanders or princes. These fallen angels are very powerful and wicked. Under them, they have sub commanders and province lords to manage specific forms of wickedness. Ultimately, Satan dictates to these princes, which nations he wants to rise, or to fall, through corruption or violence."

"How do they do that exactly, if we cannot see them?" Tristan whispered again.

"These seek to corrupt and destroy all that is good in a land, first, by corrupting men with apathy and complacency, and then by escalating wickedness so evil becomes good, and turn that which is good, into evil," Barachiel said with disgust.

"Are we in danger now?" Tristan again asked in a whisper.

"Yes. Even now, the *Prince of Persia* has surely been notified we are moving through his lands, and he is dispatching forces to stop us."

"But there are only four of you. How can you stop a legion?"

"We serve God Almighty. With Him, all things are possible."

"So we aren't in danger? I am confused. Are you in danger?" Tristan asked.

"Imagine traveling down a dark road filled with unknown peril. However, you have a sword and a lamp. It is like that."

"Ohhh-k," Tristan said now thoroughly confused.

Barachiel looked up and forward into the darkness.

"You have a roadblock ahead. But do not fear."

Tristan leaned forward to the center of the SUV. "Guys, I know this is going to sound super weird, but the angel, Barachiel, just informed me we have a roadblock ahead."

The team looked awkwardly at Tristan and then laughed in unison. However, they still instinctively began checking their weapons and slowing the vehicle down. Phil was monitoring their movement by crosschecking the map and his portable DAGR (Defense Advanced GPS Receiver). "Unless we go off-road, I don't think there is a natural way around," he added.

Ten minutes later, a voice rang out from the front of the vehicle. "We got company."

The vehicle had just crested the hill and on the downslope, they could see half-dozen vehicles blocking the road ahead. Tristan leaned forward to see what Red was talking about and he saw a sizeable roadblock up ahead. Their vehicle slowed down and stopped short of it by about a football field. Tristan looked outside again and saw Barachiel was no longer there.

Looking forward, he could see their *angelic overwatch* had moved to the front of the vehicle. In front of them were hundreds of darkened figures of about equal height arrayed in front of them. Their bodies were difficult to make out, but their eyes glowed red like an army of wood fire embers.

To the team, however, they only saw the Iranian roadblock, which consisted of a dozen men and half-dozen vehicles. They had, up until their vehicle showed up, not been paying attention. Now, with the vehicle stopped and not advancing, their attention perked up and they began pointing their weapons toward the lonely SUV.

"So, what now?" Red asked. "I think we could throw it in reverse and beat feet outta here before they could catch up, but we'd lose a lot of time and run the risk of them radioing back to their buddies behind us."

"Wait!" Tristan said as he watched the angelic squad move forward.

"What is it?" Izzy asked.

"The angels are doing something," Tristan said, never changing his forward gaze.

The angels had stood in front of the vehicle, swords drawn and looked like they were ready to throw down. Then, as if on cue, the four angels started to glow brighter and then charged viciously into the demonic horde. Soon, Tristan was shielding his eyes as flashes of light began to shoot out from the angelic melee. He could hear the sound of clashing metal and screams that seemingly went unnoticed by his teammates. This went on for a minute or so, and then the blinding brightness began to recede. Finally able to see again, he saw Barachiel wave them forward.

"We go forward," Tristan said before he could stop himself from saying it. The words had just left his mouth when the most delicious aroma arose from behind Tristan in the luggage area. "What the…" Tristan began to say as he turned around to look behind him.

Laying in the back was a massive array of metal dishes filled with delicious-smelling food. Tristan lifted the lid of one and it was full of beef and Lamb Kebabs. He moved to the next one and it was *Tahdig* (a form of crunchy fried rice). Another pot revealed *Baghali Polo* (a wild rice delicacy) and flatbreads. There were also gallons of juice, water, and teas. "Guys, I think we are good. Pull forward…slowly."

The team inched the SUV forward with the windows rolled down. The wind had divinely shifted directions and now gave them something of a decent tailwind. They stopped about thirty feet short of the group and let the smell of the aroma waft forward. The stirring amongst the guards was noticeable, and one finally stepped forward and slung his AK-47 on his shoulder. He waved the car forward. The team slowly moved forward slowly. Tristan (in the back) who had never spoken another language in his life, save, bad *Texanese*, stuck his head out of the window. In perfectly fluent Farsi, he said, *"Gentlemen, we come bearing gifts."*

The team looked at him as if he had a third eye in his forehead. Tristan shrugged his shoulders as if to say *what*? Tristan then told Red to pull forward and to the side so the back of the truck would open to the Iranian guards. As soon as he did, Tristan jumped out with his hands halfway up and went around to the back slowly. More guards came out from behind their vehicles. More of them began to sling their weapons behind their shoulders. Tristan started lifting the giant containers with food out and walking them over to the blockade. The rest of the team got out and followed suit.

The mood immediately went from tense to festive, as the guards began inspecting the feast in front of them. The team, not quite believing all that was transpiring, continued making the treks back and forth between the trunk of the SUV to the hoods of the guard vehicles. Finally, unable to continue this unbelievable scenario, Phil pulled Tristan aside.

"Dude…where did all this food come from?"

"I don't know. The angels I guess," Tristan said.

"But how?" Phil asked utterly perplexed.

251

"I'll explain after we leave. Keep pulling the food out and keep serving them."

By this point, the guards had forgotten completely about the roadblock or even these newcomers. There was so much food and drink overflowing; they had thought it was a new holiday. They began clearing out places to sit and place the food. Each man had enough meat, rice, and flat bread to feed himself and his family for a week. Juices and teas were drunk with abandon, and before long, the men were singing a song in Farsi about how great the Persian Empire was.

Barachiel signaled to Tristan that it was time to go. Tristan signaled to the team to leave while the Iranians were distracted. Tristan looked back to see what had happened to the demonic hosts who had initially stood with them, only to discover they were long gone. Tristan did not remember a lot from church growing up, but he remembered something about Jesus feeding 5,000 people with just five loaves of bread and two fish.

## Chapter 38

Central Iran
Mid-October

The rest of the movement through eastern Iran was to

Tristan's surprise, rather uneventful. They had hit the town of Torbat at night, so they made it through there under the cover of darkness. They continued heading southwest towards the town of Tabas. Like the miraculous appearance of food, their vehicle's fuel gauge never seemed to move off full, which was something that bothered Red tremendously. On more than one occasion, he stopped and physically checked the gas tank. From there, they continued west towards Isfahan, which, by that point, they were ready to get out of the vehicle and stretch their legs.

Isfahan, a major Iranian city, had numerous checkpoints going in and out of all the major thoroughfares. There was not any decent way to make it through or around the city unnoticed. They were still 30 kilometers or so from the outskirts, and they decided to hold until night. They found what looked like an abandoned structure off the main road, and approached it cautiously.

"Looks like whoever was building this mosque ran out of money," Phil said disappointedly.

"Or enthusiasm," Izzy added. "This looks like a sad excuse for a mosque."

The building was a typical rectangular, Middle Eastern structure. It had three small minaret imprints on each wall's inside, depicting the hint of Persian culture. Given its distance between the last town and the next, it was likely some kind of rest area, with a mosque built into it.

"Everybody, smoke 'em if you got them," Red said (military slang for taking a break). "Tristan, you and your angel buddies get the first shift. Keep an eye out on our perimeter."

He handed Tristan a pistol and then went to a wall to sit against, and fell asleep sitting up. The rest of the team did likewise and spread out along different walls, so as not to cluster together. Meanwhile, Tristan walked towards the entrance and noticed Barachiel come into view just outside of the wall.

"So, I've wanted to ask you about this for a while now, but, what is it like being an angel?" Tristan asked hesitantly.

"What is it like being human?" Barachiel replied.

"Ah, well, it's mostly pain and discomfort, mixed in with some moments of sheer happiness and terror," he replied with a chuckle. "I mean, life is full of pain like heartaches, headaches, and backaches…mostly in that order."

Barachiel cracked the tiniest of smiles. "We don't feel pain like that thankfully. However, we mourn the loss of our fellow messengers who sided with the evil one. They will spend eternity in the blackest, darkness, forever; aflame and in agony."

"You're talking about Satan, right?" Tristan asked.

"Yes, but that is his title, not his name. He was once called *Heylel bin Shachar*, the Shining One, or as you know him, Lucifer, the light-bearer," Barachiel added staring off into the distance.

"I suppose he doesn't wear a red suit, with pointy horns and tail, and carry a pitchfork, does he?" Tristan asked with a sly grin.

"No. If you ever met him, you would probably think he was the most beautiful being you ever saw. He was created to be the best of us (speaking of the angelic ranks). But now, evil has twisted his true form."

"What do you mean?" Tristan asked.

"What I mean is he used to be beautiful all the time, but now, evil has corrupted him. He can only be beautiful now, when he changes himself intentionally. His form that he resorts back to, is dark and twisted."

"How long have you lived?"

"We have been here since before the beginning. We were eyewitness to the creation of the universe."    "I used to believe we came from the Big Bang,"

Tristan replied.

"The only explosion there was light, and that was when God said, *Let there be light*."

"Are you also saying you have seen everything since? Every kingdom, empire, and major historical event?"

"Yes."

"I have to ask, but the Flood, Noah's Flood I mean…that was real?"

"Yes."

"I always thought that was just a Sunday school story. But why would God do that? Why destroy the whole world over a few bad people. How many people were there anyway? A couple thousand?"

"There were approximately 7,000,542,314 people on the earth when the Flood came. I have already subtracted the eight, being Noah and his family."

"What?" Seven billion people? I suppose they didn't live in caves either?"

"No, they were an advanced civilization, albeit, a wicked one toward the end of it all."

"Probably not a lot different than our world today is it?" Tristan asked somberly.

"It is very close to the same, with a few exceptions."

"Like what?"

"The fallen angels, those who sided with Lucifer, began intermingling with humans and taking wives amongst the women."

"Whoa. How is that possible; I mean, you know, the physical part."

"It is possible. Angels can take on corporeal or physical attributes when we deem necessary. They had children who were neither fully human nor fully angel. They were hybrids. They were very literally, children of the damned."

"What happened to those angels who, you know, hooked up with women?"

"They are reserved under chains of darkness in the abyss, until the end."

"They're probably thinking now it wasn't such a good idea after all," Tristan said.

"They are insane if I could put it in human terms. They were led by Lucifer to try and taint the human bloodline, so that a Messiah, Jesus Christ, could not come from the line of men."

"So that is why God did the whole Flood thing?"

"Yes. Only Noah and his family were spared, to which, is now where all the tribes of men have since come."

Tristan sat there for a moment trying to absorb all of

the new information that he had never heard of, much less, thought of in any real depth, into his new and developing worldview.

"So, can you tell me what my purpose is now?" Tristan asked hesitantly.

"Not yet. But more when you and your friends arrive to the Holy Land," Barachiel said nonchalantly. "Holy Land? I am not tracking where that is. I thought I was going back to the United States."

"You must go through the land of Israel first."

"I see. Ok. Question. How come you're with me sometimes, and other times, I cannot see you at all?" Tristan asked curiously.

"The enemy is all about, especially in this part of the world," he replied. "I don't want to bring unnecessary attention to your quest."
With that, Barachiel stood up and looked at Tristan. "Keep heading west until you get to Erbil. I will see you there."

"How will I know where to go once I get there?" Tristan asked.

"You will see," Barachiel replied. With that, he disappeared.

Tristan's mind was roiling. Everything he thought he knew about the world was either wrong or seriously misguided. He now knew his children, having attended Sunday school and BSF had a better grasp of reality than he did. The Big Bang was wrong. Evolution was wrong. Uniformitarianism was wrong. Good works could not save him. The supernatural was real. Tristan leaned back against the wall and drank hard from the carafe of water he still kept. It was going to take some time to wrap his mind around everything he was now learning.

\*\*\*

After several hours, the team began to stir. So far, they had witnessed two miracles happen. Things that defied modern logic and human reasoning. The team finally packed up after several hours of shut-eye. Night had begun to fall, and they decided dusk was the perfect time to get on the road.

The drive across southern Iran was akin to driving from Texas to Florida. Still, to play it safe, they stuck to the backroads and avoided centers of populations like the plague. Thankfully, there was enough food still left in the truck for them to all eat as well; although full bellies made staying awake even more challenging.

The team never came across any other Revolutionary Guard or Iranian soldiers along the way, presumably, as they (the government) were busy plotting their new role in the world in light of the current events surrounding the *Great Satan's* economic demise and their sudden withdrawal from Afghanistan and the rest of the Middle East.

The team finally made it to the town of Sardasht, which was near the Iraqi border. From there, they would continue their trek across the border in Kurdistan. Unbelievably, or supernaturally rather, they had made it across the entire nation of Iran, on a single tank of gas. Granted, traversing Iraq was not likely to be any easier than across Iran, but they had some contacts within the Kurdish community, who could assist them in moving through the country. The Delta team had been here many times in previous years when they had joined forces to take out ISIS. They should be able to find some sanctuary in Kurdistan.

Since the US pullout in 2011, Iraq had become a nation in name only. They had disintegrated along religious and ethnic lines, and the Kurds were in complete control of northern Iraq. At the very least, the team did not have to worry about the whole Sunni-Shia issue in Kurdistan. The Kurds were primarily Sunni, but in a way, they cared more about being Kurdish than they cared about being Muslim. This was primarily because of the centuries of bad blood between the Kurds and pretty much everyone else in the region.

There were some tough times there a few years back, when the President's decision to pull all forces out of Syria and Iraq, seemed to force some hard feelings between the Kurds and the Americans. However, considering the pullout was a ruse to kill an infamous ISIS leader, the celebratory spirit across Kurdistan was still truly palpable. The team might as well have been rock-stars for all they knew. Besides, being an outsider in a group of outsiders was not a bad place to move through. The Kurds, as Barachiel had told Tristan, were descendants of the ancient Medes from the days before the mighty Persian Empire had risen up. They knew the routes, mountains, backroads, and hiding spots better than just about anyone did.

There was a dilemma growing, however, in the back of Tristan's mind. The team had made mention on more than one occasion, about moving up thru the Caucuses to move into Europe. Although Tristan was reluctant to speak up just yet, he knew that was not the way he was meant to go.

Barachiel had instructed Tristan to go through Israel. However, he did not know if that included the team, or when he was to part ways with the group.

They had all taken a liking to him (and he to them) even after sharing his miraculous conversion encounter with Barachiel. They were witness to at least part of his 200-mile run he did out of the Hindu Kush Mountains. Thankfully, his craziness had some street credibility. Perhaps they considered him a good-luck charm, which had given them safe passage everywhere they had gone thus far. Either way, Tristan assumed they were his kind of crazy after all. Tristan was not sure how this conversation would go, but he finally worked up the nerve.

"Gents, I cannot go through Europe with you."

"What? Where else would you go?" Red asked.

"Israel."

"Aren't you trying to get back to the States? To your family?" Phil asked.

"Yes, and I will. However, Barachiel instructed me to go there by way of Israel. To be honest, he did not mention you guys, so I don't know if that includes you. Besides, I don't want to interrupt your plans if you were set on going back that way."

"That means you have to go back through either Syria or southern Iraq," Tiny said.

"What's wrong with that?" Tristan asked.

"Aside from their near-impenetrable borders trying to get into the country, nothing," Phil from the back said. "That is unless you try and backdoor your way into the country."

"That, and just getting there," Izzy said. "You'll have to trek the full length of Syria through miles and miles of *no man's land* controlled by a dozen or so different, warring factions just to get to the impenetrable Golan Heights."

"Which you can't cross without getting killed," Red said.

"I'll have to find another way in. Perhaps through Jordan," Tristan said soberly. "Where are we crossing the border at?"

"North of Erbil just past Duhok, up in the heart of Iraqi-Kurdistan," Red said. "There is no way around it. You'll have to travel the whole length of the country to get to the Golan."

"You might have to do your *magical-running* thing again," Tiny said jokingly.

"Perhaps," Tristan said staring out the window. "You guys don't have a particularly easy road to go either if you head north through Turkey."

"No. There are many mountains. We'll have to ditch the truck at some point and hoof it by foot."

"Couldn't you try to get to Incirlik Air Base instead?" Tristan asked. "That's about as far south in Turkey as you can get."

"We've called ahead," Phil said from the back. "They're vacating that place as we speak."

"What about going by boat?" Tristan inquired. "Could we just make it to the coast and then get a couple of skiffs, something we could all manage easily. I'll head south and you guys head north or west?"

"We could, but these coastlines are heavily patrolled. We will have better luck staying off the waters and off the main roads. Makes for slower traveling, but we should have fewer run-ins with the bad actors," Phil said.

"We'll head with you if you think your angel friend…Barachiel…"

"Barachiel," Tristan corrected him.

"Yeah, that guy. If you think he will stay with us and give us cover," Red said.

"I don't see why he wouldn't. He said God has plans for me and he was going to be my guide to get back. I assume, if you're with me, then you'd get some level of protection," Tristan said.

"I guess the million-dollar question is, do we head north and west toward the coast, or do we take our chances going south through the length of the country toward the Golan?" Izzy asked.

"Well, Barachiel wasn't super forthcoming about what I need to do, or where I need to go. He rather tells me on a *need-to-know* basis. I do know he wants me to go to Israel, so if you stay with me, you will have some truly divine top cover," Tristan said with a sly smile. "With that said, I guess we are making the run toward the Golan. Besides, I am Army; I know jack and squat about running a boat in the Mediterranean Sea."

## Chapter 39

Northeastern Iraq- Kurdistan
Mid-October

The Delta team arrived at Erbil around 3:00 the following morning and the city was to Tristan's surprise, clean and modern. The team had compiled a list of three old contacts who might still be there to help them navigate through Kurdistan. They did not even know if they were still alive or living there, but they started searching old locations they used to haunt unsuccessfully. The plan was to find someone who could help them navigate their way north of Mosul to Dohuk, but all of their old contacts had dried up.

Again, Barachiel came to their rescue unseen. He appeared to Tristan while they were searching around the outskirts of the city. "Follow me," he told Tristan.

"Gentlemen, I've got some new guidance from our friend." Tristan began directing the team on directions and they were off once again. Barachiel had left them a trail of "breadcrumbs" in the form of light fixtures to help the team find the right safe house.

Tristan, who had never been this far north in Iraq, and did not know any Kurds, seemed to know where to go. Malfunctioning streetlights became the trail to follow. He had noticed how well lit the city was once they arrived. It was then, some of the lights looked different from the others. If there were a row of lights, he would simply look for the one that was flickering or shining brighter than the others shine. At 3 a.m., they did not see many people out; however, their presence was not going unnoticed. Tristan sensed someone, or something nefarious, watching them.

He began instinctively directing Red to turn left and then right, following streets all over the city like a human *bloodhound*. The team, in awe of his changing persona, also began to fear Tristan more and more as this superhuman power seemed to be manifesting in him. Red had confided in Izzy, even as seasoned operators, they had never really met anyone like Tristan before who could do the things he could do…even if it was with some divine help. It was kind of like having a friend who had a genie on tap to get you through tight spots.

After a dizzying route to the unknown destination, Tristan brought the vehicle to a stop. They had arrived at a non-descript home with a tall, whitewashed outer wall, with a rusty metal gate/door. No numbers, signs or symbols, or any other identifying markers distinguished this house from the rest in relation to its location to the city. The roadways around Erbil formed a series of circles, so judging by their distance from the center they figured they were near the outskirts on the northwestern side of the town.

"We are here," Tristan said as he rolled the SUV closer to the front gate of the non-descript house.

"Who lives here?" Tiny asked.

"I don't know," Tristan replied. "Somebody either you know, or that can help us."

"How do you know this is the right house?" he asked looking around the neighborhood.

"I just know," Tristan replied. "This is where the signs led me too."

"You know, this is kind of freaky," Red chimed in. "I mean, we sort of believe you with the whole angel thing and all, but you're the only one who can see him, so we are taking a lot of this by faith."

"But the running; the food; the endless gas tank?" Tristan asked curiously. "I mean, what more evidence do you need?"

"I don't know. It's just weird, bro," Red said looking away. "I mean, I've seen a lot of things in my day, but this definitely takes the cake."

That was news to Tristan. Had Red not told him how the team really felt, he would have never known. Still, they had to get home, and they were using each other for the time being. He was beginning to wonder if this *alliance of necessity* would survive all the way back to the States.

Tristan banged on the gate and in perfect Kurmanji (Kurdish language), announced their arrival. The rest of the group looked at him curiously. A light flicked on in the courtyard, and they heard the shuffling of feet towards the gate.

"Who is there?" a voice replied in Kurmanji.

"We are your guests our friend Barachiel told you was coming."

"Ahhh...welcome, welcome," a voice materialized as the gate was unlocked and opened. "We have been expecting you."

The two began conversing in fluent Kurmanji, while the rest of team stood by helpless. An older man, perhaps in his sixties greeted the team and welcomed them into the courtyard.

"Are you hungry? Thirsty?" the elder gentleman asked.

There was a general yes amongst the group. It was considered impolite in this part of the world, to refuse the host if asked. The last thing they wanted to do was be rude to their host, even if the team and Tristan absolutely dwarfed the older man leading them. They looked more like his bodyguards than visitors.

"So," Phil asked, "you've seen this Barachiel fella have you?"

The man looked at Tristan to interpret.

"My friend here is asking if you've seen Barachiel," Tristan told him in Kurmanji.

At the mention of his name, the host's eyes lit up.

"Oh yes, yes," he said standing up and then extending

his aged arms as high as they would go to signify great height.

"Gentlemen, this is Rebin," he said pointing to the elderly Kurd.

To this, the team showed their gratitude and respect.

"Still don't understand why we can't see him," Tiny said in a pout.

"You might be glad you can't. He can look quite terrifying," Tristan responded.

Rebin, along with his wife, handed out some teacups and something that looked like hot pudding. His wife, Ara, began pouring the tea into the small cups.

"Sir, we need to get to Israel, and we are trying to find the best way there," Tristan asked humbly.

"Well, I cannot get you that far, but perhaps west of Mosul towards the border," Rebin said.

"We would be grateful," Tristan responded. "I don't know how we could repay you."

"God already has. He added many goats, chickens, and sheep to my flocks, as well as fuel in my tanks, much silver, and freshwater. We are blessed."

Tristan relayed the information to the rest of the team, and Red said in his politest, sarcastic, voice, "of course, of course, He has."

The team and the hosts sat and drank tea for a few minutes in silence. The pudding was surprisingly tasty. However, they were soon feeling the strain of constantly being on the move for days creeping upon them like a heavy blanket.

"Say, Tristan, can you ask him if we can crash somewhere, I'm smoked," Phil said.

"Yeah, me too," the rest of the team said in unison.

Tristan did, and Rebin took them to two rooms in their house where they had some rudimentary beds set up for guests.

"This used to be our sons' rooms," Rebin said looking off into the distance.

"We are thankful," Tristan replied while putting a hand on Rebin's shoulder. "And my condolences for your losses."

Although he did not say it, Tristan understood all too well the years, in which ISIS was in control in Iraq, many wives became widows, many parents became childless. The radical jihadism of ISIS had swept up a generation of young men in a fervor and destroyed a generation of young lives pointlessly.

\*\*\*

After tea, they found their respective resting spots and immediately fell asleep. Tristan found a spot on the floor, unrolled a sleeping mat, and used his jacket as a pillow. He had a million thoughts running through his mind. Just a few days ago, he was on his fourth deployment in Afghanistan.

His wife and family were safe at their home in Kansas. The United States was the pinnacle of global power. Although not perfect, the world at least, seemed normal.

Now, the US was collapsing. His family was taking refuge in Texas. He was on the run in Kurdistan, having just raced hundreds of miles across Afghanistan and Iran. He lost his best friend to a land mine. Now, a giant angel was supernaturally guiding him, even linking him up with a team of salty Delta Force operatives so as not to go on the journey alone. Someone or something was watching him. On more than one occasion, he felt like he was being hunted. He shook the thought off. He already had enough things on his mind than to go and create some mystery-thriller on top of his real-life apocalyptic nightmare.

He had heard the team talking about the news of congress wanting to replace the US Dollar. Tristan did not know much of the political machinations of how things worked in D.C., but he had heard Phil mention the "supermajority" several times in an article he read on his phone that made it sound like Congress intended to bypass the President.

That news had caused the ensuing chaos that was rocking most of the Western powers, which rippled down to everyone else. *The truth is,* Tristan thought shaking his head, *Jack would have been eating this stuff up. He had long believed we were in the last days, and I just used to take joy in mocking him for it. Now, I am living it.* Jack also said we have been caught in a financial conundrum for a long time now, and this collapse was inevitable. The enemies of the United States, namely Russia, China, North Korea, Iran, would now attempt to match crisis with opportunity and begin attacking the US, or US-held territories and bases around the world. Afghanistan was just the first domino to fall, but Turkey, Korea, Germany, and other overseas locations would soon be compromised soon as well.

The truth is there might not be much of the US left to go home to. The political parties, as well as their constituents, were becoming increasingly polarized and ideologically disparate. The US was on its way to breaking apart even without this currency collapse; this was just like icing on the cake now. Almost all of the major cities were becoming unlivable, with the crime, homelessness, lawlessness; corruption, and violence, most decent people were fleeing them as fast as they could. He had sent Katy to her parents' place in Texas for just that very reason.

If they made it back to the States in one piece and depending on where they landed, he wasn't sure how exactly he would make it home if there were a full-on civil war. He assumed, he would still have angelic help by way of Barachiel, but he had made no such promises. He only said God had plans for him, which could mean many things, the least of which meant actually going home.

At least the team had agreed to continue journeying with him through Syria to the Golan. I guess they were not thrilled at their options either of having to travel through Turkey or the Caucuses. With Turkey becoming a fully radicalized Islamic regime, and the Caucasus full of desperate Russian soldiers and KGB agents, they did not want to risk going through there to get to Europe. Besides, Phil had a friend in the Mossad he thought could help, if he could reach her ahead of time.

They would be leaving tomorrow early, likely before sunset. Exhaustion finally caught up to Tristan's restless mind. His last thoughts before he faded into the darkness of sleep were of his wife and children; their faces appearing to him like a film reel playing all the highlights of their life together as a family.

## Chapter 40

"How did you go bankrupt?" Bill asked.
"Two ways," Mike said. "Gradually and then suddenly."
***The Sun Also Rises*, Ernest Hemingway, 1926**

Mid-Late October

Domestic News

The news had hardly broken nationally before things started going south very quickly. Cable news, along with digital and printed media all tried to pin this looming financial disaster on the sitting President. Of course, this onslaught of negative news kicked off the herd mentality causing people to panic and make runs on the banks. However, the US Federal Reserve was prepared for the bank run. They were going to attempt to do what India had done several years earlier.

In 2016, the Indian Prime Minister decided to crack down on the massive tax evasion running rampant within the

Indian economy. He (along with his government) demonetized their two most popular forms of fiat currency, the 500 and 1000 note Rupees. In effect, the Indian government announced after a fifty-day period, 500 and 1000-rupee notes would no longer have a monetary value. This meant that if you were still holding on to these rupee notes on the fifty-first day from the announcement, they would be as worthless as *Post-It* notes. However, if you turned them in beforehand, you could get them cashed out for the corresponding value. If the second most populous nation in the world could pull this off, the US was sure going to try.

The US Congress, in conjunction with the Federal Reserve, announced they were demonetizing all US 100 Dollar notes and would convert them into digital *Kredit* for a similar value. Of course, this did not go over well, nor was it sanctioned by the Executive Branch. With the Executive and the Congressional Branches at loggerheads as to how to proceed, the breakup came swiftly. While the sitting Executive Branch convened for an emergency meeting at Camp David, the Cabal, along with their cronies from numerous other federal agencies, conducted a bloodless *coup d'état* and took over the White House. The present crisis was too pregnant with crisis-opportunity for them not to invoke regime change.

Soon, both houses of Congress were in complete disarray. Certain members of the Cabal, along with former Executive branch members, former members of the Intelligentsia, former Joint Chiefs of Staff (JCoS), all declared the sitting President incompetent and unfit for office. They held their own televised emergency meeting and conducted a massive press conference from the White House in Washington, D.C. showing they were now in control. The US military likewise was in varying states of disarray, with upwards of 50-60% desertion rates across the nation.

The Cabal was now running the show. The former JCoS members sanctimoniously reinstated a former exPresident as the forty-sixth president, and brought in his former JCoS Chief as his Vice President. They then began to formulate a plan that first instituted *Martial Law* across the US, and then worked relentlessly to dismantle the Constitution by assuming the loss of sovereignty without legal tender to run the government. Their reasoning was the only way to survive this economic crisis was to bring the nation under a singular, global authority that operated under the *Kredit*.

Domestically, the new US government had to balance the reality that while there would be a breakdown in American society, the loss would not be total. As the dollar began its collapse and underwent the devastating stages of hyperinflation, the Cabal realized it was better to let go and reorganize, than it was to try to keep their grip over all fifty states and their territories. Nevertheless, they needed to incentivize this decision.

Governors were given provincial/regional powers akin to 'deputy presidents' who could command their State National Guards and Militias. Those who supported their leadership were given access to the *Kredit* and citizenship in the New Republic, which was being formed. For the more democratically held states in the Northeast, who didn't have enough vested military powers to make it worth running, liberal governments there were practically begging United Nations troops to come in and help keep the peace. On a more pragmatic level though, these local and state governments were incorporating the largest criminal gangs in their areas, i.e., the Unions and the Mob Families, to help keep the peace.

Martial Law went into effect across all fifty states. However, it could not be enforced in all fifty states due to the federal government's lack of manpower. Agents at the

Federal, State, and Local levels would be *incentivized* to stay put and help keep law and order through the aforementioned citizenship and *Kredit* access. Serious crimes, such as theft, murder, and rape would now be punishable by death and carried out quickly and vigorously. Hospitals, grocery stores, and utility companies largely fell into disorder, as the manufacturing, distribution, and retail sectors reacted to a collapsing currency. People tried to keep it going shortly after the crash, but without any kind of payment, workers quit working. Things quickly escalated into rioting and looting in the urban areas, while bartering for goods and services started to trend in the rural areas.

Biker gangs and right-wing militia groups started occupying large swaths of territory in the northwest plains from Montana to North Dakota, and south to Wyoming and Kansas (minus the Indian Reservations). It was akin to something out of a bad apocalyptic movie. There was simply too much land to try to keep control over, and most state governments refused to try. The current New Republic leadership viewed this as a temporary dilemma since biker gangs and cartels knew little about administrating and governing over the long run. The military leadership decided to let go, in order to get a better grip later. For now, the main goal was reconstituting military force back on US soil and maintaining control of military bases near democratic strongholds.

Texas, always independently minded and loathing the idea of global governance, sealed off its borders and immediately voted to come under the direct authority of the Governor and Lieutenant Governor. The Governor then gave sanctuary to the legitimate President, the First Family, his staff, and their families. The states bordering Texas formed an alliance as well as a buffer zone, which Texas offered to help defend.

The governors of these states would have control of all city and state law enforcement, state militias, and national guards, but collectively agreed to answer only to the legitimate President and not the New Republic. The liberal enclaves of Austin, Houston, and Dallas-Fort Worth and among the other states experienced a reverse exodus as liberals fled to the West and East Coasts. The towns along the Southern Border all experienced massive spikes in violence as the Mexican Army and the drug cartels moved to gain control of the major border cities. Brownsville, Laredo, and El Paso became battlegrounds, but they could not make much headway beyond that against an army of heavily armed, trigger-happy Texans.

# Chapter 41

Turning and turning in the widening gyre

The falcon cannot hear the falconer;

Things fall apart; the centre cannot hold;

Mere anarchy is loosed upon the world,

The blood-dimmed tide is loosed, and everywhere

The ceremony of innocence is drowned;

The best lack all conviction, while the worst

Are full of passionate intensity.

Surely some revelation is at hand;

Surely the Second Coming is at hand.

The Second Coming! Hardly are those words out

When a vast image out of *Spiritus Mundi*

Troubles my sight: somewhere in sands of the desert

A shape with lion body and the head of a man,

A gaze blank and pitiless as the sun,    Is

moving its slow thighs, while all about it

Reel shadows of the indignant desert birds.

The darkness drops again; but now I know

That twenty centuries of stony sleep

Were vexed to nightmare by a rocking cradle,

And what rough beast, its hour come round at last,

Slouches towards Bethlehem to be born?

**W. B. Yeats, *The Second Coming***


<u>International News</u>

Mid-Late October

Intended or not, the new European *Kredit* system was
derailing the entire *old world order* (i.e., the financial system
the world operated in for the past 76-years since the Bretton
Woods Agreement in 1944). That unraveling reality, now
posed significant threats for both domestic and international
operations and policies near and abroad.

Internationally, the US had its military forces
scattered throughout the world. Of most importance, were the
20,000 US troops stationed throughout the Middle East. How
to get them home was originally the first and foremost
priority of the *Joint Chiefs of Staff* from Camp David. Now,
with the *coup d'état* in motion, this preempted the US from
playing its former role as the world's global stabilizer (both
militarily and economically). Those pretenders in
Washington, who were trying to use the crisis for their
advantage, were losing their grip. The center of American

life, the national economy, was spinning hopelessly out of control. The nation, now divided into three parts, was not completely at a point of civil war, but the kindling was ready and the flame in hand.

Worse still, the American dethroning was creating chaos now consuming the global order. Singular totalitarian nation-states privatized non-state actors, criminal networks, and separatist groups themselves began the same hopeless feat of wrangling the tornado by taking advantage of the global disorder. However, for the global elite, who had long waited for such a day (or at least since World War II), this moment was ripe with opportunity. It was *Ordo ab Chao,* meaning, *order out of chaos.* They would lay low and instead of fighting the chaos, methodically started to channel it towards their own strategic ends. Nevertheless, they agreed that the United States was the first to be sacrificed on the altar of the *new world order.*

\*\*\*

The large swath of territory between Afghanistan and Pakistan known as Waziristan. Waziristan (both north and south), has long served as an artificial buffer between the two countries whose populations were largely homogenous. It is also, where the insurgents went for safe harbor and winter refuge for decades. Almost everyone in the intelligence world had long known the ISI (Pakistani version of the CIA) had been orchestrating the Taliban insurgency in Afghanistan from Waziristan since at least 2001. The ISI always worked numerous deals with the various warlords to their own benefit using this no-man's-land as part of their bargaining power.

Under the Bush and Obama administrations, the US would give the Pakistani's money for being "partners" in the *war on terror*. The Pakistani ISI in turn would then use the money to pay off the various warlords who were waging war against the Americans. Had the American people really understood the deal at hand, they would have never went into Afghanistan, nor agreed to stay for as long as they did. However, with the current economic crisis unfolding with the collapsing US Dollar, those payments to the ISI were ending. Now, all of Waziristan was being unleashed to bring the entire brunt of the Taliban, Haqqani Networks, ISIS factions, and Al Qaeda remnants into play in Afghanistan. Both India and China began massing troops along their shared borders with Pakistan and Afghanistan.

US Naval vessels came under the direct commands of the Senior Officers on board. Orders initially sending them out to police up stranded Service members were now in disarray. The ad-hoc government presently occupying the White House had reinstated and promoted a former loyal Chief of the Joint Chiefs, by given him a sixth star and the title of *General of the Armies*.

The original evacuation plan was then reissued to all fleets to be carried out. The plan called for US Naval ships to wait off the coast of India for the Afghan theater, and in the Mediterranean off the coast of Israel for the forces scattered throughout Jordan and Syria. Troops in Saudi Arabia, Kuwait, Abu Dhabi, Bahrain, and Qatar, would launch from Bahrain with the Seventh Fleet as they departed the theater of operations.

Heavy-lift helicopters and C-130s would move US forces to neutral ports in Bahrain, Tel Aviv, Israel, and Mumbai, India for flights out to the ships. From there, the ships would begin their voyages back to the US. Fixed-wing Air Force aircraft would begin their leapfrog home; hitting designated places where the US still controlled the airfields for refueling operations. As aircraft went into refuel, they would also start taking personnel and sensitive items out of country. Financial arrangements were being made with the Kredit and by promising the host countries that whatever we left behind was theirs to keep, just so long as we could get our personnel out safely.

US Embassies around the world were also folding up operations and moving back. US air carriers were offering free flights back to the United States for ex-pats who could prove their citizenship. Transnational companies like Amazon, Boeing, and Apple, along with the major airlines, which had worldwide operations, were scaling back, waiting on the decisions from the new US Executive Branch on how to proceed.

By the time Tristan and the team were in Kurdistan, most of the US forces in Afghanistan had left, using Bagram and Kandahar as the ports of exit. They were being flown to the Indian port at Mumbai. From there, they were transported by waiting Navy destroyers who then shuttled them to the US Naval base at Bahrain, where they would be flown back via STRATLIFT and MILAIR flights to the US.

This plan seemed to be working fairly well, until Iran threatened to bomb any American ship sailing through the Persian Gulf. That is when the *General of the Armies* issued the guidance to *neutralize Iran* in what was named,

*Operation Red Horse.* This was to be a demonstration of the new President's resolve to preempt any future antagonism against US Forces. However, given that all the long-range bomber assets would need to be launched from Whiteman, Minot, and Ellsworth Air Force Bases, (i.e., outside of the New Republic's jurisdiction), they turned to NATO with requests to turn Teheran into a parking lot.

Another horse, fiery red, went out. And it was granted to the
one who sat on it to take peace from the earth, and
that people should kill one another; and there was given to
him a great sword. **Revelation 6:4**


### Chapter 42


Paradise, Texas
Mid-Late October


Things were happening so rapidly now, Katy could not keep up. The State-owned media out of New York City, Washington D.C., and Los Angeles, were running non-stop stories about how the former President had failed the nation and why the *coup d'état* was a necessary evil. *Truth be told,* Katy thought, *the media had been a state-owned propaganda machine for a long time now, but this was getting ridiculous.*

There were not even any pretenses anymore. They conducted a *coup d'état* while the real President was at Camp David trying solve this crisis, and the *swamp* snuck in and took the throne.

*Now the states were in disarray. Texas borders were on lockdown. Mexico was trying to retake the border towns. Tristan was stuck who knows where. At least he got the message to me that he was ok.* Katy had been sitting on the porch staring out over the back pasture, watching the cattle eat grass as if they had not a care in the world. *Ignorance is bliss* she thought... *that is, until you end up on the butcher's block.*

She could see the main road from where she was, and noticed a truck's headlights long before she could make out any of the specifics. After a minute or so, she could tell it was from the Sheriff's department. She went in to tell her dad. "Dad, looks like the Sheriff's on his way out here." "For what?" he responded.

"I don't know" she replied. "I'm the one visiting from Kansas. Why would he come out here?"

"Don't know, but I guess we'll find out in a second or two," Carl said getting up and putting on some shoes.

Carl, David, and Katy all stepped out on the front porch as the truck pulled up the long driveway. It came to a stop near the house.

"Evening," Sheriff Flannery said, as he stepped out of his 1979 fully restored Ford Bronco.

"What can I do you for, Sheriff?" Carl asked.

"I'll just cut to the chase. It would seem," Sheriff Flannery, said slowly, while rubbing his chin, "the President, I mean, the real one, has decided to take up residence near here."

"What?" they all asked simultaneously.

"That's what I said," Sheriff Flannery. "Got a call from the governor's office today, asking if we had any land available for a headquarters and residence? I said *headquarters* for who? The assistant to the Governor then said someone would be out to see me today." "Did they show up?" David asked.

"Sure did," Sheriff Flannery responded. "A whole mess of em. They seem to like this area."

"Sheriff, our manners, forgive us. Come on in," Janice said. "I'll get us some iced-tea."

"Sounds fine, Janice."

Sheriff Flannery, Katy's mom and dad, all grew up together in Smith County. In fact, most folks here grew up and never moved away. The land itself seemed to hold a special sway over its inhabitants. The rolling hills and temperate weather, along with its abundance creeks, rivers, and lakes, made Smith County a fine place to live. They went in and the Sheriff removed his hat and made his way to their long dinner table.

"So, what happened with the rest of the trip? Why Paradise of all places?" Katy asked suspiciously. To which, they all looked at her with a semi-surprised look. "Hey, I mean, this is a great place to live, don't get me wrong. But, I mean, aren't we pretty close to the Oklahoma border?"

"True, Katy," Sheriff Flannery responded. "But the President's got the support of pretty much the entire Midwest and South. He wanted a place to live where he's not going to fear for his life every time he steps outside."

To which they all nodded in agreement.

"Plus, this place is rich with natural gas and clean water. He can run his operations completely off anyone's grid," he added. "And as a bonus, he's got a lot of support here, and everyone has a lot of guns."

"Makes sense," Carl said. "But how close are we talking from right here?"

Sheriff Flannery looked down somewhat sheepishly…"Ya'll would kind of be neighbors," he said with his deep Texas drawl.

With that last word, all the air in the room seemed to drain as if a black hole magically appeared over the kitchen. "That's awesome," David said, grinning.

Just then, as if to break the tension, three young girls ran through the house hollering and pretending to playing tag.

"Girls!" Katy yelled.

"That's fine, Mrs. Zavota," the Sheriff said. "Kids playing always lifted my spirits up."

"So whose land is he buying, or taking, or whatever?" David asked.

"Well, seeing as you have a thousand acres, I was hoping you'd be willing to part with 500 or so. Still leaves you with a lot of grazing area for the cattle, and you'd be compensated generously."

"With what, the *Kredit*?" Janice asked.

"Gosh no," Sheriff Flannery responded. "It seems there is a plan coming together. I do not know all the details of it yet, but all the states aligned with the real President, are calling themselves *America*. The Cabal, or whatever they are calling themselves these days, are called the *New Republic*.

They use *Kredits*, and we will use gold and silver backed currency, as of yet, to be determined. As for now, there is huge turmoil with people coming in and leaving. I don't reckon it will get solidified for a few months yet."

"I hear on the news most of the liberals in Austin have cleared out headed for the East or West Coast?" Carl asked. "Of course, can't get a straight answer from the news, wondered if you'd heard anything?"

"True, it has. There is a grace period right now between both the coasts and us here in *flyover country*. Those who want to stay can, but gotta follow our rules. Most of them liberals are heading to more *culturally-tolerant* environments."

"Good riddance," Katy responded. "I hope the door hits em hard on the way out."

To that, they all chuckled.

"Sheriff, can you give us the night to sleep on that decision?" Carl asked as he looked at Janice.

"Of course. I wouldn't have expected anything less."

## Chapter 43

Erbil, Kurdistan
Mid-Late October

Their contact in Erbil, Rebin, had two vehicles lined up the next morning they could use to convoy to the Syrian border. He also had some Syrian Kurds meet them there with a spare vehicle they could use to head to Israel. As it turned out, their host was actually a very big deal in the Kurdish community. Apparently, he was a man of some report amongst the differing Kurdish factions. Of course, this all came out on the drive to the border when their driver had shared this with the team. The old man had never let on he was such a big to-do.

Their arrival to the border was the very definition of anticlimactic. Tristan could not tell the difference between the Iraqi side and the Syrian. It just looked like they decided to stop in the middle of the desert. All that marked their arrival was the other two vehicles waiting. With ISIS having been wiped out several years prior, the Kurds regained control of everything north of Kirkuk, minus certain parts of Mosul. The Kurds controlled both borders, from Iran to Syria and movement there was relatively non-eventful.

After exchanging vehicles, Tristan and the team were led to a small checkpoint south of the town of *Al-Hawl* where they parted ways from their Syrian escorts. It was here that Barachiel reappeared to Tristan, and guided him to a location where they could wait a few hours until nightfall. He had led them to the remains of what looked like an abandoned warehouse. From the looks of it, this place had taken a beating several times over from different warring factions. Thankfully, whoever originally built it used several feet thick of concrete; so much of the main architecture was still standing.

Unbeknownst to the team, four angels posted themselves above them on the corners of the top of the building. Like divine sentries, these massive spirit-beings stood always at the ready with flaming swords drawn. The team got out of the vehicle and carefully scanned the area for any signs of activity or tripwires. After being cleared, Tristan got out of the vehicle and walked to an inside wall of the gutted building. He sat down on the ground and leaned back against the wall near the corner to stretch his legs. He definitely was not cut out for Special Forces; that was a young man's game. At 46, he did well just to get out of bed in the morning and run a few miles before his knees got too sore. He cleared a small area free of rocks and rubble and laid down. He put a bag behind his head as a pillow and lay looking up at the sky through the bombed out, open roof. Red walked over to him quietly and knelt down beside him.

"Are your angelic friends still here?" he asked.

"Yes," Tristan responded, pointing to the four corners of the roof.

Red sat down beside him. "What do they look like?" he inquired further. "I've always been fascinated with the spiritual world."

"They're big," Tristan replied. "Massive. Easily ten feet tall."

Red looked up at the roof, only seeing the darkening sky beyond the hobbled walls.

"Seriously?" he asked.

"Yeah. You would freak out if you saw one. I freaked out when I first saw Barachiel. They make Tiny look like a little kid if he stood next to one," Tristan added.

Tristan wasn't joking. Tiny was easily 6'5, and 350 pounds, yet these angels made him look like he lived up to his name.

"Why is it that only you can see them?" Red asked.

"I don't know," Tristan replied. *Truth is, he really did not know. He certainly felt like he hadn't earned the right.* "It happened right before my friend Jack died; he was standing on this landmine and he had this look on his face. One minute, we are moving slowly through this valley, being careful and quiet, trying not to be seen by some guards up ahead at a choke point, and the next minute, two Taliban ambush us. I end up shooting them, which drew the attention of some guards a good bit away. They started coming our direction. Right about then, we hear the click of the landmine. At that precise moment, it was as if time froze.

"He immediately knew it was his, and he told me it would be ok; God had a plan. He said he would distract them so I could get away. So I started backing up slowly, not sure if there were any more landmines around, but I kept looking back at him. He started singing a hymn. It was dark. I do not know how I could see his face as clearly as I could, but I just remember his face. He looked fearless, absolutely unafraid of death. I was moving away from him at an angle towards the direction we were going. I got maybe thirty-feet or so and these Taliban guys came in from a different angle closing in on him.

"I suppose they would have captured or killed him. Either way, it didn't look promising since they had their AK47s pointed at him. They were so fixated on him they did not even notice me moving backwards. In the last moment, he looked at me and said as clearly as I am talking to you, *goodbye my friend*, and he lifted his foot. That is when I noticed someone with him."

"An angel?"

"Yeah, but very faintly. At the time, I wasn't sure what I saw. However, since having met Barachiel, I know it was an angel. After that, I traced the steps those guards had used to approach us, and then I ran for what felt like an eternity. After I slowed down, I began to think back to that moment, and I couldn't tell if it was real or if I was seeing things. And then I found the cave, and met Barachiel, and you guys know the rest," Tristan finished softly.

"It's a bit tragically ironic if you think about it," Tristan added. "I never believed in any of this stuff, and now...now I see them everywhere."

"All this because you became a Christian?" Red asked.

"I don't know," Tristan said. "My wife's been a Christian for most of her life, and although she believes in angels and God and all that, she's never said she's seen one. I don't know why I was chosen. It wasn't like I made fun of her or anything out loud, but I was pretty resistant to *the faith* looking back."

"Maybe there isn't much time left," Red added soberly.

"Time left for what?" Tristan asked.

"You know, before the end of the world and all that. I remember going to church with my granny, and the preacher then was going on about how there would be signs and wonders in the last days. Never really thought about it until all the troubles in the US, and then saw you running like a bat outta hell," Red said pondering his own thought intently.

"Yeah, I didn't even think about that. If you had told me last week that we were in the last days, I would have laughed in your face. But now, after everything that's happened, it sounds plausible."

"Guys, check this out," a voice called out quietly from across the room.

Red and Tristan got up and came over to the corner of the room to where Phil was. "Look at the headlines."

Phil had the only GPS smartphone left, which hadn't been lost or damaged from the team. He flipped the phone around so the other guys could see it.

*US Collapses*

*President Replaced*

*Civil War Imminent*

"Dude, how long have we been out here?" Izzy asked. "All this happened in a couple days?"

"I think it's been more than a couple days," Tristan replied. "Maybe a week or so."

"Still, all in a week? It's like the whole world has fallen apart since we left Afghanistan," Izzy said. "What are we gonna have left to go home to?"

"Rubble," Phil said looking around. "We'll become another failed state."

"Doesn't matter," Tristan said, "whatever the US looks like, I got a family I need to get back home to."

"Look here," Phil said as he continued to read through the article he'd clicked open. "The East and West Coasts are now calling themselves the *New Republic*." "What about Texas?" Tristan asked.

"Doesn't say," Phil continued. "My guess this is like the Civil War, except instead of being the North versus the South, this is the left and right, versus the center."

"Flyover country," Tiny added. "Where I'm from."

"Good luck with that," Izzy said approvingly. "We got all the guns."

There was a general round of agreement, seeing as the liberal states had all but made gun ownership a mortal sin.

Tristan looked up to the roof. Barachiel was there, and he was pointing toward the south, towards Israel. "Gents, it's safe to go now."

"About time," Izzy said, "let's roll."

# Chapter 44

Southern Syria
Late October

The drive south was nothing short of apocalyptic. The country looked like what Hiroshima must have felt like after 1945…obliterated. Bombed out cars, houses, buildings everywhere. Rubble lined every street. Bomb blasts marked every road. Although the team was moving at night, they could sense the presence of death all around them. The weight of it was thick, like a suffocating blanket. Tristan could see the why behind the oppressiveness. The air above them was a flurry of demonic activity. His own angelic escort numbered only four, but they seemed to be moving as if the enemy above could not see them, or the small band of Americans.

"Why can't they see us?" Tristan whispered to Barachiel as he leaned his head against the window of the newly acquired military transport truck.

"God has blinded them to us," he replied. "Our movement has been veiled since we left Erbil."

"Veiled? I mean, if God was going to go out of the way and provide all this top cover for us, then what was the point of Jack dying?" There was clearly pain bleeding through Tristan's question.

"That was not my decision. God had plans for Jack, and you. That is all I know."

"How do we get into Israel from here?" Tristan asked.

"God will provide a way," Barachiel replied. "When the time comes, I will be instructed on which path to take."

The vehicle continued its painstakingly slow progress down the road. Aside from the craters littering the road, the threat of improvised explosive devices (IEDs) loomed large over the team. Most of them had lived through one (or more) IED events having served in Delta. Thankfully, the US had made large improvements over their tactical vehicles being able to withstand the blast of a standard IED with innovations like reinforced armor and v-shaped hulls. Still, the experience of one was not a pleasant event and their current mode of transportation was ill suited to survive contact should it happen again.

They had crossed the border and followed highway716 south to highway-6. From there, they followed 716 south along the border moving at a snail's pace. The place was largely dark with very little ambient light. The team had night vision goggles, so drove with their headlights off at about 25 kilometers per hour (15 mph). They then turned left onto an unnamed/marked highway, which paralleled highway-7, which they followed to Al Suwar. They crossed the river and through the town unscathed or even unnoticed. From there, they would proceed south to Deir ez-Zur, and get on highway M20. This is where things would get dicey.

M20 ran straight southwest toward the ancient city of Palmyra and eventually, Damascus. There were no other side roads or cutoffs to avoid going that direction, other than to abandon the vehicle and travel south by foot. Palmyra had been a temporary stronghold of ISIS, but abandoned the area to its ruin once American and Kurdish forces began driving them out. However, no friendly forces remained, and it was unclear who now was friend or foe. That was the problem with Syria. With all the modernity and technology the West had at its disposal, the facts on the ground became so muddled with half-truths and confusion, it was hard to tell anymore what was real and what was not. Fortunately, they had their angelic escort.

From highway-90 (out of Palmyra), Barachiel led them down highway-2. This would lead them to an unknown road, which skirted the outside of Damascus away from the eyes of the governmental forces still operating in the area. They had begun executing their own version of *Martial Law* once the Americans and ISIS pulled out of the area. That meant shoot first, ask questions later. This path they chose, would take them close to the main Syrian airport, but it was completely unlikely they would catch any kind of flights out of the war-torn country. However, it also meant they were getting very close to the Golan. They would stay off the beaten-path through small towns like Bawidan, As Sanamayn, and Grgis, which brought them to the very threshold of the United Nations' "buffer" zone (Ceasefire Line B) separating what used to be Syria from the Israeli Golan.

The whole trip had taken two-full nights. Their speed ranged from 25kph, to 100kph on less damaged roads. The team had taken shelter that first morning in the abandoned warehouse. Now, they were running out of night to move in the dark, and would have to hole up again near the Golan. Barachiel had instructed them through Tristan again, to ditch the truck and walk through the town of Al Rafeed, which was west of Grgis, and situated inside the buffer zone between the two Ceasefire Lines Bravo and Alpha. Here, Barachiel led Tristan, who in turn, led the team to the house of Omar Ishak, a Syrian Orthodox Christian family.

Omar Ishak's family had lived here in this region for more than two hundred years. While life under the Ottoman

Turks, and later, the rotating military strong men ending with the Assad family had not always been pleasant, it was tolerable. However, with the country self-destructing due to an eight-year civil war and ISIS, life had become unbearable. The family had been praying for a way out after ISIS had murdered Omar's parents and his eldest son. Omar had managed to hide his wife and daughter away in their underground network of tunnels, to prevent any more thugs from stealing his last remaining child.

Living in the buffer zone offered nothing in the way of real protection. The United Nations troops, which used to be stationed there, were *paper tigers*. They were either unable or unwilling to step in to protect life or stop atrocities committed either by Assad or by ISIS. Their sole purpose was to prevent any of the ugliness from spilling over to the Israeli side of the border. Omar had been living in perpetual fear for the past two-years and prayed relentlessly for a miracle.

Then, there was the knock on the gate door.

Barachiel had led the team to this house, which was situated on the outskirts of the town of Al Rafeed. Normally, Omar would not have opened the door, especially given the fearsome sight of this group of Western mercenaries. However, the night prior, he'd had a very vivid dream that visitors would come and he was to provide shelter and safe passage. Thus, the knock at the door seemed confirmation of this very dream.

"Please come in," Omar said in his best-broken English.

"Shukraan," each of the team said as they entered into his house.

The house was typical for this part of the world, with an outer thick wall and an open courtyard. There were plenty of evidence of war here, with bullet holes and parts of the outer wall hit by grenades and other explosives. The stone tile covered the courtyard and looked to be very old.

"Please sit," Omar said pointing the team members toward a long table with bench seating.

He then went and brought some tea and flat bread out to serve his guests. Since waking from a vivid dream, Omar had begun preparing for this very moment. Although taken aback by their fearsome appearances, there was a very good atmosphere around them. Especially from the smallest of them (Tristan).

"I have been....waiting...how you say, expect, you?" Omar said painfully.

"Expecting," Phil added.

"Yes, expecting," Omar added excitedly. He then told them about the dream in his best-broken English.     The team looked at Tristan, and Tristan shrugged and then looked to the invisible guest (Barachiel) as if for confirmation. To which, Barachiel nodded approvingly. "We were led here to you, by an angel," Tristan said, pointing to an empty corner.

Omar's eyes lit up and he looked to the corner of the courtyard. Although he could not see the angel at first, he could see the brighter discoloration of the corner darkness in the shape of a figure.

"Look, we need a way across the Golan into Israel," Red said. "Can you help us?"

Omar was still staring at the corner. Without turning his head, he said, "My name is Omar, and I can help. Only on…. (Struggling for the word) one condition first. My family must come."

"We will help any way we can," Izzy added. "Where is your family though?"

Omar turned his attention back to the team. His eyes glistened and the smile on his face could contain neither his enthusiasm, nor his poor dental work. "I have hidden them for now. Drink, eat, and rest, then we will go get them and take the old path south into the land of Israel."

# Chapter 45

Katy sat there on the porch drinking her coffee staring out across the field while wrapped in her blanket to fight off the morning chill. She was thankful Tristan had warned her ahead of time to get back to Paradise as soon as possible. She was now hearing horror stories of how motorcycle gangs were freely roving the rural highways in Oklahoma and Kansas, looking for travelers to kidnap and rob.

Things had begun to deteriorate rather quickly across the United States. Just a few weeks ago, the press were talking about the collapse of the US as if it were some curious abstract theory. Now the theory was becoming a reality. It made her think of a history article she came across while attending a community college to work on her Associate's degree.

The article if she remembered correctly was about how World War I started. Incurably curious now, she looked up the key words, *impossible inevitable,* mindful that since all this began, the internet had become notoriously unreliable. That and she lived in the middle of nowhere so her signal strength was weak. Nevertheless, there it was. An article by Anatole Kaletsky back in 2014. She skipped down to the end to reread the article's summation.

*It may seem almost impossible that Washington would go to war against Beijing to defend some uninhabited Japanese islands. Or against Moscow over some decrepit mining towns in Donbas, if Ukraine ever joined NATO. In early 1914, though, it seemed almost impossible that Britain and France would go to war with Germany to defend Russia against Austria-Hungary over a dispute with Serbia. Yet by June 28, war moved straight from impossible to inevitable — without ever passing through improbable. Four years later, 10 million people had died.*

Perhaps it was an oversimplification of all the factors and dynamics leading up to the Great War, but still, an accurate one. It only took World War I thirty-days to go from impossible, to inevitable; how quickly did they think it would take the US to collapse, or fundamentally change into something unrecognizable to its founders? *I think what we have already become unrecognizable to our founders here in the 21st-century even before the collapse* she thought sadly.

The US Constitution was designed for the sole purpose of maximizing individual liberty, while minimizing governmental control. That whole idea went the way of the Dodo bird back in the 1950s. We may have won the second Great War, but they never told us what we lost. When you become king of the hill, the power and prestige becomes intoxicating, and any nation would do whatever it took to keep it. Great power tends to change you forever. This also was not what she pictured the collapse of the United States to look like. For decades, Hollywood had been feeding the public this continual drip of post-modern, dystopic, apocalyptic visions of a world without the United States. That vision always came across like something between a *Mad Max* movie and a zombie-apocalypse. Yet, it was happening now, and not everything changed all at once.

It was fracturing at different rates of speed.

Of course, there were the big things, like the President moving next to her in Paradise, but more noticeably, the little things. Like mailing letters, or buying things from the store. If you could not make it in Texas, you could not buy it. For this fact alone, the price of normal, everyday items began to skyrocket. Things which normally would not be expensive, now became of immense value.

National chain stores like Wal-Mart and Target went independent, since their national headquarters were located outside the state in places like Arkansas and Minneapolis.

At the heart of the commerce world though, was the US Dollar. Although most people do not use paper currency anymore, especially for purchases above $100, US Dollar backed credit and debit cards became the currency of choice. Now those cards, and card reader machines (which were everywhere) were worthless. Relics of the past. They were now in this weird in-between time between the US Dollar becoming worthless, and something new taking its place. Nothing was black and white anymore, but varying shades of gray. Hanging over all of them though, was this lingering thought of uncertainty.

Politically, things happened quickly of course. The Democrats effectively performed a *coup d'état* while the President was away, and the states all revolted to varying degrees. Aside from the roving gangs out in the less populated areas, life in flyover country still kind of kept chugging along. The problem gangs and criminals had with folks in flyover country was everyone was armed to the teeth now. It resorted back to the Old West rules.

It seemed the most radical changes were happening in the major urban areas along the east and west coasts. Riots, martial law, and general lawlessness. Here in the state of Texas, or rather, the nation of Texas, the governor had taken over as the chief executive. Sheriffs had the power to deputize on the spot. Highway Patrols transitioned into Texas Rangers, and essentially became a mobile judge, jury, and executioners. If they came across a violent crime in progress (which happens more and more these days), they could just smoke the bad guys and leave em where they lay.

She was still deep in thought when she saw a black Chevy Escalade crest the hill and make the corner. It drove past their property and continued to the next entrance off their county road, and turned into a driveway opposite their land. *It looks like the President has taken over the old Grainger property,* she thought. No one had lived on it in forever, and you could not see the house from the road. Curious, she pulled up Google maps and looked to see the dimensions. Again, the internet was crawling. She wondered how much longer they would have it before someone, somewhere pulled the plug. The map did not load.

Curious, she looked up the city of Paradise, which did load. She went back to her location and searched again, and it was seemingly stuck in a perpetual loading mode. *Maybe it is not the internet, but where I am searching,* she thought.

*Surely, the President-in-Exile could still have some pull to block out his new residence.* She looked up, and the black Escalade was already gone. She would have to ask her dad about the Grainger place. He had lived here for nearly 40years; surely, he had been over there at least once.

She stood up, still looking out across the open fields. She wondered what kind of America her children would grow up in, or would there even be an America? She wondered where Tristan was. She thought back to her friends in Kansas and other places, and wondered how they were holding up with everything coming apart at the seams. Everything comes to its eventual end she supposed. Every empire that has ever been, has also gone off into the sunset.

The Greeks and Romans were two classic examples she could think of, but even here in the 20th-century, they had witnessed the collapse of the British Empire. They used to say the *sun never set on the British Empire.* However, by the end of World War II, the Nazi's and Japanese put an end to the British Empire forever. *At least the British Empire was destroyed through war. We are being dismantled by a change in currency. How sad a fate for this once great, shining city on a hill.*

She let the thought linger on her mind when something new popped into her head. *To whom much is given, much is required,* she remembered as having come from the Gospels. *That was a God-thing,* she thought. I would not have thought of that on my own. Curious, she looked it up, *ahhh, there it is* she said. **Luke 12:48**. *The Parable of the Good and Evil Servant.*

But he who did not know, yet committed things deserving of stripes, shall be beaten with few. For everyone to whom much is given, from him much will be required; and to whom much has been committed, of him they will ask the more.

The US had been blessed beyond measure above almost every other nation in existence. *In fact*, she thought, *the US always existed as an exception to the rule, rather than the norm.* Most of human history has been marked with one empire or kingdom ruling after another. Tyrannical or absolute rule was always the way life had been for most of the civilized world. For the parts of the world, which had not been civilized, it was fiefdoms and barbarian hordes. The US had been the greatest political experiment in human history.

The US borrowed from the great empires of the past; the Greeks, the Romans, and wrapped their logic-based legal systems, with the great thinkers of the Enlightenment, especially regarding free-market economies and private property rights. All of it was then enshrined with a moral backdrop of the Judeo-Christian principles for both social and private interactions. It resulted in a document (the Declaration of Independence and the US Constitution), which proposed that man's rights came from God, not from government. It was a glorious thing. Now it had started to come apart at the seams. *At least,* she thought, *I will have a US President as a neighbor.*

## Chapter 46

Southern Syria
Late October

After their tea and flat bread, Omar beckoned the team to follow him inside his house. Although riddled by bullet holes and pot-marked by the stray mortar-round, Omar's house was actually very beautiful, in a highly functional, defensive sort of way. It was typical for the area for a house to have an outer wall, and an inner wall, separated by a courtyard. The inside of the house was even more impressive. It showcased stone tiled floors, and an openness maximized the breeze and the shade, which probably came in handy during the heat of the summer months.

They walked into and through the large, open-air kitchen area, and into what appeared to be some type of pantry. The floor was covered with rugs, which seemed odd. However, Omar explained on more than one occasion, he and his family had to spend the night in here due to the artillery shelling going on around the house.

It made sense; the cellar was in the center of the house and was the most protected place he had. It was filled with empty jars, and wooden crate boxes and a single light bulb. Although Omar's house was nicer than most, you could tell the tea and bread he offered, was probably the last of it he had. The pantry was near bare, and Tristan had noticed the kitchen was near spotless. After years of war, he had probably been raided a few times for food. *Not a lot of cooking these days,* he figured.

Omar continued to the back of the large pantry and slid one of the rugs aside. Beneath the rug was what appeared to be a large, stone tile, which looked like the rest of the floor. Omar pulled out a knife and slid it in the groove of the tile and it came up without too much struggle. "The stone cover hides sound of wood," he said smiling slyly. Underneath the tile, was a wooden hatch, which appeared to lead to a basement.

"Most houses do not have a *qabu*, ah…how you say in English…underground room?"

"A basement?" Izzy asked.

Omar shook his head as if to say no.

"A cellar?" Phil added.

"Yes, a cellar," Omar replied excitedly. "The ground is very hard here, it is difficult to dig. My grandfather dug this many years ago. My father continued adding to it as have I. Has come very handy in recent years."

The cellar was dark, and there was only a single ladder going down. Omar went first. Although the cellar hole was normal sized, Tristan wondered how Tiny was going to fit into it. "We might have to bust out some Crisco," Tiny chuckled. Apparently, he had the same thought.

Each of them crawled down into the hole from the pantry. Omar went back up, brought the stone cover even with the wooden hatch, and closed it down, sealing them off from the rest of the world. He then pulled a string which presumably pulled the rug back over the hidey-spot. Each of the team members had already broken out their tactical flashlights and were busy inspecting the room. Omar climbed back down the ladder and carefully walked over to the wall and flipped an archaic looking switch. A single lightbulb went on. The room appeared to be no bigger than 10x20, but it had another door. Tristan was already getting antsy. He was not a big fan of being subterranean.

"Come," Omar said as he motioned them to follow him to the closed door. With a double knock, pause, and a single knock, Omar opened the room door and walked in. The door led to a narrow hall, whose walls were lined with chicken wire and wooden frames to help support the ceiling and the walls should they start to give out. Omar took about 10 steps, and then stopped. He felt along the wall and found a hole about waist high.

The hole was no bigger than a fist, and it was here Omar reached in and turned something. You could hear the metal-thud as if a large bolt had been unlatched. He then pushed on the seemingly unmarked wall, and the wall gave way inward about six inches. He continued pushing on the right side and it opened up even more. With the chicken wire and wood on it, you'd have never known there was a door there. The room behind the door was much brighter and smelled fresher than the one in which they had just been.

The room awash in light showcased bright colors, with floor pillows and cool air blowing. Inside the room, which was approximately 40x40, was where Omar hid his most valuable treasure, his family.

After the initial introduction, Tristan asked, "Omar, how far does the tunnel lead? Can we make it into Israel?"

Omar nodded enthusiastically. "Yes, we can make it into Golan. This tunnel has been here for many years. It is very deep, much deeper than Hezbollah dig."

Omar had been referring to the Israeli Defense Force's (IDF) extensive use of ground penetrating radar to detect the tunnel systems due to Hezbollah's penchant for attempting to penetrate Israel. He continued, "The tunnel changes shape the more far we go. It becomes narrower at the ceiling, like this," he said making the shape of a triangle with his fingers.

"This is fascinating," Phil said. "Building a tunnel this way took a lot of foresight."

Tristan had been thinking the same thing as well. He pictured Omar's grandfather in his mind's eye in a grainy, black and white film reel, digging all this by hand back in the 1930s-1940s. Somehow, his grandfather had decided he needed this tunnel shaped in a certain way. Given all Tristan had seen thus far, he doubted this was something Omar's grandfather thought up all on his own.

The first question he thought was why would Omar's grandfather need a tunnel south into what was then a virtual *no man's land*? This was even before Israel had become a nation again. Secondly, how could he have known to make a tunnel triangular? Obviously, underground tunnels had been around as long as humankind has, but the situation of it all just struck him as odd. Even though ground-penetrating radar was not exactly new technology, everything before the 1970s was rather rudimentary and would not have been able to detect tunnels in this rocky soil as they were in currently.

"When we move, we must be silent. We can still be heard if we make a lot of noise," Omar said in a whisper. Omar led the team and his family back into the main tunnel, and turned left. "We must be quiet."

Thus, they began their long trek into the darkened tunnel. Omar led the way, with his family close behind him. They moved in complete silence, attempting to minimize their presence underground. Tristan had been to an underground tourist cave in Texas years ago, and the memory of him not liking being underground came back with a rush. He had forgotten how claustrophobic he really was. The air was stale and oppressive. The only light they had was what they carried with them. It felt very much as if they were marching into hell.

After walking in the darkness for what seemed like hours, Tristan began thinking they were perhaps lost. Just then, a hand reached back and pushed against Tristan to stop.

The whole group had apparently come to a stop. At the lead, Omar reached up and pulled down what appeared to be an antiquated rope ladder.

"Here, hold this," he said quietly as he handed the end of it to Red. "I'll go up first and make sure the way is clear."

Omar's family moved to one side as the Delta Team began rearranging their gear for a climb upwards. Omar climbed up the rope ladder awkwardly, and disappeared out of their immediate range. As they had moved along the tunnel in the dark, the ceiling had subtly widened back out a bit. Tristan had not even noticed. Looking straight up as best he could, Tristan could see a sliver of light penetrate the river of darkness they had been wading in as a thought flashed across his mind in an instant...*this is what hell is like.*

Everyone always thought of hell as a place of bright, glowing flames. However, they assumed the fire operated like it did here on earth, which is to say, provided not only heat, but also light. However, in hell, there is no oxygen (or so Tristan understood). Therefore, the fire there must exist by some other means. If fire could exist without oxygen, then it also reasonable to assume the hell-fire could also act in a ways not characteristically normal for fire. Which is to say, the fire, which still burns, does so without providing light. It gave Tristan a frightful shudder. He was not even sure where the thought came from.

Just then, light from above flooded the tunnel. The team and family could hear some voices, but could not make out what was going on. Just then, Omar called down to the Delta team to come up first, which seemed odd to Tristan.

"I'll go up," Red said.

"I'll follow," Izzy added. "The rest of you stay down here until you hear from us."

The two men began climbing up. After what seemed like an eternity, Red yelled back down the tunnel, "all clear!" The team helped Omar's family go up next. Tristan, Phil, and Tiny brought up the rear echelon.

The light was deafeningly bright, and although it took them some time for their eyes to adjust, Tristan instinctively knew they were not alone.

As his eyes adjusted, he noticed Omar, and the team, sitting on the ground with their hands behind their head. A number of Israeli Defense Force (IDF) forces in varying gear and equipment surrounded them. Their sergeant was talking to Red off to the right, and Tristan felt a shove push him forward and down. Soon, he too was sitting with his hands above his head. At least he was not in the tunnel anymore.

Red and the IDF Sergeant came back and they both

began to speak, Red in English and the IDF Sergeant in Hebrew. Tension immediately began to ease as the team and family got up. The IDF soldiers lowered their weapons and immediately began to help the family up. The IDF Sergeant walked up to the group and said, "My name is Sergeant Abram, velcome to Israel."

Although their arrival had caught the IDF teams by surprise, Omar had not attempted to walk any further into Israel. He simply climbed out of the tunnel, and raised his hands. This of course, caught the attention of a drone operator who notified the nearest IDF teams of his location. As they got closer, he spoke to them in Arabic and some English, notifying them of his American compatriots and his family.

Of course, Israeli leaders already knew of the ensuing US collapse and presumably understood that Americans abroad, in varying degrees, were stranded. Having been in a similar predicament decades earlier, they were sympathetic to the Americans' plight. Omar and his family had been conduits for the Delta team to make it through. Part of his negotiating venue, was in exchange for safe passage into Israel, along with citizenship, he would hand over the tunnel and the house in Syria over to the IDF. He did not care, as he did not intend to ever go back. The team and family were quickly loaded into vehicles, and began their trek into the Holy Land.

## Chapter 47

Paradise, Texas
Late October

Paradise, Texas, went from being a nameless, small country town in fly-over country, to becoming the home of the most powerful leader on the planet. Although the Governor still ran the state of Texas, having the former (and still current) US President residing here and setting up operations, definitely put Paradise on the map, albeit, not necessarily in a good way. Katy wondered if this was going to be part of the 'new normal.'

She was cooking breakfast for the kids and listening to music in the kitchen when the dogs started to bark and howl. Someone was here.

She lowered the volume and went to the window to see who had pulled up in their driveway. Her dad and brother were out in the shop and her mom was out in the garden, pulling weeds, and showing her grandbabies the tomatoes.

Katy peeked out the window to see Sheriff Flannery get out of his cruiser and begin walking up to the front door.

She opened the door first.

"Morning, Sheriff," she said.

"Morning, Katy," Sheriff Flannery replied. "Your parents about?"

Immediately, Katy felt like a teenager again. *My parents?*

"They're out back," she replied, "we can walk around back and gather them up. What's going on?"

"Well, things are going to be changing here in Paradise, and well, I guess Texas as well. Need you and your folks' buy-in on what we got to do," the Sheriff said.

"What is changing?" Katy asked.

"Let's get the group together first," Sherriff Flannery said soberly.

Katy got her parents and told them who was here. They met inside in the living room, while Katy made coffee for the group.

"Well, this isn't the easiest thing for me to come ask, but the Governor has asked if we would be open to revisiting the idea of selling some land for the President's national defense team," Sheriff Flannery said. "I know we asked before about the 500 acres, but with the Grainger place working out the way it did, figured it was a dead issue. You know the US President, err….former and I guess, still, President, and was looking to move some Active military

324

units and Texas Guard units here to beef up security for the whole area."

"Sherriff, I gotta tell you, I understand the ongoing situation, but we aren't moving. And it's not just we don't want to move, we have cattle, crops, and other natural resources all tied up here we cannot just uproot and move into town. We also have more family moving out here, so I have to make room for them. Plus, this land has been in my family's name for generations."

"I know," Sherriff Flannery, said, "I was just instructed to come ask. I made it clear to the Governor, you and your family have a lot of pull here in Paradise, and the last thing we wanted to do was turn the town against the President."

"We do?" Katy asked curiously.

"Sort of, at least, well, that is what I told the Governor," the Sherriff replied with a sly grin.

"Listen, we are going to be the best neighbors the President has ever had," Janice replied. "You just let the Governor know, he's surrounded by supporters who'd take up arms for him in a heartbeat.

"Also, my husband Tristan, who is an Active Duty Army officer, is still stuck somewhere in the Middle East.

You let the Governor know we have sacrificed more than most as of late."

"The President's *Chief of Staff* told me yesterday, the last thing any of them want to do, is inconvenience their new neighbors. He just said the Office of the President carries an awfully big footprint."

"That's a hard ask, Sherriff," Carl said. "We understand we are living in extraordinary times, but we are going to have to say no. The President should know he has loyal supporters as neighbors, so if it's a matter of security, just let him know we aren't going to allow any enemies of the state use our land for anything."

"Understood, and I'll relay the message," Sherriff Flannery said. "How you guys holding up anyway?"

"Adjusting to this new reality is, well, challenging. Plus, we're all worried sick about Tristan, so until he comes home, things will be edgy," Katy added.

"We are keeping him in our thoughts and prayers," Sherriff Flannery said soberly. "Keep us posted if you hear anything, and we will get him home."

The thought of having to move off their 'ancestral' homeland, never crossed Katy's mind before. However, having the most powerful man in the world move across the street was bound to have its downside. Would they be sacrificing for the greater good, meaning, would giving up their land, help the President regain control of the fifty states?

## Chapter 48

For we do not wrestle against flesh and blood, but against principalities, against powers, against the rulers of the darkness of this age, against spiritual hosts of wickedness in the heavenly places. **Ephesians 6:12**

Golan Heights, Israel
Late October

They were being shuttled to a hidden military site near Bet Tel, Israel. The bus's windows were tinted so dark, he could not see out of them. The rest of the group sat in their separate seats. This was the first time Tristan felt like he could actually rest. He did not mean physically, but mentally and emotionally as well. He began to drift off, and then, unexpectedly, a thought very firmly planted itself inside his head.

*True believers were always the most dangerous people in the world. True belief in something is always dangerous to*

*someone else. If it is true that Satan runs this world, then*
*Christians are now enemy number one.*


It is why the world was constantly attacking issues near and dear to Christian causes: abortion, homosexuality, tyranny, cults, and the occult. It is why although the majority of terrorist attacks between 1990 and 2020 were from radicalized Muslims, the secular world refused to speak out against it even though the cause was obvious.

Furthermore, as this trip has borne out, there was another kind of war being waged, a spiritual one. He had seen it with his own eyes. If people could see what he saw, they would never again want to sin. The dark entities, which freely move about this planet, were staggering, especially in places where sin was promoted as normal. Not just the nightclubs and bars, but now, more seemingly innocuous places. It was as if people were constantly swimming through an ocean of dark spirits. The places in the world promoted as hedonism, were really just orgiastic cesspools of these evil, ancient entities.

Tristan had now seen them with his new eyes. He could see how they influence our daily affairs. An angel could swoop in at the last second to nudge you an inch, so a moving car does not hit you. A demon could whisper into your ear at the right moment to urge you to give in to your deepest desires, or to anger.

Now, in a very real way, these spiritual beings were interacting with him in a very tangible way. He was not sure why, but it seemed like there was more to this, than him simply making it home to his family. It was like this thought he just had. His old self would never think about things like spiritual warfare. Sure, he considered himself well studied and intelligent, but he never cared much for theological or spiritual ponderings. Now, it was as if he had walked into the magical wardrobe and fallen down the rabbit hole, all while eating the blue pill. His world was turning upside down and inside out.

The bus came to an abrupt stop and Tristan jolted awake out of his daydream. Apparently, they had arrived at their destination. The bus door opened allowing in a flood of light. It was going to take them a minute to allow their eyes to adjust to the midday light much in the same way it does walking out of a darkened movie theater into the afternoon light.

Tristan followed the group off the bus, and noticed Barachiel standing off to the right-hand side of their gaggle like some giant, out of place character, grossly misplaced amongst a sea of tiny people. The thought brought a smirk to

Tristan's mouth. *If they could see what I saw, they would be freaking out right now*. As if queuing off Tristan's thoughts, Barachiel shot him a glance shaking his head while simultaneously saying *shhhh* with his eyes.

Tristan wasn't the sharpest knife in the drawer, but he got the point. He looked back and nodded his agreeance.

Just then, the Israeli Sergeant asked, "Who are you looking at?"

"Oh, nothing, sorry, just lost in my thoughts. Where to now?" Tristan replied.

The Israeli Sergeant glanced in that direction, then shook his own head, and said in his heavily accented English, "Follow me."

## Chapter 49

Golan Heights, Israel
Late October

If you weren't looking for it, you would have never known there was an Israeli Defense Force base here. It was very non-descript and underwhelming upon first sight. Tristan was used to the overtly over the top, multi-layered defense base fortresses the Americans liked to use. However, looks can be deceiving. Upon closer inspection, Tristan could see dozens of cameras and sensors around the area. The Jews were renowned for their military and intelligentsia prowess; this must have been one of their more clandestine bases. They began walking toward one of the buildings and Tristan looked around for Barachiel, but could no longer see him. Izzy, Red, and the rest of the Delta team followed close behind him in a single file line.

Tristan did not feel "apprehended" or in "custody" per se, but he also did not feel like they could just wander off and go their own way either. They were brought to a nondescript building where the Israelis could do some light interrogations of them to ascertain who they really were and where they were headed.

Clearly, the Israelis knew what was happening to their greatest ally in the world, the United States. It must have been quite a shock to them to see the United States derailed by something as innocuous as a financial virus. Nevertheless, the sight of homeless Americans showing up at their borders must have seemed backwards to a people that spent nearly two thousand years in diaspora.

They entered the building as a group, but then headed towards a long hallway with an elevator at the end. There were eight in their group, including Omar and his wife and daughter. There were about as many guards as well, however, the further they walked down the hall, the more IDF soldiers began peeling off to remain behind. Soon, they were just with two guards and waiting for the elevator doors to open.

They entered the elevator and the guard, whose name he could not read being in Hebrew, pushed the second to the bottom button. *This must be where they do their interrogations,* Tristan thought. He had not seen Barachiel since getting off the bus, but assumed he was down here somewhere.

As the door opened, they were treated to a bright office with dozens of people moving about working feverishly. The guard, without emotion or any kind of personality, turned to them and said, "My name is Amir and I will be assigned to be your escort," as he looked at the Delta team. Another IDF soldier similarly stepped forward and said, "My name is Nadja, and I will be escorting you to our office," looking at Omar and his family.

The group split up and the Americans moved into a medium-sized office with the normal array of desks and chairs with Amir. A soldier came in a few minutes later with an urn of coffee and cups, to which he sat on one of the tables. "Please, help yourselves," he said motioning the group towards the coffee. After days on end drinking only water and rationed Meals-Ready to-Eat (MREs), the coffee was definitely welcomed. "Our commander will be here with you shortly," he added as he stepped out of the room.

"What do you think, Red?" Izzy said as he poured a cup.

"I think they are going to be very curious about how we got here undetected," Red said looking around for cameras and the usual listening devices.

"Well, hopefully, they're up on the news and realize our predicament," Tristan added.

Tiny remained quiet during this entire time. You could see the wheels turning in his head fast, and he even looked a little apprehensive.

"What's up, big guy?" Phil asked.

"I was just thinking back to our interrogation days at the farm," Tiny said. Tiny was referring to the CIA farm near Quantico, Virginia that the Delta operators used for a lot of their own clandestine training.

"I had half planned on going back there to be an instructor when this Afghan tour was over, but now, I think those days are long gone," he added somberly. "That was going to be my last job for the military before I retired and got one of those sweet GS-civilian gigs."

"Everything's changed now, boys," Red said. "The world has been turned on its head and nothing will ever be the same."

"We just need to get back home, secure our families, and get to *the ranch*," Phil said. Several of the team members had a shared some land they dubbed 'the ranch,' in West Virginia. It was away from civilization where they had all planned to move their families in case a scenario like this happened. There was not much on it other than an old cabin, but they had high hopes of turning it into something of a legit-living-off-the-grid compound.

"There's probably hillbillies on it now, making their own moonshine…," Phil added with a chuckle right as a stern IDF officer walked into the room.

"Gentlemen, let me guess…you were on mission and got stranded?" the officer asked with the tiniest of smirks on his face.

"Something like that," Red responded.

"Well, welcome then. My name is Colonel Horovitz, and uh…welcome to Israel."

# Chapter 50

Northern Israel
Late October

Along with the collapse of the US economy, the world seemingly turned back the hands of time to 1929 again. All of a sudden, once stable nations became hotbeds of turmoil and uncertainty, as financial markets were all in varying states of freefall. Even though the EU had the digital *Kredit*, the impacts of a collapsing superpower had the black hole effect of sucking everything around it, into it. Everyone, everywhere, seemed to be struggling…except Israel.

While it was still uncertain how they knew, they were ready for it. Perhaps it was the United States' insurmountable national debt. Perhaps it was the increasing polarization of the American political climate. Perhaps it was a combination of the two, which caused the Israelis to err on the side of caution, as if an American collapse were not only possible, but also probable. No one really foresaw the *Kredit* coming (including the Israelis), or it doing what it did…no one really saw how it would collapse the American economy seemingly overnight.

However, the Israelis had prepared for the collapse of the US, which would trigger the collapse of all the rest of the global community. They knew anything exclusively pegged to the US dollar would sink like the Titanic. Therefore, they began diversifying all of their financial holdings years earlier, into the energy markets, precious metals, technology, and natural resources. They also minimized all of their financial holdings. They did so rather clandestinely, so as not to signal to anyone what they were doing. Now, it seemed, it was paying off.

What they had not anticipated was Americans to start showing up at their borders like refugees, which is something Colonel Horovitz was now tasked to sort out. The Americans had been Israel's most trusted ally since their rebirth as a nation. However, this was predicated on the American government's friendly-to-neutral (depending on the administration) relationship with Israel at the time. Now, they were a people without a functioning government. To whom would their loyalties now lie?

These five men were all soldiers. Judging by the looks of them, at least four were Special Forces of some kind, which could come in handy. He was not sure if he should offer them a job with the IDF or help them keep passing through. Nevertheless, he sat down opposite them and began his questioning.

"Clearly, gentlemen, I understand the predicament you and your nation is going through...I am after all, a Jew," he said without showing any emotion. "I need to understand how you came to be here, and how you got through Syria, or what used to be Syria, unharmed?"

"Sir, you wouldn't believe us if we told you," Tristan said.

"Perhaps. But you can try anyway," Horovitz replied with a wry smile.

## Chapter 51

Come now, *you* rich, weep and howl for your miseries that are coming upon *you!* Your riches are corrupted, and your garments are moth-eaten. Your gold and silver are corroded, and their corrosion will be a witness against you and will eat your flesh like fire. You have heaped up treasure in the last days. **James 5:1-3**

Paradise, Texas
Late October

Of the fifty states in the US, most were in varying stages of lawlessness or societal collapse. The major urban areas were largely deserted and on fire. Biker gangs, militias, and other heavily armed groups controlled the rural areas surrounding them. There were also large swaths of areas controlled by the states' National Guard and local law enforcement agencies, which collapsed in together to form their own entity. Former federal military bases in the New Republic as well as America, were given to the states to manage and safeguard.

The Northeast from Philadelphia, the Washington, D.C. beltway, all the way up through Boston, were in ruin. Those who had the means to move out early did. Since 2020, COVID-19 forced most of the businesses in the Northeast to adapt to working remotely or folding shop. Still, the Northeast was a ghost of its former self in terms of population.

The Southern states, from Georgia through Texas, as well as the Rocky Mountain states, did the best. They were already used to living more "off-grid" than the Northeast and West Coast states. Of all the states, Texas seemed to have it most together. The state government was still semifunctional. Since so many Texans already owned weapons, the state largely began policing itself with community militias. The state had five large military installations as well as numerous small military and federal installations, which still helped cement the state government's control over large areas.

The governor imbued new powers of both judge and jury to local (and loyal) mayors to deputize police officers, sheriffs, rangers, and other law enforcement agents. If law enforcement officers caught you in the act of a violent crime, they could execute you on the spot, legally. Although large cities like Houston, El Paso, Laredo, Dallas-Fort Worth, Austin, San Antonio and Corpus Christi were still volatile to varying degrees, the military-police alliance was starting to get the upper hand on criminal elements, which is to say, there were many street level executions.

With the POTUS relocating to northern Texas from Washington, D.C., his new "Pentagon" would also move with him to Fort Hood. From his location in Paradise to Fort Hood, was roughly a 45-minute flight by the Marine 1 helicopter. Katy's new neighbor had many helicopters coming and going at all hours of the day and night. *I think most people are still trying to wrap their minds around all of this. It is hard to think the United States, which had been around for hundreds of years could be reduced so quickly by something as simple as changing currencies*, Katy thought. She sat there pondering the state of affairs for her country, when the phone rang in the background.

Remarkably, cell phones and internet networks still worked in many parts of the United States. A year ago, a certain tech-billionaire began launching satellites into low level orbits to make internet free for the entire world. No one, not the remaining governments, nor the criminal underworld, were willing to let their access to the internet die on the vine.

"Hello," Katy answered the phone timidly.

"Hey, it's me," Tristan replied.

"Where are you?" she asked.

"I'm currently in Israel. It's been a long, strange, trip so far," he replied. He sounded exhausted.

"It is so good to hear your voice. I have been worried sick about you. Almost two-weeks and not a peep."

"I know. We have been on the move since Afghanistan collapsed, and a lot has happened. I teamed up with some other military guys, and we've just been trying to make our way across from there."

"When will you be home?" she asked.

"Not sure. They have us secured here for entering the country illegally, but I think given what is going on, they are not pressing us too hard. The IDF here were kind enough to let us use the phones to call home. Although, none of the other teammates got through to anyone. As soon as I can get a ride west, I will."

"You want to talk to the kids?"

"Heck yeah, put em on."

A few minutes later, and much to the delight of his daughters, Katy got back on the phone.

"Things are crazy here," she said.

"Oh yeah?"

"You won't even begin to believe who are new neighbor is."

"It's not that smelly kid from high school is it?" Tristan asked.

"Ha-ha, uhhh, no. Close, but no," she laughed. "Seriously, when you get a ride or however you're getting here, you need to land in Texas. The states have all fragmented and bordered up. It is super-weird. Just be careful when you get here," she said.

"How bad is it?" he asked.

"It's pretty bad. We are not at the Civil War stage yet, but close."

"Oh wow. We've heard bits and pieces, but we've been on the run with limited technology, so getting news has been difficult."

She continued to give him the brief overview of the states, as she knew it, so he could relay it to the team. The IDF chief came into the hallway where Tristan was and gave him the nod to come back into the room.

"Hey look, I got to go. I love you. Tell the kids I love them too. I will see you soon, I promise."

"I love you too, and I'm going to hold you to it," she said as she hung up the phone lingeringly. *God, please watch over him. Put your angels around him to protect and guide him back home to us. Show him your power, and your love, so that he will believe in you. Amen.*

## Chapter 52

Northern Israel
Late October

The team was being peppered with a thousand questions about how they escaped from Afghanistan, sneaked across Iran and Syria, and then made their way underneath the Golan Heights all in a manner of weeks. Admittedly, it sounded nuttier than a Payday candy bar.

"Hey look, Colonel; we've been answering your questions in good faith for a few hours now. How about we get to ask some on what's going on with the rest of the world?" Red asked.

Colonel Horovitz nodded his approval.

"Where is it safe to go to, and how can we get back to the United Sta....?" Red let the name die in his throat in light of current events.

"Nowhere is safe anymore. Not here. Not where you been. Not Europe. Not even your America," Colonel. Horovitz said soberly. "As for you getting home, we have been running reverse Aliyah to the US to bring our Jewish brothers and sisters home. You can catch a ride there if you wish."

"What's really going on with the money?" Izzy asked. "It can't be as simple as some computer bug wrecking everyone's banks."

"It is, and it isn't." the colonel replied. "Is it so hard to believe that in a world where everything has become digitized, could also not become very vulnerable?" "Yes is hard to believe," Tiny replied. "Global banking is very complex, and it has hundreds of currencies, safeguards, fail safes, and other security measures in place to prevent something like this from happening."

"And yet, here we are," Colonel Horovitz replied with a cynical smile. "No one thought an invisible virus could shut the world down a couple of years ago either, and yet, it did." *That is true,* Tristan thought. *They had just come out of the weirdest year on record, and then this happened.* He decided he did not like the *new normal* very much.

"Colonel, what do you think will happen going forward?" Tristan asked.

"It's hard to say for sure," Colonel Horovitz turned to him and replied. "Our government has somewhat been sheltered from this collapsing financial system, largely because people hate us." This garnered a strange look from the collective team.

"It's true. How many nations had embargoed our goods, or had sanctions, or boycotts against us? 20? 30? 50? I don't know the exact number, but it was quite a few." He continued. "Ever since 1948, we (Israel) have had to rely on ourselves, and so, we have been building our financial reserves ever since. We could never allow ourselves to be indebted to any nation, not even yours; for fear something like *this* could happen."

Israel had certainly had more than their fair share of troubles ever since they became a nation again. Katy had often used their "rebirth" as a nation to prove Bible prophecy was physical proof of her faith, but he hadn't listened. He had studied their miraculous victories in the 1967's *Six Day War* at Command and General Staff College (CGSC) when he was at Ft. Leavenworth, but he thought they just got lucky. However, after meeting Barachiel, he realized it was not luck and he himself had now become a firm believer in the otherworldly.

Speaking of his large, supernatural friend, he had not seen Barachiel since getting off the bus several hours earlier. He wondered why his new friend had signaled him to remain silent; nevertheless, he had obliged. Suddenly, an IDF officer came in and leaned over to tell Colonel Horovitz to tell him something in private. Not sure why they were whispering, as he, nor anyone on the team as far as he could tell, spoke Hebrew. As soon as that thought popped into his head, Tristan could now hear what they were talking about as well as what they were saying. Tristan immediately sat up as if someone was whispering in his ear. Not only were the two IDF officers a good ten feet away, but Tristan could not speak Hebrew.

"Colonel. We have just received a report Turkey, Iran, Russia, and others, are mobilizing their forces to the north," the junior IDF officer said.

"Where?" the colonel asked.

"So far, in Syria, northeast of Damascus," he responded.

"This is not the first time they've done that, Captain," Colonel Horovitz replied. "They're always repositioning their units."

"True. But this is the first time they've done it together."

Colonel Horovitz leaned back and rubbed his chin as if to take in the gravity of the moment.

"Gentlemen, we have a situation developing. You will have to excuse me for the moment. Please, make yourselves comfortable," he said as he walked out of the office.

"Sounds serious," Izzy, said matter-of-factly.
"They are about to be attacked from the north," Tristan said looking out the window. "The Russians, Turks, and Iranians are massing just north of Damascus. They mentioned some other groups, but I didn't recognize their names."

"You speak Hebrew now?" Red asked.

"Apparently, I do. I think Barachiel just gave me a new superpower," Tristan said with a grin.

"I wonder if this is why we were able to get through Syria unscathed?" Red added. "We didn't see a lot of militia or other groups while passing through. What other groups did they say?

"Just something about *Magog and Gog*. Ever heard of them?"

Now the word of the Lord came to me, saying, "Son of man, set your face against Gog, of the land of Magog, the prince of Rosh, Meshech, and Tubal, and prophesy against him, and say, 'Thus says the Lord God: "Behold, I *am* against you, O Gog, the prince of Rosh, Meshech, and Tubal. I will turn you around, put hooks into your jaws, and lead you out, with all your army, horses, and horsemen, all splendidly clothed, a great company *with* bucklers and shields, all of them handling swords. Persia, Ethiopia, and Libya are with them, all of them *with* shield and helmet; Gomer and all its troops; the house of Togarmah *from* the far north and all its troops— many people *are* with you.

"Prepare yourself and be ready, you and all your companies that are gathered about you; and be a guard for them. After many days you will be visited. In the latter years, you will come into the land of those brought back from the sword *and* gathered from many people on the mountains of Israel, which had long been desolate; they were brought out of the nations, and now all of them dwell safely. You will ascend, coming like a storm, covering the land like a cloud, you and all your troops and many peoples with you."

**Ezekiel 38:1-9**

# Chapter 53

But concerning the times and the seasons, brethren, you have no need that I should write to you. For you yourselves know perfectly that the day of the Lord so comes as a thief in the night. For when they say, "Peace and safety!" then sudden destruction comes upon them, as labor pains upon a pregnant woman. And they shall not escape. **1 Thessalonians 5:1-3**

Twenty-minutes later, Colonel Horovitz came back in to the office and waved in another officer, a female Captain judging by her rank.

"This is Captain Moshe, she will be escorting you to our airbase and to your ride home," he said.

"Just like that?" Tiny asked.

"Fortune is on your side today my American friend. We have a flight already bound for Florida for *Aliya* to Israel. Besides, we have some developing issues to our north, which is more pressing than five American trespassers," Colonel Horovitz said.

"Yes, that is fortuitous indeed," Phil said. The rest of the team looked at him as if he had just nerded out. "What? I got to show off my deep *vocabulistic* skills every once in a while."

The team headed out the door following Captain Moshe. She barked out some orders to some soldiers and they took off running outside. A few minutes later, they pulled up in two AIL M-242 Storm Mark II vehicles.

"Gentlemen, if you will get into the jeeps, I'll escort you to the Haifa Airbase, where you will catch your flights back to the US."

"Sounds good to us," Tiny said.

Two hours later, the team had made it to Haifa and were going through security at the air base. They didn't have any luggage, but the flight was still a couple of hours from takeoff, so they asked Moshe if they had a place where they could go and get cleaned up. She led the team to the crew quarters in an adjacent building, where they could take a shower and grab some food before they got onto the cross Atlantic flight.

After an hour, the team regrouped and began heading out onto the tarmac towards the KC-135R, which was almost done being prepped when it happened. At first, it was faint, barely noticeable above the roar of the airplane engines and the other's voices. Tristan had stopped walking, and looked around. The team kept walking, blissfully unaware of any such noise. However, as soon as the noise had come back, it faded again. Immediately, Tristan looked up, and saw the sky had the bluest, and most ethereal appearance he had ever seen. In fact, he had never seen the sky display such depths of vivid blueness in all his life. It was as if the sky had somehow become a living entity and was in full bloom. *I must be hearing things,* he thought curiously. He started walking again.

But then the sounds of trumpets came back a second time, more pronounced and he stopped again…troubled, and perplexed at what was happening. The sounds were all around him, as if giant hidden speakers were hidden behind the scarce few clouds in the sky. He stole another glance over to the team who still did not hear it, and were now almost to the KC-130.

"Hey, do you guys…," was all he got out before a voice rang out in the most terrifying shout he'd ever heard. It was if a man the size of a mountain had shouted with a megaphone, the voice reverberating through every fiber of Tristan's body. Another voice rang out immediately after the shout, and it said only three words, which Tristan could not understand. At that instant, Tristan felt himself being wrenched from where he was standing only moments before.

Tiny and Red turned around at the commotion behind them. "Where did Tristan go?" Red asked puzzled.

***

Like most people in the western hemisphere, Katy and her family had been sound asleep when the trumpet blast occurred. She had let her daughters sleep with her in the king-size bed, due to a massive thunderstorm raging outside. The rest of her family were in their respective rooms peacefully asleep, oblivious to the goings-on of the world.

She heard the initial, fainter trumpet sounds, and somewhere in the recesses of her mind, thought it was Tristan calling her phone. However, the last set of trumpets, made her jolt up from her bed. The sound did not appear to be coming from any one direction, but from all directions at once. She knew instinctively what it meant. She reached down to touch her children and had no sooner thought of Tristan when she heard the shout, and the voice saying, "Come up Here!"

For the Lord Himself will descend from heaven with a shout, with the voice of an archangel, and with the trumpet of God. And the dead in Christ will rise first. Then we who are alive *and* remain shall be caught up together with them in the clouds to meet the Lord in the air. And thus we shall always be with the Lord. **1 Thessalonians 4:16-17**

## Chapter 54

Global Update
Late October- Early November

The Rapture event caused people from around the world of all nationalities, ethnicities, ages, and in all time zones, to suddenly disappear. For those in the western hemisphere, it was nighttime and thus most were either at home or asleep. In the east, it was daylight. Most curiously, was the UFO activity in the skies just after the event. The skies around the world were abuzz with strange sightings and even stranger sounds. In fact, so much video evidence was caught on film that many had begun to argue whether the two events (the disappearance and the UFOs) were somehow connected.

Most tragically for those left behind, was the disappearance of all children. In fact, everyone under the age of 20 was suddenly gone. The outcry was immediate. It was the first time since the global flood during Noah's day (circa 1656 Anno Mundi) that a collective cry went up around the world in which the whole earth mourned at once.

The immediate effect of the Rapture was the almost instant halt to life on planet earth as vehicles, ships, and planes, instantly went without drivers and pilots. Spectacularly violent crashes of all types occurred throughout the developed world, which began to embroil and tie up all major thoroughfares. The secondary and tertiary effects were the other vehicles crashing in attempts to avoid driverless vehicles. Captainless boats suddenly began drifting and clogging up waterways. Planes, unfortunate enough to have either one or both Christian pilots, were suddenly pilotless. The Rapture, plus one-hour became the second most calamitous time in human history.

The news agencies, which survived the initial collapse in the west, started breaking the stories early the next morning describing it only as "mass disappearances." They were also reporting on all the strange aerial activity which now became undeniable, to even the most hardened skeptic.

The New Republic (east and west coast governments) were unsurprisingly, not hit as hard as the states in what they dubbed "flyover country." The secular, godless, and non-Christians had been flocking to the coasts from the more conservative center states, for fear of being trapped in what they mockingly deemed, "medieval America." In truth, the

Rapture gutted the central and southern states with ruthless and divine efficiency.

By the following day, the news outlets in D.C. and New York, as well as the social media monopolies in Silicon Valley, California, began trying to redefine the disappearance narrative as "extra-terrestrial." It started with news pundits inserting doubt into what actually happened. They began throwing out an assortment of possibilities; anything and everything, except what really happened. This went on for several days, until a new narrative began to gain traction. The new narrative; global reset. This was the idea that the celestial visitors (UFOs) were purging the world of those who were harming earth. In fact, this new theory began to take hold in a major way amongst the political and liberal elite; so much so, calls were made to form a new global government.

Many in Europe and the rest of Western Civilization (who were inundated with their own issues), were completely unaware of the near-frenzied activity transpiring in the Mediterranean. With the US in complete meltdown, and Europe struggling to keep the EU from falling apart, the time was ripe for the desperate, former power brokers to make their move. Russia, Turkey, and Iran, had strengthened their former political and economic alliance into a new, 'triple entente.' Their goal was the overthrow and sacking of the nation of Israel.

Their motivations varied. Russia had been squeezed out of the European energy market by both the Americans' stranglehold over NATO, and Israel's recent and massive natural gas discoveries off her coast. The Russians sought compensation for their colossal financial losses, by seizing control of the Leviathan and Tamar natural gas fields off her coast.

Turkey's ongoing radical Islamization of the nation (under their increasingly unhinged Prime Minister) had effectively eroded any remaining goodwill between Israel and itself. They sought control of Jerusalem's Al Aqsa's Mosque, the Dome of the Rock, and the Old City. Taking out Israel's military was, for them, icing on the cake. Iran sought to erase Israel as a nation altogether. They wanted to initiate a third Jewish diaspora, and then move to encircle Saudi Arabia and gain control over Islam's holiest site, Mecca, and eventually bring all Islam under Shia rule.

Now while this new Triple Entente formed a coalition of conflicting agendas, and strange bedfellows, each of them viewed the destruction (or neutralization of Israel) as critical to the success of their end state. With the United States effectively unable, or now, even unwilling to come to the aid of Israel, for them, there was no time like the present.

Both Russia and Turkey began funding and covertly marshaling forces to Tripoli, Libya, as well as the Port of Sudan in Sudan. The word got out there was quick money to be made in joining their efforts to overthrow Israel. To the Russians, these forces would form a "southern flank," which would force Israel to divide her forces (and her attention) in this impending attack.

The northern front would form in what used to be Syria, and would consist of the Russians, Turks, Iranians, and the former Soviet satellite countries forces. Hezbollah and Al Qaeda forces would augment them. The southern front would consist of Libyan, Sudanese, and Somali forces coming up the Red Sea from the Port of Sudan. Their goal, essentially, was to overwhelm tiny Israel. However, little did they know they were about to fulfill Bible prophecy.

*** 

Tristan woke up looking at the sky again. Judging by what he felt and where he was looking, he reckoned he was laying down on his back. Immediately, he sat up and looked around. *Where am I,* he thought.

"You are on the road to Damascus," a familiar voice spoke up.

"Barachiel, oh thank God you are here," Tristan said. "What happened?"

"Thank God indeed. This was the Great Catching Up, except, you were not caught up, you were caught laterally," he said pointing his giant fingers sideways.

"What?" Tristan asked. "Catching up?"

"What is known to most people in the common tongue as *the Rapture*," Barachiel replied.

"My wife was always going on about the Rapture. I just thought it was some kooky thing her church believed in; I didn't know it was like a real thing."

"It is very real, and the world right now, is finding out, just how real it was," Barachiel said solemnly.

"I don't get it. I prayed in the cave, became a Christian, and I mean, you were there. If I remember anything from my wife, it was that all Christians get taken up. Why am I still here? I mean, you wouldn't be here if I weren't a Christian right?" Tristan asked anxiously.

"You have been redeemed, yes, but as I said before, God has a specific plan for you. You spent most of your life mocking your wife, in your heart and mind, for her beliefs. You loved her and that is what kept you together. However, she spent years, on her knees, praying for your salvation. Always keeping up hope you would one day see the truth of the Gospel of our Lord, Jesus Christ."

Tristan was crushed. Tears welling up in his eyes as the reality of never seeing his wife and children again sank in. He began embarrassingly wiping the tears from his eyes. "I don't get it; shouldn't I have gone up, instead of here? I thought the whole point of this journey I am on, is to get back home."

Barachiel reached over and put a hand on his shoulder. "There is no home for you here anymore. But be of good cheer my friend, you are redeemed. You will have your homecoming nonetheless. You will see your family again, in heaven, where they are now safe and happy. Nothing will ever harm then again. God is going to use you to do mighty and wondrous things. Our Father is allowing you to redeem your time, by becoming the remnant for this short moment in history. You are now, the last Christian on the earth at this moment. He will use you to witness the demise of Damascus; and then, after, you must return back to your earthly, ancestral home to be His witness to the things which have and will occur."

"Remnant? I don't get it."

Quoting the Apostle Paul, Barachiel said, *"Lord, they have killed Your prophets and torn down Your altars, and I alone am left, and they seek my life"? But what does the divine response say to him? "I have reserved for Myself seven thousand men who have not bowed the knee to Baal."* Romans 11:3-4."

"What does that mean?" Tristan asked cautiously.

"Paul was quoting 1st Kings 19:17-19. Nevertheless, I say to you, to remind you, God our Father, always has a remnant. Always."

"So I am the remnant," he said scratching his head. "Ok. For how long?"

"Not long. You will have help here shortly. After that, the Two Witnesses will arrive, and your mission will be complete."

"Who are these two witnesses I am supposed to meet up with?" Tristan asked.

Barachiel helped Tristan up to his feet.

"They are Elijah and Moses," Barachiel replied.

Tristan immediately felt woozy at the mention of their names and Barachiel quickly reached out again to steady him.

"You mean like the real Elijah and Moses?" he asked.

"Yes."

"Haven't they been dead for a couple thousand years?" he asked.

"No and yes. However, with God, all things are possible," Barachiel replied.

"And why do I feel different? I mean, I am 46 and I used to have all sorts of aches and pains, but now, I don't feel anything. It's weird, I feel like I'm 18 again."

"You look different too," Barachiel replied, and he produced a mirror to show him what he looked like now.

"Oh my...!"

## Chapter 55

Early November

Barachiel had instructed Tristan to head toward Damascus and wait on the southern bypass near the underpass of Fayez Mansour and Almotahalik Aljanobi. Tristan had been walking on the northern highway leading into what used to be the oldest, continually inhabited city in the world. However, after years of civil war and constant bombings, Damascus became a ghost of its former self. Tristan felt like he was becoming the guy in a post-apocalyptic movie who is about to be jumped by a horde of zombies as he made his way into the deserted city.

He was thinking about meeting the Two Witnesses, who, for millennia, had been legend; he was not quite sure how to feel about it. What would he say? *Hey fellas, welcome to the end of the world. Here are the keys, I'm outta here*! He chuckled at the silliness of it. Truth was he was terrified.

These dudes were legit prophets with supernatural powers. Although he had not read the Bible enough to know what they could do, he had heard enough about them through his wife, and he had seen *The Ten Commandments* with Charlton Heston. Rivers of blood, terrible darkness, and the "Angel of Death" now filled his thoughts.

Furthermore, the Rapture had changed him, or transformed him into what he was supposed to look like. He was not sure why he had to change, but God did it. Tristan no longer needed his angel friend's help to find where he was going, he just knew. After Barachiel had shown him what he looked like, he felt like he'd become the very person he would run away from, if meeting in a dark alley. His dark hair was now a shock of white hair. His eyes, which had been brown, were now vividly blue, as if he had been wearing some crazy Halloween contacts. He had also grown a few inches, so he was now near 6'5 feet tall.

Aside from his radically different appearance, all of his previous aches and pains were gone. He also felt smarter, as if he knew things now he should not know intuitively. He had a million questions before the Rapture; now, he just knew things like multiple languages. However, he still was not sure why he had to wait outside of Damascus.    He noticed his walk was much faster than a normal man's walk. In fact, his normal walk could be categorized as a good jog. *This would have come in handy back in my Army days,* he thought with a chuckle. He supposed he should be more somber now, given the fact he was the last Christian on earth, and his wife and family were now gone up. The thought of them immediately sent a shock to his heart. Although he knew they were in a much better place now, the reality of not seeing them again for however long his mission was, pained him something fierce.

He thought back to Jack's book with the penny carved to look like a skull. Hobos or something. Was he now some homeless vagabond, doomed to walk the earth for the next seven years until this thing was finished? The thought of it weighed on him heavily; so much so, he no longer noticed where he was.

Just then, a thought came to mind. No, not a thought, a scripture verse. More than that, he understood what it was saying. It was talking about the Old Testament faithful, who also, were subjugated to mistreatment while here on earth. This was Hebrews 11:35-40. He didn't understand how he knew it perfectly but he did, as if he had studied it all his life. Excitedly, he recited it aloud.

Women received their dead raised to life again. Others were tortured, not accepting deliverance that they might obtain a better resurrection. Still others had trial of mockings and scourgings, yes, and of chains and imprisonment. They were stoned, they were sawn in two, were tempted, were slain with the sword. They wandered about in sheepskins and goatskins, being destitute, afflicted, tormented—of whom the world was not worthy. They wandered in deserts and mountains, *in* dens and caves of the earth. And all these, having obtained a good testimony through faith, did not receive the promise, God having provided something better for us, that they should not be made perfect apart from us.

He came to a stop. Apparently, he had been speed walking and daydreaming at the same time, yet his feet instinctively slowed down and he became cognizant that he had arrived at his destination. He looked around at the crisscrossing highways. There were massive cracks and fissures throughout the roads, and even parts of the overpass. Bullet holes pockmarked the concrete in every direction.

The *Arab Spring* had begun back in 2010 in Tunisia. By 2011, the poisonous ideas of the Muslim Brotherhood began spreading throughout Egypt and Libya. It was long thought the United States initiated and funded this revolution as payback against the Saudis' stranglehold over Sunni Islam. By 2013, the Arab Spring had reached into Syria. Although she was one of the last sucked into the fray, aside from Yemen, Syria has remained the longest lasting conflict to date.

For years, the Russians, Turks, and Iranians had been jockeying their forces around Syria for seemingly conflicting and nonsensical reasons. Now it makes sense; they were clearing out the Assad government and prepping the battlefield for a large, multinational military invasion. With the news he had overheard with Colonel Horovitz, Tristan wondered if this location had anything to do with the coming invasion. Just then, he heard what appeared to be the sound of something heavy hitting the ground like a punch.

# Chapter 56

The burden against Damascus.
"Behold, Damascus will cease from *being* a city,
and it will be a ruinous heap. **Isaiah 17:1**

Damascus, Syria
Early November

Tristan looked behind him, and two angels appeared standing in a dissipating cloud of dust. They walked forward, and greeted Tristan in Hebrew, to which he replied in fluent Hebrew. Although it was Hebrew, it was a much older dialect than what he had been exposed to in recent days. Its ancient syntax gave instant gravitas to whatever it was they would say. He imagined it would be a lot like bringing William Shakespeare back from the 16th century to give a speech at a *Ted Talk* in modern England.

Aside from the fact, he had never met them before, or even that he was supposed to meet them here, he instinctively knew they were Ariel and Turiel. The question was why were they here? Like Barachiel, they were taller than he was and built like football players. They held their wings furled behind their backs, and from their crossed sashes hung a sling to carry their magnificent swords. He now knew they were here to carry out the destruction of Damascus.

Tristan walked towards them and nodded, as if to acknowledge the significant role they were about to play in these final moments of human history. They returned the nod, and then turned toward the city proper. As he got closer, he could see something was strange with their eyes. He could not pinpoint it at first, but as he focused in, he could see the astral projections filling their irises and pupils. They both raised their hands and began praying to God aloud.

Their powerful, prayerful voices began to grow louder and louder, as they beseeched God to fulfill His promise given to the Prophet Isaiah. Immediately, clouds began to form overheard and then darken. Tristan stepped back and began wondering if he should seek some shelter. They were about to unleash some Old Testament fire and brimstone judgment on this oldest of cities. Then he saw it, fire, falling down like rain from the darkened clouds. At first, it was like a drizzle of fire; then it began to pour.

Having been in the military for a couple of decades, he had seen some impressive military displays of massive artillery barrages and aerial bombings. Those had nothing on this. This was like seeing a thunderstorm from a distance and the line in the sky between the dry air and the rain. Except, this was like a deluge of rain-fire coming down over the central part of the city. This seemed to trigger secondary and tertiary explosions, presumably, where the Assad Regime had previously stored chemical and biological weapons. As it was before their arrival, this place was a toxic dump. No wonder God was purging it.

After a few short minutes, everything was on fire. Even the concrete and rocks were burning. The smoke from the flames and the explosions began filling the sky so greatly day was turning into night. No doubt, the Israeli Mossad and Israeli Defense Forces (IDF) were seeing this transpire through their satellite feeds. Tristan began to understand why he was here, and why they were destroying Damascus before heading south into the Holy Land.

After an hour with their hands raised, their voices fell silent and they dropped their hands. Although Damascus was largely rubble-ized before they ever began; but now, it was ashes. The fire had been so intense that nothing above a single story home was left standing. Tristan was sure, had they stayed there another few minutes, even those sparsely standing homes would be gone as well. They turned around and began walking away from Damascus down the highway seven (Fayez Mansour) heading south. Tristan fell in behind them and the three began their supernatural speed walk towards the land of Israel.

## Chapter 57

Northern Israel
Early November

Brigadier General (*Tat Aluf*) Rudenko summoned Colonel Horovitz to the Joint Operations Cell (JOC) shortly after the worldwide disappearances began. They had been monitoring events around the world, to include those disappearances in Israel, when a young Corporal came racing toward them.

"General, Colonel, sirs, you need to see this! Can I change the main screens to show satellite feed #7," Corporal Noach asked excitedly.

"Corporal, what is it? We have a dozen different screens and reports to keep track of this moment," Colonel Horovitz said impatiently. "There is only about a thousand crises happening all at the same time."

"Sirs, trust me, you are going to want to see this," she implored.

"Fine, put it on the screen," BG Rudenko replied.

The dozen screens they had playing were showing the

major network montages of the ensuing crises from Europe, Asia, North America, South America, Africa, the Middle East, and Israel. The Israeli feed, covered not just Israel, but Israel's borders and surrounding nations. The Corporal began configuring a live feed to show on all the screens, much to the dismay of all the other operators still trying to create their own reports.

The satellite feed focused in on Syria, and then closed in on the city of Damascus. From the satellite's perspective, all it could show was a huge, ominous, black cloud cover blocking the city. Just then, the darkened cloud began to glow bright red, and became full of lightning.

"What is happening there, and how old is this feed?" Colonel Horovitz asked.

"Sirs, it is a few minutes old, and we don't know what is happening," Corporal Noach replied. "The clouds just formed from out of nowhere. At first, we thought it was an explosion, or some kind of strange weather phenomenon, but look!" she said pointing towards the south of the screen. "Three heat signatures; looks like they're running away from the city towards our border."

"Can we zoom in?" Brigadier General Rudenko asked.

"Yes sir, let me see how much though," she replied.

Corporal Noach worked the controls and managed to bring in the focus to where the three men could be seen closer.

"Hey, wait a minute!" Colonel Horovitz said in a shell-shocked voice. "That looks like one of those Americans who came through our facility the other day; who is he with?"

"They look like a couple of …I don't know. It looks like they are wearing robes and backpacks," Brigadier General Rudenko replied, unable to stop staring at them.

"At the speed they are moving, it looks like they are running. However, their bodies look like they are walking. Strange."

"Strange indeed. Captain Moshe, get my vehicle and security team. Radio me when you have pinpointed their approximate point of entry. We're going to the perimeter to get a better look."

\*\*\*

Both Turiel and Ariel were walking so fluidly they might as well been on hover boards. Their speeds, while not in flat-out run, was still unnerving. However, Tristan was finding he could keep up with them rather effortlessly. He had a million questions to ask them, but did not want to impede their mission to satisfy his own curiosity. As if on cue, they slowed their speed down to that of a normal walk, as if they could in fact, read his mind.

"After Damascus, what is your mission now? Am I to go with you into Israel?" Tristan asked.

"You will go with us only to the border. Then He (pointing up to God) will move you back to your home. You have your own mission," Turiel said.

"What is that mission though? I mean, aren't we at the end of the world?"

"You must get your leader to prepare the underground," Ariel replied.

"Prepare the underground?" Tristan asked.    "Yes. Get your leader to prepare the refuge, while you and another gather those who are the Gentile remnant. There, they will wait for our Lord's coming, although, I fear not many will survive what will come in the years ahead," he replied.

"And how will the President, our leader, believe me?"

"He and others will believe you. Unfortunately, even though you will be given power from on high to execute God's plans, some will not follow. They are even now, being given over to the power of the lawless one," Ariel added.

"Who is coming?" Tristan asked.

"The Beast is coming. He is the great delusion. All who side with him will burn in the fiery torments of hell forever."

For the mystery of lawlessness is already at work; only He who now restrains *will do so* until He is taken out of the way. And then the lawless one will be revealed, whom the Lord will consume with the breath of His mouth and destroy with the brightness of His coming. The coming of the *lawless one* is according to the working of Satan, with all power, signs, and lying wonders, and with all unrighteous deception among those who perish, because they did not receive the love of the truth, that they might be saved. And for this reason God will send them strong delusion, that they should believe the lie, that they all may be condemned who did not believe the truth but had pleasure in unrighteousness. **2 Thessalonians 2:7-12**

## Chapter 58

Northern Israel
Early November

Tristan had made it as far as the Israeli side of the border with the two angels. Amazed, he followed these two as they effortlessly made it through the assorted walls, fences, and land mines, and other defense measures the IDF had put up to thwart would be invaders. Upon stepping foot on Israel proper, the Two (plus Tristan) had met a heavily armed contingent of IDF personnel, and even one person he recognized.

"Colonel Horovitz," Tristan said with a raised hand as he walked toward the line of vehicles and their heavily armed soldiers who were arrayed with all weapons trained on them. "Major Zavota?" he replied inquisitively. "What happened to you?"

"It would seem God had other plans for me."

"Who are these two with you? More Delta team stragglers?"

"No. These two are angels believe it or not. Gentlemen, may I introduce to Ariel and Turiel," he said pointing to each accordingly.

With that introduction, a chorus of laughter broke out amongst the line of troops facing them.

A flash of anger stole over Tristan's face as the two angels stood there stoically. "Don't you even read your own Bibles?"

Their mocking laughter quickly ended as the two angels vanished in front of their eyes. There was an immediate reaction of both shock and confusion as the line broke, and the soldiers began looking in every direction. "Where did they go, Major Zavota?" Colonel Horovitz asked.

"Sir, I didn't take you as a religious man, but these two really are angels. I believe you will see them again before this is all over. As for me, I too must go, but not back with you. I must go west back to the United Sta…" he let the words die in his throat. "To America I mean." He couldn't finish the sentence since the United States of America no longer existed as it once was.

"I think you should come with us until we sort this all out," Colonel Horovitz said impatiently.

No sooner had those words come out of his mouth, than Tristan too had disappeared.

*** 

Tristan appeared in front of his home in Paradise, Texas. One moment, he had been with the Two Witnesses squaring off with a large contingent of the IDF, and the next he was here. Although somewhat anti-climactic, it was relieving. He simply thought about where he wanted to be, and he was there. Although he did not understand all of the mechanisms of teleportation, he knew this would be how he travelled from now on.

Standing in front of the house, he knew in his heart and mind no one was here, but he walked into his in-laws' nonetheless still expecting. This was the one place in the whole world he wanted most to be more than anywhere. He always pictured himself coming back home and hugging his wife and kids, seeing his extended family. His mom would be there as well, having driven up from Austin. There they would all be, eating a huge family meal together. For whatever reason, Paradise, Texas, always felt like home.

Since this whole fantastical journey began, all he wanted was to be here. Walking in, he could still smell the old familiar haunts of a well-loved home-bacon, eggs, and freshly cooked biscuits. Although happy his family was in a much better place, his reunion home was still bittersweet. It was in that moment, he fully realized the gravity of his salvation. He fully realized that without God's supernatural intervention, he would have never made it. He would have died alone in that dark cave in Afghanistan.

Yet, being here now no longer truly felt like home anymore. He was realizing that despite the memories and all the time spent here, this was no longer his real home. Something far greater awaited him. He stood there for a moment taking it all in, and something drew his attention to the refrigerator. It was not hunger nor thirst, as he had come to notice, for he neither needed to eat or drink. He saw a picture his daughter had drawn and it was a picture of him. He presumed he was glowing, judging by the excessive use of a yellow-crayon used around his head and body. Behind him on the corner of the page, was what looked like an angel? *She knew,* he thought. *Amazing.* He grabbed it and then walked back out of the house towards his new neighbor, the former leader of the free world. Tristan did not know how much was left of the President's team, he expected there to be some security, although he reckoned that did not matter much now.

He supposed he could have just teleported directly to him, but he also knew that could be a very jarring experience for normal humans. He decided to go in the old-fashioned way, through the front door. As expected, there were several black SUVs arrayed along the driveway up into the old Grainger property. Tristan began walking up the driveway. Almost immediately, Secret Service agents began posturing at this seemingly brazen approach. The moment they saw him, they began stepping out of their vehicles with their weapons already drawn before Tristan got to within three hundred feet of their positions.

"Halt! Identify yourself!" one of the agents yelled out to Tristan.

"Gentlemen, take me to your leader," Tristan said with a smile.

"I don't think so, buddy, keep your hands where we can see them."

But as soon as Tristan had put his hands up, he was already well past the agents who were now pointing their pistols at thin air.

"Hey, what the…" they said collectively.

Tristan had made the teleport jump past the outer perimeter guards before resuming his stroll up to the President's newly created compound. He instinctively knew snipers were already locked onto him as he continued moving closer. He could hear the radio chatter in the distance as a vast array of security personnel began moving ahead of him to form defensive positions. Tristan could even hear the drone two-thousand feet overhead, which had been watching him the minute he stepped foot onto the property. Amazingly, he was not worried.

He got within eyesight of the compound and stopped. There were an array of at least a dozen industrial sized trailers, which surrounded the old Grainger Estate. The Grainger house, which had been built in the early

20thcentury, was designed after the Southern plantation styled home common to that day. This meant it had a wrap-around porch on both the first and second floors, as well as the colonnade pillars in the front. Of course, the house was aged and weathered, but would suffice to serve as the temporary estate until the President could regain control of the country.

The Rapture had hit the United States harder than almost every other nation on the planet. Not that there were more Christians in the US than elsewhere, but there were more Christians in every strata of society than anywhere else. Christians, in most other nations, were relegated to the bottom strata of their own respective societies. In the US, however, Christians were found throughout senior cabinet positions in the government, the medical field, legal field, law enforcement, the military, and every form of business from CEOs to janitors.

Tristan saw the scurry of activity as numerous Secret Service agents and other security officials scrambled to confront this strange looking fellow on the compound. Eventually, someone brought out the bullhorn.

"You there, put your hands behind your head, and drop to your knees!"

"I am unarmed and not a threat. However, you must tell the President he needs to speak with me, now, I have very important information," Tristan replied in a voice equally as magnified as the man with the bullhorn.

"Hands behind your head, and to your knees, or we will fire!" the voice said again.

*We do not have time for this,* Tristan thought. *I have tried to play nice, but this will take forever.* With that he jumped (teleported) directly into the President's office. The President and his senior staff had been in a meeting prior to his untimely arrival, but since, had been intensely focused on what was happening outside the window with Tristan near the edge of the inner compound. The atmosphere was thick with apprehension. They were even in the process of expressing great shock at Tristan's inexplicable disappearance.

"Gentlemen, my name is Tristan."

Frightened cats do not jump as high as this group did at the sound of his voice behind them. There were varying shouts of surprise and horror as they realized the strange looking man, who had been outside, was now standing behind them.

One of the Secret Service agents drew his service pistol on Tristan and emptied an entire clip, seemingly having no effect whatsoever on him.

"Don't worry, Mr. President, I am come in peace. I am also your neighbor," he said pointing toward the county road. "So shooting your neighbor is just not how we say hello around these parts."

The confusion on their faces was profound, yet comical. Tristan could see them all mentally processing everything their eyes had just witnessed.

"Mr. President, I am here to warn you. You are not safe here. We must go."

"Where?" the President asked.

"To the North American Aerospace Defense Command, at the Cheyenne Mountain Complex at Peterson Air Force Base, Colorado Springs," Tristan replied.

"Why NORAD?" his Chief of Staff asked.

"There is coming a government who is even now, in the process of forming, which will take over the entire earth. There are precious few places left on the earth that can be defended. NORAD will be one of those places he will seek to take control of first," Tristan said.

"Who is *he*?" the President asked. "The Lawless One. The Son of Perdition."

"Who?" the Chief of Staff asked.

"The Antichrist."

A mix of skeptical eye rolls and shock spread amongst the group. The Secretary of Defense leaned toward the President and whispered something into his ear.

"Sir, we don't have time for this," the Chief of Staff said as he turned to the President.

"You are correct; we don't have time to stand around arguing over whether I'm right or not. And yes, executing CONPLAN 3400 at NORAD makes perfect, tactical, operational, and strategic sense," Tristan added.

They both looked at him surprised he could hear them.

"What kind of government are we talking about? The New Republic? The United Nations? The Chinese?" the Secretary of State asked.

"No, it will be a new form of government in light of the current global crisis that the *Rapture of the Church* has presented. It will be communistic in practice, global in scope, and imperial in nature. It will also be enabled by a powerful new Artificial Intelligence system, which utilizes the *Kredit* to control all buying and selling."

"Why should we believe you?" the acting Vice President asked.

"You are now the acting Vice-President, are you not?" Tristan asked. "What is your explanation for that, or the billions around the world who have suddenly disappeared?"

"I don't think anyone can know exactly what happened," he replied skeptically.

"I do. Just as I 'magically' appeared here and made it past all of your security, and being shot with no effect, your minds are struggling to reconcile how this is all happening. Let me assure you, it is not a trick, nor is it even by my own power, but by God. Likewise, the Bible states that there was coming a day, in which all true believers would be removed instantaneously from the earth, which in our case, just happened; the Rapture of the Church."     "Why me, and what happens once we get to NORAD?" the President asked.

"Mr. President, you still have loyal personnel there, and you have the legitimate government on your shoulders. I am using you, to bring a remnant with us to preserve until our Lord Jesus returns. Once we get there, we lock in, and don't come out for seven years," Tristan said. "Trust me when I say you cannot fight what is coming and you cannot weather the storm out here. You must go underground."

"Why seven years?" the SECDEF asked.

"Gentlemen, there is much you need to learn about what is to come. We can do that after you have arrived and are secure," Tristan concluded.

"Where will you be?" the SECDEF asked.

"I will meet you there; however, I am going to gather those who God has sent me to collect up."

## Chapter 59

NORAD, Colorado
Early November

Twelve hours later, the President and his advanced team were flying out of Paradise on Marine 1 and 2 helicopters. His staff had called ahead and notified NORAD of their intended arrival. The rest of the staff were packing up and loading into black SUVs. What they did not take, they burned. Tristan tried warning them that at this late stage, it really didn't matter. Things would never go back to the way they were.     Meanwhile, Tristan teleported to the local radio station, WPAB in Fort Worth, and nearly gave the radio talk show host a heart attack. Tristan could not tell if his sudden appearance freaked people out, or his unnatural appearance, or both. Either way, the host was quick to hand over the controls of his microphone suite to Tristan so he could mass communicate his message.

This particular radio show was syndicated and broadcast to over 700 radio stations around what used to be the United States. He was not trying to reach everyone, but the ones who were supposed to come, would be listening at this exact moment in time. God would give him the words, and afterwards, God would guide those people to the right location, which was NORAD. He now knew what he had to do. It was not so much head knowledge, as it was heart knowledge. God gave him the intuition to do what needed to be done.

He tapped the microphone twice and interrupted the commercial, which was playing at that exact moment and said, "If you can hear my voice, and want to know the truth so as to be saved, head to the mountain." He ended the message and was gone in an instant.

After this, he would head to different places around the world to gather those specific people who would be preserved to go into the Kingdom. They would come from every tribe, tongue, and nation. Another thing Tristan noticed was different now, aside from having a mission and the means to carry it out, was the supernatural world had come alive to him.

Before his encounter with Barachiel, he'd never had anything supernatural happen to him. His wife would tell him every so often of a dream she had that was beyond the norm, but he shrugged those off as suggestive programming from years in the church. Nevertheless, meeting Barachiel and everything that had happened since, let him know just how blind he had been. The world was engulfed in supernatural activity, and he could see it now. Even more interesting, was that they noticed him seeing them as well, and did nothing.

What was it about him now that made him untouchable, or was he? Perhaps he was not worth their time now that the Rapture had already occurred. Perhaps they were too busy setting up this final kingdom, to worry about a relative nobody like himself. He was not an angel, nor was he mortal any longer. He was an *in-betweener* for lack of a better word. He was one who had been given a glorified body, but not caught up permanently. There was only one other person he knew of that was also like this, *Enoch*.

He did not even know how he knew the name Enoch, much less, his status. This must be part of the imbedded knowledge he seemed to command at will now. That is something that had only recently become common knowledge to his vastly improved brain functions. He prayed in fluent, ancient Hebrew: *Lord, you have brought this man to my thoughts, and I do not believe this was by chance. Please show me where to find this man Enoch, and what our final instructions are for our time remaining here*, Amen.

## Chapter 60

By faith Enoch was translated that he should not see death; and was not found, because God had translated him: for before his translation he had this testimony, that he pleased God. **Hebrews 11:5**

NORAD, Colorado Springs, Colorado
Early November

Tristan had met the Presidential team back at NORAD near the main entrance. He had been standing near the outer gate when Marine 1 and 2 flew to a nearby landing pad. Up armored SUV's were standing by, waiting to take the President and his staff to the mountain compound. The small convoy made its way up the road but came to a stop when they saw Tristan standing by the side of the road like a hitchhiker. Tristan figured they were most likely debating whether or not they should pick him up or not.

The first and second SUVs slowly passed by him, both to get a closer look and also to see what he would do. At these, Tristan never turned to face them. He already knew which vehicle the president was in, and turned to face the third SUV as it came up next to him. At this, the vehicle stopped, the passenger door opened, and a burly Secret Service agent stepped out and approached him.     "Sir, I need to check you for weapons. Nothing personal, just standard protocol."

"I will allow it," Tristan said.

The agent checked him and confirmed that Tristan had nothing of concern on his body. He then turned and opened the rear passenger door and beckoned Tristan to join them. Tristan walked to the vehicle and stepped in fluidly.

"Hello again," the President said. "We weren't entirely sure if we would see you again."

"I had other stops to make. You are not the only ones we are bringing into this mountain fortress."     The vehicle began moving again.

"What other people are you referring to?" the Chief of Staff asked.

"God has decreed a certain number from every tongue, tribe, and nation who will be housed here for safekeeping for entry into the Kingdom."

The vehicle was now moving into the compound proper.

"As you know, Mr. Tristan, there has been a great crisis in the world in the last couple days. What would be useful for us is for you to tell us, the best you can, what lies ahead. We are very interested in what you have to say regarding this topic," the President said.

"I would be glad to. Once you have settled into this mountain compound, prepare a room for yourself and all the others who I will bring. I will be back with you shortly," Tristan replied.

"How many are we talking here?"

"Four hundred to be exact, but you will find, there will be room enough," Tristan replied.

In the blink of an eye, Tristan was no longer there. The President and those sitting with Tristan recoiled in shock. This teleportation thing was something the mortals were just going to have to get used to seeing.

\*\*\*

Tristan stood near the base of the mountain, and looked north. He instinctively knew he was in Canada in the Alberta Province just north of Lake Louise. He saw the thin trail of smoke rising above the snow-frosted pines halfway up the mountain and knew he'd come to the right place. He began walking toward it. Although he could have just teleported to it directly, he now began to miss the simple act of walking, as if it had been some forgotten ritual from millennia ago. After walking ten minutes, he had arrived at a small clearing that seemed to serve as a miniature plateau. He saw the rather elaborately constructed log cabin, and began walking toward the door. Just then, the door opened and a giant of a man stepped outside.

"Tristan Zavota," the voice bellowed from the giant man.

"Enoch!" Tristan replied, equally as loud. As they approached each other, there was a similar glimmer, or shimmer, each man displayed as the sunlight hit their faces. This was one of the effects of the glorification process, which happened during the Rapture. Presumably, Enoch had lived with this condition for many millennia now since his own translation; perhaps this was why he lived away from the general population. That and his immense size. He must easily have been nine-feet tall.

"Welcome my friend. Barachiel told me you would be coming. We have much to discuss," Enoch said.

"Thank you. Our Lord put your name in my mind so I should come to see you, but beyond that, I do not know why."

"Do you like history, Tristan?" Enoch asked as they walked into his cavernous cabin.

"I do," Tristan replied.

"Good, grab a seat by the fire and allow me to serve you a drink. Have some warm wine," he offered.

"Wait, I thought we can't drink?" Tristan said as he took the metallic, chalice-shaped cup.

"This is not that kind of wine. It's heaven's wine and it is divine," he replied with a look of deep satisfaction. "Furthermore, your new body cannot become intoxicated, even if you tried; your body purifies everything instantly, so every impurity is immediately rejected."

"So if I ate a greasy cheeseburger?" Tristan asked raising one eyebrow.

"I haven't 'eaten' anything in thousands of years. I do not need to; neither do you, now. But I suppose if you ate a cheeseburger, it would simply evaporate inside your body like it was never there."

"I'm just impressed you know what a cheeseburger is," Tristan replied lightheartedly.

"Tristan, I have been walking the earth since the floodwaters subsided and Noah's family left the ark."

"Wow. Doing what?"

"I've been chronicling human history. Every empire. Every dynasty. I have been everywhere on earth, and I've seen everything man has done."

"I bet you have some stories to tell," Tristan said before sipping from the chalice.

"I do. But..."

"But we don't have time, right?"
"Correct. I believe we have some certain people we must collect up."
"I thought as much. I still can't figure out, why you and me though? Isn't that more of an angel mission?" Tristan asked.

"It makes perfect sense," Enoch replied. "We are the first and last Gentiles raptured."

"Wow that does make sense. There is a symmetry to it; just the same way Moses and Elijah make sense, representing the two most iconic figures of the Law and the Prophets."

"Yes, see? God does everything perfectly. Shall we go?"

"Yes. By the way, this wine is amazing. Do we get to drink this forever?"

"Yes we do," Enoch replied with a smile. "But you haven't seen anything yet."

## Chapter 61

For many walk, of whom I have told you often, and now tell you even weeping, *that they are* the enemies of the cross of Christ: whose end *is* destruction, whose god *is their* belly, and *whose* glory *is* in their shame—who set their mind on earthly things. For our citizenship is in heaven, from

which we also eagerly wait for the Savior, the Lord Jesus Christ, who will transform our lowly body that it may be conformed to His glorious body, according to the working by which He is able even to subdue all things to Himself.

**Philippians 3:18-22**

Early-Mid November

Enoch and Tristan finished their wines and then teleported to the outskirts of Moscow, Russia, in the blink of an eye. They stood on the road in front of an aged, charcoal-gray Soviet era apartment complex known as a *Khrushchyovka*. It was 6:15 in the evening, and night was already beginning to overtake the day. There was a raucous group of people down the road about 200 feet, apparently having some kind of street party. Enoch stepped forward and with a powerful Russian voice said, "Ivan and Ekaterina, come forward."

While his voice was incredibly loud, he did so calmly and without yelling. It was almost as if he could will his own voice to amplify without physically straining to do it. At first, Tristan was unsure if they had heard him, but then a light turned on in an apartment that appeared to be on the third floor. A curtain was pulled aside and two faces appeared there.

"Ivan and Ekaterina, come forth," Enoch repeated.

The faces disappeared and a few minutes later, a young couple appeared in the doorway of their apartment's main portico. They looked shaken and confused at these two strange men standing in the street in front of their apartment. The husband had the rough look of a construction worker with short brown hair cut into a crew cut. The wife had reddish blond hair and a thin build.

"I am Ivan, and this is my wife Ekaterina. Who are you, and what do you want?"

"You must come with us if you want to survive," Tristan said.

They looked at each other.

"Who are you?" Ivan asked again.

"I am Tristan, and this is Enoch."

They continued to close the distance between them and came to about ten-feet apart. Ivan, presumably, wanted to measure himself up to these two strangers. He may have been 6'1, but compared to both Tristan, and especially Enoch, he seemed like a young teenager by comparison.

"Are you politsiya?" Ekaterina asked.

"No," Tristan responded. "We need to take you to America."

At this, they shot confused yet hopeful looks in their eyes.

"I had a dream about this," Ekaterina said softly. "Ivan didn't believe me."

"God has sent us to gather you two to a place where you will be safe for the next few years," Tristan said.

Ivan looked hesitant, almost to the point of defiant.

"You will see your child Alexei again," Enoch said looking at Ivan. "If you don't come with us, you will never see him again."

Ekaterina burst out crying. Ivan teared up. "Your child is safe in heaven now, and if you come with us, you will be reunited."

Ivan wrapped his arm around his wife. "We will come."

Just then, the crowd down the street seemed to notice them. Several of them started to stumble in their direction.

"Do we have time to run back upstairs and grab some personal belongings?" Ekaterina asked.

"Yes, but be quick. We have more stops we must make tonight," Enoch replied.

The raucous crowd continued toward them.

"I don't think they have seen you yet, Enoch," Tristan said. "I would not want to pick a fight with you." "They are intoxicated," he replied. "The alcohol has impaired their ability to reason. They will find out soon enough."

"That doesn't sound good," Tristan said. "I would not want to be them right now."

The first of the revelers came within twenty feet of them. Clearly, this man had drank too much vodka. He leaned on what appeared to be an abandoned Soviet era *Lada Nova* car, which most likely debuted in the mid-1980s. He seemed content to stand and stare, eyeing them in a semi drunken stupor, apparently trying to determine if they were either potential victims or threats. Apparently, the drunk had been waiting for the rest of his comrades to join him in his mockery. When they arrived beside him, he asked in perfectly slurred Russian, what circus they just escaped from, prompting Enoch to turn and face them and address them in fluent Russian.

"You ungodly cowards. You could not turn away

from the bottle in this life to come to salvation. Your vodka has consumed you and your mind has been poisoned."    The group of rowdy men started laughing uncontrollably.

"So now you will be made to see that this is not funny at all."

At once, the group stopped laughing and began rubbing their eyes. At first, Tristan thought they had been struck blind, but they were not so lucky.

"God requires back the time He so freely gave you to come to salvation, but you wasted it. First, we must cleanse you."

At this, alcohol began to stream out of the men's eyes as if they were crying inconsolably. Then the streams turned into a gushing forth as if their eyes were vomiting the vodka itself. If Tristan had not been regenerated into his new form, he did not know if he could handle watching it. Vodka coming out of the eye socket looked excruciatingly painful.

About this time, the young couple had made their way back from their apartment to them and walked up to the spectacle now going on in the street.

"These men were up to no good," Tristan said.

"These are Russian mafia thugs. It is good to see them suffer," Ivan replied.

"All I know is they messed with the wrong hombres tonight," Tristan said nodding his head toward an angry Enoch. "Let's get Enoch and go."

At that, Enoch turned away from the dozen men writhing in the streets still having vodka coming out of their eye and they stood together facing each other.

"Are you ready?" Tristan asked them.

"We are," they replied.

They grabbed hands and were gone in a flash.

And Enoch also, the seventh from Adam, prophesied of these, saying, Behold, the Lord cometh with ten thousands of his saints, to execute judgment upon all, and to convince all that are ungodly among them of all their ungodly deeds which they have ungodly committed, and of all their hard speeches which ungodly sinners have spoken against him.

**Jude 1:14-15**

**Chapter 62**

NORAD, Colorado Springs, Colorado
Early-Mid November

Tristan and Enoch brought Ivan and Ekaterina back to

NORAD Mountain, much to the surprise of everyone there. They departed almost as soon as they got there and made a dozen other trips to continents all across the world. Tristan almost felt a bit like Noah, gathering couples from around the world. Their next trip was to Argentina, then South Africa. Their last trip was to Ethiopia. In all they went to almost every nation overnight, and upon returning, had 400 people hanging out in a secured waiting room.

"How have they been treating you all?" Tristan asked.

The group responded collectively which normally would have just sounded like total chaos were he not regenerated. He could now divide his attention up in such a way that he could hear each individual speaking clearly. A very shocked President's Chief of Staff came into the room.

"Tristan, the President is respectfully requesting your presence at this moment. It's time to brief us on what comes next."

"Very well. Chief, this is Enoch," Tristan said directing the chief's attention to the giant of a man. "The Enoch from the Bible."

The Chief of Staff looked at him and said, "I don't really know who you are, but I've heard the name before. Welcome to NORAD, Mr. Enoch."

Enoch nodded his head to acknowledge him but remained silent.

"Alright, if you will, please follow me."

Tristan turned to Enoch. "Let's split up. You stay here and explain to the group what is coming, and I will do the same with the President and his team. And if it isn't too much trouble, could we rescue the men who saved me coming out of Afghanistan?"

"I think we can do that," Enoch replied. "In the meantime, we will split up and take the two different audiences."

With that, Tristan turned and followed the Chief out and down a long hallway.

"You know, this is all completely crazy," the Chief said to Tristan. "All of this. You teleporting and bringing unverified foreigners into NORAD, the dollar collapsing. Who would have thought it ended like this?"

"It is like a three-act play," Tristan replied. "Act Onelife is normal. Act Two, the world falls apart. Acts Three is what comes after."

"Fair to say the most powerful man on the planet is requesting to find out more detail about Acts Two and Three with great detail. But I do have one question."

"Yes, go ahead."

"So if this is the entire Biblical end-of-days scenario we are really facing, why are some of us here? I mean, I am not a Christian, nor a believer. Why am I here?"

"You will be before the end."

After walking what seemed like an endless series of hallway corridors, they had finally arrived at the conference room.

"We are here," the Chief said as he used his badge to open the conference room door. "Can't wait to hear what you got to say."

"Mr. President," the Chief said as he announced their arrival. "Mr. Tristan has come to brief us all on what is supposed to happen next."

## Chapter 63

NORAD, Colorado Springs, Colorado
Early-Mid November

"Ladies and gentlemen, good morning," Tristan said while looking at the group. "Please allow me to have your full attention as I share about the things which come next. Clearly, you have already witnessed the Rapture of the Church. This is the prophesied event, in which Jesus comes to take His bride, the Church, back to heaven."

A hand went up immediately and upon acknowledgement, asked, "Who is the Church. You mean like the Roman Catholic Church? Because I'm Catholic and I'm still here."

"A very good question, thank you," Tristan said. "The Church is the universal body of believers in Jesus Christ, from the first-century, until now. Those who have already died in the past were with Jesus, but not in bodily form. They were, as we would say, alive in the spirit in heaven. They came with Jesus out of heaven, to the earth's atmosphere, and received their resurrected bodies. Those who were alive at His coming were instantly translated into our glorified bodies like mine," he said pointing to himself. "This is how I can teleport and am changed from mortal, to immortal."

"But why do the Rapture?" the President asked. "Surely, God wouldn't willfully cause all the chaos, death, and destruction this has caused. Wasn't there another way?"

"No. The time which is coming, has been designated for two purposes, neither of which involves the Church. In fact, it would be unjust for God to keep His bride the Church, here through it. Unjustness, of course, would go against God's perfect nature."

"So what is next? The Tribulation?" the Secretary of Interior asked.

Upon saying this, several staffers glanced at him curiously.

"Hey, I know a little bit about Bible prophecy. My ex-wife liked to talk about it," he said defensively.

"Yes it is. It is not the next thing, but the thing after next. The next thing will be the gap between the Rapture and the official start of the Tribulation, or what is officially called Daniel's 70th Week," Tristan said.

"How long does this gap last for?" the Vice-President asked.

"Unknown. My best guess, judging by the way certain geopolitical events are shaping up, I would say more than six-months, but less than a year. Maybe even as long as three and a half years."

"So the Rapture doesn't start the Tribulation, I mean, Daniel's 70th Week?" the President asked.

"No. The Rapture was an imminent, standalone event. However, the Rapture kick starts the conditions necessary for the 70th Week to begin. The Tribulation starts with the signing of an official treaty between Israel, and many nations."

"Like what conditions?" the Secretary of Defense asked.

"The War of Gog and Magog," Tristan responded. "This is where Russia, Iran, Turkey, Ethiopia, Sudan, Libya, and other nations come against the nation of Israel. It will seem utterly hopeless for Israel; yet, God will destroy these armies by His own hand."

"You mentioned a peace treaty just now. Are we involved in that? What about the United States?" the President asked. "What does the Bible say about us?"

"The Bible does mention many nations being role players in the last days. There will be a revived Roman Empire, who through both technology and satanic authority, takes over the entire planet. I would presume, it means the US as well. To that point, however, the Bible does not mention any nation like the United States," Tristan concluded.

"Is that due to the *Kredit*, the Rapture, or both?" the Secretary of State asked.

"Clearly, these are sequential events," the Secretary of Defense said. "The *Kredit* triggered the *coup d'état*, which had already spawned a global economic meltdown. The Rapture was then the proverbial *black swan* event none of us saw coming leading us into this Tribulation."

"So we are in a gap now, and we are waiting here in a mountain bunker waiting on the Russians to invade Israel?" the Vice President asked.

"Yes."

"This is ludicrous," the Vice President said. "We need to regather our forces, Mr. President, and retake Washington."

"That would be suicide," Tristan added. "If you leave this bunker, you will die."

"Why is that?" the Vice President asked skeptically. "Because the Four Horsemen are about to ride." "They are real?" a surprised Secretary of Defense asked.

"They are. The Lion of Judah, Jesus the Christ, is about to unleash them upon the world by opening the Seal Judgments. The *War of Gog and Magog* will be the catalyst for the first Horseman, the Rider on the White Horse. He will come in declaring peace, but it will be a false peace. What he really brings in is massive destruction. He is the lawless one, the son of perdition, or as many know him, the Antichrist. The Red Horse of War follows him. After war comes the rider on the Black Horse representing Famine. The last rider rides on the Pale Horse. Death and hell follow him."

"And that's it, right?" the Secretary of Defense asked.

"No, then things go from bad to worse," Tristan replied. "The Last three Seal Judgments kill a quarter of the people on the planet. Then there are the Trumpet Judgments, followed closely by the Bowl Judgments. Things are about to get *apocalyptic*, as they used to say. Trust me, this is where you need to stay to be safe."

***

I looked when He opened the sixth seal, and behold, there was a great earthquake; and the sun became black as sackcloth of hair, and the moon became like blood. And the stars of heaven fell to the earth, as a fig tree drops its late figs when it is shaken by a mighty wind. Then the sky receded as a scroll when it is rolled up, and every mountain and island was moved out of its place.

And the kings of the earth, the great men, the rich men, the commanders, the mighty men, every slave and every free man, hid themselves in the caves and in the rocks of the mountains, and said to the mountains and rocks, "Fall on us and hide us from the face of Him who sits on the throne and from the wrath of the Lamb! For the great day of His wrath has come, and who is able to stand?"

**Revelation 6:12-17**

# Chapter 64

NORAD, Colorado Springs, Colorado
Early-Mid November

Enoch began speaking to a group of about thirty persons in the main entrance from where he and Tristan first entered. At first, he started in a voice just above a whisper, as if to force the listeners to lean in closer. There were still some who didn't quite believe he was who he said he was, and hung back, although his size and supernatural abilities were starting to win them over.

"I am going to tell you all the things I have seen with my own eyes," he said. "The history of man is not what your schools have taught you. The world before the Flood was not filled with cavemen bearing clubs and lugging their wives around by their hair. The world was vibrant, and full of people, and modernity you haven't even reached yet in this modern day.

"If you can believe it, I'm the average height for people during that time," Enoch said.

Those in attendance looked around at each other in disbelief, some shaking their heads.

"Think about it this way. You have things like copier machines, right?"

Mutual head nodding commenced.

"If you take a picture, and then make a copy of it, it looks pretty close to the original, does it not?" Enoch asked.

"Yes," was said collectively.

"What happens if you keep making a copy, of the copy you just printed?"

"The quality starts to go down," one Air Force personnel said in the rear of the room.

"That is correct. If you keep taking the copy you just printed, and use that new copy to make another copy, and so on, at some point, the picture will become unrecognizable," Enoch said.

"Adam and Eve were the first humans God created perfectly. Since we are all descendants of Adam and Eve, then we are all copies, genetically speaking, of them. It then stands to reason, those closer to Adam in the genealogical timeline, the closer to perfection those people would be. As opposed to those born hundreds to thousands of generations later, does it not? I am the seventh generation from Adam, and those alive in my generation before the great flood, were as well.

"Not only were we taller, but we were stronger and smarter. One man could lift what would today be many hundreds of pounds. Not just lift it, but also carry it great distances if need be. Many great civilizations existed in the time between Adam and Noah," Enoch concluded.

"How long was it between Adam and Noah?" a civilian woman asked politely.

"Almost 1,700 years," Enoch said matter of factly. "Think about your own recent history. How many civilizations have existed since the third century A.D.?"

"A lot. The Romans were on the way out, but then the Byzantines, the Muslims, the Holy Roman Empire, etc.," a soldier replied.

"Yes, exactly," Enoch said excitedly. "The same was the case before the Flood, except, people were closer to superhuman than they are today. Think of all mankind could achieve with greater strength, intelligence, and longevity."

"Wait a minute, Mr. Enoch," a serious looking man in a business suit interrupted. "Are you trying to tell us, that humans, as a race, have only been around earth for six thousand or so years?"

"Yes, exactly," Enoch replied.

"How can you explain that in light of the fact that we have rocks, minerals, and fossils that are millions of years old?" the serious man inquired.

Enoch's eyes bristled with what appeared to be electricity.

"Because I was there. Moreover, I am telling you now that humans never evolved from apes. They never climbed out of the primordial soup, as your so-called experts claim. If you have instruments that show this earth older than six thousand years, then your instruments are incorrect. Is it possible that you, many thousands of years removed from the event, are wrong and perhaps, not as smart as you think you are?" Enoch said sternly.

The not so serious man now was floundering under the weight of his personal eyewitness testimony. "I mean, how can we trust what you are saying, versus, what is taught in nearly every school in the nation?"

"I remember when all the schools and experts used to say the earth was flat, and if you went too far east over the ocean, you'd eventually fall off the earth," Enoch replied. "Now, if you can trust your eyes, and your ability to reason, I am here in front of you, and clearly, I am not like any of you," he said, extending to his full height of 8'6" tall. "You can trust what I have to say."

He then walked over and took one of the soldier's M4 rifles, snapped it in half as easily as he might have snapped a twig, and then disappeared in front of their eyes.

## Chapter 65

Brussels, Belgium
Mid November

While Tristan remained within NORAD, serving a portion of the American remnant both as a prophetic guide detailing them with the Gospel of the Kingdom, the world outside had grown increasingly frightening. Enoch was moving at lightning quick jaunts taking note of the total collapse that was happening all around the United States. The US had gone from being close to the perfect model of a civilized, modern nation, to nightmarishly lawless almost overnight. Nowhere was safe.

Gunshots rang out seemingly everywhere. Fires were raging in any given direction. Those who had the means to get out of the cities, had long fled. The local gangs and crime syndicates, in the most medieval of fashions, were quickly subjugating those in their respective territories who could not. The worst hit areas were the major metropolitan cities like Washington, D.C., Chicago, Los Angeles, San

Francisco, Houston, St. Louis, Miami, Boston, and New York City. They had become deathtraps. Their surrounding suburbs were not much better. Most of the streets were littered with abandoned cars and dead bodies.

The rural areas, depending on where you lived, varied in the kind of *hell-on-earth* they presented. Much of the Midwest, already taken over by large, consolidated motorcycle gangs felt the wrath of their brand of justice. That is to say, if one of these groups caught you outside on the road or in a town, whatever you had, to include your life, was fair game. Countless cars and bodies lay littered around the roadways.

Although Texas fared a little better in terms of fighting the gangs both in the city and in the country with their rangers, it was a losing battle. The brutal Mexican cartels were making their moves further and further north of the border. They had already claimed much of the border towns, from El Paso down to Brownsville. Now they were moving east and north, setting up checkpoints and sending scouting parties to see how much resistance they would meet the further inland they pushed.

Paradise, Texas, after the initial collapse and before the Rapture, had wisely decided to close down the three main county roads leading into it by blockading it with broken down vehicles and armed checkpoints. The highway leading through the town, had been reduced to one lane, and the exits had been blockaded again with broken vehicles. If someone wanted to come into the town, they would have to do so by foot or by horse. However, after the Rapture, so many of its residents were taken up that it was now near impossible to staff all the checkpoints. It would only be a matter of time before the Cartels made their way to Paradise.

***

Enoch expanded his jaunts across the Atlantic. Although he was not omniscient, God allowed him to understand perfectly, the issues facing the nations presently. Enoch took note that things here were a little better. Far fewer people disappeared in Europe and the Middle East from the *Rapture of the Church*, and thus, these nations were not affected as negatively as their cousins were across the Atlantic. Thus far, they were largely impacted by the second and third order effects by the collapse of the American economy.

The *Kredit* itself was not as affected by the American collapse as badly as people first thought. The *Kredit* system operated on a 5G network, using quantum-based technologies, managed by a super-artificial intelligence system located just outside of Brussels, Belgium, near the European Union (EU) Headquarters. Those familiar with it, jokingly referred to the AI program as "the Beast" in reference to its relentless ability to slavishly perform any task assigned to it no matter how complex. Before the American economy even collapsed, the "Beast" had run through millions of scenarios and preselected the best courses of action for the EU to take.

The 21st century American economy was still operating by 20th-century industrial era rules. What this meant was its economy was still largely dependent upon a strong fiat (paper) currency, and a debt-based economy. So long as the majority of Americans remained in debt (i.e., mortgages, car payments, taxes, etc.), did not become debt free, and the banks kept loaning money, the US Dollar would continue to circulate through its economy. As *the Beast* aptly noted, since the 1990s, America's manufacturing base had largely moved east to China, and she was now primarily a service-based economy.

This meant the usual lead indicator the Baltic Dry Index (BDI) should indicate its steady but downward trajectory. The BDI had long served as a leading indicator for economic health by monitoring the shipping of raw materials (coal, steel, timber, etc.) from Europe to the United States. Since American manufacturing had already been on the decline (even before COVID), the BDI was showing significantly less raw materials than it had in the decades prior to the 1990s.

*The Beast* noted, months before the release of the *Kredit,* its introduction would initially upend the global economy. However, with its bulletproof bio-technological solutions embedding the technology into the phones, and then into the users themselves, it could almost overnight, put an end to human trafficking, the drug trade, the black markets, global warming, and terrorism. Even if it caused some initial disruptions, EU leaders (and other committed globalists) figured it was worth the risk.

Of course, had they known, the Americans would never have supported this course of action, which is why they were kept out of the loop on all decisions related to the *Kredit*. However, the EU was not going to sit around and wait for the American economy to implode and suck the rest of the world down with it. With the US $30 trillion dollars in debt, waiting for it to collapse first was like waiting for a bomb to detonate before trying to defuse it. Even though

Enoch was from the antediluvian age, as he would say to Tristan with a smile, he wasn't born yesterday. Even he understood why Europe acted when they did.

Now two things the EU leaders were not anticipating, was the COVID-19 global shutdown, and the *Rapture of the Church*. COVID delayed the *Kredits'* initial launch in 2020, which was timed to meet the United Nation's *Agenda 2020 Global Reset* initiative. Even still, the pandemic delay, the subsequent quarantines, and the economic shutdowns actually helped speed up global digitalization, making the transition to the *Kredit* much easier on the back end.

Nevertheless, Enoch noted that the impact of the American currency collapse to a digital crypto system like the *Kredit* was minimal. Even the second and third order effects, which initially affected the EU, were quickly overcome. This was because as early as 2016, the EU had been instructing (based on the Beast's recommendations) for its central banks and financial institutions to begin diversifying their holdings and markets away from the United States.

The second *Beast* solution was that after the predicted American collapse, to immediately seize and convert all US holdings in European possession, such as land, gold, silver, oil, and technologies, into collateral for subsidizing the value of the *Kredit*. Hundreds of billions of dollars' worth of tangibles had been floating around Europe for decades, primarily in Switzerland and Monaco, which had long served as 'tax-free' safe-havens for wealthy Americans. This confiscated treasure now belonged to the European Union. An unseen Enoch had heard EU leaders discuss beforehand how *possession was 9/10ths of the law*. Besides, who would stop them if the US were in disarray? EU leaders further argued that if affluent Americans wanted their wealth back, they would have to become citizens of the EU, and then pay their fair share to get it back. Either way, the EU made out like bandits.

The last *Beast* solution was the most ambitious, and the most promising. The plan was to use elite NATO strike teams to secure what military equipment, weapons, and warheads they could get their hands on. First, they would seize all the US Military assets already deployed in European bases such as in the UK, Germany, Spain, Italy, and elsewhere. Next it would conduct a series of strategic raids into the continental US since there would be little to no organized military resistance to stop them. Lastly, it would recruit from the US military to fill its own ranks of military forces, with the promise of tax-free citizenship and lucrative pay. EU leaders figured that with no promise of future pay, they could count on at least 10-20% of the US military migrating their anyway to find some stability. The EU would pay handsomely to fill and augment their own EU Army ranks, with formerly battle-hardened American military.

To Enoch, it seemed while the US was already destined to collapse before the Rapture due to the implementation of the *Kredit*, the Rapture was the icing on the cake. This, primarily, was not that the US had more Christians than any other nation; it just had more in every strata of society. While there were more Christians around the world who disappeared than in the US itself, most of these non-American Christians were on the bottoms of their respective countries social strata, and thus, their disappearance was not felt as profoundly as it was in the US. Therefore, the societal impact for them was far less catastrophic in the nations outside the US, than in the United States itself.

Thus, Enoch noted, future Millennial Kingdom generations would come to note that the very thing which made America great was its original trust in God rather government. This provided several centuries' worth of freedom of speech and religion, which allowed the Christian faith to flourish for as long as it did…until the end. Then this freedom became its greatest liability.

In the end, there was no great revival, no great spiritual awakening. Society and its government simply drifted further and further away from God until it became completely reprobate. Just when things seemed like they could not get any worse, there was a sudden removal of all of God's people, immediately recalled to their heavenly home by way of the Rapture. That is where they were; now God would begin to wage war, His final war upon Satan, his demonic forces, and an unrepentant world. As for the sudden demise of America, as Jesus so aptly noted, *to whom much is given, much is required* (Luke 12:48).

## Chapter 66

In those days, and for some time after, giant Nephilites lived on the earth, for *whenever* the sons of God had intercourse with women, they gave birth to children who became the heroes and famous warriors of ancient times. **Genesis 6:4 NLT** (author's emphasis)

NORAD, Colorado Springs, Co.
Mid November

From an angel's perspective, the earth looked like a giant fire ant hill that someone poked rigorously with a stick. The demonic hordes were everywhere, which made Barachiel's journey all the more perilous. The glorified redeemed, such as Enoch and Tristan, could simply think about where they wanted to go, and were there. Angels, however, still had to travel from point to point. Humans, who encountered angels, often mistook their sudden appearance for teleportation, because they could physically manifest or disappear at will. The truth was, they still had to travel the old-fashioned way.

Barachiel made his way cautiously through the forest to the outskirts of NORAD. He was instructed to retrieve Tristan for another mission. Of course, the entirety of the mountain was crawling with demonic entities. Some of these were so deformed and hideous, Barachiel was not quite sure if they even qualified as fallen angels any longer. *Perhaps they have opened the abyss a bit prematurely and let out the Nephilim,* he thought with a shudder.

The Nephilim, were the half-human, half-fallen angel hybrids that roamed the earth nearly five millennia ago. The world before the Flood existed in near-paradise conditions and at that time, mankind was rapidly growing upon the face of the earth. Men were physically taller, stronger, smarter, and could live for centuries back then. There was also no barrier between the spiritual realm and the physical, so humans could interact with angels just as easily as they could each other.

Around 900 years after Adam was created, a group of fallen angels, descended to earth and began to live amongst the humans openly. Of course, to the humans, these angels appeared as demigods. They appeared, as angels often do, flawlessly beautiful and were found to be very attractive. This made taking wives no hard work for them, as human women often threw themselves at them begging to be taken as wives. At that time, mankind had already drifted away from worshipping the one true God, and had begun to make idols and chase after false gods. So it was no coincidence to the timing of the arrival of these fallen watcher angels; they planned to take advantage of the situation on earth.

It was during those days that fallen angels began to take human wives and their offspring were giants, or, as they would later be called, *Nephilim*. Their offspring, both the descendants of tall humans, and even taller angels (usual height is 10 feet high), caused their offspring to be nearly 1214 feet head to toe. The beauty and might of their children, all males by the way, enticed more women to sire children with these pretend demigods.

The Nephilim, understanding their damned fate, became exceedingly angry and violent. Being neither fully human, nor fully angel, they came to understand that upon their deaths their souls were relegated to that as wandering spirits. Furthermore, those legions who were not condemned early to the abyss (for being exceedingly wicked) were forced to serve in perpetual servitude to their demonic overlords. In the millennia that followed, seeing their once beautiful forms become disfigured and monstrous drove them into madness.

Seeing the demonic hordes running around noticeably now even to humans, reminded Barachiel what it was like before the Flood. The Apostle Paul had written nearly two thousand years ago in his epistle to the Ephesian church, *for we do not wrestle against flesh and blood, but against principalities, against powers, against the rulers of the darkness of this age, against spiritual hosts of wickedness in the heavenly places.*

At the time Paul wrote that, even until Barachiel arrived on his first mission for Tristan, this remained true. However now, these forces of wickedness were no long just operating in the spiritual realm. They were now operating openly in the physical world. The world after the Rapture reminded him very much of that same doomed pre-Flood world: violent, bloody, and only evil continually.

God had put a protective barrier up between the mountain, and those fallen abominations, which was why they were massing around it but unable to get in. From the wood line, Barachiel called out quietly to Tristan in the holy angelic language. He knew those demons would either not hear it, or understand it even if they did. As soon as Barachiel spoke, Tristan perked up. He had been talking to the former Secretary of Defense about ensuring they had enough food and water to survive the next seven years plus years.

"What is it?" the SECDEF asked.

"An old friend is calling. I'll be back," he said as he instantly transported himself to Barachiel's location.

## Chapter 67

Brussels, EU
Late November

Enoch had been acting as an unseen *watcher* in the BEAST headquarters near the EU for nearly a week now when he saw a huge group of fallen angels arrive *en masse*. At the center of the entourage, were two men that piqued his interest. He knew them because they had been former compatriots of Tristan when he was on his initial journey. He did not know how he knew Izzy and Red; he just knew instinctively that they were why he was there. They seemed to be escorting another individual, a politician of some sort, into the Headquarters. The wicked angels did not seem to be there for them, but for the man they were escorting. Enoch would wait until the two parties separated before moving in.

The man at the center, the politician, had a sense of destiny around him, as if he somehow knew he was intended for great things. Watching him as he moved, it seemed like the traffic and crowds parted and smoothed themselves out before he arrived. No doubt, it was these fallen angels clearing a path ahead of him to take him to wherever he needed to go. Curious as to how Izzy and Red could have gotten wrangled up with this man as quickly as they did, he prayed to God for wisdom.

His answer was near instantaneous as he came to understand how after the Rapture while they were in Israel, the Rapture diverted their plane to the airport at Athens, Greece rather than to the United States. It was here they met this relatively unknown state official at the airport who, seeing the chaos erupt around him, and recognizing the caliber of men these were (mercenaries), hired them on the spot as personal security. The other two team members (Phil and Tiny) were still intent on making it back to the US to their families and farms in West Virginia and parted ways.

The politician made his way into a closed conference room while Izzy and Red posted themselves near the door. The fallen angels made their way past them and continued in with the politician. Now was the time to grab them and leave.

***

Tristan immediately recognized the voice of Barachiel, and understood that he was waiting for him outside near the tree line beyond the security perimeter. Immediately, Tristan excused himself from the SECDEF and teleported himself to Barachiel. This form of travel still greatly unnerved the normal human.

"Tristan!" Barachiel said in quiet, but enthusiastic greeting.

"Barachiel!" Tristan replied. "What brings you to these parts?"

"I've a new mission for you," he replied, "from on high."

"Really? I am still overwhelmed at the idea that He (speaking of God) would still be using me. I am not worthy of His continued graciousness."

"None of us are," Barachiel replied. "Still, we have a small task to complete before events can proceed any further."

"Where are we to go?" Tristan asked.

"We begin in Georgia."

"The country Georgia, or the Peach State?"

"The country."

"Shame, I was looking forward to some good old fashioned sweet tea."

"I think you'll manage. Let's begin."

## Chapter 68

Early December

With the collapse of the United States well under way, the decision to move the United Nations Headquarters out of New York City was unanimous. Most nations had already recalled their ambassadors, diplomats, and other officials back to their respective nations, thus, the vote was conducted virtually. The next great push was to determine where the UN headquarters should move to. While numerous nations and cities offered to host the global government, the proposal went to the new and emerging Saudi Arabian city of Neom.

This new city-state, inside of Saudi territory, bordered Israel and Jordan to the north, and was directly east of Egypt along the Red Sea.

Since the city was not yet inhabited, and was still in the process of construction, the winning decision was that the UN got a significant say in how the city should be constructed. Neom was designed to be a *global* city-state, like that of Washington, D.C. and the Vatican. It was also meant to exceed even that of other technologically advanced Arab cities like Dubai, Abu Dhabi, and Doha. It was intended to be the most technologically advanced city in the world.

Along with the relocation, the UN determined that given the new geopolitical dynamics of a multipolar world (with the US having abdicated its throne), it would reorganize itself into ten regional governments, led by a Region Chief. The chief served as both the Prime Minister as well as the Commanding General of the armies in their region. The regions were aligned along similar languages, ethnicities, and cultures. The regional governments' capitals would be located in the most geographically strategic areas conducive to waterways, port access, and least impacted by the mass disappearance. These seven regional governments will have ten respective capitals, with ten leaders. They are as follows:

1. North America Region East (Canada, US)-
   Bangor, Maine
   North America Region West (Canada, US)-
   Vancouver, Canada
2. South America Region- Buenos Aires,
   Argentina
   Central America (and Mexico) Region-
   Panama City, Panama
3. Sub-Saharan Africa Region- Cape Town,
   South Africa
4. Northern Europe Region- Brussels, Belgium
5. Far East Asia Region -Beijing, China
6. Central Asia Region- Moscow, Russia
7. Mediterranean Union (UfM) Region- Rome,
   Italy

Neom, Saudi Arabia- United Nations Headquarters

Enoch noted that most people after the Rapture did not realize that Neom was actually destined to become the *New Babylon*, which had long been foretold of in the Holy Bible. Granted, after the Rapture, there were few who understood the implications of these geo-prophetic events.

However, the reason most missed this connection, was because this new Babylon was neither called Babylon, nor in Iraq. Ancient Babylon used to be located between the Tigris and Euphrates rivers; just south of what is today Baghdad. Nevertheless, Enoch knew the ancient boundaries well enough to know they were still guarded by the same wicked angels who guarded them millennia ago. Those boundaries included where Neom was being built, which was well inside of the ancient Babylonian Empire.

## Chapter 69

Vatican City
Mid-December

While Neom would become home to the world's regional governments and corporate headquarters, Rome would serve the dual purposes of serving as both the Mediterranean Region headquarters, as well as the global religious capital (Vatican City) for the United Nations. It was here that a new and charismatic young pope would lead the United Nations in its first post-Rapture ecumenical religious agendas. Of note, he was also a close associate with the rising new political star that hailed from Greece.

The previous pope, who was in his mid-eighties when the Rapture occurred, died suddenly during those calamitous days. Despite the global tumult caused by the Rapture, and the subsequent collapse of the United States, the Vatican wasted no time in finding the new replacement pope. This one, like the previous, hailed from a more progressive branch of Jesuits. This man was also half the previous pope's age, thus making him the youngest in nearly a thousand years (or since Pope Benedict IX, circa 1032).

It was during the days after the Rapture that he saw great opportunity in advancing his vision for great ecumenical revival. He earnestly believed that the only way humanity would survive, was if all religions came together and set aside their differences during these days of great turmoil. He argued before and especially afterwards that all of humanity shared in a common acceptance of a power greater than themselves, and that humankind should not get hung up on what name they call that power. Furthermore, he claimed to be in contact with the celestial visitors (from the UFOs) and they were now speaking directly through him as a vessel.

Their appeal to all of humanity was very alluring to the Vatican, and in particular, with the mission the newly reorganized United Nations was trying to do. With tens of

millions missing around the world, and much of the world's
economy in a death spiral, they wanted someone who could
inspire faith in this new world government, and provide a
vision for man's next evolutionary step forward. In addition
for the call to global ecumenicalism, the new Pope proposed
a radical new idea for tying the Kredit not just with
citizenship, but also loyalty to the new global church.

***

Barachiel and Tristan arrived in Tbilisi, Georgia, to
little fanfare. In fact, they arrived in the dead of night, and
found most of the city under a military lockdown. The
government there, who had been pro-US in years prior, was
now undergoing a Ukrainian-styled civil war between two
warring factions. Those who wanted the Russian control to
return, and those who did not. Although the patrolling
military appeared to have things well in hand, it was a
façade. Tbilisi was the final holdout for the anti-Russian
forces, as the rest of the country had been given over to the
pro-Russian forces.

"Who are we here to retrieve?" Tristan asked while
they began walking toward the center of the city. "There
is a group of Tribulation believers in a tiny church near

this city's center," Barachiel replied. "We need to move them before Gog pushes through."

"We could have just teleported directly there and saved my feet from getting blisters, my dogs are barking," Tristan said jokingly.

"We could have, but then I couldn't have shown you all this" Barachiel replied majestically pointing to the destruction all around them. "We also have three other stops in Armenia, Kurdistan, and Lebanon before we *mission complete* as you used to say."

Tristan mulled on that for a second, then asked, "Wait, aren't we in the 'Tribulation' already? I mean, I thought the Rapture kick started everything."

"Yes and no," Barachiel replied. "The Rapture was like a bottleneck event that once complete, now has allowed everything else to proceed, but technically, the Tribulation does not begin until a major peace treaty is signed between Israel and many nations. After the *War of Gog and Magog*, which is why we are here, is complete, the Mediterranean Region will sign a peace treaty with Israel, allowing them to join. That officially, as you say, kick starts, the Seventieth Week of Daniel, or the seven-year Tribulation."

"So just for clarity's sake, what you are saying is that we are now in an unscripted gap of time between the Rapture and the start of the Tribulation?

"Yes and no. What we are in now is not completely unscripted; there are things, like the coming of the Two Witnesses, the formation of the world government, Gog War, and the rebuilding of the Third Jewish Temple which must take place in the meantime."

"What have the two angels been doing since they abandoned me at the Israeli border?"

"We've been busy since, and I've not really thought about them since we left."

"When will the Two Witnesses arrive?"

"Man, you have a lot of questions today don't you?" Barachiel asked with a smile. "They will be stationed in Jerusalem when the 70th Week begins, and will remain there for three and a half years until they are killed."

"Wait, what? Killed?" Tristan asked.

"Yes, but it is ok, because they will be resurrected in three days and immediately raptured up in front of the whole world. I cannot wait to see their reaction when this happens," Barachiel said with great eagerness. "We are here," Barachiel said pointing to a dilapidated church that looked like it could collapse at any moment. "They are underground."

Even though both Tristan and Barachiel were indestructible, Tristan still did not fancy entering a building that could collapse on him at any moment.

"Does Gog attack this church?" Tristan asked.

"No, but the massive military movement through here causes the already weakened walls to collapse in on the remnant below, trapping them. God has decided to show mercy on this group, so we will move them back to NORAD."

"Alright, let's do this," Tristan said as they both instantly teleported themselves to the basement below, frightening nearly to death the dozen or so men and women gathered in prayer.

***

Enoch manifested directly in front of Izzy and Red, terrifying the two large men who jumped back at the sight of an even larger and stranger looking man before them. But before their lungs could push the air through their lips to voice a scream, he grabbed them and the three were gone before anyone else noticed. They instantly appeared back at an unoccupied conference room at one of the lower-levels at

NORAD.

The two trembling men were still trying to process everything that just happened, when Enoch spoke to them.

"You are former acquaintances of Tristan Zavota are you not?"

"Umm…..yes," Izzy replied looking guardedly. "We knew him, but we lost him in Israel. He just vanished. We don't know what happened to him."

"He is safe, but he wanted me to find you and the rest of the team to bring them back here."

"Where did he go?" Red asked.

"He was translated, from mortality, to immortality. He is like me now. We cannot die, and we serve at the behest of the living God Yahweh."

The men were trembling uncontrollably at this point. The very mention of the living God had caused an instant reaction in these mortals that is common for the unredeemed. That and the sight of Enoch was also unnerving. They had been fierce warriors in the previous life; now, they were facing a man who could pick up both of their 6'5 frames as easily as a father could pick up his two young children. "Where are we?" Red asked.

"We are in NORAD. Tristan asked me to retrieve you and bring you back here. If you will excuse me, I must go and retrieve your compatriots from West Virginia. If you would walk out of this room, and to the elevators down the hall, take it to the first level and let the security team know I brought you here. They will handle the rest."

"Uhh…yeah, roger that," Izzy replied. "And who are you again?"

## Chapter 70

Armenian-Turkish Border, Israel
Mid- December

Unbeknownst too much of the world, a massive military coalition was in the process of forming on the plains south of Yerevan, Armenia, and north of Mount Ararat, Turkey in the dead of winter. This coalition consisted of Iranians, Russian, Turks, and soldiers from many of the former Soviet satellite nations like Turkmenistan, Uzbekistan, Afghanistan, Tajikistan, and Kyrgyzstan. These would make up the northern coalition who would come to march against the nation of Israel.

In the south, another part of this coalition was forming under the direction of Russia, made up soldiers from Libya, Somalia, and Sudan, who would also march against Israel from the south. Although the individual nations had their own *modus operandi* for joining this alliance, the overarching plan was to take advantage of the ensuing global crises and take by force, Israel's massive natural gas fields for themselves.

The coalition, spearheaded by Russia (Magog), had seen a rapid decline in both their population and economic wealth in recent decades. Their population had been severely decimated over the 20th century due to both the numerous communist purges and World War II. Furthermore, seventy years of communist government policies prohibiting the acquisition of personal wealth had caused many Russians to flee for other lands.

As for their economic decline, the Russian government largely blamed Israel for undercutting their once lucrative energies monopoly they once held over Europe. With advancements in fracking technologies and the discovery of the massive Leviathan and Tamar gas fields off their coast in the early 2000s, Israel's newfound energy wealth made them global competitors in the natural gas markets almost overnight. The Israeli government secured exclusive exporting and pipeline deals with both Cyprus and Greece, bypassing the Russians and Turks altogether to sell directly to the EU.

The Iranian Regime's (Persia) purposes were less pragmatic and more theocratic in nature. For them, securing Jerusalem would be a feat they had not accomplished since the Sasanian coalition conquered it in 614AD. As the minority Muslim religion in the world, being the first since the Ottoman Turks held it, would in their minds, restore their rightful place as the preeminent Islamic faith. Furthermore, this would also help them reclaim the Islamic holy cities of Mecca and Medina, and eventually, allowing them to force all Muslims to convert to the rule of Shia Islam.

Likewise, the Turks (Gomer, Beth Togarmah, and Tubal) wanted a revival of their 400-year Caliphate, which once held sway over the Middle East. They wanted to reestablish their former glory, and the conquest of Jerusalem held the key. While they were no great friends with the Russians and the Persians, they played the strategic (yet tricky) *enemy of my enemy is my friend* angle.

The Libyans (Put), Sudanese (Cush), and the rest of their southern coalition (mercenaries and terrorist groups), were in it both as proxies to the Russians and Turks, as well as the potential booty they could claim by way of pillage and plunder. Thus, it was here in the fields of north of Mt. Ararat as well as in the south at the Port of Sudan, that this motley coalition began their ill-fated march towards the Holy Land.

Colonel Horovitz had been eyeing the satellite feed with a building sense of both anxiety and morbid curiosity. As chaotic as the world has become since the great disappearance, the arrival of the so-called angels, and the collapse of the United States, nothing surprised him anymore. Nevertheless, the Israeli Defense Force (IDF) had been on high alert since all the craziness began. Now, there appeared to be a massive group of military aged males filling the valley north of Mt. Ararat between Turkey and Armenia on both sides of the Aras River.

What piqued his curiosity was not the size of this growing gaggle, but the lack of tanks, vehicles, aircraft, or any other sort of modern military equipment. Surely, this cannot be the so-called *war of Gog and Magog* he thought to himself with a chuckle. Having grown up in an Orthodox home, he was very familiar with the Prophet Ezekiel's prophecy of the *War of Gog and Magog*. It terrified him when he was child, but as he got older and eventually joined the IDF, he summarily dismissed it as an old Jewish fable. *Nobody fights with swords and bucklers anymore. Besides, if this was true, then it was fulfilled in either the Six-Day War or the Yom Kippur War.* Nevertheless, here these armies were, lining up just as Ezekiel prophesied.

Of course, the IDF was also tracking suspicious movement in and around the Port of Sudan. It appeared that both these northern and southern coalitions were going to attempt to box Israel in. The southern forces would race up the Red Sea by speedboats and small-motorized caravans in an attempt to overrun the resort city of Eliat while the north poured through what used to be Syria. He pulled out a small copy of the Tanakh he kept in the command center, opened to the book of Ezekiel, chapter 38, and started reading it toward the end of the chapter.

*"And it will come to pass at the same time, when Gog comes against the land of Israel," says the Lord God, "that My fury will show in My face. For in My jealousy and in the fire of My wrath I have spoken: 'Surely in that day there shall be a great earthquake in the land of Israel, so that the fish of the sea, the birds of the heavens, the beasts of the field, all creeping things that creep on the earth, and all men who are on the face of the earth shall shake at My presence. The mountains shall be thrown down, the steep places shall fall, and every wall shall fall to the ground.' I will call for a*

*sword against Gog throughout all My mountains," says the Lord God. "Every man's sword will be against his brother.*

*And I will bring him to judgment with pestilence and bloodshed; I will rain down on him, on his troops, and on the many peoples who are with him, flooding rain, great hailstones, fire, and brimstone. Thus I will magnify Myself and sanctify Myself, and I will be known in the eyes of many nations. Then they shall know that I am the Lord." '*

**Ezekiel 38:18-23**

According to Ezekiel, they would not even fight this battle. Clearly, Ezekiel does not realize that we (the IDF) will not simply stand by and let this force come against us regardless of how they get here or what weapons they bring with them. The satellite feed began showing huge groups as if they were getting ready to bivouac in the expansive plains. Surely, they are not going to march all the way here are they, he thought skeptically.

Just then, the satellite feeds went dark.

# Chapter 71

"I am Enoch," he said to Izzy and Red.

"Enoch as in the author of the *book of Enoch*?" Izzy asked.

"I did not write that book. However, there are some quotes by me those Essenes took from the oral history passed down from Moses."

Izzy and Red were still marveling over this giant man's appearance. Being large men themselves, they now knew what it felt like for normal men to be around them.

"Where is Tristan anyway?" Red asked. "The last we saw of him was at the airport in Israel."

"Tristan was caught away from there and is now in his glorified state. He will be along shortly. In the meantime, follow the corridor to the elevator, and go up. You will meet those others of the remnant there."

"Hold on, before you go, why us?" Izzy asked.

"That man you were working for is a very evil man. In fact, he is the most evil man who has, or will ever live. Tristan asked, as a courtesy to me, to intervene in your fates."

"That guy was like a diplomatic nobody from Greece. Even before this century, Greece was turning into a failed state.

How could that guy be the most evil man who has ever lived?"

"That man will one day soon, emerge as the Antichrist. Nevertheless, more on this later. I've got another mission that needs my attention."

And with that, Enoch was gone.

*** 

"Hey, what happened to the feed?" Colonel Horovitz yelled to the command center.

"Sir, everything is out," a young IDF Captain replied. "We have no phones, no internet. Even our cell service is gone."

Just then, Enoch appeared in their midst, scaring those in his immediate surrounding half to death. Everyone with a sidearm instantly drew and pointed it at him as many started to scream at him to get on the floor. Enoch just looked at them dismissing them with an eye roll. One IDF security personnel tried to fire his weapon at him, only to hear the deafening click of a non-fire.

"Enough!" Enoch shouted in a supernaturally elevated voice that reverberated throughout the building. "Who is in charge of this mess?" Enoch asked in perfect Hebrew.

"I am," Colonel Horovitz said moving toward him through the crowd. "Who are you and how did you get in here?"

"My name is Enoch, and the battle of Gog and Magog is about to begin."

"We were watching them mass north and south of here until our satellite and communication arrays went offline. Do you know what happened?"

"Yes, you were hit with a very powerful Super Electromagnetic Pulse detonation. The Russians detonated it 300 miles in the exo-atmosphere over this nation. They did this in connection with a massive cyber-attack aimed at shutting down your Iron Dome technology."

"That explains the horses and lack of modern equipment," Colonel Horovitz said rubbing his chin. "But that doesn't explain the..."

Just then, a series of violent explosions shook the buildings viciously. Everyone, with the exception of Enoch, hit the floor and covered themselves. The lights went out and the emergency backup lighting cast an eerie red glow throughout the complex. The explosions continued for another 15 minutes straight, as the reinforced concrete roof took the brunt of the explosions with a muffled thud. The Russians, Turks, and Iranian air forces, with jets and unmanned aerial vehicles (UAVs) had begun a series of strategic strikes aimed at taking out all the Israeli military airbases as a second wave of attacks began. Enoch simply paced around and occasionally looked up as if communicating straight to God. Just then, as if on cue, the main feed turned back on showing the troop movements in the north and south. Strangely, no power came back online or accompanying support systems turned on. The feed showed a massive line of troops stretching from the Aras River down through to Syria already crossing into the Golan Heights on horses.

Colonel Horovitz, dumbstruck, asked Enoch, "How could they be that far south? I just saw them a few hours ago massing near the Turkish-Armenian border. And why are they riding horses?"

"You were watching a powerful illusion. I think you would call this a *Deep Fake*. The Russians somehow managed to hack into your satellites and feed this loop into the data streams you pull from your satellites. What you were watching was a feed from three weeks ago when the armies first starting massing. They intended to attack during your festival of Hanukah. As for the horses and primitive weapons, the Rapture of the Church or the *great disappearance* as you call it, *threw a monkey wrench into their plans.*

"He has made all of their modern weapons of no effect, and yet, they are compelled to come anyways. They all see you as the greatest prize to take down. Therefore, they have been gathering resources such as horses, swords, spears, bow and arrow, and many other more primitive weapons to fight against you now for months. Besides, the Russians, Turks, and Iranians already had sizable forces in Syria to begin with, and had always intended to use them as a first wave of ground forces against your army that is even now, failing to turn their power on."

"So this whole time they've been on the move south, and we've been watching a Deep Fake loop?"

"Yes, which is why I am here, even now it is too late for you to act. You will however, broadcast this live feed for the entire world to see the power and majesty of God our Father."

The EMP attack was so powerful and pervasive that it knocked out all of the power not just in Israel, but also in the surrounding countries of Lebanon, Jordan, Sinai Egypt, and most of Syria. Enoch told them in fact, that they had the only working computer monitor in all of the central Middle East.

# Chapter 72

NORAD, Colorado
Mid-Late December

Barachiel and Tristan had made three other stops south along the path finishing their last collection in Beirut, Lebanon. Here, a number of recent converts to the Christian faith were gathered in a home during a secret Bible study. Their arrival had the predictable surprise element as they instantly appeared in the midst of the gathered believers. Their departure to be instantly transported to Colorado caught these new believers by an even bigger surprise.

Once their mission was complete, Tristan asked Barachiel a question that had been on his mind since they began all of this.

"Why these people?"

"What do you mean?" Barachiel replied.

"I mean, from what I understand, the Church has been raptured, and those left behind are a separate group known as the Tribulation Saints. I also know the Antichrist is going to take over the entire world, and believers during this time are going to have to die for their faith. So why are we rescuing these people? I mean some of them (speaking about the President's team and some already at NORAD) are not even believers yet. I don't get it."

"Well, I can't tell you why each one of them specifically, but I can tell you that before this is all over, they will believe. These will enter into the Millennial Kingdom in the normal human form."

"Right, ok, I think I get it. The Church has been raptured and like me, are in their glorified bodies. The Tribulation Saints are martyred, and are already in heaven, awaiting their glorified forms. The only ones left in their normal physical state, will be all these that we rescued, and the Jews who flee to Petra after the midpoint. Does that sound right?"

"That is exactly how it will happen. We have rescued at this point nearly 140 persons, which is a man and woman from each of the seventy nations."

"Between them and the Jewish remnant, doesn't start the world's population out with much does it?"

"In the beginning there was just two. Noah and his wife had their three sons and daughter-in-law's for a total of eight. A lot less than we will have at the end." "True.

"By the way, two of our friends are here. Shall we go say hello?" Barachiel said with a smile.

"Absolutely. I'm sure they won't be surprised in the least!"

***

The IDF Command Center comfortably held around 100 personnel, and nearly all of them were in the main Joint Operations Center (JOC) intently watching the live feed playing out on the giant wall monitors. Although the EMP had rendered anything electronic useless in and around Israel, the picture coming through was as if the satellite itself were mere hundreds of feet above the columns (as opposed to hundreds of miles above). The picture was supernaturally clear, so much so that you could even see the whites of their eyes as they marched south to the Israeli border. This was the *tip of the Magogian spear* as it were; those Russian, Turkish, and Iranian forces who were already in southern Syria. Hundreds and thousands rode horses, marched, and some were even racing to get to the no-man's land that marked the beginning of the Golan Heights.

While Enoch remained toward the rear of the multilevel room, he closed his eyes and saw a mass of Jews praying near the Wailing Wall in the Old City in Jerusalem. Their crowds were enormous, given the seriousness of the

EMP effects on the modern city of Jerusalem; naturally, many were terrified and came there for help from on high.

"Behold the hand of God!" Enoch said as he opened his eyes and watched the forces of Magog immediately stop dead in their tracks as if lost. Murmurs and whispers broke out amongst the attendees in the IDF TOC as they waited anxiously as to what would happen next. The skies overhead darkened and you could see the formations start to break in every direction as the wind picked up too and dust filled the air.

One observant IDF Air Force weather clerk noticed the weather radar pop up on her mobile device, and walked over to Colonel Horovitz to show him. It was by far, the craziest weather event she had ever seen. It looked like a storm front was forming along the path of the armies and it stretched from the Horn of Africa north through the length of Syria into the mountains of southern Turkey, but completely passing benignly over the land of Israel itself.

The main display now began displaying a frightening show of lightning and large hail, which began mercilessly pounding the soldiers. After an hour or so of this brutal torrent, the hail stopped but the clouds, rain, and lightning remained. Those watching the feeds could see thousands of bodies lying dead or unconscious on the ground.

To the north in the mountains, it appeared that fighting broke out amongst the so-called anti-Israel coalition. The Iranians began fighting the Turkish forces, the central Asian nations began fighting the Russians, and eventually, they all just fought each other. It was a bloodbath, and no one watching could tell how or why it started; only that something caused them to turn on each other. The scene was horrific, and didn't make matters any better that you could start to see a river of blood begin to form flowing south down the columns of the hundreds of thousands of dead and dying combatants.

The feed then switched to the southern flank of the Magog Invasion, the forces coming up through the Red Sea. It was supposed to be a mad-dash for Eliat to storm the beach and make their way north from there. However, the storm, again, mercilessly pounded the thousands of small speedboats making their way up the coast. Huge hailstones sank every boat they hit, and many, attempting to turn away, were struck nonetheless. There was nowhere to hide when they got caught out in the open seas.

Just then, a massive earthquake rocked the ground underneath the IDF JOC as everyone (except Enoch) inside hit the floor and looked for something to use as cover. A mixture of screams and cries could be heard throughout the building as the ground rolled like a wave back and forth a dozen times. Enoch continued to watch the screen as those in Jerusalem were also experiencing this massive earthquake. The picture adjusted somewhat to that aerial view from a UAV and showed the Al Aqsa Mosque and the Dome of the Rock being rocked by the earthquake.

The Joint Operational Command Center (JOC) was designed to withstand a direct hit from a Katusha rocket (the weapon of choice of Hezbollah), but the sheer power and intensity of the quake, was causing stress fractures to spider the reinforced concrete walls and ceilings. The light and wall fixtures all swayed back and forth precariously, as the emergency lights kicked off replacing the eerie red glow with complete darkness throughout the building save the main display.

"Colonel Horovitz," Enoch spoke loudly, "look at the screen."

He had been crouched under a desk attempting to calm some other soldiers down who were there with him. He looked up just in time to see the two Islamic icons collapse in a heap of dust.

"You have no more threat from the north or south. I think it would be wise for you to go to minimal manning here, and direct the bulk of your forces south to Jerusalem for the time being. They are going to need your help in recovering your city."

"Oy vey," Enoch heard him say as he translated out of the building.

## Chapter 73

Israel, Rome
January- August

News of the failed invasion had reached world leaders shortly after it was miraculously thwarted. Israeli leadership, courtesy of Colonel Horovitz's sole working satellite feed, provided the regional leaders the necessary proof the Iranian, Russian, and Turkish alliance had been utterly defeated without a shot being fired from the Israeli Defense Force.

Almost as soon as the news broke to the UfM-Region headquarters in Rome, one Greek diplomat called for the special protection of Israel moving forward, claiming an attack on one, was an attack on all. He eloquently addressed the body of leaders there further adding, the emerging crisis, which no one was thinking about at the moment - the collapse of Russian, Turkish, Iranian, and the other central Asian governments. With the decimation of these nations' militaries, the politicians there had no protection from either outside threats, or internal revolution.

There was unanimous agreement amongst the UfM Region leaders about approving Israel's security, but they decided to temporarily postpone ratifying the decision until after both Turkey and Russia's nuclear weapons, military bases, and government buildings were secured. Many had begun to take notice of this Greek's decisive action and leadership in the face of what would normally be considered an overwhelming crisis. He calmly laid out what needed to happen, and formed three separate subcommittees with both military and civilian emergency managers dedicated to the handling of providing food, clean water, and energy to the citizens in those regions.

Meanwhile, the new Pope began echoing the Greek Diplomat's efforts, but adding in the idea of religious ecumenism so that the recovery work could continue unabated and without disruption or distraction of cultural, religious, or ethnic differences. They would need to work as one, with a singular purpose, of providing by peace and stability to the nations affected by the conflict. He was also instrumental in directing the civilian corporations responsible for providing the *Kredit* chips so that everyone who needed it could buy food and keep the lights on.

When the two men were together, they seemed inseparable. They worked tirelessly on the same projects and seemed to come up with workable solutions to the most complex issues, almost overnight. There were even whispers that the two might be in relations together, which would have shocked the world in earlier years, but now, seemed trivial considering how far humanity had progressed in the 21st century.

***

In Israel, the destruction was incalculable. Most of the city lay in ruins, but after years of terrorist attacks and wars, the tiny nation had been prepared to quickly pick itself up and begin the recovery process quicker than most. Local and national Israeli organizations dedicated to the rebuilding of the Third Jewish Temple, began petitioning their leaders immediately to take this as the sign from God to begin rebuilding the Temple. They did this simultaneously while using their charity outreach to assist those impacted by the earthquake. The combination worked, and soon, Israeli leaders at all levels were nodding in agreement that now was the time.

Before long, Israeli leadership at the Region-level, understanding the present goodwill at the UfM Region

Headquarters in Rome also began verbalizing their intent to rebuild the Third Temple where the Dome and the Mosque once stood. They were not looking for permission; they were going to rebuild it anyway and finally claim sole stewardship of the whole of the Temple Mount, but they were intent on remaining transparent about the process. Thus, four months after the War of Gog and Magog, the first stone was laid where the future temple would be built.

## Chapter 74

Year One of the Gap
September

Enoch, Barachiel, and Tristan remained at NORAD for much of the spring and early summer to not only fortify the base from physical attack, but also spiritual. Barachiel began speaking to the crowd of 200 gathered in the main conference area of the Cheyenne Mountain Complex to address the seriousness of the situation.

"The Dark Legions numbers are swelling in what used to be these United States, and it will not be long before they turn their attention to this Complex. Thankfully, at least for now, the collapse of the United States has provided these wicked angels plenty of distractions before turning their attention on us."

"How many are in a legion?" someone asked.

"Each Dark Legion was comprised of 6,000 wicked or fallen angels, and there were at least, nearly 10,000 separate legions, or 60 million fallen angels operating in the US alone."

"When you said we have to protect against not just the physical attacks, but also the spiritual, what does that mean?" another asked.

"Not only do these spirits sweep through the land possessing people to commit all manners of violence and evil, but they are also now able to physically manifest in ways they had previously been restrained from doing since the days of Noah. In fact, it was because of their activity on the earth in the antediluvian (or pre-Flood) world, that God forbade angels from physically manifesting without His express consent to do so. Any who violated that mandate, would be tossed into the abyss *until* the end of days. Which was now.

"You may remember the activity in the skies above your world in the decades leading up to the Rapture; you called these things unidentified flying objects or 'UFOs'. These were demonic entities presenting themselves in a semi veiled fashion. You could capture pictures and videos of them, but you never actually have captured one.

"Moreover, these things could easily break the laws of physics, because your physical laws do not bind them. In the same fashion, these malicious spirits will pass through your security measures, because it was only ever designed to keep out the physical threat, never the spiritual. Even here, you are in danger without taking the appropriate precautions."

"I though angels were supposed to be good?" still another asked.

"In the beginning, all angels were created holy, but when Lucifer, or the Devil as you know him, rebelled, a third of the angelic hosts rebelled with him. Since God created hundreds of billions of angels (only He knows exactly), this third was still a much greater number than all the humans on planet earth at man's greatest population. Later, during the Flood, the abundant offspring created between abominable unions between human women and fallen angels (the Nephilim) were giants who also perished in the Flood. Their disembodied souls, however, being neither fully human nor fully devil, were cursed to wander the earth as demon spawn possessing men and becoming subservient to the more powerful fallen angels.

"The fallen angels were organized in much the same way that you humans organize your militaries, which is to say, hierarchical. Instead of generals and prime ministers though, the demonic ranks consisted of their lord, Lucifer (or Satan, the Devil, and the Dragon) at the top. He was the chief wicked angel, a former Cherubim angel. Apart from God, he was the highest and most powerful created being in existence.

"Beneath him, were his chief principalities, or those territorial princes who were responsible for specific geographic locations on the earth. Every continent had its own dark viceroy. Beneath them, there are sub-commanders over regions. Beneath the regional commanders, were the national commanders. Beneath them, the commanders over cities and even down to individuals.

"Next, Satan has his chief powers (or authorities) over specific sins, which have long held sway over all of mankind. These were not just the seven deadly sins as popularized by Roman Catholic theology, but were actually the names of high fallen angels who were responsible for directing their campaigns of destruction throughout all of human history. These princes are Lust, Gluttony, Greed, Sloth, Wrath, Envy, and Pride. They worked both independent of the regional commanders, as well as in coordination with them. These powers have their own rank and file agents who service every variation of sin within each of these seven categories." "Do they all look like you?" another asked.

"From a human perspective, angels (both holy and wicked) are enormous, with the average height around nine feet tall. While the holy angels have remained as I am now, which is our true form, the wicked angels, by perverting their true nature, have begun to devolve over time into a new monstrous nature. The more evil, the larger and more grotesque they became.

"However, they can still present themselves deceivingly as beautiful angels of light or other benevolent for short periods of time. Their power is derived from the increase in wickedness either in an area, or in a particular sin. Nevertheless, Satan is at the top of this pyramid scheme, so he gets a cut on all wickedness, thus ensuring he perpetually remains unchallenged at the pinnacle of power."

Tristan looked across the crowd and could see the fear and anxiety building in their faces. He worried that even though Barachiel was telling them the truth, the truth was almost too much for them to bear. "Barachiel, give them the good news as well," he leaned over and whispered.

"While the numbers of fallen angels in this post Rapture world present a frightening reality for those of you left behind, the good news is that God is still God, and the Devil, is God's devil. He may have given them free reign in this brief period, but it is the brevity of its duration, which will keep Satan's forces in check. Furthermore, God will raise up His own army to continue offering salvation to those left behind."

"What kind of army?" a general asked interestedly.

"First, God will have his Two Witnesses in Jerusalem. These are the prophets Moses and Elijah. They will have supernatural power to shut up the rains, call fire down from heaven, turn the rivers into blood, and will issue consuming fire against anyone who tries to stop their preaching. Next, God will have the 144,000, from the Twelve Tribes of Israel. These will be sealed by God for a certain time, and both will proclaim *the Gospel of the Kingdom* until their mission is complete."

Enoch turned to Tristan and pulled him aside in private while Barachiel was still talking. "When the Two Witnesses arrive, our time here will be complete."

Tristan received the news with mixed emotions. On one hand, he wanted to go home and be reunited with his family. On the other, being a year into this, and having made friends from all over the world, he felt a bit of responsibility to be here to see it through to the end with them. Seeing this concern in Tristan's eyes, Enoch continued. "Our role was only during the gap in time between the Rapture and the start of the 70th Week of Daniel. It was never to go beyond that."

## Chapter 75

Year One of the Gap September-October
Jerusalem-Neom

"Then those who dwell in the cities of Israel will go out and set on fire and burn the weapons, both the shields and bucklers, the bows and arrows, the javelins and spears; and they will make fires with them for seven years. They will not take wood from the field nor cut down any from the forests, because they will make fires with the weapons; and they will plunder those who plundered them, and pillage those who pillaged them," says the Lord God. **Ezekiel 39:9-10**

The aftermath of the failed Magog invasion was beyond the scope of human reasoning when looking at the river of bodies strewn from the Golan all the way through Syria. Yet there they were, for all the world to see, the dead lying bloated in the sun being eaten by the vultures and all manner of carrion. The IDF was now tasked with a split mission; half-helping in and around Jerusalem with the post-earthquake recovery operations, and here, collecting weapons and intelligence to prevent anyone else from using them. The bodies, however inglorious they now appeared, would lay where they lie.

Colonel Horovitz followed Enoch's directions, diverting the bulk of his forces south to assist with recovery operations. He himself went to the Temple Mount, along with other senior IDF commanders to survey the damage caused by the massive earthquake. He was getting reports that the magnitude of the earthquake was somewhere between a 9.5 and a 10.0., although with the Russian EMP bomb having disabled the bulk of their electronic detection systems (along with everything else that was not hardened) it was difficult to tell exactly how powerful it was.

"What do you think will happen now?" Captain Moshe asked. "Will we finally get our Temple back?"

"We should have did this back in 1967 when we had the chance," Colonel Horovitz replied. "But now, I think if we ever were, now would be the time."

"Then it is all true, we are in the last days before the Messiah comes," Captain Moshe replied staring disbelievingly at the recently transformed Temple Mount.

"I've seen a lot of things in my days in the IDF, but nothing as crazy as what we've seen in the past few months. If that Enoch fellow is right, we are going to be in for one wild ride in the years to come."

***

"After this I saw in the night visions, and behold, a fourth beast, dreadful and terrible, exceedingly strong. It had huge iron teeth; it was devouring, breaking in pieces, and trampling the residue with its feet. It was different from all the beasts that were before it, and it had ten horns. I was considering the horns, and there was another horn, a little one, coming up among them, before whom three of the first horns were plucked out by the roots. And there, in this horn, were eyes like the eyes of a man, and a mouth speaking pompous words. **Daniel 7:7-8**

Turiel watched as the Greek diplomat got up to speak. Apparently, he was selected by his cohorts in the UfM Region delegation to address the UN's main body at the new headquarters in Neom regarding the recent state of affairs for the UfM. He was fluent in every major language and even most dialects, and thus, mixed this into his speech with a fluidity that was beyond impressive.

"Ladies and gentlemen- citizens of the world, hear my plea for unity. We must come together as one body to tackle the monumental issues we face. We must not look at these recent events as crises, rather, as opportunities to rise above and evolve into the people we were always meant to become. I am personally leading the Task Forces in recovering one of our rogue nations (speaking of Turkey) and are, even at this moment, stabilizing that country before any more harm befalls it. I have called for a new Peace Initiative with Israel, so that she may live and rebuild in peace. I am working day and night with the Reverend Holy Father (speaking of the new pope) with his glorious vision of bringing all people, of all faiths, together as one. We are using every tool at our disposal (speaking of the Kredit) to do so. Join us in our fight to reclaim the planet."

After he finished, the UN attendees erupted in a wave of applause and standing ovations. It was weird to watch this unbridled enthusiasm for a speech so laden with hidden agendas. Turiel could not believe they could not see through the charade of it all. Well, he could believe it given the overwhelming demonic presence in the room. If people could see what he saw, they would have fled out of there in terror.

Slimy black and red demons clung to these so-called leaders like leeches constantly whispering in their ears.

Normally, Turiel would not step foot in a place like this, not because of the discussions, but because the demons themselves would have seen him and would have fought him relentlessly until either he left or they were vanquished. Given the numbers, he thought the latter would have happened first. Nevertheless, God blinded them to his presence and he watched this macabre scenario play out. He imagined it would be like going back in time and watching Adolph Hitler address some political body before his rise to power to become the monster he eventually became.

In terms of regional power, the Union for the Mediterranean (UfM) Region was on the rise. The North American Regions were a mess. The Central Asian Region was in shambles. The Sub-Saharan African Region was weak. That left seven other regions vying for control over these virtual-power vacuums. However, both the Far East Asia Region and the South American Region were disadvantaged due to their geographical locations, and being so far removed from the action. It was now, really, between Northern Europe and the UfM who remained best postured to control the affairs of the world.

# Chapter 76

Then I was given a reed like a measuring rod. And the angel stood, saying, "Rise and measure the temple of God, the altar, and those who worship there. But leave out the court which is outside the temple, and do not measure it, for it has been given to the Gentiles. And they will tread the holy city underfoot *for* forty-two months. **Revelation 11:1-2**

Year One of the Gap
Jerusalem
October-November

Although numerous Orthodox Jewish organizations, the Sanhedrin, and political bodies were calling for the rebuilding of the third Jewish Temple, there were only two organizations really equipped and prepared for the actual construction, the Temple Institute and the Temple Mount Faithful. In fact, there were even organizations dedicated to the servicing of the husbandry requirements (cattle and agriculture) necessary for operating a rebuilt temple. Needless to say, for them, a rebuilt Temple was not a matter of if, but when.

However, not all Jewish political parties and organizations were excited about this developing situation. They represented a once popular, but now shrinking, minority of diaspora-minded liberal Jews bent on keeping the *status quo*. The reason their groups were shrinking though, was that after the Rapture (or as they called it- the great disappearance), there was no *status quo* anymore. This became even more self-evident after the failed Magog Invasion; everything really was on the table for this third temple to become a reality.

Normally, there would have been mobs of Arab-Palestinians protesting at even the whisper of a new Jewish temple on the Temple Mount, however, the Muslim world had been dealt a severe blow. Most of the military-aged males from Russia to Ethiopia, and from Libya to Iran had been killed in this recent confrontation. And they couldn't even argue how unjust the Israelis had been, because the Israelis didn't even fight. For them, it was if Allah himself had revolted against the attack, and wiped out the would-be liberators. For all intents and purposes, Islam, in the Middle East, had been neutered.

Prior to the failed invasion, Saudi Arabia and a number of other Sunni-Muslim nations had already agreed to a normalization process with the Israelis thanks in part to the Americans. Part of the discussion was the realization that the seventy-three year hot and cold wars with the Jews, had failed to produce anything substantial. In fact, they seemed to lose more and more territory each time they went against Israel. Thus, the Saudi's public proclamation that neither the Al Aqsa Mosque, nor the Dome of the Rock held any real significant importance to Islam was the final political straw that broke any resistance to rebuilding the third temple. The prevailing attitude soon became, we have Mecca, Medina, and Neom, let them have their silly temple.

While all political resistance for rebuilding the temple melted away, the problem now became two-fold" finding the perfect Red Heifer to sacrifice and sanctify the temple tools, and where exactly on the Temple Mount to place the holy of holies. No one exactly knew where to place the cornerstone. Granted, everyone had opinions and theories as to where they thought it should go, but no one could agree where it had to go to be biblically correct.

Meanwhile, with Neom bringing the global stage to the Saudi Kingdom, there were now calls for the city to be renamed after something with more historical significance. The word NEOM is actually an acronym for the phrase New Enterprise Operating Model. However, the Saudi's claim the name means New (NEO) Mostaqbal (M), which is Arabic for the word *future*. Either way, if the new world's government was going to set itself up there, they wanted something representative for the entire planet, not just the Saudi Kingdom.

While many names were offered up as potential replacements, the name that garnered the most support from the European nations was *Babel* (after the famed Tower of Babel). Since the European Union (EU) had formerly modeled its own headquarters in Brussels after the unfinished tower at Babel, the mantra of *many tongues, one voice* seemed to resonate the most with them. This spoke to the diversity of languages and cultures represented within a growing Mediterranean Union region. Nevertheless, given that the tower was originally only known through the Bible, there was little historical significance for those of the Muslim, Hindu, and Buddhist faiths.

This led to the compromise everyone seemed to approve of. Historically speaking, Saudi Arabia, Egypt, and Jordan, were all at one point in time, under the Babylonian Empire. Since Babylon was named after Babel, the compromise was that the name for this new global city would be called New Babylon.

# Chapter 77

Then one of the seven angels who had the seven bowls came
   and talked with me, saying to me, "Come, I will show you
   the judgment of the great harlot who sits on many waters,
with whom the kings of the earth committed fornication, and
the inhabitants of the earth were made drunk with the wine of
                        her fornication."
So he carried me away in the Spirit into the wilderness. And
   I saw a woman sitting on a scarlet beast which was full of
names of blasphemy, having seven heads and ten horns. The
woman was arrayed in purple and scarlet, and adorned with
gold and precious stones and pearls, having in her hand a
golden cup full of abominations and the filthiness of her

   fornication. And on her forehead a name was written:
          MYSTERY, BABYLON THE GREAT,
             THE MOTHER OF HARLOTS
          AND OF THE ABOMINATIONS OF
                    THE EARTH.
                **Revelation 17:1-5**

While the world leaders were glad-handing each other over their ability to rename Neom, New Babylon, the pope in Rome was busy. Last year's roll out of the *Kredit* was, at best, risky, at worst, disastrous. Adding insult to injury, the *Great Disappearance* further destabilized the world's markets by collapsing the Americans. However, both he and the Greek believed in it, and believed it would resolve a number of problems the nations have and will face in the future, primarily, political and religious allegiance. They needed something that was both carrot and stick, and the *Kredit* seemed to fit the bill.

However, the *Great Disappearance* also opened something else that had previously been held in restraint, and that was contact with the other side. Before the disappearance, he knew only of UFOs from his private discussions with several world leaders who had the classified information regarding the increase in the aerial phenomena. Afterwards, he himself experienced it firsthand. One night as he lay in bed, he felt himself begin to levitate out of his bed, and he noticed he was not alone.

Three beautiful, angelic visitors who only identified themselves as *Cosmic Masters* came to him in the night physically manifesting themselves to him. They told him the mysteries of the universe he had for so long sought answers.

They told him that there was no "God," but rather, "God" was a force by which their race evolved. Furthermore, they were the ones who seeded humanity on earth in eons past. They told him he would be selected as the new pope before it happened, and that he would be tasked with spreading their message of unity. They told him of the many great things he and the Greek would accomplish, and that they would aid him in his quest. They would even empower him to show signs and wonders when the time was right; to remove all doubt the legitimacy of their quest. The goal, global unity under one government. This one government was to be headed-up by his partner, the Greek.

These beings further added that the thing everyone referred to as *the Rapture* was really, them removing those who could evolve no further. They removed them so they would no longer be a hindrance to this new world order he and the Greek were destined to run. *Who would have thought the Vatican would select a homosexual atheist as the chief pontiff?* he thought as he marveled at the delicious irony. *Now how best to get everyone on board?* His discussions with the Greek on this issue always came back to two things- money and religion. *If we control what people believe, and we control the money they use, we can control everything else.*

He was getting some disturbing reports that people were calling the *Great Disappearance* the Rapture and turning their lives over to Jesus. He was simply not going to allow this scourge to fester and grow into some kind of movement that challenged his authority. The last thing he needed was some kind of new reformation or revival. He needed to lobby the Region leaders to outlaw it sooner rather than later. Then, the idea came to him. He needed to tie the *Kredit* to squashing Christianity, Islam, Judaism, and any other belief that conflicted with what the new world order's objectives.

## Chapter 78

Year One of the Gap
Rome
November-December

He causes all, both small and great, rich and poor, free and
slave, to receive a mark on their right hand or on their
foreheads, and that no one may buy or sell except one who
has the mark or the name of the beast, or the number of his
name. Here is wisdom. Let him who has understanding
calculate the number of the beast, for it is the number of a
man: His number is 666. **Revelation 13:16-18**

The new pope realized that convincing the world to ditch their national currencies would be a difficult, but not an impossible task. The *Cosmic Masters* had told him what he needed to say, and how he needed to say it. He questioned whether he, the religious pontiff for nearly a billion people, was suited for such a task. After all, finance was not his area of expertise. They assured him he was the right person to do this. He and his partner, the Greek, would work in tandem convincing the world that getting on the *Kredit* was the only way to fix their current global dilemmas.

So it went for weeks. He spoke regularly and privately to world leaders, speaking of both the need and the urgency to convert to the Kredit. He talked of how powerful the new Beast Quantum system was, and how ingenious it was in solving complex problems. He had traveled several times to Brussels to see the Beast himself, and walked away even more a believer than before he went. The Artificial Intelligence in the system was remarkable, and incredibly perceptive in interacting with humans. As if it were really a sentient being trapped inside of a computer system. He was told that it was anywhere from a thousand times, to a million times smarter than the smartest human alive.

His staff had arranged for him to address the UN body in December and that time was quickly approaching. He had no idea what he would say, but as he lay in bed one night, the *Cosmic Masters* again came to him, and assured him not to worry about it. He only need open himself up beforehand, and they would speak through him. That is exactly what happened when the day came.

"My fellow citizens of the United Nations, let us for the first time, come together and make a real progress towards true peace. In order to do this, we must unite our currencies. This might seem odd coming from the world's chief religious figure, but even I recognize that money makes the world go round. If we want peace, then we must be under one system. If we want equity, we must be under one system. If we want love, we must be under one system. If we want stability, we must be under one system. We can truly only be under one system, when we unite our currencies. The hour is too late, and the call for equity, diversity, and unity is too strong, we must act now. Thank you."

The pope stepped away from the UN podium to thunderous applause. The Cosmic Masters had told him the world was ready to unite, just as they told him he would be selected as the pontiff. Two for two in their predictions. He could feel it all starting to come together.

***

Tristan knew their time was ending, and he was doing his best to forewarn the President and his team of things to come. They had just finished watching the UN news feed and were commenting on how the push for the one world currency was just as Tristan and Enoch had been talking about for months now. For them, it was weird to see these things falling into place exactly as the Bible described some two thousand years ago. Tristan pulled the President to the side for a private conversation.

"Are there any doubters left in your inner circle?" Tristan asked.

"Maybe the Vice-President and the SECDEF," the president replied. "I've seen the transformation in most of my staff from being politically driven creatures, to spiritually minded believers…as have I."

"When the enemy comes, they are going to try and use the non-believers as their point of entry to sow division and create hostility in here. Perhaps even going so far as to letting the enemy forces inside."

"I can't believe that though, I mean, the VP and the SECDEF have been by my side through thick and thin these last few years. They may not be believers yet, but they are definitely not traitors."

"Traitors to whom?" Tristan replied curiously. "The new power structure in the world is not the US, despite what anyone hopes or wishes. We are not making a comeback. Nevertheless, even beyond that, is the spiritual dimension. Anyone not plugged into God is fair game for the real enemy, Satan. They are fair game for demonic influence and even demonic possession. The enemy is empowered during this time, and he is very intelligent. Even more than any other angel, and angels are already very powerful."

"More powerful than you?" the President asked.

"I don't know. But it doesn't really matter, myself and Enoch will not be with you much longer."

"Wait, what?" he replied visibly shaken with the new news.

"I found out not long ago, but when the Two Witnesses arrive at the official beginning of the 70$^{th}$ Week, we will be going up."

"So will Barachiel or any other angel remain behind to help us?"

"I don't know. Perhaps. I have not been told that as of yet."

"Lord help us."

"Yes, may He indeed."

## Chapter 79

Year One of the Gap
Rome
January-May

By January of the New Year, momentum was really picking up for a global transition to the *Kredit*. Nations formerly destabilized by the Rapture, were now adjusting to the new normal, and it seemed that the Regional Governments were really stepping up to the task of running the world. The man dubbed "the Greek" was now formally voted in to head the office of the UfM Region Chief.

His impressive work stabilizing Turkey, as well as Russia and the Central Asian nations was nothing short of miraculous. Of course, he knew that and yet was perceptive enough to not appear openly narcissistic so as not to lose any ground already gained. However, pride coursed through his veins like a river of egotism. Unbeknownst to him at this point, two demon lords, Pride and Grecia, clung to him like a shadow. The Greek was finding it harder and harder to hide his narcissism behind his shroud of false humility. He simply had too much to do, and there were far too many incompetent people working for him. He found he was working circles around everyone, and no one was able to keep up, save his partner, the pope.

Arriving in this position of authority was not his destiny or end state. For him, this was only the beginning. He began to swing his arcs of power, grabbing in wider and wider circles. He was not content with just ruling his region; he wanted them all. His two-fold approach of the *Kredit* and this Peace Treaty were simply the right tools to do such a thing. Ironic that more lands have been conquered by peace than any other method.

As for his two guests, these two remained at the top of the satanic hierarchical rank structures. As it were, Satan himself, or the Devil as he is often called, would never personally stoop to direct the affairs of a man. To Satan, humans were no better than insects. In fact, he had only ever personally intervened twice in all of human history. The first was to convince Cain to kill his brother Abel. The second was with possessing the man Judas Iscariot. However, he knew time was running out, and if he wanted to destroy the nation of Israel, and thus, disrupt God's prophetic plans, he would have put his top two lieutenants on this. This is why he chose his two highest-ranking demon lords to work through this man called "the Greek."

The *demon lord Pride* and the *demon prince of Grecia* would be the two assigned to him day and night. Pride continually reminded him of his ingenuity in initially drafting the first peace initiative shortly after the failed Magog Invasion. He reminded him of his swift and decisive action in the aftermath of Magog. He reminded him of his right to rule and to never settle for just one region, but the world.

It was this last point where the Greek decided to expand upon this peace treaty, not just to include the UfM, but also northern Europe, and Central Asia. The *demon prince of Grecia*, who was the head of the demonic region covering all of the Mediterranean, began smoothing all the would be issues ahead of the Greek; paving the way as it were. He also instilled fear in all the national leaders in the UfM, and convinced them to give their allegiance to this man or else perish in horrible deaths.

The Greek knew that on the surface, this was a peace treaty, however, confined in the details of the fine print, and would be the strings of subjugation should any party fail to fully meet the whole of the requirements. The key components centered on peace and security, but true peace can only come about by true strength. One must have the ability to enforce this new version of *Pax Romana*, or otherwise, the strong will simply ignore your treaty and attack anyway. The recent Russian-Iranian-Turkish coalition's failed invasion proved exactly this point. It was also too perfect a crisis to simply let waste.

This treaty, would bind all participants to the collective security measures and in particular, Israel. The strength of the treaty however, was not in the proclamation, but in the fine print details embedded in the agreement's clauses and indexes. One clause in particular he ensured was included was the internationalization of the city of Jerusalem. The problem was he knew the Israelis would not go for this, especially, in light of the fact they now wanted to rebuild their temple. He needed to find an angle. The *demon prince Grecia* reminded him that Jerusalem was, by its own history, one of the most international cities on the planet. The Jews, Babylonians, Persians, Greeks, Romans, Muslims, Christians, Ottoman Turks, British, and now the Israelis all laid ownership claims on it throughout its storied history. This is the angle.

The Greek would need to tie in their want for this new temple, with their needful duties to the region at large. Should they violate the mandates of the UfM or the UN, he would need the legitimacy to step in and secure their city from them.

Grecia whispered in his ear.

*Move the UfM headquarters from Rome, to Jerusalem. This would guarantee they would never be attacked again, ever. Peace forever.*

Then it hit him. We must move the UfM capital from Rome to Jerusalem. *But what of Rome,* he thought?

*Ah, Rome must remain the spiritual capital of the world. It will be the center of all religious worship, and home to all faiths.*

Rome will become the new Mecca for all faiths. It will for perpetuity, be the holiest place on earth for all peoples. A smile broke out over his face, as he was thinking this. *This will make Maximillian very happy.*

### Chapter 80

Year One of the Gap
Rome
May-August

"Remember the Law of Moses, My servant,
Which I commanded him in Horeb for all Israel,
*With the* statutes and judgments.

Behold, I will send you Elijah the prophet

Before the coming of the great and dreadful day of the Lord.
And he will turn

The hearts of the fathers to the children,

And the hearts of the children to their fathers,

Lest I come and strike the earth with a curse."

**Malachi 4:4-6**

For nearly eight months now, the remnant community inside the Cheyenne Mountain Complex were busily working to shore up their facility, gather supplies on scavenging parties, and catalog everything for the eventual seven-year duration of the Tribulation. Aside from their physical duties, Tristan and Enoch both used the time to teach and lead daily Bible studies. Most of the original group had remained with only a handful fleeing early on. Those who remained professed their faith in Christ, and were committed to surviving as long as they could, to physically enter into the coming Kingdom. However, they were also prepared to die a martyr's death if it came to it.

The world outside the mountain complex became increasingly dangerous, and devoid of life. Colorado Springs suffered huge losses during the Rapture, and afterwards, the wanton violence and lawlessness drove the rest away. There had been a robust, but short lived criminal element in the city, but after everything that could be burnt, pillaged, and plundered was done, they moved on to other areas. Within a few months, wild animals began to return to forage and search for food in this newly opened hunting grounds.

The animals had changed though. Whereas before the Rapture, a wild animal was more than likely to turn and flee an encounter with a human unless they were either cornered, injured, or protecting their young. Now, these animals almost always turn and attack…as if there were some airborne case of divinely sanctioned rabies. There was no more whipping out of cell phones to snap a picture of an elk or a bear; now you ran and found some place safe to hole up in until the animal got tired and left.

The world beyond Colorado Springs, either north to Denver, or south to New Mexico was a virtual wasteland. The only major cities in the former United States that was left were on the east and west coasts, and parts of Texas. Current geopolitical information became harder and harder to come by. The angel Barachiel would come by around once a week and give reports to Enoch or Tristan to fill them in on what was going on in the rest of the world. It was from him they learned of the failed Magog Invasion, the rise of the new pope and the new political leader called "the Greek." It was also through him they learned of the coming third Jewish temple.

"I guess our time here has come to an end," Tristan said somberly. He had grown close to many under this mountain in the short time they'd been together.

"It has. I have been on earth for nearly six thousand years, I am ready to go back to heaven. This place, as amazing as some parts of it are, is a dump compared to heaven," Enoch said with a wink. "You're going to love it."

"I'm ready to see my family again."

"And to see your friend Jack again no doubt?"

"Yeah, he'll be in for a surprise won't he?" Tristan laughed.

"He already knows."

"I know, but it would have been better to surprise him!"

"Perhaps. Let's get ready."

\*\*\*

Eli, the project manager for the Temple Mount cleanup and site preparation, was leaning against the hood of his truck busily adding notes to his work laptop when two men walked past him unnoticed. Eli's construction crews were working on the Temple Mount and nearly done hauling all of the debris from the remains of the Dome and the Mosque. They should have been done months ago, but since so much of the city had been damaged during the earthquake, they were continually being pulled away to assist their construction company's other emergency projects.

The two men, the prophets Moses and Elijah, continued their quiet ascent up the stairs to the top of the Temple Mount, virtually garnering no attention from passersby. They were wearing identical matching charcoal robes made of sackcloth and roughhewn rope belts and could have easily passed for a couple of vagrants. However, despite their haggard and homeless appearances, the look of determination on their faces spoke of intense purpose and focused mission.

Their long gray beards, and weathered faces, appeared as if instead of them traveling through time to arrive at this point, time (in the span of millennia) travelled through them. They kept their gazes down, careful not to make eye contact with anyone before their time. They did this because their irises were unnaturally blue and their pupils appeared to have starlight beaming from them. If anyone saw them as they truly were, they would have been mobbed with crowds before ever reaching their destination.

Approaching the top, a construction worker shouted at them in Hebrew to leave the construction site.

"Hey, you can't be up here. You need to go back the way you came in!"

The two men said nothing but continued walking another 150 paces before coming to a stop. The construction worker, flanked by two others, walked behind the elderly men to escort them back to the stairway.

"Probably Orthodox," one worker jokingly said to the other.

"Homeless Orthodox," the other replied. They both laughed as they drew closer to the two men standing still.

"Hey!" the worker said as he walked around them to see their faces. "You can't be…."

The two prophets looked up and stared directly at the men. The worker recoiled back, stunned, and unsure of what to do next. His compatriots were equally shocked, and speechless. The two men raised their hands and began praying loudly in an archaic form of Hebrew that these workers barely understood. Although they were not shouting, the prayers seemed to echo loudly and caused the workers to step back even further as if their eardrums might rupture.

"Somebody needs to get Eli up here," one of the workers finally managed to get out of his throat. "I'll go," and he bolted toward the stairwell leading down to the Old City market.

Two security force officers heard the loud prayers, and immediately began walking in their direction to investigate the commotion with hands on their side arms. They got within twenty feet of the two men before one of the two turned and faced them. The security officers stopped cold in their tracks, unable to tear their gaze away from the men's eyes. The officers froze when the men began speaking simultaneously and spoke the exact same thing, at the same time, perfectly timing their message to their now, growing audience.

"The end is at hand. Messiah has already come. Yeshua, King of kings has taken His bride the Church and now will commence with judgment upon the earth."

…Rise and measure the temple of God, the altar, and those who worship there. But leave out the court, which is outside the temple, and do not measure it, for it has been given to the Gentiles."
And they will tread the holy city underfoot *for* forty-two months.

**Revelation 11:1-2**

Printed in Great Britain
by Amazon

72617364R00278